By JOEL SKELTON

NOVELS
Dress Up

Beneath the Palisade: Reliance
Beneath the Palisade: Courage

Published by DREAMSPINNER PRESS
http://www.dreamspinnerpress.com

Beneath the Palisade

Courage

Joel Skelton

Published by
Dreamspinner Press
5032 Capital Circle SW
Ste 2, PMB# 279
Tallahassee, FL 32305-7886
USA
http://www.dreamspinnerpress.com/

Beneath the Palisade: Courage
Copyright © 2013 by Joel Skelton

Cover Art by Catt Ford

ISBN: 978-1-62380-293-6
Digital ISBN: 978-1-62380-294-3

Printed in the United States of America
First Edition
January 2013

Dedicated to my father, Jess:
Although the road was often rough,
I could not be more thankful for the journey.

Acknowledgments

I'M VERY grateful for adept critiques from Ann Hinnenkamp, Jennifer Hutchins, and Kris Radcliffe. The story is so much stronger because of their involvement.

Contributions from my bud, Kristopher Krentz (aka Str8 Cat) have strengthened the story in ways that can only be whispered in a poorly lit hallway.

Thank you to Jennifer Hutchins (aka my niece) for research, and more importantly, her unyielding enthusiasm and encouragement.

My dear Patrick—thank you for your love and support. I know I'm the luckiest.

CHAPTER

One

YOU'RE staring at his crotch. Again!

Theo Engdahl shook his head in an attempt to delete the image. *Dude, what the hell is your deal?*

Checking out the bulge in Adam Walburn's navy shop pants had become a real problem. An addiction. Despite telling himself how wrong it was to stare at his friend and coworker... down there, Theo was helpless to stop it. *It's just not right. He's another dude!*

"Grab me a couple of B7s, will ya?" Adam had labored over a dirt bike engine for the better part of the morning.

Theo grabbed two spark plugs from the bin on the wall and walked them over.

"Thanks." Adam placed a plug between his teeth while installing the other.

In need of a distraction, Theo looked over to the riding mower parked in front of the motor oil rack. *Stay focused on work.*

Adam removed a rag he kept in his back pocket and wiped the grease from his hands. Returning the rag, he rolled the bike out into the lot. Signaling for Theo to join him, he fired it up. "Let's go for a spin."

Most of Theo wanted to refuse the invitation, but a small part of him, the part giving him all the trouble lately, couldn't say no. *He's your friend, idiot. Stop acting so weird.* Pushing past his apprehension, he climbed onto the back of the bike.

"Hang on," Adam hollered back before he opened the throttle, causing the bike to surge forward. Theo plunged his arms around Adam's waist as they tore out of the parking lot and onto the highway.

With his nose inches from his friend's back, Theo inhaled a tantalizing combination of machine oil, cologne, and sweat. He fought off an unexpected urge to rub his face on the faded orange cotton shirt in front of him. As he became conscious of his arms wrapped tight around Adam, an unwelcomed feeling of shame spoiled the ride for him. *What's wrong with me? Why won't these feelings stop if I don't want them?* Even worse, he was aroused.

"Dude, you'd better head back," Theo yelled into the wind. "I don't want to keep anyone waiting for us. Artie would blow his stack." Artie, the owner, was on vacation this week, leaving Theo and Adam alone in the shop.

"Stop being such a pussy!" Adam shouted, turning the bike around and speeding past the shop at full throttle.

Theo felt a pang of relief when, after racing them a half mile down the road, Adam turned around again and eased them back into the parking lot. The erection he experienced showed no signs of letting up as he jumped off the bike. "Gotta pee! Be back in a minute."

Thankful for the privacy of the bathroom, he leaned back against the door and shut his eyes. There was a time, maybe even a few short weeks ago, when he could laugh away or, better yet, control these evil thoughts. Something had changed. The temptation was stronger than ever and the bouts more frequent. Today was the worst urge he had ever had and it scared him. *How did I get to be so disgusting?*

Furious, he splashed water on his face and reached for a handful of paper towels. In the process, he caught a glimpse of himself in the mirror. The image staring back was pathetic. Weak and helpless. *I don't want to be this way. Please, just let this be some kind of fucked-up phase I'm going through.* He slammed the door and stormed out of the tiny sanctuary at the same time a car pulled into the parking area. Theo recognized it immediately. *Oh God, not that nosey old hag.*

A middle-aged woman, her hair piled halfway to the sky and framed on the sides by tight ringlets, slid out of the car and walked back to her trunk. "Hello, Theodore."

"Hello, Mrs. Kettleson. Let me guess, won't start?" Theo lifted the ancient lawnmower out of Sally Kettleson's banged-up silver Buick Regal and slammed the trunk closed.

"There isn't a lifetime of prayer going to get this here machine started. It needs your help."

"Probably just needs a tune-up is all. I'll call you when it's ready. Should be tomorrow sometime."

"Tell your mother I'll see her tonight at Prayer Potluck." Sally smiled, a quick maneuver that involved scrunching her face up into a tight little ball until her eyes squinted.

The only person in town more active than Sally Kettleson at Palisade Baptist was Theo's mother, Darla. One or both of them could be seen up at the church practically every day. For the Engdahls, the Kettlesons, and a host of other locals, life revolved around their church.

Despite fierce parental concern for his spiritual well-being, Theo had begun to drift away from his religion at the same time he started to realize something wasn't right. A little voice deep inside kept getting louder and louder, and, no matter what he did, it taunted and teased with increasing frequency. *Whatever this is, just fight it!*

Since graduating from high school three years ago, he had seized every opportunity to avoid Palisade Baptist, and now found himself precariously close to being thrown out of the house for what was perceived as disrespect for his family's strong religious commitment. Theo waved to Mrs. Kettleson and wheeled her older-than-Jesus mower into the shop.

There would come a time in the very near future, he thought as he pushed the mower over to his workstation, when he'd have to move out and say good-bye to the comfort and affordability of living in his parent's basement. In his own special way, he prayed that, when the time came, it would be his decision and not theirs. For now, life was still tolerable. But just barely.

"You want to start on that or the big rider we got in yesterday?" Adam gestured to the large mower parked next to the oil shelf.

"Hang on." Hearing the phone, Theo jogged across the garage to the little side office and picked it up. "Artie's Small Engine Repair, this is Theo."

"Hi. I'm calling from the Palisade Beach Cabins. We have a tiller that's acting up. How soon could you guys take a look at it?"

"One sec." Theo looked over at a clipboard hanging on the wall to make sure there weren't any rush orders he wasn't aware of. Nothing. "I can start on it now if you can get it down here."

"Oh, great. I'm on my way."

Theo returned the phone to its mount and strolled out to the garage. "I got a tiller comin' in the next few minutes. I'll start on the rider after that if there's still time today. Do you want to work on the mower that just came in?"

"Funny, we sit around twiddlin' our thumbs the first part of the week, and now it's binga banga, one job after another. Sure." Adam grabbed the Kettleson mower and pulled it over to his work area.

Theo cleaned and organized until a truck pulled into the lot. The driver climbed out as Theo approached.

Dressed in faded red sweatpants cut off at the knees and a navy hoodie with a bright white T-shirt underneath, the dude looked over and smiled. Theo gazed at the man's mop of dirty blond hair. When his hair was long, it flopped over his head in the same way. The other thing Theo noticed, but quickly pushed away, was the bulging calves and muscled ass. *Get a grip.*

"I called a few minutes ago." The man hoisted a tiller out of the back end of the truck and stood it upright on the ground. "I'm Ian."

"Right. Let's see what we have here." Theo walked over and squatted down for a closer look. "What's it been doing?"

"Nothing, that's the problem. It just quit on me."

"Could be a clogged gas line, or maybe a plug. Do you wanna hang around while I take a look at it?" The engines on these tillers were simple, and Theo figured his chances of fixing it in a few minutes were good.

"Oh, that would be great. I've got a ton of work to do."

Theo left the man in the lot and carried the tiller into the garage and examined the fuel and oil levels. "Must be the plug. Everything else looks fine," he speculated as he passed Adam, who had already begun work on Sally Kettleson's mower, on the way over to the plug station.

"Hey, you know who that is, don't you?" Adam flashed an evil grin, nodding past the open garage door.

"Haven't a clue. He a friend of yours?" Theo snatched the plug he needed and walked back.

"That's pretty frickin' funny." Adam shook his head in disgust. "No friend of mine. He's one of the fags who own those beach cabins. Be careful not to drop anything around him. You're liable to wind up with a chubby up your ass."

Theo glanced out to the parking lot. The dude leaned against the side of his truck, looking at his phone.

"Paula, that bitch I dated a few years ago from Two Harbors, dragged me over there for their grand opening." Adam hovered as Theo unscrewed the old plug. "They got the place looking like a fairyland. Couldn't wait to get the hell out of there."

Theo took another look and then hated himself for it. He wanted to look for all the wrong reasons. *Knock it off.* Like Adam, this guy—Ian, was it?—made him nervous. As far as he could tell, it was something to do with looks. Or, maybe not looks, but attitude— masculine and confident. Although Ian had a few years on Adam, Theo noted their similarities. There wasn't a thing faggy or wimpy about either of them. If Adam hadn't mentioned it, he would have never guessed the dude was a fag.

Theo felt his confidence bottom out. *Nothing feels right anymore.*

He tried to focus on his work. Screwing in the new plug, he gave the small engine a once-over with his rag, removing the grease and dirt buildup. "That should do it." He lifted the tiller off his worktable and wheeled it out of the garage.

"Remember, no bending over if you know what's good for you." Adam snickered.

"Wow! That was quick." Ian, who appeared impressed, shoved his phone into his pocket.

"I'm pretty sure it was the plug. Let's see." Grabbing the starter cord, Theo placed a foot on the machine and gave it a tug. The engine turned over a few times and stopped. He made an adjustment to the choke and tried it again. This time it fired right up. "Yep, that was it." He reached down and killed the ignition.

"I really appreciate you fixing this so fast." Ian lifted the tiller into the truck bed. "How much do I owe you?"

"Twenty-five will cover the labor and the plug." Theo looked back to Adam to acknowledge solidarity against the fag, only to be overcome by a fear of guilt by association. *He's so good looking.* His face warmed.

"Can I put it on my card?" Ian took out his wallet.

Take your tiller and get the hell out of here. "Sure." Theo snatched the card from the customer's hand and hurried into the office, acutely aware the gay dude was hot on his trail. *I bet he's staring at my ass.* He swiped the card, entered in the required data, and waited for the machine to process. *Could you be any slower?*

"Do you set up accounts? You're a heck of a lot closer than Two Harbors." Ian rested his large, weathered hand on the counter.

Unwilling to make eye contact, Theo focused on the hand that had just violated what he considered to be his personal space. *Nothing faggy about that hand at all.*

"You'll want to talk to Artie about that. He's out for a couple of days on vacation. Here's his card." Theo handed Ian a business card from the stack by the till.

"Great. I'll wait until next week and give him a call."

Theo ripped off the receipt from the printer and slid it across the counter along with a pen. "Need a receipt?"

"Yes please." Ian signed. "I'm sorry. I didn't catch your name." He stuffed his receipt into his wallet.

"Theo." *Why the hell does he want to know my name?*

"Theo, okay. Hey, Theo, thanks for the great service." Ian extended his hand.

Show him how a real man shakes. Theo wiped his hand on his pants and executed a good, hard shake.

"If you need a place to stay for a weekend getaway, stop by and we'll give you the neighbor rate."

Theo looked away, too embarrassed to acknowledge how the handshake had mysteriously become something more meaningful to him. A brush with the forbidden or some shit like that.

"Take care." Ian left the office.

As much as he tried, Theo was unable to take his eyes off the attractive man as he walked to his truck and pulled out of the lot. Catching himself in a sigh, he stared down at the signature on the receipt. Ian Burke. The penmanship was precise. Masculine. Not flowery or ornate. Theo threw the receipt in the till and slammed it shut when he'd realized that, for the last several moments, he'd been touching himself.

"Just a minute, I'll ask. Theo, Theo you there?" Adam hollered.

"What's up?" Wiping the perspiration from his brow, Theo returned to his friend in the garage.

"It's Monica. She wants to know if you and Lucy want to join us for something to eat and a movie Friday night."

"Sounds like the ticket. I'm sure Lucy will be up for it. Nothin' else planned." He reasoned a foursome would be less stressful than the recent dates he'd had alone with Lucy. A tension, an unspoken anxiety, had developed between them. The easy friendship they'd enjoyed for so long seemed threatened. Theo understood that to "go there" with her would somehow be the beginning of the end for them. He planned to ignore her frustration for as long as he could until he could work it out. Work himself out.

"Yeah, I know she'll be up for it." Adam laughed after ending his call. "Lucy called Monica last night."

Theo knew that as damaging as this revelation was, Lucy talking to Monica, he could never let on the effect it had on him. His chest tightened, and his breathing became labored. He felt light-headed as he struggled to maintain his composure.

Oh God, what did they talk about?

Up until now, Lucy and Monica had been acquaintances, enjoying time with one another whenever the two men in their lives brought them together. Nothing more. For Lucy to call Monica, well, it had to be something important. Theo felt like he'd been kicked in the stomach. There was only one reason for her to call. It wouldn't be long, he feared, before Adam would know. Lucy wanted what every other woman her age wanted, but because... *I'm so screwed up...* she wasn't getting it. She wanted to know the reason for his sexual disinterest in her. When he had that figured out, she'd be the first to know.

Theo had no place to turn. Feeling betrayed, he walked over to the rider and began taking it apart.

"PETRA?" Harper called out. "Anyone home?"

"I'm coming. I'm *coming*!" the Palisade Beach Cabins' new office manager hollered.

Harper walked behind the desk. Next to the computer, he spotted a picture. *I don't remember seeing this before. Sure, now I remember.* It was a picture Ian had taken of Petra and Emily at the resort Christmas party last year.

"Hey, Harper. Sorry, I'm ready if we need to get going."

"This is a very nice picture of you both." Harper placed it back where he found it. When no response was forthcoming from Petra, he looked over. "Problems in paradise?"

"Paradise, no. Problems, yes. Being with Emily is like working in phone sales. Every move I make is a frickin' hard sell. Anyway, she's visiting her parents and plans on moving back to the Twin Cities for the summer. Ian already told me she could work here if she wants, but I guess that's not an option she's interested in. I'm not an option she's interested in."

"Sorry to hear that."

Harper felt bad. On the sturdy side, Petra possessed a kind, loving face. Her dark, naturally curly hair framed it nicely. She was witty, smart, and competent. *Just be you, Petra. Someone will eventually cross your path and, without trying, you'll find yourself linked to an equally marvelous person.*

"Have you seen the gardener?" Respectful of Petra's space, he moved back out into the center of the room.

"Ian's running an errand. He should be back in a minute." Petra gathered up papers and piled them into her bag. "Oh, that reminds me. I haven't printed out the resort schedule you asked for."

"Yep. We'll need that for the meeting." Harper sat down on one of the chairs at the front window.

He had arranged to have food delivered from the Lip Smacker because Alex, who used to have Petra's job, was racing around trying to get their first newsletter out for the Men's Center they were in the process of opening. Harper smiled. He and Alex had been teased mercilessly over the fact they'd purchased the old Odd Fellows meeting hall in Two Harbors for their new project. Everyone agreed the choice couldn't have been more fitting. They still had daily responsibilities with the resort, but progress on the Center was steady. The newsletter going out was a very big deal to them.

"Man, does it ever feel like spring." Ian came through the door and walked around the end of the desk as pages noisily spewed out of the printer. "Here's a business card for Artie's Small Engine Repair. Can you give them a call to set up an account? Artie is supposed to be back from vacation in a few days."

"Absolutely. Anything else?" Petra took the card and placed it on the keyboard.

"Nope. What up, stud?" Ian saluted his partner.

"Hey, handsome." Harper got up from the chair. "Are you riding with us, or do you want to drive alone? Wait, I can answer that. You should drive alone so you can bring Petra back when our meeting is done. Alex will have my ass if I don't roll up my sleeves and help him out."

"Sounds like a plan." Ian strolled to the door. "Shall we?"

He and Ian watched as Petra stuffed the last printout into her large lime-green purse and dashed around the counter. "I'm all set."

"After you my… dears." Harper held open the door for Petra and Ian.

"TURKEY, for the turkey." Harper delivered a box lunch to Ian.

"Crap, that was funny. Not." Ian opened his box and proceeded to unload its contents onto the long folding table they were all seated at. "Where's Alexaaaandra?"

"Alexaaaandra?" *I don't want to know.* Harper placed a box lunch at an empty place and took his seat. "Alex ran the Center's newsletter over to the post office. He'll be right back." Harper went about arranging his own lunch to his liking and then went right for his cookie.

"What's this Alexaaaandra shit all about?" Petra cracked open her soda.

"I'm trying to talk Alex into doing drag at the Main Club. There's an amateur night coming up next month. With those legs and that slender waist, he'd knock 'em dead." Ian chuckled. "He's oh, so close. I told him I'd help with his outfit…."

"Oh, that reminds me. Sorry to interrupt, Ian." Harper glanced toward the door anxiously.

"No, you're not." Ian ripped open his packet of chips.

"You're right. I'm not. While we're all together, let's talk a minute about Alex's twenty-first birthday before he gets back."

"Man, does time fly when you're having fun." Ian put his hands behind his head and leaned back in his chair. "You know what I've noticed lately? Our boy's starting to get man features."

"Man features?" Petra perked up. "As opposed to…."

"I know what you mean." Harper laughed. "He *is* starting to get man features. When we scooped him up out of the wilds three years ago, he was just a kid, not even eighteen, but he looked, what?" Harper looked over to Ian for his opinion.

"He was like this little kid with man-size problems. It was so strange." Ian dove back into his lunch.

"Exactly, and now he's filling out and has this great swimmer's look going on. I think it's safe to say there'll be more than a few hearts broken by Alex along the way." Harper was aware of how prideful he sounded, and that made him smile.

"Those green eyes. You could lose yourself in them." Petra launched into her chicken salad with wild abandon. "Are you guys planning something fun?"

Harper couldn't remember anticipating an event more. Since hiring Alex as their first office manager when the cabins opened three years ago, the talented young man had become an important part of their lives. Alex was their friend and a trusted business associate. He was a younger brother, and in some respects, a son. They were excited to do something very special for his milestone birthday. "Yep. For starters"—he looked over to Ian to confirm their plan still needed work—"bar hopping, even though Alex doesn't drink." Harper sipped his diet soda for emphasis.

"He dinks a plenty, let me tell ya," Ian piped up in Alex's defense.

Harper's hand went to his mouth as a safeguard to block the cola he was close to spitting out. "Oh man, I can't believe I just said that." When he felt it safe to release his hand, he threw his head back and roared.

"What's so funny?" Alex breezed into the room, launching everyone into fits of laughter. He pulled his windbreaker over his head and tossed it onto a chair, revealing a now-vintage Palisade Beach Cabin Resort T-shirt from their first season.

"Oh, nothin'," Ian eked out.

"Petra, what are these guys laughing at?" Alex opened his box lunch and examined its contents. Like Harper, the first thing he plucked out was his cookie.

"Alex." Petra snorted, adding fuel to the silly.

"Forget it." Alex reached over and snatched away Harper's clipboard. "Okay, let's get this meeting started. I'm extremely busy today."

"Right, no more dinkin' around." Ian appeared to have pulled it together. "What's the first order of business, boss man?"

"The *soft* opening," Alex read from the clipboard, cracking everyone up again. "Okay, someone better tell me what's going on."

"Soft opening sounds pornographic. Everything sounds kind of pornographic today." Petra shifted in her seat and then looked up as if to see if her attempt at explaining their bout with the giggles was a success.

"It does?" Alex laughed, not offended but clearly not getting it.

"Okay, first of all, it's off-season opening, not soft opening. I don't know why I wrote that. Now, if you would be so kind." Harper took back his clipboard. "Petra, what's left to do on cabin repair?"

"The roof leak on three is done, but the roofer dude suggested we plan on having all the cabin roofs replaced soon."

"Really? I don't think they look that bad." Ian took a huge bite out of his sandwich.

"Me either. I think he's fishing for work. Cabin three got nailed by a frickin' branch during that big storm last year." Petra shoved a few chips into her mouth. "It was my first week working for you guys. I'll never forget how scary—"

"Working for us is scary?" Harper pouted from the end of the table.

"The storm. The storm was frickin' scary," Petra admonished.

"Let's see." Harper looked over the list. "Ian, how are you doing with the gardens? Do you need extra help this year? We can all pitch in if you need it."

Working through the University of Duluth, Ian had received his Master Gardener certification a few weeks earlier. Harper had encouraged him to do this because he had felt it would be another marketing feather in their cap, and frankly, more impressive for visitors to know a gardener of Ian's caliber was on staff. The landscaping and gardens, all designed and maintained by Ian and a small crew, were the primary reason many of their guests chose the Palisade Beach Cabins over their competitors. The grounds had become a popular destination for a variety of fund-raising and special events.

Alex pointed to himself and mouthed, "No way am I planting this year."

"Yes, you *are*." Ian pounced for Alex's lunch.

Alex managed to nab his box before Ian could get his hands on it. "No, I'm *not*!"

"Come here." Ian stood, pushing his chair out from under him.

"Lick me!" Alex taunted, retreating to the other side of the room.

"You're never too old for a time-out," Harper reprimanded sternly.

"He started it," Ian said, sitting back down.

"God, this is worse than kindergarten." Petra shook her head.

"Seriously, let's get through this. Ian, do you need help with the gardens?" Harper peered across the table, waiting for his partner to answer.

"No. I want to do it all myself."

"Fine. Alex, talk to me about the software update." Harper motioned for Alex to sit back down.

"The manufacturer's update"—taking no risk, Alex sat next to Harper, as far away from Ian as he could get—"arrived yesterday. I can take a look at it tonight, maybe even get it loaded onto the system, and by next weekend, we can have everyone trained."

"Perfect." Harper scratched one off the list.

"Petra, how are we looking for reservations?"

"Reservations are strong. We're close to being full through the middle of July, and off-season is selling really well. Here's the most recent printout you requested." Petra slid the document across the table.

"That's awesome." Ian threw a chip at Alex.

"And another one for Petra, how are we doing with staffing?" Harper flipped through the pages to make sure he hadn't forgotten anything.

"Not so good. I've got a few more interviews this week." Petra pushed back her chair. "I'm trying not to be picky, but man, there's a lot of lazy and helpless out there. It's housekeeping. Changing sheets, scrubbing toilets. I can tell by the look on some of these kids' faces when I run over the list of expectations that the thought of doing anything with a toilet other than their own business is incomprehensible to them."

"Well, let me know by the end of the week if you're still having problems."

"Will do. I'm trying to get a crew the first time around I know will last the season." Petra pocketed her cookie.

"Understood." Harper enjoyed their office manager's common-sense approach. With Alex spending more and more of his time at the Center, finding someone as dedicated to keeping the internal workings of the resort running smoothly had been a miracle. Who would have thought a thirtyish ex-roller-derby lesbian would meld so nicely into their irreverent, all-male mix. *I hope you stick around for a while, Petra. You make a great addition to the team.*

ALEX rinsed the last of the salad plates and loaded them into the dishwasher. Ian had cooked—Harper had a free pass for cooking over the weekend—leaving cleanup tonight Alex's responsibility. Grabbing his soda off the marble counter, he walked down to his room at the end of the hallway.

Do you really want to do this, man?

He'd agonized over this decision for weeks. It was time to make his move, well, almost time. He needed a minute to collect his thoughts. *Don't make up a bunch of excuses. They'll see through that in a second, and it will probably piss them off. Just tell them what's on your mind.*

Sitting on the corner of his bed, Alex did a quick tour. The guest room had been his for over a year. When the time arrived to open the Men's Center, Petra was hired on as his replacement. As the resort's operational manager, Alex still had a full list of responsibilities, including all of the technology upkeep, but running the day-to-day office would now be Petra's job, and it only made sense for her to occupy the office apartment. She'd jumped at the opportunity.

There was nothing wrong with his current setup. Everything he could possibly need was here, including a small refrigerator for his soda supply, a Christmas gift from Ian and Harper.

And he adored his housemates. Idolized them. They were his family. With his father's passing a few years ago, a tragic suicide when he jumped off the palisade, and his mother's death years earlier to cancer, Alex was left with nobody to fill in the gaps. He still marveled at how lucky he was to have crossed paths with Ian and Harper and all of their wonderful friends. His life had never been better.

You don't have to do this, you know—yes, I do. I want to be on my own.

For all of their wonderful love and support, Alex couldn't shake the feeling he was living with parents. There were no rules, nobody to scold or punish him if he screwed up. He was living with two other men, granted, older men by ten years, but that didn't mean anything. He was given as much space as he needed. They had their own thing going on. On the rare occasion when the dude he invited to spend the night crossed paths with them, both Ian and Harper had always been polite and gracious.

Alex chuckled. Ian had gotten into the habit of rating all of Alex's dates he came into contact with. While they were still in the house, Ian posted a sheet of paper on the refrigerator with a large number between one and ten written in marker. So far, the lowest score was a four (bad hair), and the highest, a nine (nice car).

I want to set up my own house. Make all my own decisions. That's it! He needed to feel more like an equal rather than a younger brother, or… *say it! I'm not their son.* In a few weeks, he'd be twenty-one. Financially, he'd done very well for himself over the last several years. A generous salary, the bonuses, coupled with his frugal nature, added up to a nice balance in his savings account. He was independent, except… *except for living here.*

Harper will understand this more than Ian.

Ian and Alex were the best of pals. A marvelous bond had developed between them over the years; they were like brothers. Whereas his relationship with Harper resembled that of a father and son. Harper was more paternal, more protective.

Okay, you have to do this!

Nervous, Alex paced around in a circle a few times to gain momentum and then headed to the entertainment room located on the opposite end of the house. "Hey!" He walked in and sat across from his housemates, who were curled up on the couch. "You guys look like monkeys grooming each other."

"You look like beef stew vomit." Ian smooched his hand and blew the kiss toward Alex.

"We've been channel surfing, waiting for you to finish cleaning up." Harper sipped his beer.

"Man, you're slow." Ian whipped an accent pillow in the air, missing Alex's head by inches.

"Anyone got a movie in mind?" Harper looked around the room for suggestions.

That's your cue. "You guys mind if we talk for a minute?" Alex patted his hands on his knees and then stopped, understanding Ian would be all over his weird nervous shit if he gave him a chance.

"What's on your mind?" Harper reduced the volume on the remote and tossed it on the table next to his feet.

Despite all the planning and rehearsing he'd done over the last few days, the very thing Alex had worked so hard to avoid, profound nervousness, came rushing over him like a tsunami. No matter how hard he tried, he was unable to lift his eyes off his shoes and face the two most important people in his life.

"Are you pregnant?" Ian asked suddenly, sitting up straight. "Damn it, how many hundreds of times have Harp and I told you to stay away from that turkey baster?" Turning to face Harper, he added, "I suppose there's some clinic, God knows where, we can take him."

Several seconds passed in silence while Ian's silly joke gained momentum. Harper lost the straight-face battle first and started to giggle. "Where... does this weird shit come from with you?"

"I don't know." Ian laughed. "I just think this way."

"Alex, do you want to walk out and come back in again? Ian promises to behave himself." Harper flicked Ian's ear.

This is as good as it's going to get. Go for it!

"I love you guys, but...." Finding the right words seemed impossible. He couldn't look across the room.

"Take your time. We love you too. You know that." Harper sat up in his chair and reached for his beer.

"I hate that I'm such a wimp." Alex found the nerve to look up from the floor.

"We don't, dude. We love wimpy." Ian looked around the room, displaying his "I'm serious now" look.

"Okay, I'm just going to say this." Alex decided if he sat forward on his chair, somehow what he had to say would come out easier. "I love it here, but I'm thinking I want a place of my own."

There. Finally, it was out. Ian and Harper reacted by looking over at each other.

"Makes sense to me," Ian said after several moments had passed.

"Me too. I mean, I think it makes sense. We're going to hate like hell for you to move out, but I get it. I'd want my own place too." Harper reached for his beer and nodded over to Ian as he tucked his leg under his butt. "Watcha got in mind?"

Alex detailed his plan to start looking in the Silver Bay-Two Harbors area for a small house, or at the very least, one of the nicer apartments.

"I like the house idea better than the apartment one," Harper confessed. "It's a buyer's market, and depending on what's out there, I bet you'll end up with a good deal. If you need us to cosign, say the word. We'd feel like shit if you had to pass on something you wanted because the bank put the brakes on it."

"If you want a second opinion, I'd love to help." Ian stood and walked past Alex as he strolled over to the fireplace. This was typical of Ian. He had reacted by showing support, but seconds later he was having buyer's remorse. *Ian, I had to be honest. This is really hard for me too.* Alex couldn't help but feel for his friend, who would never admit he was hurting.

"Alex, can I ask you one thing?" Ian turned, resting his elbow on the mantel.

"This isn't going to be good, is it, Harper?" Alex asked warily, standing to try to displace the nervous energy that was attacking him from every angle.

"Nope! Keep your 'Ian' shield up, by all means." Harper rose from the couch to join them.

"It's good," Ian whispered as he looked over with a droopy smile. "Will you stop by now and then for a sleepover?"

"Sure," he answered softly. "Sure I will. I'll be back in a minute." Fearful he might self-destruct and start to shed a few, Alex strolled back down the hall to his room. *Sleepover... thanks, guys, for being so cool. Damn, that was hard!*

CHAPTER
TWO

THEO drove around to the back of the shop and parked. He yawned, rubbed his eyes, and fell back hard against the seat. *What an awful night.* Worried to the point of feeling sick to his stomach, he had tossed and turned, hoping to latch onto a solution for the mess he found himself in.

A call with Lucy earlier in the evening hadn't provided him with anything concrete to fuel his insecurity, but the more he dissected and analyzed the tone of her voice and her responses, the more his confidence dwindled. His biggest fear—Lucy, Monica, and Adam, secretly behind his back, were coming to conclusions. *About me!*

Shit bubbled up all around him, he thought as he stepped out of his truck. Before leaving for work, he'd gotten into it with his mom over a stupid-ass church program she wanted him to participate in. Darla Engdahl's brainchild "What's Next?" paired teens with young adults to help the teens navigate through those first few years when they were out and on their own. *What a bunch of crap! How the hell am I supposed to help someone else out when I don't even know who I am? Give me a break!*

"You're being very selfish. You must use a part of your life to help others. That's what we do. That's what our family does because we are good Christians," his mother had lectured angrily.

When he told his mom no way, she had started to cry. Darla crying wasn't anything new. Crying was her stock defense whenever she wanted to prove a point or reinforce the chances of getting her way. *My days of giving in to her are over.* Of course this would escalate up to his dad, adding another strike against him and another piss stain to his welcome mat. Theo shook his head in disgust as he walked through the door of the shop.

Twisting the closed sign around to open, he hit a switch igniting a band of florescent lights spanning across the water-stained ceiling of the front office. He'd have an hour on his own before Adam rolled in. The two mechanics were taking turns opening up the shop while Artie was on vacation. If Adam confronted him on anything, he'd shrug and laugh. *Nothing wrong with me, dude!*

The mail from yesterday sat piled on the counter. Looking for something to keep his mind off his troubles, he sorted through it. A few pieces down from the top, he came across a bright red flyer from the Men's Center. *What the hell is that?* A Two Harbors address was listed on the bottom, along with a phone number. He'd never heard of any Men's Center before. *Must be new.*

Inside was a list of activities and who to call if interested. Theo read down the list, expecting to encounter the deal breaker, an affiliation with a church. Bowling, biking, fishing, weekend camping trips, the list went on, and still no religious reference. The Center offered weeknight discussion groups: single parenting, substance abuse, and help with sexuality issues.

Sexuality, what does that mean? Theo wondered. *Is it guys who can't get enough pussy?* He'd heard about sex addicts who had to have it day and night. Reading on, he soon discovered exactly what it meant: Explore with other men the challenges of living gay in your society, including the coming-out process. Share your stories and learn from your peers. Moderated by Mark Middleton, Psy.D. Tuesday Evenings, 7:00-9:00 p.m.

Theo's heart pounded against his chest. *Too bad I'm not gay. Where's the support group for guys who are confused?* He stuffed the brochure back into the stack where he had found it.

You know, maybe it's Lucy, Theo told himself when he had opened the large door, letting light from the outside flood into the garage. *Most dudes don't want to screw nice and sweet. They want...*

no, wait, they need nice tits and a hot ass. Theo's new revelation had an extremely short shelf life after he reminded himself Lucy *had* nice tits *and* a slender, curved ass. Frustrated, he kicked a can, spewing bolts across the floor in all directions. *Damn it!*

His head began to ache. Soon Adam would show up and he'd have to pretend everything was okay. There was no way he was going to make it until quitting time at four. The day would only go from bad to much worse.

Theo's stomach cramped the same now as it had when he was little and was forced to wait for his father to get home from work. Every second of the day spent in fear as he tried to come up with the best excuse he could think of, in hopes Carl Engdahl would show mercy for his son's misdeed and spare him from a trip down to the basement for a meeting with his thick leather belt. *This is crazy. I'm not a little boy any longer.*

Switching on the shop light, Theo walked over to the riding mower he had left half torn apart and started working. An excess of oil putting pressure on the crankcase kept him occupied until the sound of Adam's pickup pulling into the lot caused him to drop his wrench on the cement.

You can do this, dude. Just act natural. It's their word against yours. You're confused. Everyone gets a little confused now and then.

"Hey, butt licker, how's the rider comin' along?" Adam walked over to the back counter and deposited his lunch cooler.

Butt licker? Is he calling me a fag name because he thinks I'm one of them? They'd called each other a million stupid names, but today it seemed different. Theo couldn't let his anxiety show. Not this early in the game. He searched the archive for an appropriate response and settled on, "Hey, hoser."

"Damn, I'm tired this morning. Glad *I* wasn't the one that had to open up."

What do we normally talk about? "Do anything fun last night?" Theo buried his nose in the engine he was dismantling.

"Monica, I don't know what got into her. Get this." Adam took a soda out of his coat pocket and snapped it open. "We went over to

Mickey's for pizza. She wants us to take a trip this summer to the Badlands. She had some maps to show me. You ever been there?"

"Nope."

"Me either." Adam walked over to continue his conversation. "Looks fun. I told her, yeah, okay. Let's do it. Made her night. Anyway… whoa, hang on."

Huh?

Adam scurried across the garage, trumpeting out a fart when he reached the other side. "Pizza and beer. Could be a lively day. So where was I?"

Out of the corner of his eye, Theo watched Adam pace back and forth to clear the air before heading back. "You guys are going to the Badlands."

"Yeah. Going to the Badlands. Made her night. Anyway, I go to take her home, and she changes the plan on me. Monica wants to spend the night at *my* place, dude. On a work night!"

"Wow," Theo answered, knowing Adam would expect a reaction.

"Well, let me tell ya, we got back there, and I barely got in the door. Dude, she was all over me. She shoved her hand right down the front of my jeans and shook hands with the johnson. We were naked by the time we hit the kitchen, so, dude, I've always wanted to do this. I lifted her up and sat her right back down on the table. Shit went flyin' everywhere."

Adam was so wound up, he began weaving back and forth between the toolboxes and engines scattered on the garage floor.

"Oh God, she was so hot for my rod she grabbed my ass with both hands and pulled me in so hard I almost had the wind knocked out of me."

"Wow," Theo answered again. This time he knew he needed to add more. "I wonder what got into her?"

"Oh, man," Adam continued, oblivious to Theo's lack of interest. "Harder! Harder, Adam! Fuck me harder! Dude, you should see the scratch marks on my ass."

Adam's last comment cut him to the quick. The problem, oh God, the problem, he *wanted* to see Adam's ass. Wouldn't mind it at all. Recently, he'd found himself imagining what his friend and coworker looked like naked. Theo gulped. *It's all I think about.* Not a day went by lately when Adam naked didn't float up to the surface and tease him. *It's the devil.* Every time this nasty thought found a way to the surface, he stomped the living shit out of it, hoping it would give up and die away. *Say something, you idiot.* "Sounds like a movie I saw once." Theo held his breath, hoping he'd passed the test.

"Oh yeah, dude, that's exactly what I was thinking. This is like a porn. Shit! I'm boning up again just tellin' ya about it."

Yesterday, before the call between Monica and Lucy, he could have looked over at Adam's crotch, no problem. They would have both laughed. Today, it was different. Everything was different. Theo bit his lip. Was Adam telling him about last night's exploits with Monica for a reason? Was Adam looking for a certain reaction from him? *Like the reaction you're already giving him? Pull it together!*

"Dude, you okay? You look kind of funny." Adam stood right over him.

Theo had thought earlier in the morning about faking sick. Now he didn't have to. Adam's fuck tale had made him physically ill. He was hot. He blinked several times to try to clear his vision. *Am I going to pass out?* Struggling to stand, he wiped the perspiration from his brow. "Sorry, man. I woke up this morning feeling like crap. I need to get out of here. Maybe go home and sleep for awhile."

"Dude, sure. Don't worry, I can handle it. We're keepin' up good. I'll finish this mower and then move over to the rider. What's going on with it?"

Theo pointed out what was wrong with the engine he was working on and thanked Adam for covering for him. *Get me the hell out of here.* Picking his truck keys off the counter in the office, on impulse, he dug out the Men's Center flyer he'd shoved back into the mail and fled out the door.

ALEX looked over at the piles of pamphlets stacked in front of him and scooted his chair up closer to the table. Each piece needed to be folded into thirds and a computer-generated address label affixed to the middle section. Sounded simple enough when he and Harper had first talked about it, but like everything, it took much longer than either would have thought.

Yesterday's newsletter went out to interested parties located within a hundred mile radius of the Center. This much larger group he was working on went out to everyone else. It had been a stroke of genius to collect addresses at Duluth Superior Pride the last two festivals in preparation for the Center becoming a reality. Alex grinned. Harper had a solid vision of what they were trying to accomplish, which made barreling through this busywork tolerable.

Both years, their little Pride booth had a steady stream of curious visitors. Surprisingly, many of the people they met over the course of the festival weren't locals. These folks had made, in some cases, a considerable effort to make it to Pride, and those same people, understanding the importance of Pride, might also appreciate the importance of the Center. Down the road, they might become financial supporters. In addition to their monthly flier, another mailing project in the not-so-distant future would be their first request for donations. They'd have to be up and running for a while, and be able to detail some success related to the Center before they could start asking for financial help.

Alex was startled when Harper poked his head in for an update. "Hey, how's it going?"

"It's going… monotonous." Alex got out of his chair and stretched.

"Please don't ask me to help." Harper sighed and fell back onto the doorjamb. "I've got my own special kind of ugly going on. Take a break, and let's go for a walk."

"What's your ugly?" Alex asked when they had ambled down the hall to the open area they hoped would soon be ready to host dances and other events involving large groups.

"I spent the morning watching an online CLE. It was dreadful. The facilitator was god-awful." Harper picked up a box containing a wall sconce.

"What's a CLE?" Alex had never heard the term before.

"CLE stands for Continued Legal Education," Harper explained. "An attorney is required to take a certain number of classes over a period of time so they can stay admitted to the bar. Every three years you have to report your attendance. If you fall short of having the required number and type of CLEs by the reporting cut-off date, you're in violation of the rules, and eventually you'll lose the right to practice law."

Alex thought about this for a minute and then asked, "Are you going back to being a lawyer?" *Is he thinking about opening up some kind of law office here at the Center? That would be pretty cool.*

"No plans at the moment, but someday maybe. In the scheme of things, it's really nothing to keep up your CLEs, just, well, monotonous." Harper laughed. "Let's pick a night next week and work on getting these lights up. The resort has to be our number one priority, but I'm hoping we can wedge in a few small projects here too. Maybe we can get Ian to help."

You guys are so lucky to have found each other. You're perfect together.

Occasionally, Alex found himself watching Harper and Ian for no reason other than to admire how easy they made their relationship look. It wasn't that they never had bad days or got snippy with each other. That happened. Usually Ian was the snippy one, and Harper just got quiet and frowned a lot. These spells rarely lasted more than a day.

Someday I hope to have what you guys have.

Alex looked over to Harper and smiled. "Sure, whatever works best. I'm there."

"Great! Now follow me. We've got a call to make." Harper charged off in the direction of his office.

What's this all about? Alex followed him into one of the rooms off the big open hall, and at Harper's prompting, sat in the chair across from his large oak desk.

"I think you're going to like this." Punching a number into the phone, Harper crossed his eyes while he waited for the other party to pick up.

"Mark's Realty. Tiffany here," a voice on the other end answered brightly.

"Tiff, it's Harper Callahan. How's it going?"

"Harper, great to hear from you. When my secretary told me she'd set up this call, I knew there'd be at least one bright spot in my day. What's shakin'?"

"Well, I have you on speakerphone, and along with me is my colleague, Alex Stevens."

Alex giggled. He couldn't help it. He'd never been referred to as a colleague before.

"Oh, hey, Alex. How's it going?"

"Hi, Tiffany." Alex wanted to die when his voice cracked. "I'm good."

"Alex is interested in becoming a homeowner, and who better, we thought, to help him get there but you, my dear."

Awesome! Alex was about to burst. He had no idea Harper would offer his help and support so soon.

"Oh wow, that is exciting. I'd be honored to help out."

"Perfect." Harper beamed. "How should we start this?"

"Alex, why don't you give me an idea of some of the things you're looking for in a home." Tiffany paused to blow her nose. Harper flashed a look of utter disgust, which made Alex giggle again.

"Sorry, my allergies are really bad. Anyway, it doesn't have to be too detailed, but the more you can give me to work with, the better idea I'll have out of the gate. I don't want to waste time showing you properties you're not going to like."

Alex didn't need any further prompting to launch into a well-thought-out list of amenities he'd envisioned for his first home. They included an attached garage, fireplace, screened porch, an entertainment room, and an updated kitchen.

"He'll have what we're having," Harper joked when Alex had come to the end of his list.

"I like a man who knows what he wants," Tiffany cheered. "Okay, give me a few weeks to scope out the market. Does it have to be in the Tettegouche-Silver Bay area?"

Alex looked over to Harper. The Palisade Beach Cabins were there, but the Center was in Two Harbors, a good half an hour away.

"Alex, I don't want to misrepresent you, so pipe up if I'm taking this somewhere you don't want it to go." Harper smiled.

Alex nodded back, a silent communication to Harper indicating he was cool. This was his deal, but to not take advantage of Harper's ability to steer a discussion in the right direction would be stupid. He was sitting across from the master.

"Tiff," Harper sat up in his chair, "Alex has a very clear idea of what he wants. Let's not limit the search to Tettegouche. Ideally, that's where he would like to be, but on the other hand, if you found him his dream home, and it meant he had to spend some time on the road going to and from work, well, it might be a compromise he'd be willing to make."

One of the things Alex admired most about Harper was his practicality. Alex flashed an enthusiastic thumbs-up.

"Gotcha. Guys, let me do some searching around"—paper rustled on the other end of the call—"and I'll get back to you in a week or two with, hopefully, a few properties to look at. If anything comes up earlier, I'll give you a call. Sound good?"

Harper gestured over to Alex for a response.

"That sounds great, Tiffany." Alex couldn't keep the excitement out of his voice.

"Good. Who should I call?"

"Call this number. Harper and I are never too far apart." Alex smiled, hoping he'd answered correctly. Harper returned a thumbs-up.

"Well, thanks again for thinking of me. I appreciate the business."

"It's the least we can do for all of the lodgers you and your friends have sent to the Beach Cabins." Harper leaned as far back in his chair as he could and stretched.

"Have a great rest of the day, guys. We'll talk soon."

"You too! Bye!" Harper and Alex said in unison.

Alex sprang up from his chair the moment the call ended, too excited to sit.

"You okay with how that went down?" Harper stood and tossed his soda can in the garbage.

"That was so cool. Thanks!" Alex fought off an urge to walk over and hug Harper. *You're such a dork.*

"If there's a house to be found that comes close to having the *multitude* of amenities you've assembled, Tiffany will find it." Harper stepped out of the office. Alex followed. "Oh, did including a bidet slip your mind?"

"What's a bidet?" If it was something really cool, he'd make sure to put it on the list.

"Google bidet, B-I-D-E-T. It's got you written all over it." Harper led the way back to the small conference room Alex had been working in. "Wanna grab some lunch?"

Lunch would be great, Alex thought, but, knowing Harper, they'd get sidetracked on some special mission, and his afternoon would be lost before he knew it. He needed to stay focused on the mailing or the brochures would never get out.

"Naw, I'd better stick around." Alex plopped down in his chair and familiarized himself with where he'd stopped prior to Harper's impromptu visit.

"You and Todd doing anything tonight?"

Harper was clearly on the hunt for a distraction. But Todd—did he want to go there?

After dating the handsome veterinary assistant on and off for several months, Alex had come to the conclusion that the primary thing on Todd's mind, and probably the only thing he would ever have on his mind, was sex. Sick of Todd's pawing and begging, Alex had grown tired of the shallow relationship they had formed. To make matters worse, when Alex compared it to what Harper and Ian had, spending any more time with Todd was pointless. There would be no future with Todd.

"Was that a frown I just spotted?"

Harper smelled blood. He and Ian could be relentless if they thought Alex had a problem and hadn't come to them for help or advice. It wasn't that they were nosey. It had more to do with their not wanting him to spend a minute of his time distressed. Another reason for wanting a place of his own.

"I need... more." Alex sat back, knowing he would be forced into having this conversation whether he liked it or not. Mostly, he liked it. He valued Harper's opinion, and he trusted that, when it was all said and done, Harper would always have his back. His boss and friend provided a great sounding board. Ian too, but his time with Ian was limited in comparison to how much he spent with Harper. Time spent with Ian was dedicated to fun and games. A serious discussion with him wasn't impossible, but it was highly improbable. It all balanced out.

"You mean he's tiny, you know, where it counts?" Harper's concern was contradicted by the familiar wrinkle on the corner of his mouth, signaling either a chuckle or, at the very least, a grin.

"Harper, quit. The dude is *all* about sex. It's all he thinks about." Alex looked over to see if he'd made his point. "I'm bored," he added for extra emphasis.

"Oh, I get it." Harper stared into the air.

Alex was familiar with this response too. Harper would not advise or comment until he'd searched the database for his best shot.

"I feel trapped," Alex offered.

"Smothered," Harper countered.

"Trapped," Alex repeated, knowing it would delight Harper he was holding his own.

"Smothered trapped," Harper added brazenly.

"Sure," Alex relented. He'd already scored the victory.

"Have you spelled this out to him? Your needs? Alex, he seems like a really nice dude. He's nuts over you." Harper picked up a brochure from the pile in front of him and glanced over it.

"His nuts are all over me night and day. That's the problem." Alex looked over to see what effect his comeback would have.

Harper chuckled. "Seriously, have you spelled it out to Todd what you're looking for in a man?"

"It's not worth it." He waved his hand as if shooing away a fly. There was no point in spending time on Todd. Their time together, Alex had concluded, was time he'd never get back. *Cut your losses.*

"Why?" Harper crossed his arms and looked over. "Because you're too busy to really talk to him? You've decided Todd isn't worthy of your respect? Or is it Todd lacks the prerequisite mind-reading skills needed to qualify as a Mr. Right candidate?"

Cautious and careful wasn't Harper's style, no matter how much a person meant to him. His last comment stung, as it was intended to. Alex hadn't invested the time in Todd, and because of this, Todd didn't have a clue what was going on. Harper had spotted Alex's shortcoming in record time.

"Can I say one more thing?"

Harper paused long enough to force Alex to give him a reluctant nod. Anger percolated from every pore. If Alex allowed it to best him, whatever defense he might be able to present would be worthless. Harper would cash in on his lack of self-control in a heartbeat.

"I don't want this to sound flip, but you're fucking with him even though you're accusing him of fucking you too much. It's not fair. Alex, it's mean. In a way, what you're doing is lying to him."

Alex avoided eye contact with Harper. Noise from the street filtered into the room. This wasn't the first time Harper had attempted to set him straight, and it wouldn't be the last time either.

Alex wished like hell he could see it coming so he would at least have a chance to turn things around before Harper nailed him.

"I didn't intend to make you feel bad, sport," Harper continued, "but Todd could be planning a future with you and have no idea you've already moved on. How would you feel if someone did that to you? I'd be pissed as hell."

Another stinger. Alex knew Harper was right. He hated himself for appearing so thoughtless and self-centered when Harper and Ian were anything but. It was okay to be angry at himself, but he didn't have to search very far—only a quick glance at the concerned face staring back—to be reminded he was with a friend and not the enemy. He sighed, thankful to have averted a meltdown.

"Dude, I know you hate hearing this. I can see it on your face. But it's important you do." Harper tapped the brochure in his hand until Alex was forced to make eye contact. "Besides entertaining various ways you can off me, what are you thinking? Can you see what I'm talking about?"

Being scolded by Harper, no matter how gently, frustrated him. It didn't happen often. It didn't have to. Alex was a good guy too, he knew this, but his age and inexperience, the culprit every time in these situations, pushed him back a few steps just when he thought he was making strides forward. He could lose the battle but still save a few nuggets of self-respect by taking the tongue lashing like a man and not the threatened little boy who screamed for release.

When am I going to grow up?

Harper's comments began to germinate the seeds of guilt. Alex felt like crap for the way he had dealt with his "Todd" situation. "I wasn't trying to be mean to Todd," he offered, grabbing a stack of mailings only to put them back. Harper was watching him, and it made him uncomfortable.

"I don't think you're capable of consciously being mean. And I wasn't trying to make you feel bad by picking on you. But you have to ask yourself, what kind of person do you see in Todd? I mean, looking past his constant need for sex, what is it you see in him?"

"That's the problem." The sting was starting to wear off. "I don't see much past the sex. He's not like you...." Alex stopped himself. He hadn't intended for his last comment to leak out. Too revealing. He felt his face flush from embarrassment.

Again, the noise from the street took over where Alex had left off.

"Toward the end of my first year of law school"—Harper took the seat across from him—"I was lucky to fall into favor with a professor whom I greatly admired. Charles Berkin. Professor Berkin became my mentor. It was almost the same setup you and I have. He was roughly ten years older. This relationship lasted past the day I graduated. We e-mailed one another frequently until his death from a heart attack a few years ago. He was only forty-two. I still feel the loss."

"That sucks." Alex knew Harper was sharing this with him because there was a lesson to be learned. It wouldn't be a waste of his time. Harper's stories never were.

"Like me, Charles was *very* handsome." Harper paused until Alex rewarded him with a smile. "The combination of his looks and his superior intellect held me captive. Again, it's probably impossible for you to overlook the similarities."

"Harper...." Alex laughed, unable to resist his boss's charm.

"Anyway," Harper continued, "he wasn't married, and I'm not sure he was gay, but I held out a secret hope that, down the road, we would end up together." Harper laughed. "Man, am I glad that didn't pan out."

Without having it spelled out, Alex knew there was only room for one man in Harper's heart, and his name was Ian Burke.

"You and I are more alike than you might think, Alex. We're both very intuitive, and we both set very high expectations for ourselves. And I recognize you look to me for leadership like I looked to Charles, and that makes me enormously proud. You have to know that."

"I know that." As frustrated as Harper, or on a rare occasion Ian, could get with him, their love was unquestionable. They were family.

"Take this however you want, but don't search for a Harper or an Ian to spend your life with. Trust me, you'll never find anyone who completes the match to your satisfaction. If you don't know it already, we're just too damn special."

There was no confusing the message in the joke. Harper's observation couldn't have held more truth.

"Keep an open mind. Take the time to have the important conversations you need to have with the guys you're dating so you can unearth the potential in someone. Don't be lazy, and don't mislead. If you follow this advice, you're going to end up with someone that is so right for you he'll take your breath away. Ian and I will be left standing in the dust in tears."

"Okay." Alex wasn't sure what else he should say.

"Lip Smacker?" Harper stood. "I'm famished."

"Sure." Harper wasn't perfect, Alex thought as he walked out the door. But he was damned close to it. *Thanks, Harper.*

STARING blankly into the abyss, Theo watched a tanker, miniaturized by its distance, slowly approach the Port of Duluth. He was suffocating. Unable to stand it any longer, he cracked his window.

"Baby, what're you doin'?" The warm, clingy body pressed firmly against his shoulder asked. "It's freezin' out there, sweetie."

Theo didn't care. He was miserable. Miserable and mad. Mad at himself for not jumping at the opportunity to end his date with Lucy after the movie and head home to the sanctuary of his room. Instead, he'd led himself into battle. Now, there was no turning back.

"Come on, shut the window. I'm chilly," Lucy begged.

I can't do this any longer.

Lucy, his girlfriend of almost two years, had in one short week gone from being one of his best friends, someone he looked forward to spending time with, to an annoying, whiny chick whose every move repulsed him. No gray area here. He knew their relationship could not go back to what it was. Not now, not after she had become so… needy.

Dinner with Adam and Monica had been fine. They'd settled on Dusty's, just outside of Silver Bay. The beer was cheap, and Dusty's served up a respectable burger. Most of the conversation was centered around Adam and Monica's upcoming trip to the Badlands. The movie, an intense espionage thriller, managed to take his mind off his troubles for a few more hours. But in a weak moment, after saying good-bye to Monica and Adam, he'd agreed to drive Lucy up to the palisade overlook. *What the hell was I thinking? You're a complete moron.*

Now he was knee-deep in the very situation he had hoped to avoid. Parked alone with Lucy. To make matters worse, she was doing everything in her power to get him to perk up and play. She needed him. She wanted him. Using her fingers, she probed and explored, hoping at some point he'd show her some attention.

To avoid her sniveling, he rolled up the window and hoped she'd soon grow tired and ask to be taken home. Home to her own house. Her own bed. And this, Theo swore to himself, would be the last time he'd *ever* let himself get talked into being alone with her.

"What's wrong, sweetie? You mad at me or somethin'?" Lucy shoved her body up tighter against his.

Yes. No. How the hell am I supposed to answer that?

When he didn't answer, she tried another tactic. He heard her unzip her coat. She sat forward and pulled herself out of it. A wet tongue taking a swipe on his neck caught him off-guard, and he banged his head against the window.

"Boy, are you jumpy tonight." Lucy giggled.

Bitch!

Lucy wiggled out of her sweater and mashed her tits against his arm.

I want to die.

There wasn't time to die, because she was already on to her next move—to pick his hand up off his lap and place it on her bra-covered boob.

"Lucy, stop it!" Theo removed his hand and stuffed it between his legs.

"What's your problem, Theo?" Lucy exploded, her stark white bra glowing in the low light. "You've been an asshole all night. Did I do something? You're treating me like shit."

"Lucy...."

"Is there something wrong with me?"

Oh God, please don't start that.

"Tell me what it is. If you don't tell me, I won't know. Theo!"

"It's not you... it's me," Theo snarled, unable to filter his emotions.

"Right! You lying prick."

"Lucy—"

She cut him off while at the same time diving into her sweater. "You don't even have the balls to tell me you want to break up. You fucker. That's what you are. You're a fucking lying prick."

"I'm confused...." Theo struggled to find the right words that might appease her and buy him some time.

"No, you're not, but I sure as hell am. You told me you loved me. Love, Theo. And now you don't? *Fuck off!*"

Lucy grabbed her jacket, opened the truck door, and jumped out.

"Where are you going? Get back in here." Theo leaped over in hopes of snagging a section of Lucy's coat and pulling her back in.

"Go to hell." Lucy slammed the door.

Theo got out of the truck and followed her. "Lucy, where are you going? You can't walk home. Come on. Get back in the truck and we can talk."

There's no quick way out of this one.

Sobbing, Lucy charged ahead. Theo ran back, fired up his truck, and circled out of the parking lot in pursuit. He drove alongside of her with his window open. "Lucy, I'm so sorry. I'm not sure what's going on with me. Please get back in the truck."

In the chilled air, Lucy walked a few hundred feet farther and stopped. Theo applied the brakes and waited to see what her next move would be. Lucy walked around the front of the truck and climbed in, sitting as far over on her side as she could possibly get. "Take me home."

Theo put the truck in gear, and they drove several miles in silence. Lucy quietly sobbed.

Theo's feelings of anger and repulsion had now morphed into blame and disappointment. Theo had no intention of hurting her like this. "Lucy, I know you're mad as hell right now, but will you please just listen to me for a minute?"

Silence.

"I'm very confused... right now. There's no one else. You have to believe that. I'm just going through some kind of weird phase."

"A fucking phase, Theo? Is that the best you can do?" Lucy hissed.

Theo bit his lip. "Something is wrong with me. I'm not myself." *Lucy, give me a break here.*

"Why don't you want to have sex with me?"

Theo could feel her eyes bore into him. *Oh God, please don't push me.*

"Here's something for you to think about. There're plenty of guys who want to take me out. I'm not a dog, Theo. I get hit on all the time."

"You're not a dog." Theo had to do something. He couldn't end the night like this. He turned into the parking lot of her apartment complex, pulled into a space, and put the truck in park.

"Lucy"—he turned in his seat to face her—"I'm really scared. Something in me has changed. I'm not the same guy you—"

"You can say that again. You're an asshole." Lucy crossed her arms and stared out her window.

"Lucy, I'm scared. I'm scared I might be... gay."

Once the word had exited his mouth, a tremendous sense of regret enveloped him that quickly morphed into panic. He gulped to rush much-needed air into his lungs. He'd had no intension of going there; it just happened. He was up against a wall, and he chose the truth. Darla Engdahl would be proud.

"Gay?" Lucy looked over, incredulous. "Gay? Oh that's a good one, Theo. Do you think I'm that stupid? You're one sick, pathetic dickhead." For the second time that night, she swung her door open and hopped out. "Have a great life, sicko," she hollered, at the same time slamming the door with all her might.

Theo sat, stunned. He'd played what he thought would be a winning card. He had lost miserably. The worst part, he was confident Lucy thought she had caught him in a lie as opposed to a heartfelt disclosure. She would share his failed strategy with Monica, who would share it with Adam, who would confirm what he probably already suspected. It wasn't a lie. He watched until she had let herself inside before he drove out of the parking lot and back onto the highway toward Two Harbors.

At this point, he didn't care who thought what about him. His life, as he knew it, had just blown up. Where the pieces fell was anyone's guess. Well after midnight, he drove his truck up and down the deserted streets until he came to a parking lot, where he pulled in to turn around. A freshly painted sign, "Men's Center Parking Only," greeted him.

CHAPTER

Three

"OKAY." Harper put his fork down. They were all gathered in the office for an early-morning celebration, sipping orange juice and stuffing in the last few bites of an artichoke and feta quiche he had whipped up the night before. "Petra's the newest kid on the block, so she should be awarded the honor of officially kicking off the season." Harper was excited for her.

A Chicago native, the North Shore had been Petra's home while attending the University of Minnesota in Duluth. She'd moved back to the North Shore from Shakopee, a southwestern suburb of Minneapolis, after sustaining a career-ending injury on the roller-derby circuit, playing for the Minnesota Roller Girls. Parlaying a front desk job at the Lift Bridge Inn into a management position, she had responded to their ad for an office manager after it was decided they needed to replace Alex in that position.

"You go, girl," Ian shouted, clapping his hands together. "Let's get this party started."

Petra laughed. "This is so exciting I can't stand it."

"Come on, Petra," Alex hollered, "rock our world, girlfriend."

"Hit it," Harper chimed in as he joined the group peering over the reception desk.

Stepping back so everyone had a clear view, Petra, with an impressive hand gesture that drew oohs and aahs, flipped the silver toggle switch on the wall below the thermostat to its "on" position, igniting the "Vacancy" section of the welcome sign up on the highway. Everyone in the room whooped with excitement.

"Can one of you guys check out the ice machine and make sure it's running like it's supposed to be?" Petra asked when the commotion had finally ebbed. "I noticed a buzzing sound coming from it, and possibly this isn't a good thing?"

"Dang, it's buzzing again?" Alex asked, busing the paper plates from breakfast.

"What's up with that?" Petra asked.

"Not sure, but it does it every year until it's been running for a while. I'll try and keep an eye on it. Let me know if there's a change and it sounds worse." Alex walked around the back of the counter to grab a garbage bag.

"Before you guys leave, I have to ask your opinion on something." Petra reached for a note she had taped to the monitor.

"The new key chain, it's perfect," Ian teased. "It's girly in a manly way."

"A lesbian joke by a gay dude. It doesn't get any better than that, let me tell ya." Petra rolled her eyes before continuing, "I got this call yesterday from... Harold."

"Harold?" Harper looked around the room to see if the name registered with anyone.

"Yep. Harold called to inquire about the possibility of spending the entire summer here." Petra looked for a reaction.

"The entire summer? Seriously?" Ian chuckled. "What's up with that? Kinda weird."

"Apparently, friends of his spent time here last year, raved about it, and now Harold, along with his partner, want to spend the summer with us." Petra gave her shoulder a shrug.

"Well, we're sold out until the middle of July, right?" Ian downed his last swig of juice.

"Yes and no. Remember, we hold open a cabin each week until the last minute in case of a fuck-up, which, knock on wood, we've never had and I don't plan on ever having," Petra reminded them. "Bottom line, we can make it work. I'm just not sure it's the best idea."

"Why don't you think it's a good idea?" Alex went around the room collecting glasses and tossing them in his plastic garbage bag.

"Having one cabin tied up for the entire season robs us of who-knows-how-many guests, who will hopefully go back home and tell their friends about how groovy we all are. It's a marketing thing."

Harper, always interested in the marketing aspect of the business, appreciated her logic. "That's a good point, Pet," he confirmed. "Did Harold give any reason for why they want to be here the entire season? It seems a little odd, given the fact they haven't spent a night with us before."

"I say we make it work," Ian chimed in. "We're not exactly hurting, and it might be a good idea to experiment with an extended stay to see how we like it. Not that we have to make a practice of it or anything, but it might not be bad to have the experience of doing it one time at least."

"And that's also a good point," Harper confirmed. "Alex, care to weigh in?"

"I can see it both ways." Having cleared up the breakfast mess, Alex fastened a twist tie onto the large bag and tossed it outside the office.

"You're supposed to always agree with *me*." Ian pouted. "You promised. I don't want to play with Alex anymore."

"I say we leave it up to the office manager," Harper offered. "Petra, you call it."

Petra laughed as everyone awaited her decision. "Well, even though it was over the phone, I got a good vibe from Harold. Once July hits, we can hold out another cabin for last-minute screwups and emergencies. I'm game. Let's do it!"

"Do we offer a special rate or a discount?" Alex walked around to Petra's side of the counter and hit a few keys on the computer.

"Did Harold ask for a special rate?" Ian followed Alex and began rubbing himself against him.

"Get away from me, you perv!" Alex swatted.

"Both of you, get the fuck out of my space. *Now!*" Petra barked, shooing Alex and Ian around to the customer side. "No, price wasn't discussed. I got the impression it didn't matter. Harold had his heart set on spending the summer with us."

"Okay, this is what I'd like to do." Harper grabbed his coat off the back of the chair nearest the window. "Let's offer a cabin to Harold on a weekly basis. He'll always have the opportunity to renew his lease, but we'll have the opportunity to boot him out if, for some reason, he proves a nuisance. Sound like a plan? I can draw up a makeshift contract for him to sign back at the Center. I'm thinking it might be best if we have a little protection. It could get to be a very long summer if we got saddled with an asshole or *two*."

"Works for me." Ian licked his finger and attempted to insert it into Alex's ear.

"Okay." Petra placed her note back on the computer. "I'll call him back with the good news. Should I tell him we'll be ready by the weekend? Can you have the contract drawn up by then?"

"Sure, that's no problem." Harper zipped up his coat. "I'll do it today and drop it off tonight. Hey, do we have any guests checking in today? I forgot."

"That would be an affirmative. The Lingles, from Majestic Pines," she confirmed after double-checking the computer screen.

"Lingle, sounds like a potato chip." Harper located his keys. "Alex, are you heading into the Center with me or hanging back?"

"I'm going with you." Alex grabbed his jacket. "I have to run up to the house and grab some stuff. I'll be right back. Have a good day everybody!"

"You too, Alex." Petra waved.

"Is he gone?" Ian asked as he watched Harper move over to the side window that faced the house.

"Yeah, he's halfway down the trail already." Harper came away from the window with a devilish look.

"Pet, Harper and I bought Alex a boat for his birthday." Ian jumped around the office like he was on a pogo stick.

"You bought him a boat? Are you frickin' serious?" Petra looked over in amazement.

"He's going to poop his pants." Harper chuckled.

"Twice," Ian confirmed. "It's a little motorboat he'll be able to tool around in with his friends, which I'm sure includes *moi*." Ian continued to jump around the office with wild abandon. "A vintage Chris-Craft with just enough oomph to handle the big lake."

"Are Chris-Crafts the boats with the cool wood?" Petra asked.

"Exactly. This one's a little beat-up, but it will give Alex something to do." Ian walked over and put his arm around his partner's shoulder.

"The seller is in Duluth. Anyway"—Harper smiled— "his birthday is a couple of weeks away, but we'll have to figure out how to hide it around here. We want to put a big bow on it and surprise him. Will you help us out?"

"Oh, sure. I love surprises. Let me think on that one. Alex, such a lucky guy." Petra laughed.

"Damn right," Ian agreed. "Harper gave me an electric toothbrush for my last birthday."

"Come on," Harper coaxed. "You got more than that and you know it."

Ian laughed. "Oh man, you're right. I did get more. I was walking funny for days afterward."

"Quit!" Petra begged. "Not only is that TMI, but I have a ton of work to do around here. Go! Leave!"

"Bye, Pet," Ian and Harper called out as they left the office. "Have a good day!"

THEO looked at his watch. Twenty minutes and counting. Nerves churned his stomach.

You have to do this. Have to. Don't even think about wussing out.

Earlier in the week, he'd made a call to the Men's Center to ask about the session that met every Tuesday night. The sexuality session. A guy—Theo looked down at the piece of paper next to him on the seat—"Alex," he'd written down, told him to come a little early so he could fill out paperwork. The paperwork was for the Center's records only, and he was assured that nothing would be shared with an outside party.

Lucy avoided his calls, and Adam had noticeably distanced himself. Theo had thought about talking over the fight he and Lucy had with his friend, but wasn't sure he could do that and not alert Adam to the bigger problem. He hoped a session or two at the Center would help him understand what was happening to him. He made a deal with himself to find the courage to at least go into the Center and attend one of these meetings. If he felt uncomfortable, he'd just get up and leave, knowing he gave it a shot. The front end of this bargain was turning out to be harder to honor than he had expected.

You need help.

Concerned he might be late, Theo stuffed his notes into his pocket and stepped out of the truck. His knees shook as he walked the distance of the parking lot to the Center's front door.

"Hello," a voice greeted him as he entered.

The doors opened into a cavernous room lit by big silver flying-saucer-shaped lights hanging from the high ceiling. Off to the side, a young guy sat at a small table.

"Let me guess. Are you Theo?" The dude, who looked to be about his age, had a friendly smile.

"Um... yeah... Theo. Theo Engdahl. I called earlier in the week." Theo walked over to the table.

"Right. You talked to me. I'm Alex." Alex stood and offered his hand. "Welcome to the Men's Center."

"Thanks." Theo shook hands. *I've never seen eyes that green before.* His cousin Andrew had blue eyes that were kind of intense, but nothing like these.

"How you doin' tonight?" Alex asked. "The rain still holding off?"

"Yeah, no rain yet. Might get some later."

Despite his anxiety, Theo could feel his body begin to relax. He had visions of walking into a room full of freaks and immediately being put on the spot. So far, the place seemed okay. Nothing like he had feared.

"Okay, I need you to fill out this form." Alex handed him a clipboard. "Include all the information I've put an *X* by. You can sit here." Alex gestured to the empty chair next to him. "Oh, and we have soda and waters. Thirsty?" Alex smiled and pointed to the cooler at the end of the table. "We're working on getting coffee, but so far, this is the best we can do."

"A water would be great."

Theo sat down next to Alex and opened his water. Nerves had dried his throat. After downing a few healthy swigs, he placed the bottle on the floor and began to fill out the form. Halfway down the page, he stopped. *This feels weird.* He couldn't put his finger on it. There was something strange, good strange, about being seated so close to this dude. When Alex moved, Theo caught a whiff of some aftershave or something. It smelled good. Not girlie. And it made him want to get closer. *Adam would shit his pants if he knew what I was thinking.*

Pretending to contemplate how to answer one of the questions, Theo turned his head just enough for Alex to come into view.

Perhaps sensing he was being watched, Alex glanced up from what he was doing and looked over. "Any questions?"

"No. I was just...." *Get a grip.* Caught in an awkward moment, he added, "Had a brain fart," to cover his tracks.

Alex chuckled and returned to his work.

Your green eyes, dude, they're awesome. Theo had to resist the temptation to look again. *Stop this shit right now!*

Forcing himself to focus on the remainder of the questions, Theo stood after finishing and presented the form to Alex.

"Great. Thank you." Alex removed the form from the clipboard and stuck it in a folder.

His teeth are perfect. Theo looked away because he couldn't believe this dude's teeth had made an impression on him. *I'm doomed.*

"Tonight's meeting is around the corner and down the hall. You can't miss it." Alex stood and pointed in the direction Theo should go. "Mark, the facilitator, is already there, along with a few members of the group. Why don't you head in and introduce yourself."

"Sure. Sounds good." Theo looked down at the table. The time had come to face his fears and confront the horrible, confused feelings he battled. One more sip of water. Theo turned away and drank from the plastic bottle. *Dude, grow a pair and do this.* He couldn't believe how helpless he felt. His nervousness was embarrassing.

"Hey," Alex seemed to pick up on his apprehension. "Mark's a great guy and really good at what he does. You'll be fine."

"Thanks." For a fag, this Alex dude was cool. *At least I think he's a fag. Has to be if he works here.*

The nerves revved up again as Theo walked to the meeting. Only one room, about a third of the way down the hall, had light shining from it. As he approached, he heard voices. *Be a man.* With an unprecedented jolt of fortitude, he entered.

"They have to improve their pitching if they're going to get very far this season," a guy seated at the head of the table explained. Theo was surprised to discover the group only consisted of three men. Two other dudes were seated halfway down the table across from each other.

"Are you Theo?" the guy at the head of the table stood and asked. He was dressed in jeans and a University of Minnesota hooded sweatshirt.

"Yeah, I'm...." Theo choked on his own words. "Excuse me, I'm Theo Engdahl."

The dude, who appeared to be in his thirties, extended his hand. "Hi, I'm Mark Middleton. Welcome!"

What gives with all this hand shaking? Is it because gay dudes like to touch each other so much?

"I'll let these other guys introduce themselves." Mark gestured down the table and walked back to take his seat.

"Hey, I'm Ted."

Theo nodded.

"Steve here," said the other guy.

"Theo, grab a seat. It's early. We'll wait a few minutes and then get started. Where're you from?"

"Silver Bay." Theo forced himself to smile. Everyone in the room nodded.

Moments later, another guy waltzed in. Jerry—followed seconds later by Doug, he learned once they had sat down.

With introductions completed, Mark started the session. "Because Theo is new to us, let me take a minute to talk about our objectives and how we work together as a group."

Mark ran through a set of rules which, to Theo's surprise, included a ban on dating or having sex with anyone from the group. *Is he serious?* Meetings began with each member giving an update on their status. Theo was given a pass for this first meeting, but Mark made sure it was understood that in the future, he'd be required to share. After this initial update from everyone, each session was then dedicated to one specific member and his issue, or issues, if needed. Everyone would contribute to the discussion with the goal of the target person benefitting from the feedback.

Theo was equally fascinated and freaked out as people opened up about their particular struggle. Steve was into fisting, and Mark, seeing the blank look on his face, explained to Theo what this involved.

Are you shitting me?

Jerry, a man in his sixties, was finding it next to impossible to come out to his family, which by now consisted of only one brother and one sister who were still living.

Dude, just do it.

Doug was married with children and found himself caught between two worlds. He enjoyed sex with his wife but found Herman, the next-door neighbor, equally appealing.

He's bi. What's the mystery?

Finally, the group worked around to Ted, who admitted being addicted to an online affair that had been going on for over two years with Glen, who Ted assumed was another man. The fact that there was any doubt about Glen's gender was in part because Ted was falsely portraying himself to Glen as a much younger man than he actually was, by twenty-some years. Glen was probably doing something similar to Ted.

What a frickin' waste of time. This whole meeting setup is stupid. Theo had already decided to bolt at the first opportunity.

Ted was asked to detail any improvements he may have made to his situation since the last meeting. Ted sheepishly admitted he had made none and, if anything, found the need to connect with Glen stronger today than at any time before.

Mark cautioned him, and the group, that what Ted was doing was substituting a real need for something much safer, a fantasy life online. Theo noticed how the other group members offered their sympathies about his problem as well as encouragement to come clean and end this relationship. Mark explained the goal would be for Ted to meet a *real* person he could start building a *real* relationship with. Ted, Mark advised, should never lose track of this objective.

"Okay, that was a good session tonight." Mark seemed pleased, making eye contact with everyone at the table. In a brief recap, he pointed out to Ted that he had all of the necessary tools to make this change. He just had to do it. The group was his safety net, and they would be there to help him get on with his life.

When the meeting ended, several people wrote down their e-mail addresses and handed them to Theo, so that if he felt the need between sessions for a buddy who would listen, to not hesitate to give them a shout. Mark asked Theo to hang back and waited for everyone to leave before moving down and taking a seat across the table from him.

"So, Theo, you can see how we work here. Do you think you'll be able to let these guys into your life? Nice group of men, don't you think?"

They're fucking nuts. "Yeah," Theo answered, because he didn't have the balls to tell this guy no.

"You said yes, but your eyes and body language are telling me no." Mark folded his hands and waited for Theo to respond.

Theo felt his face heat up. He thought about running out of the room, but couldn't bring himself to do it. The ache in his stomach intensified.

"What brought you here tonight, Theo?" Mark sat back in his chair.

This is so embarrassing, I want to die. How could he answer? *It's complicated. More complicated than you could ever believe.*

"I'm a therapist. I guarantee you there's nothing you can say that will shock or disturb me." Mark chuckled. "Just not possible. Take a minute, but before you leave tonight, I'd like you to be as honest with me as you can and tell me why you're here."

I'm trapped. I feel trapped. Theo's eyes darted toward the door. *Run your ass off and never look back. Maybe you'll wake up tomorrow morning and this will all be one fuck of a bad....* Theo was blindsided by a surge of emotion. *I'm going to cry. I can't help myself. I'm so weak.* His eyes welled up, and he began to weep.

Mark did nothing. Each time Theo stole a brief glance across the table, he saw the same thing—Mark looking back, concerned.

Theo cried for several minutes before he was able to regain control. When he attempted to wipe his face on his sleeve, Mark got up and found a box of tissue on an empty chair and handed it to him.

"Whatever it is, Theo, we'll fix it. You have to trust me on that." Mark sat back down.

Theo blew his nose but still found it impossible to look at the man sitting across from him.

"Do you want me to ask you some questions?" The therapist leaned in and folded his hands on the table.

Theo nodded, wiping his eyes with a tissue.

"Are you here because you're confused about your sexuality?"

Theo nodded again.

"Are you experiencing feelings you don't understand or that are unwanted?"

"Yes." Theo was relieved he only had to reply to the questions.

"Are you scared or frightened you might be gay?"

Gay. The word triggered another intense attack of emotion. Theo was helpless to fight it off, and, once again, he broke down. *I don't want to be gay. Please fix me. I don't want this. I didn't ask to be this way. It's not fair.*

"Here's what I'd like to do," Mark offered. "Your instincts were right. The group isn't a good fit for you, at least not now. I have an hour open on Wednesday evenings. Would you be willing to meet here on Wednesdays at six? We'll take this one step at a time and see where we end up. Don't worry about a fee or your insurance. The Center provides me a blanket salary that, for now, will cover our sessions. We could start tomorrow night. You interested?"

Theo reached for more tissue and blew his nose. "Yeah."

The tension he'd felt earlier had mysteriously started to lift. He was able to look across the table. *Please fix me.* The man seated across from him was his only hope.

"I'm looking forward to working with you." Mark stood and walked toward the door. "We'll make it better, Theo. I promise." The therapist winked. "Now, I need to head home. Haven't had a chance to grab dinner yet. See you tomorrow, then?"

Theo stood and followed him out. "Yeah, you can count on me being here."

"Great!"

Theo walked with Mark to the front of the building. Alex was still seated at the same table he was at when Theo first arrived, only this time he was huddled over a laptop.

"Alex, Theo is going to take my 6:00 p.m. slot on Wednesdays, beginning tomorrow. We've decided to keep him out of the group, at least for now."

"Oh, okay. Sounds good. I'll put him on the schedule." Alex smiled, making Theo almost feel at home. Almost.

"Theo, the only thing I ask is that you give me at least a one-week notice if you are unable to make one of our sessions." Mark looked over to Alex and grimaced. "I hate being stood up. Is that a deal?"

"Oh sure. Thank you." Theo shook Mark's hand.

"Thanks for your help tonight, Alex." Mark held open the door, and Theo followed him out.

ALEX grabbed his laptop bag and swung it over his shoulder. Taking one last peek down the hallway where tonight's meeting had been held, he confirmed all the lights were off. Outside the building, he dug his keys out of his pocket and locked the Center's front door. A very light mist was falling. It was more refreshing than annoying, he thought as he headed toward his truck. Turning the corner, he noticed another truck on the opposite end of the lot from where he had parked. The early spring air was cool enough for him to see plumes of exhaust curling slowly up into the dark night air.

I wonder what this is all about? Strange place for someone to park.

Reaching down, he patted his pocket to make sure he had his cell phone, just in case. You never knew what kind of nut jobs you could run into these days. He and Harper had had at least one conversation about the reaction the community might have toward their Center. They had speculated there could be some fallout, although, so far, there hadn't really been any response. There was a good chance many of the locals didn't even know the Center existed. Add to that the positive mark on the community Harper and Ian had made with the cabins, and they thought in all likelihood, if something nasty were to happen, it probably already would have.

I better check this out.

Once he had gotten closer, it appeared only one person, the driver, was seated in the truck. Alex made a slight arc in his approach to avoid being an easy target. This tactic would also allow him to approach the truck from the driver's side. When he narrowed the distance to within ten feet, the driver lowered his window.

"Theo?" Alex advanced a few steps. *Something's not right here.*

"Hey."

"Everything okay?" Alex walked up to the side of the truck.

"I guess. About as good as it's going to get."

Alex could hear the emotion in Theo's voice. He'd been crying.

"I'm in no hurry, if you need someone to talk to." Alex knew he sounded like he was fishing for a better explanation for why Theo was still here, but he wasn't sure how else to handle this.

"That's kind of the problem. I don't know what to talk about. I don't know what's happening to me right now."

Damn, you're hot. Stop it! But it's the truth. "We could talk about something else and see if anything gets figured out that way?" Maybe if he could just get Theo talking about anything, what was really bothering him might surface.

"Okay. You wanna hop in? It's warm." Theo gestured over to the passenger side of the cab.

"Sure." Alex walked around the back of the truck and opened the door. Sliding his computer bag off his shoulder, he placed it on the floor, leaving plenty of room for his feet, and then jumped in. "I like nights like this, the mist, I mean. Always have. Kind of weird, I know."

"I like night better than day for some reason," Theo said.

"I never thought about liking one better, day or night. That's a tough one. I like things about both." Alex was surprised at how chilled he'd gotten in the brief time he had been standing outside. The temperature inside the cab was perfect. It was clear that if the conversation had any hope of continuing, it would be left up to him to push it along. "How did you hear about the Center?" *That's it, start with the exploratory questions first.*

"I was going through my boss's mail and found your brochure."

Why haven't I crossed paths with this guy before? I know I'd have remembered him.

"That's our first flier. We're planning on others once the Center is up and running a little longer."

Alex had hoped for a comment back, but instead they sat in silence. *We graduated the same year.* He had read over Theo's intake form and was amazed he hadn't at least partied with this guy at some point. Alex knew if he had, he would have remembered it. Theo had that look, that certain something that made Alex curious and wanting more. Up until now, he'd only come across this look on movie stars. It was a moody, quiet kind of thing, but not psycho. Throw in a generous handful of macho, and he was getting close to hitting the nail on the head. He turned to face Theo. "Wow, I can't believe we haven't run into each other before."

"Where did you go to high school?" Mist had collected on the windshield, making it impossible to see out. Theo activated the wipers for a couple swipes back and forth and then sat back. "You in sports?"

"Two Harbors." Alex struggled to stay focused. *I would have remembered you, Theo.* "Yeah, wrestling. I wasn't very good, though. How about you?"

"Baseball."

"Okay." *What do we talk about next?*

"Must be nice."

"Huh?" *What must be nice?* Alex wasn't sure where this one was going, but Theo had initiated it, so that was something, at least.

"Must be nice to work here. Interesting." Theo looked over and smiled for the first time all night. "I work on small engines in a grimy garage."

"Yeah, it's nice." Alex didn't want it to sound like his gig was better, even though that's exactly what he thought. "I have two jobs. I work here, and I also work at the Palisade Beach Cabins."

"Wait." Theo produced another weak grin. "Ian?"

"You know Ian?" It was Alex's turn to smile. Theo knowing Ian certainly was a surprise.

"I think so." Theo's confidence seemed to teeter before he added, "Some dude named Ian brought a tiller into the shop this week. He said he was from where you work—the Beach Cabins."

"Oh sure. I work with Ian. He and his partner, Harper, own the resort. They're great guys."

Let's see. Where can we go from here? Alex ran through a list of favorite topics in hopes of latching onto something appropriate.

Theo tapped his fingers on the steering wheel.

What's running through your mind, Theo? Because of the nature of tonight's meeting at the Center, Alex wasn't sure what was fair to talk about. His guess—Theo had some issue with his sexuality or—*yeah that's probably it*—he hadn't come out yet. Alex sensed he had it right. He felt more than a vibe but refused to allow himself to go there.

"Listen, Theo. I don't want to intrude on your privacy, but, are you doin' okay? I mean, is there anything you want to ask me or talk about? I'm good about keeping stuff to myself."

"You're gay, right?" Theo wasted no time getting back to Alex.

"Yep. Does it show?" Alex laughed, hoping Theo would lighten up.

"No, I didn't mean it that way. You... you're... you look like a regular guy." Theo sighed, the way people sigh when they think they've said something inappropriate.

"For the most part, I try to be myself." Alex wanted Theo to know that, if his struggle was coming out, there was nothing at all wrong with being a gay dude. "I came out my senior year of high school to my best friend, Colin. Now it just seems like being gay is the most natural thing in the world."

"Colin Henderson?" Theo looked over, his eyes wide with amazement.

"You know Colin?" *Of course he does. Who doesn't know Mr. Popular?*

"Yeah. Our teams played against each other in high school. He could really hit the ball."

"I'm tellin' ya, Colin is gifted when it comes to sports." Alex felt a pang of sadness. It had been several weeks since he'd talked to his buddy.

"Is he still your friend?" Theo could not have sounded more serious.

"Who?" Alex didn't understand the question. *Oh, I think he means Colin. Does he think Colin ended our friendship because I came out? Because I'm gay? Wow!* "We're still best friends," Alex was happy to report. *Dude, you might be hot as hell, but you need some work.* "I don't see him much these days. He's in the Twin Cities—premed at the University. We hang out every time he's here or I'm there. I'll say hi to him for you."

"Not sure he'll know who I am." Theo gave the wiper blades another shot to clear the window.

"What position did you play? He'll probably remember you. He's good that way."

"I was our catcher senior year. Had a pretty good batting average too."

Theo appeared to relax, stretching his legs out as far as they could go.

"Cool." Alex needed a minute to regroup. He wasn't sure what else they could talk about.

"God hates gays. Doesn't that bother you?"

Alex felt Theo's eyes bore into the side of his head. He resisted the urge to blurt out his reaction to this but, instead, chose to peer out his own window while he hoped the awkward question would dissipate and die. *This poor dude, he's been brainwashed.* When he finally turned back, Theo's eyes locked with his for the first time. Alex saw someone looking back at him who was hurting. For the first time since they had been talking, he was introduced to Theo's sadness. It resonated from somewhere deep within. Alex softened. His knee-jerk reaction to the God comment seemed harsh. *He can't help himself.*

"The last thing I want to do is offend you, Theo. But I have to be honest. I'm not so sure that's true. I know there are tons of people out there who believe that, that God hates gay people, but I still don't think it's true."

Theo looked away just as a police car crept slowly along the street outlining the Center's parking lot. When it had reached the middle of the block, it stopped.

"Oh shit." Theo forced his body lower into the seat.

Alex followed Theo's lead and lowered himself as far as he could go while still being able to see out. The mist had intensified, coating the windshield and making it next to impossible to keep an eye on the movement of the squad car.

"This really sucks." There was no mistaking the panic in Theo's voice.

Normally, the sight of a cop car checking out the Center wouldn't make Alex nervous. Prior to the Center opening, he and Harper had met with local law enforcement to let them know what they had planned at the Center and, to the best of their ability, the hours they intended for the Center to be open. If there was unusual activity of any kind, the last thing Alex wanted was for the cops to drive by and not check it out. The challenge right now for Alex wasn't combating a fear of being caught in a truck talking to another man; it was the onslaught of the giggles.

"What should we do? Should I run the wipers?"

Theo was self-destructing. Alex tried to put himself in Theo's place, to go down the pathway of fear as a way to control his own emotional breakdown which, of course, left unattended, would blossom into an epic case of hysteria. "Oh God," Alex said out loud without realizing it.

"Oh God, *what?*" Theo reached over and grabbed Alex's arm and, in the process, accidently triggered the wiper. "Fuck! We're so screwed now." The world stopped for a brief second until it was revealed that the cop car had moved on.

Made nervous by Theo's very real fear and fueled by his own nerves, Alex burst out laughing.

Theo, responding to Alex's outburst, let loose a squeal and doubled over. Alex, coming up for air, tried to speak, but the rocking of the truck made him roar even harder. Tears streamed down his face as he struggled to regain his composure. Theo was weathering his own giggle fit, pounding the dashboard in hopes of bringing it under control.

"That's some funny shit," Alex whispered after his laughter had subsided.

"Wow, I was so scared," Theo confessed.

Reluctant to end this chance encounter, Alex wiped his face on his coat and said, "Dude, I'm not sure how to say this, but I've enjoyed talking with you." There was more to say, but he waited to see what Theo's response would be.

"Me too." Theo mimicked Alex and dried his face with his sleeve. "I was so fucked up when I left the Center. Now, well, I don't feel so lost. I don't know what the hell I'm going to do with myself, but for some reason, I don't feel anywhere near as shitty as I did earlier."

"Theo, I'm not sure if you're straight, gay, or a little of both, and to be honest...." Alex stopped short of completing his sentence, knowing if he continued, he'd be dishonest.

"What were you going to say?" Theo looked over, and for the second time that night, their eyes met and locked.

"I was going to lie and tell you I didn't care if you were straight or gay. I care." Alex felt his face warm. "To be honest with you, I'm hoping you're gay." Alex waited to see what kind of reaction this might have. Seconds ticked by and still no response. "I'm sorry. What I think doesn't mean anything more than to let you know that I'm glad we've met. And I really like you."

"Thanks. I'm glad too. Listen"—Theo sat up in his seat—"can we do something together sometime? Hang out?"

Alex felt his heart soar. *You have no idea how much I'd like that.* "Sure. I'm at the Center pretty much Monday through Friday, and when I'm not, I'm working at the Beach Cabins. Do you have a pen and something to write on? I'll give you my cell."

Alex waited for Theo to fish out a pen from a compartment below the dash. "Call the Center or my cell. If I don't answer, leave a message and I'll get back to you as soon as I can." He wrote his number down on the rumpled envelope Theo had handed him.

"Great!" Theo smiled, pocketing the scrap. "I'll call you soon."

"Perfect. Hey," Alex thought to add, "don't feel you have to call just to hang out. If you're feeling bummed and need someone to listen, I'm there."

Theo turned away. Alex knew he'd embarrassed his new friend, but that was okay. It was worth the momentary discomfort for Theo to know that Alex really cared.

A million scenarios flashed up for review as Alex navigated his way home. The mist had turned to a steady rain by the time he pulled into the driveway. Looking down at the clock on his dash, he was surprised to see that it was past midnight.

Entering the house, Alex could tell by the stillness his roomies had already gone to bed. Everyone was working hard these days. Getting the grounds and the cabins ready for a busy season was a monumental effort, even though they were successful enough now to employ a staff to help out.

After hanging his coat up in the mudroom, Alex followed the path of light into the kitchen. On the center of the counter was a plate of cookies. Next to them a note: "Eat them up. Eat all of them up or you're dead! Hugs, Ian."

Do I really want to leave these guys?

Alex picked up the plate and headed down the hall to his room.

CHAPTER
Four

THAT last round pretty much did you in, didn't it, Radish?

Harold Benedict reached over and brought the woolen blanket up over the shoulder of his partner of thirty-three years, Quentin Cornelius Devereux. Decades ago, Harold had affectionately nicknamed Quentin "Radish" because of his love of radish and honey-butter sandwiches. The struggle to stay positive became more challenging for Harold with each passing day.

I can't go there to save my soul. Not yet. To go there is to give up hope. I will not give up hope.

Tired of Ravel's "Sheherazade," Harold pressed a preset on the dash, and Sinatra's lush voice came oozing out of the surround system. How many times over the years had they sat in front of the fire, their glasses filled with a robust red, enjoying the timeless crooner and his trademark Nelson Riddle arrangements? *I'm not ready to give that up yet.*

Out of the corner of his eye, Harold thought he spotted movement. He looked over to Quentin, who remained fast asleep. *Radish, I know I've told you this time and time again, but you can't imagine how much you mean to me. Please don't give up. Life would be so incredibly empty if you were gone. I don't know what I'd do.*

Younger than Harold by two years, Quentin, at sixty-five, would need nothing short of a miracle to make it to sixty-six. Late last winter, after having tolerated a stubborn sore throat for several months, he was diagnosed with level-four throat cancer. A nonsmoker for more than two decades, the news had hit them both hard. Getting Quentin past the fourteenth of December, his birthday, had become Harold's primary goal. If they could make it through the next couple of months without any serious setbacks, there was a chance. *A better chance.*

In his darkest moments, he hated himself for allowing the thought to surface that perhaps Quentin's chance to improve no longer existed. It was hard being supportive every second of every day. But that's what he needed to do. Wanted to do.

Harold stifled a yawn. *Gosh, it's warm in here.* He reached over to adjust the temperature but then stopped when he realized it wouldn't be a good idea. Quentin was so easily chilled these days. The last thing he wanted to do was to add to his partner's discomfort. The only way to make absolutely sure he was comfortable was to overcompensate. He was sure Quentin, never one to complain or make himself a burden, was making a greater effort to appear unaffected by the disease than he was letting on.

Once the reality of the cancer diagnosis had set in, and the realization that, although beatable, it would be literally the fight of his life, Quentin had pulled himself together and started to make plans. He moved on as if nothing had changed. Today's journey to the North Shore was a big part of those plans.

Raised on the North Shore, Quentin's parents had once owned a chunk of land along the lake adjacent to a majestic palisade. The parcel had changed hands several times over the years, and now, most recently, it was the site of a lovely resort. Friends had visited the Palisade Beach Cabins the previous summer, and their pictures had reminded Quentin of the incredible beauty he had left behind for a life in the big city.

Faced with a future of uncertainty, Quentin had expressed a desire to revisit his past and his memory of the palisade. Was this a last-minute addition to his bucket list, Harold wondered? For as long as he could remember, Quentin had avoided any discussion of his childhood. To Harold's knowledge, the reluctance had nothing to do with painful memories but with the fact that there always seemed another, more exotic destination that called out louder. But now, things had changed. The energy wasn't there for adventure. It made sense, the more Harold thought about it. Quentin may have been saving this reunion with his past for—he bit down on his lower lip—*the end.*

Closing in on a rent-a-truck, Harold either had to change lanes or disengage his cruise control, which he was loath to do. Checking his rear and side mirrors, not once but twice, he eased the car into the passing lane and sped past it.

"Honey, I'm very thirsty." Quentin sat partly up and turned away while he released a series of shallow coughs.

"Hi there. I was getting lonely." Happy to see his partner coming around, he reached down to a pocket in his door and brought up a thermal mug of ice water prepared especially for this moment. "I'm all ready for you."

Quentin guided the straw to his lips. "Oh, water tastes so good to me these days. Thank you."

"Radish, you've never met a beverage you didn't like," Harold quipped.

"That's not entirely true. How easily you forget my dislike for warm milk."

"I'm glad you're awake. We're just coming into Duluth. According to the map, the resort is about forty-five minutes from here." Harold, having never been to the North Shore, was anxious to see for himself what all the talk was about. "How are you feeling?"

"Like a million dollars," Quentin teased. "You know, actually, not too bad. This morning, right before we left, I was having second thoughts. So achy all over, you know."

"Are you hungry?" Lately, it seemed he was always asking if Quentin was hungry. One of the pesky side effects of the disease he found most troubling was how it destroyed one's appetite. Never being a big eater to begin with, keeping a steady flow of nourishment into Quentin was a nonstop challenge. No way in hell was he going to allow him to grow weaker because he wasn't eating properly. This was one aspect of his health maintenance Harold *could* control. The trick was to find ways to bring it up that didn't come off as nagging or bothersome.

"I think I will be soon, but I'm fine for now." As if meeting his match, Quentin was already discovering ways he too could offer some encouragement without actually having to commit to eating.

Harold thought about insisting they grab a bite now while the choices were greater, rather than waiting until they were back in the sticks, but decided against it. "I think," he suggested after tabling the food issue, "what we do is take this adventure one day at a time." On this one, Harold had to admit it was more for his benefit. Giving up the comforts of home, and he had agreed to this wholeheartedly, was still going to be a challenge. "I'm not sure I mentioned this to you, but we are on a week-by-week lease with the resort. There's no obligation or money lost if we decide it's not our thing and want to head back home."

"If it's anything like I remember, the pictures Alan and Rick brought back from their stay here last summer don't even come close to doing the place justice. It's very unique. I can't wait to see it again." Quentin took another sip.

"Do you think we should try and locate Dr. Routhier while we pass through Duluth? You're scheduled to meet with him on Friday." Harold had planned to ask someone at the resort if they could direct him to the office of the renowned cancer specialist recommended by Dr. Katzburger, their physician in the Twin Cities. "It might be nice to know where we have to go so there isn't any confusion."

"Oh, honey, I know that's a good idea, but I just want to get to the palisade. We're so close. Is that all right with you?" Quentin reached over and gave Harold's arm a gentle pinch.

"Of course it is."

Harold was forced to disengage his cruise control as the traffic increased, leading into the city. "Oh my, isn't that absolutely amazing?" The freeway had brought them to the edge of a bluff overlooking Duluth and the harbor.

"I'd forgotten about this view. Or maybe I never really noticed it because I was so hell-bent on heading south when I left here.

Gosh, this is lovely." Quentin bunched up the blanket and rested it on his lap. "Harry, look at the cargo ships lined up to enter the harbor. It's like being on the coast. I can't believe we've waited so long to visit here."

That was the other thing about Quentin, and today it made Harold smile. Whenever a thought or behavior of Quentin's missed the mark, the acceptance of blame was always shared. The inclusion of Harold in Quentin's comment was intentional.

They wormed their way through the city and eventually traded the freeway for a residential street that ran along the lakeshore. The homes, many large, beautiful mansions built a century ago or more, captivated them until they had to decide whether to take the expressway, which took them away from the scenery, or stay on the old highway, a slower but more picturesque route to the resort.

"We're not in any rush, are we?" Quentin weighed in but then asked, "What would you like to do?"

"I'm really enjoying the drive. It can't be that much longer if we take the route closest to the lake."

"Harry?" Quentin looked over and placed his hand on Harold's knee.

"Yes, my little radish?"

"Thank you."

Harold smiled, patting his partner's hand. "We're in this together, sweetie."

THEO was about as ready as he'd ever be. Working with Adam had been strained the last couple of days. But he sensed something had changed. Hopelessness had been mysteriously replaced with a hint of optimism. Alex. He'd gone to sleep thinking about the dude, and it was his first thought when he awoke this morning. The memory of his conversation a few nights back was still crystal clear. In particular, it was Alex's easy response to his remark that God hates gays. Not sure what he was expecting in return, the minute it came out of his mouth he knew the accusation was false. It was somebody else talking, perhaps his mom, his dad, or more likely, the church. Alex had been cool. Theo could tell by the look on his face that, even though he appeared to understand how someone could say such a thing, he didn't believe it. Deep down, Theo knew Alex was right. The next time they met up, he was going to say something. He was ashamed of himself for sharing this fear. This was another sign he was weak. He needed to be strong.

Alex was strong, and this fascinated him. He wasn't a squirrel or a pansy ass. He didn't seem to have any of the characteristic fag-like behaviors Theo had expected. *Nope! Alex is a hot-looking regular dude who is into other regular dudes and....* Theo sat up as he turned the corner onto the highway. He *never* would have dreamed of allowing thoughts like these to surface without a good fight, but now, they emerged without resistance. Alex.

From the minute he'd sat down on the fold-up chair next to him to fill out his forms, Theo recognized an attraction. Well, at the time it seemed more like a curiosity. He was too nervous then to pay much attention to it. But now, with this first meeting distanced by time, his initial fascination with Alex resurfaced. *The dude was very cool.* There was more to this, and Theo couldn't bullshit himself. *Holy mother of Jesus, can you frickin' believe it? I'm turned on by a gay dude. Unbelievable.* As wrong as this sounded in his head, a better than equal amount of voices told him it was okay. It was right.

Theo hit the brakes and swerved into the center of the highway to avoid hitting a deer who had miscalculated its opportunity to cross safely. Reaccelerating to the speed limit, another thought surfaced. This one wasn't as welcome. The Lucy thing wasn't working. It was never going to work. *Girls aren't ever going to work, are they, Theo?*

The fear that drove these internal battles had diminished. Theo was surprised to find he was more intrigued than freaked out by the recent events surrounding his sexuality, the Men's Center, and.... "I'm gay," he mouthed out of the blue within the safety of his truck cab. His foot hit the brake again, but this time there was no deer in sight.

I just said it. I said I was gay.

Theo gripped the steering wheel with all his might. He could continue to ignore it, he could even continue to put up a fight, but there was no way in hell he would ever be able to look at himself in the mirror and argue otherwise.

Even if you are gay, you're a good guy, Theo. Stick with the plan. Let Alex and the Men's Center help with this and everything will be fine.

Theo pulled into his parking spot and stepped out of the truck. It was Adam's turn to open up. Thankfully, this would be the last day they would be on their own. Artie, the owner, would be back in the shop tomorrow. Yesterday was painful. They'd danced around each other, barely saying a word. Today needed to be different. Today he didn't care. The air had to be cleared. He was nervous about a confrontation but anxious to find out what Adam was thinking. Knowing his friend as well as he did, once he had a chance to speak his mind, Adam would let you know exactly where he stood. Theo thought it would probably be best to decide on the spot what to share and what to hold back, depending on how the conversation went down.

"Yo, dickhead, what's shakin'?" Theo was surprised he didn't have to force a smile as he walked out of the small office into the garage. This burst of confidence, this energy, he couldn't explain where it was coming from, but he sure hoped it held up.

"Hey," Adam looked up for a second before returning to his work. The large riding mower he'd taken over from Theo was dismantled, with the pieces scattered all around him.

"Anything else come in?" Theo placed his lunch pail on the counter and took off his coat. *What? No snappy come back this morning? Come on Adam, what's on your mind?*

"Old man Becker brought his asshole son's dirt bike in. It's still outside in the lot. I told him we'd try and get to it today but wasn't sure." Adam reached over for a hunk of engine and began cleaning it off with a rag.

Theo walked outside the garage and around the building to where Brian Becker's dirt bike sat. Becker, the son of an area dentist, grew up with a sense of entitlement that was legend. He was closer to Adam's age. Theo didn't know him very well, but he still hated him. It was cool to hate Brian Becker because he was such an asshole.

"Did Daddy Becker say what the problem was when he dropped it off?" Theo parked the bike in his work area and reached for a handful of clean rags from the bin on the wall.

"Acting up."

Theo contemplated giving Adam shit for not knowing much, but it was more important he got him to start talking. "So"—sucking air into his lungs for confidence, he began examining the bike—"has Monica talked to Lucy? She won't return my calls." He waited to make sure he was being ignored before he added, "Sucks it had to end like that. Trust me. It was for the best, dude. She can move on now."

A few agonizing seconds passed before Adam threw down his tools with a grunt. "So, what'd you do? Wake up one day and decide to tell people you're frickin' queer? Is that how that works?" Adam stood and walked over to his lunch box, pulling out a soda. "Hey, I don't want to go out with you anymore because I *might* be gay. How whacked is that?" Adam threw his arms out for added emphasis.

Theo wasn't sure how to answer. As much as he dreaded where this was headed, it was better to get it out in the open. He needed to find out where he stood. He hoped their friendship could survive, but Adam had a strong dislike for fags. To find out one of his friends was the enemy could be a deal breaker.

"I was trying to be truthful with her. She kept blaming herself." His face warmed, but he had to say this. He had to say it all. "That's not fair, dude. It's not fair that she should think there was something wrong with her. It's all me."

"So, all this time, you were just faking it with her? Is that even possible?" Adam cracked open his soda and sipped. "Seriously, you'd actually tell someone you were gay?" He shook his head in disgust and walked back over to the dismantled rider. "Just to get her off your back?"

It was hard for Theo to determine whether or not Adam was mostly pissed he had used the honesty route with Lucy, or just angry that his friend was probably gay. He wasn't given much time to analyze it.

"And how the hell do you know what you are or not?" As anticipated, Adam had been set loose. "I mean, are you suddenly an expert on fags and what they're like? Dude, this is so insane. Why didn't you just tell her you needed to break it off? You made things so complicated now." Adam kicked a drawer shut.

"It's complicated because... it's what it is. I sure as hell didn't wake up one morning and decide to complicate my life." Theo thought for a minute before adding, "This thing, it's been brewing for a long time. The fight with Lucy made it all come to the surface."

"Whatever." Adam's voice dripped with disgust.

For the next twenty minutes the two worked in silence. Theo was surprised to find small bursts of anger butting into his thoughts. He didn't expect any grand gesture of sympathy, but at the same time, he did expect his friend to have more questions than attitude. The more he thought about it, the angrier he got. In Adam's mind, the real issue here was what to do with a friend who might be gay. *So sorry to inconvenience you, dude.*

"I'm really fucking sorry this involves you." Theo found his voice. "How shitty it's going to be to admit to people that your friend is gay. That's got to really be tough. Wow, sorry for not understanding that, because if I had understood it, I would never have said it to Lucy." Theo gasped. *How did that just come out of my mouth so easily?* He closed his eyes and waited for Adam to retaliate. He didn't have to wait long.

"You asshole! Haven't you ever heard of guilt by association?" Adam shook his head with an incredulous look. "People don't just wake up and decide they're gay." Adam went on, his voice building with anger, "Don't you see? How could one of your best friends not know this about you? Or, and here's what sucks, they're all going to think I knew, and either I'm okay with it, or, worse, I might be a faggot too. I can't fucking believe what you're doing."

"You don't have to convince me. I know you're not okay with it." Running out of patience, Theo waved Adam off.

"Don't get fucking pissy with me. I have cut you so much slack. I knew something wasn't right with you for a while now, but I never said a thing. Not one fucking thing!" Adam slammed his soda can down on the counter and retreated to the opposite end of the garage.

"What do you mean, you *knew* something wasn't right with me? What is that supposed to mean?" Theo had somehow found the fuel he needed to hold his ground. "Explain that to me, because I sure wish I'd of fuckin' got the memo."

"Okay… I can't even count the times I've caught you staring at me, at my dick to be specific. Go ahead and try and tell me you weren't, but you know something, Theo? No matter what you say to me, we'll both know you're a lying motherfucker if you try and deny it."

Theo was stunned. He couldn't believe this whole time Adam was aware he was checkin' him out, and said nothing. Devastated by this revelation, he turned his back to try and regroup. He'd always trusted that if he'd slipped up, Adam would have called him on it, would have innocently teased him about it.

"Yeah, I'm not making it up, am I?" Adam took a couple steps toward him. "Dude, take a good look."

Theo winced when he heard the sound of a zipper going down.

"Come on! Here, I'm pulling it out for you so you can get a really good look. Oh yeah, here we go… where do you want it? Come on, Theo, turn around so you can see my cock. You want it in the mouth first? Is that what you want, dude? You want this fucking pole in your mouth first so you can suck on it like a lollypop?"

"Adam, please…."

"Oh no, wait, that's not it, is it? No, you want it up your ass, don't you? Big ol' man cock thrusting in and out of your crap hole. Oh, that's fucking hot, isn't it? Yeah, that's what we're talking about, isn't it, Theo? Oh, baby."

Theo moved toward the door of the office. He had to get out.

"Well, you know what?" Adam yelled, following him to the door. "It's never going to happen, because to get this in your ass it has to be hard first, and dude, you better believe me, there's not a fucking thing about you that turns me on. Faggot!"

Theo bolted through the office and out the door. Somehow he made it to his truck, where he jumped in, closed the door, and locked it for protection. He felt like vomiting as he peeled out of the parking lot onto the highway. Angry tears welled up in his eyes. Unable to keep the truck steady, he turned off the busy highway onto a dirt road and slammed the truck into park. Numb and desperate, he reached for his cell phone and scrolled through his contacts until he found who he was looking for. He placed his thumb on top of the dial button.

HARPER shuffled through the mail and pulled out anything that looked like a bill. It was his job to approve them before either Petra or Alex sent off for payment. *So far, so good.* After subtracting payroll, including token salaries for both he and Ian, the resort was consistently earning a gross profit margin of nearly thirty percent. *You've got a respectable operation here, Mr. Callahan.* The next phase, if they were really going to grow, was to aggressively cultivate the wedding and special occasion market. Ian had worked his magic, and the grounds were steadily gaining notoriety. Another coup, the resort had become a favorite of local tourist publications. Photographs of the landscaping were popping up all the time.

"Thanks for covering for me, boss." Petra bounded into the office, tossing her car keys on the counter. "I love shopping in the morning."

"Me too. Before all the crazies come out. Do we have anyone checking in today?" Harper asked after Petra had scooted behind him over to the computer.

"We might meet Harold and his partner today." Petra sipped from a glass of ice tea. "He called here last week with a few questions and mentioned that it would be either today or tomorrow, depending on how organized they were."

"Oh, fun. I'm really warming to the idea of hosting someone here for the entire summer. Speaking of." Harper walked over to the window after hearing a car pull up. "Unless Harold's a cross-dresser and he's decided to leave the partner at home, someone else just pulled in."

"That's right. We have someone going into Cabin six. Come on, computer, wake up." Petra, in a flurry of activity, went about organizing the office for her day.

"I'm going to hang out here for a while and catch up on some of the invoices. Let me know if I get in the way." Harper cleared the pile of bills and mail out of Petra's way and moved down the counter to work.

They both watched as a woman with plump, rosy cheeks, a fun mop of frizzy blonde hair, and deep brown eyes entered the office.

"Betsy Bender?" Petra asked.

"Yes. That's me," she answered.

"Welcome to the Palisade Beach Cabins," Petra said cheerfully.

"Hello." Harper smiled.

"Okay." Petra slid the reservation form across the counter. "Let's get you checked in and into your cabin. If you would, please write your address here."

"Do you want my home address or work?" Betsy appeared to be all about the detail.

Harper listened to the exchange between Petra and their guest. *Petra has a nice welcoming quality.*

"Oh, either one," Petra answered. "Occasionally, we mail out coupons, if that helps. Otherwise, we don't use your address for anything else. It's never shared with anyone."

"I live in Ohio"—the guest giggled, causing Harper to look up— "but I'm stationed this summer in Bayfield. I'm in the Coast Guard."

This is getting interesting. Harper was intrigued by the change in Petra's tone. *If I'm not mistaken, Betsy and Petra play for the same team.*

"The Coast Guard, really? That sounds very exciting."

Petra's playing it cool. I love it.

"It's my first assignment, and I'm so thrilled."

Sneaking a glance over to his office manager, he was amused to see that Petra's cheeks had colored. *Something's going on.* She had definitely dialed it up.

"I thought I'd come up a week early, before I have to report, so I can drive around and look at other areas of the lake. Last fall I spent a weekend in Bayfield, so I already know what it's like there."

Harper was aware of the attraction the area held for lesbians.

"Well, I'm so glad you decided to stay here with us." Petra smiled.

And I don't think she's kidding, Betsy.

"Okay." Harper watched Petra staple the credit card receipt to the reservation form. With a newfound flair, she added, "You're in Cabin six, which is at the end of the road leading down to the lake. Here's your key, and here's one of our complimentary S'more kits. There should be plenty of wood if you feel like having a fire. Charcoal for grilling is located in the broom closet of your kitchenette."

"It's so beautiful. I can't wait to get organized." Betsy smiled in a way that lit up her entire face.

"If you need anything at all while you're here, please let me know." Petra handed over the cabin key.

Something tells me we might have just expanded our list of guest services.

"I will." With a wave, Betsy turned and left the office.

Harper bit his lip. *This is too good to pass up.* "Coast Guard. Sounds interesting." *Let's see what that buys me.*

Petra looked over and nodded. "Yeah, pretty cool."

"She had a nice look about her, didn't you think?" Harper, aware the intention of his last inquiry was neither subtle nor appropriate, kept up his inquisition.

"If I tell you I thought she looked hot"—Petra leaned over, forcing Harper to make eye contact with her — "will you stop this little game?"

"I knew you thought she was hot." Harper laughed. "I just had to give you shit."

"Betsy definitely got this old girl's juices flowing," Petra confirmed.

"Romance strikes the Palisade Beach Cabins. I love it!"

The playful jousting was interrupted when another car pulled up to the office.

"It's a Lexus with two old guys in it," Harper announced from the window.

"Harold," they both chimed at the same time.

"Harper, get away from the window." Petra motioned for him to join her behind the counter at the same moment they heard a car door slam.

"Here they come. This is so exciting." Harper winked.

The screen door opened, and in walked a dapper, handsome gray-haired man dressed in white pants and a navy sport coat.

"Good afternoon, I'm Harold Benedict. Are you Petra?" he asked as he walked over to her end of the counter.

"Yes I am. Welcome to the Palisade Beach Cabins, Mr. Benedict. I'd like to introduce you to one of the owners. This is Harper Callahan."

Harper reached across the counter and offered his hand. "Welcome."

"Harper, what a marvelous name." Harold shook his hand with an unmistakable air of refinement.

Petra reached behind to retrieve her reservation paperwork. "Did you have any trouble finding us?"

"Not at all. My partner, Quentin, who's a little under the weather right now, grew up around here. I believe at one time his family may have owned this parcel of land. It's a homecoming for him. It's been many years." Harold surveyed the office, his eyes landing on Alex's watercolor of the palisade hanging on the wall. "What a marvelous painting. Was it done by a local artist?"

Harper stepped out of the way so Harold had an unobstructed view. "The painting was done by our very own Alex Stevens. If you see a young, lanky guy with green eyes roaming around, it's Alex. He can really paint."

"He certainly can." Harold leaned across the desk for a closer look. "I hope to meet him while we are here. I paint a little too."

"I'm sure he'd love to meet you." Harper smiled.

Petra took over, sliding the reservation materials toward their guest. "I'm sorry your partner isn't feeling well. If there is anything we can do for him, please let us know. We make trips into town periodically throughout the day if you'd like us to pick up anything."

That was an awesome gesture, Petra. Well done. Harper was impressed with Petra's willingness to please their guests.

"That's very sweet of you. We'll be sure to let you know." Harold began looking over the documents. "This must be the contract you mentioned."

Petra shot a glance over to Harper, who returned it with a nod.

"Great. This looks fine." Harold took a pen out of his pocket and signed.

"Terrific." Petra signed the contract under Harold's signature. "Let's make a copy of this for your records." She placed the document in the fax machine behind her and initiated the copy. "I'll need a credit card from you as well. One night will be charged now, and per our agreement, we will charge the remainder of your stay at the end of each week."

Harold reached inside his coat, pulled out his wallet, and handed Petra a card.

"We have you in...." Harper looked over to Petra.

"Cabin five," Petra said over her shoulder as she processed the reservation.

"Cabin five is the second to the last cabin you reach before the service road ends. There's a gravel pad for you to park on. I'd be glad to follow you down to help get you moved in." Harper stepped toward the opening in the desk.

Harold signed the receipt and handed it back to Petra. "That's very kind, but we should be fine. One thing you might be able to help with. Could you recommend a place where Quentin and I can lunch? Somewhere that isn't too far from here?"

"Absolutely." Harper reached under the counter for a map. "The Lip Smacker should do the trick. They have fantastic food, and all of their baked goods are made on site by the owner, Audrey. If you're lucky enough to be there on the day they're featuring Audrey's famous chicken pot pie, you're in for a real treat. It's memorable." Harper circled a spot on the map and then turned it around for Harold. "When you head back up to the highway, turn left and go about eight miles back toward Duluth. It's on the right before you get into Silver Bay. You can't miss it. The Lip Smacker."

"Oh, that sounds marvelous. Quentin loves a good pot pie." Harold folded the map and put it in his coat pocket.

"Here's your receipt, a copy of our agreement, and your key to Cabin five, Mr. Benedict. Oh…." Petra turned to head into the apartment.

"I got it," Harper chimed in. Seconds later, he returned. "Our complimentary S'more kit. There's firewood piled outside the door and charcoal for grilling inside the broom closet located in your kitchenette."

"Marvelous." Harold let out a little laugh. "And please call me Harold."

"Would you like a second key, Harold?" Petra held the spare in her hand.

"Not necessary, I shouldn't think. Cabin five it is."

"We hope you enjoy your stay with us, and, please, if there is anything we can do to make it more enjoyable, just let us know. The office is open twenty-four hours. Just ring the bell." Petra stepped back from the counter.

"Will do. Nice meeting you both."

"What a nice man," Petra offered after Harold had left the office.

"He really is nice. I hope his partner is feeling better." Harper resumed his paperwork until he was interrupted by a soft knock.

"I hate to trouble you, but I've lost my key. I've looked everywhere." Betsy peered through the screen door.

Harper looked over to Petra. *Already? That's a new record.*

"Do you think it might be somewhere in the cabin?" Petra asked.

"I haven't gotten in yet. I couldn't locate the key to open the door. I'm sorry."

Is she too embarrassed to come in, Harper wondered.

"I remember giving you a key. Could it be in your car?" Petra walked around the desk to the door.

"My car, that's it! I looked in my jacket, but I know it's in the car. I remember now putting it up on the visor. Sorry, I'm a little flustered."

"Oh, don't worry about it." Petra looked over to Harper. "I need a walk. Let's go take a look."

"I've got you covered." Harper waved her out.

"Are you sure? That's so nice of you, Petra." Betsy stepped away from the door so Petra could step out.

"I'm misplacing things all the time," Petra offered.

This could be the start of something big. Harper chuckled.

"I'M GAY." Theo looked over to Mark for his reaction.

"I have to tell you, that's a very short journey to get from where you were the last time we talked to 'I'm gay.' Care to share the high points of your travels?"

Theo liked Mark. The therapist had an easy way about him that didn't threaten or challenge.

"I don't know. It's like I came to the end of the road or something. I just don't feel like fighting it any longer. I want to move on." Theo was proud of his response, and he could see by the look on Mark's face he approved.

"Congratulations, Theo. But I have to caution you about moving forward. Have you told many people in your world the news yet?"

"There's no one to tell." Theo went on to explain his encounter with Adam in vivid detail.

"I'm sorry that happened." Mark shook his head. "With a strong reaction like that, I wouldn't expect the chances to be good for him to come around and embrace your sexuality. So, there isn't anyone else? Family?"

Theo hadn't speculated on how his parents would react to the news he was gay. He didn't have to. "My family is going to freak. They're big into the church."

"I see. Keep in mind that parents travel remarkable journeys themselves very often to be supportive to their children. It might not be as bad as you envision. So that's it?"

Theo was forced to break eye contact when guilt overtook him. Alex. How inappropriate was it to talk to him? And what about the attempted call? He had come so close to calling Alex after his confrontation at work.

"Whoops. Something just happened." Mark folded his arms across his chest and raised his eyebrows. "Feel like letting me in on the secret?"

Tapping his fingers on the table, Theo spent a moment staring at the ceiling and decided to go for it. Nothing had happened during their talk in the truck. But his incriminating urge to touch Alex, to see his strong, lean body naked fueled his bout of shame. "After our last meeting, I spent time in the parking lot trying to sort things out. That dude who works here, Alex, came up to my truck. We ended up talking. He's a cool guy."

"Do you have feelings for Alex?"

"Yeah, I think so." Theo resumed his nervous tapping until Mark reached over and silenced his hand.

"Alex is a good guy to know. I'm not talking about whether or not he's good boyfriend material. I'm commenting on his levelheadedness and the fact that he's got a very strong support group to fall back on. I encourage you to be his friend, but don't project yourself into being linked to him in any other way. Keep things simple for now. With that said, if something happens regarding romance, you'll have to decide whether or not to pursue it. I wouldn't stand in your way."

"Okay, thanks. He's easy to talk to." Theo was relieved. It was nice to hear that Mark supported the friendship and wouldn't put the stops on something more. The projecting point was troubling because, without having it spelled out further, he knew he was already guilty of this.

"Let's take this route, if you're comfortable. Don't come out to anyone else before we talk about it first. I don't want you to get hurt. That includes family, unless you're really confident they'll support you. If there's any doubt at all, we'll tackle that one later. I want you to become confident and strong without having to deal with a ton of outside distraction. As far as Adam and work, you don't owe him anything else. Do you understand what I'm telling you?"

"Yeah, I think so." Theo knew the hesitation in his voice wouldn't get past Mark.

"It's up to Adam now to bridge some of the gap he created by reacting so strongly. It could happen, but I don't expect it to be soon, and frankly, from my experience, the chances are slim. How do you feel about potentially losing his friendship?" Mark folded his hands and waited for Theo to think this one over.

"Adam and I were never close buds. The only reason we got to know each other was because we worked together. People don't treat their friends like crap."

"That's a good point. What's work going to be like for you if Adam remains angry? Will you be okay?"

"It should be fine. I'm just going to keep to myself. My boss really likes me, so that should help. He's back tomorrow. Adam won't do anything with Artie around." Theo was surprised at how easily he gave up on his coworker.

"Great! Here, let me give this to you." Mark took a card out of his notebook and wrote on the back. "I don't do this too often, but I want to make sure you have someone to talk to when you need it. This is my cell. Feel free to call me if you're struggling. And, Theo, I want you to never lose track of the fact that being gay, despite what others might think of it, is nothing to be ashamed of. It's merely a component, a part of you that makes you different from many others. And lastly, keep in mind that this isn't the easiest area in the world to go about life as a gay man. But you'll soon find that a comfortableness will replace your anxiety. Especially if you work toward building a support group for yourself. Meeting and getting to know Alex is a healthy step forward. I wouldn't say that if I didn't think it to be true."

"Thanks, Mark. I feel pretty good right now." Theo couldn't stop himself from smiling.

"It's a huge weight to get off your back, I'm sure. But this romance notion you might carry toward Alex, well, you're on your own there." Mark laughed. "And don't worry, I won't say a word. What we talk about here doesn't leave the room. You can count on it."

"Okay." Theo stood because he was unable to stay seated. He was revved. There was a world out there he needed to conquer, and he wanted to get started.

"Next week, let's talk more about that support group. Give it some thought. Also, if bumps come up along the way, we can hash those out too. Sound like a plan?"

"Yes. Tonight was really great." Theo reached over to shake Mark's hand.

"I'm glad it was helpful. See you next week." Mark returned a good shake back.

Theo wandered out of the room toward the Center's entrance. Alex wasn't around when he had arrived earlier, but laughter coming from the large hall intrigued him. It was worth checking out.

Turning the corner, he almost stumbled into a wooden step ladder with Alex perched on the top rung. Standing next to him was an older dude.

"Theo! Hey, how's it going?" Alex looked down and smiled.

Theo could feel his heart race. "Hey," he answered shyly.

"Theo, this is Harper Callahan, the Center's director."

"Hi, Theo." Harper stepped forward, offering his hand.

"We're trying to get these lights up so we can use this space for something fun." Alex climbed down the ladder, grabbed his Dew off of the floor, and took a long sip.

"You guys need any help?" Theo had a ton of energy to burn off as well as a need to be around Alex.

"Truthfully, yes." Harper winked and then socked Alex in the arm. "I'm only half as talented with this stuff as this guy is, and that's not saying much at all."

"I struggled with the first one, but I'm gettin' it, I'm gettin' it." Alex gave Harper a playful shove back. "I'd love some *real* help."

"Fine, if you're going to be that way." Harper stuck his nose in the air. "I'm going back to my office to do a few things before heading home." Turning back with a smile, he added, "Give me a shout if you need me. Nice to meet you, Theo."

Theo observed the easy relationship the two men shared. The other thing that caught his attention—how handsome that Harper dude was. *Wow!* Slightly taller than Alex, gray pants and a black sweater accented the guy's lean build perfectly. His hair was cut short in a way you didn't see much around here. *This guy's stylin'.*

"I'd like to get a few more of these up before calling it a night. Could you un-package the sconce and hand it to me when I'm on the ladder?" Alex moved the ladder down to where the next box sat up against the wall. Theo could see there was still a majority of the project to complete. "I have to connect the wires, drill two holes, and screw the thing in. It goes pretty fast."

"Sure." Theo picked up the box and examined it. "Do you have a knife or something I can use to break the packing seal?"

"It should be lying on the floor next to the last box."

Back where he first encountered Alex on the ladder, he found a small penknife. When he returned, he was treated to Alex climbing up the ladder. His eyes instantly went to Alex's ass. His jeans did an excellent job of hugging his butt. *Don't go there, Theo. Remember what Mark said; keep things simple.*

"I really appreciate you helping out. Harper's a super good guy, but he hates doing stuff like this."

Opening the box, Theo pulled out the light fixture and handed it up to Alex. "Glad to help. I'm kind of charged after my meeting tonight, so this is good for me."

"Okay, great." Alex took a pencil out from behind his ear and marked where the holes needed to be. Reaching into a tool belt attached to the ladder, he pulled out a cordless drill and went to work. "There should be a packet in the box that has the screws and some electrical thingies," he said when he'd finished drilling.

"Yep, here it is. Screws and wire nuts. You probably need those first."

Alex took the packet from him and laughed.

"What's so funny?" Theo looked around for a clue.

"Sorry. Wire nuts, I didn't know they were called that." Alex was laughing harder now, "We're really juvenile around here, and that struck me funny."

Theo laughed out of relief the joke wasn't on him but then frowned after realizing he had no idea what was funny in the first place.

"There, another one done," Alex announced when he had tightened the last screw. "I don't know if I can go on. I'm starving."

You hungry at all?" Alex climbed down from the ladder and patted his stomach.

Theo looked around the hall at the remainder of the lights that needed installation. If they buckled down, he estimated they could probably have them all up in under two hours. This gave him an idea. He removed his phone and checked the time. *Great, this will work if Alex is up for it.*

"How about we call Patsy's and order a pizza to be delivered. They're open for another hour. That way we could keep going on these and probably finish tonight. Not sure if you have plans, but I'm game." Theo watched as Alex surveyed the room.

"Wow, it sure would be nice to get this done. Are you sure you want to stick around and help?" Alex threw his soda can into the empty light box.

"Sure. We can take turns on the ladder if you want." Theo was pleased Alex was receptive to his idea.

"Deal. What kind of pizza do you like? I'm treating. Well, actually, we'll make Harper and the Center buy dinner. He'll be so glad this got done." Alex moved the ladder down to the next box.

"Not too fussy." Which was a lie, but he figured he'd struggle through anything to have the opportunity to get to know Alex better.

"I'm kind of picky," Alex admitted. "How about plain pepperoni?"

Yes! "Sounds great." Theo found the number and dialed.

"Hey, make sure to tell them to bill it to the Men's Center. We have an account there."

Alex was back on the ladder when Theo had finished ordering. They installed four more lights before the pizza arrived.

"You mind if we sit on the floor?" Alex had gone off to see if Harper was still around.

"Not at all." Theo plopped down, the pizza box separating them. "Do you live in Two Harbors?"

"I live on the Palisade Beach Cabins property with Harper and his partner, Ian. They're really fun roomies. Anyway"—Alex chuckled— "I know Harper was glad you took over for him so he could get home. I'm getting pretty good at predicting when they have sex. It's like you can feel it when you're around them. Oh God, I sound like a demented perv." Alex laughed while he chewed.

Theo was starved to hear about other guys having sex. "No big deal." His mind was bombarded with images of the two handsome men fondling each other. *I wonder how they do it, exactly?* He needed to change the subject or risk poppin' a woody. He had the perfect topic. It had been on his mind since first talking to Alex in the truck.

"You know when we were talking the other night in my truck. I said something to you that I didn't mean."

"What's that?" Alex cracked the top on his new soda.

"I told you God hates fags. I don't believe that. I'm not sure why I said it."

"It's cool. I've heard it before." Alex tore off another slice.

Taking a piece for himself, he nodded back, understanding he didn't have to elaborate. Alex seemed to understand his reckless comment was stupid.

"I like Patsy's because the crust is so thin," Alex noted between bites. "This is really nice of you to stay, Theo. I hate doing this stuff on my own. I'm enjoying it."

"It's the least I can do." Understanding that he might have to explain his comment, he added, "Mark's been a great help. Things are going well."

"Oh, good. You seem a lot better than you were the other night."

There were so many things Theo wanted to ask Alex but thought he should probably hold off until they knew each other better. His gut told him they could become good friends. Even the little time they had spent together felt easy. Almost like they had known each other for years. It was a good sign. *He's easy to look at. Those eyes.*

The sound of techno rock blaring from somewhere on Alex startled them both. "Hang on, it's my cell." Alex jumped to his feet and fished his phone out of his pocket. "Hey!"

Theo watched as Alex walked to the opposite end of the hall. He didn't want to eavesdrop but couldn't help himself. Anything he could find out about his new friend would be interesting and maybe useful down the road. Quickly, it became apparent the call wasn't going well. Alex was flailing his arms in the air, and more than once he heard him say the name Todd.

Is Todd his boyfriend?

Several minutes passed before he heard a loud "Good-bye." Alex, obviously agitated, came walking back shaking his head. "Sorry about that."

"No problem. Everything okay?" Theo didn't know how to respond. He couldn't ignore the fact that Alex's mood had changed drastically from before the call.

"It's fine. I'm having some issues with a friend. It's my fault for not being up front with him from the beginning. Anyway, it's a long story."

"Okay." The call was personal, and Theo didn't want to pry further.

"Theo, grab that last piece. I'm going to go back to work. Don't rush."

"No, that's fine. I'm stuffed. Sure was good. Thank you, or I should say, thank you, Men's Center, for treating."

The rest of the lights went up much more quickly once Theo had assumed the installation role and Alex his helper. He was thankful to have more to do. When Alex had been on the ladder, there was too much time for his mind to wander. His eyes insisted on exploring either Alex's ass or his crotch. Both were equally satisfying. *Keep it simple.*

When all the boxes had been hauled to the trash and everything put away, they walked to the door together. Theo recognized an awkwardness as they stepped out into the night. For more times than he cared to count, he stopped himself from doing what Mark had cautioned against—projecting himself as something more than a new friend for Alex. This rule was challenged when Alex paused after locking the door and patted Theo on the shoulder.

"Thanks again, man. I never would have thought we'd finish tonight."

"These fixtures go pretty fast once you know what you're doing." *If you moved to kiss me right now, I'd let you.* The attraction was almost more than Theo could manage. Flustered, his eyes darted to the ground. "It was fun," he added when he knew his best bet would be to head to his truck. "Have a good night, okay?" He looked up and smiled.

"You too. Have a safe drive home."

Alex began walking toward his own truck. They had parked on opposite ends of the lot again. Discouraged by the discovery that Alex was already involved with someone, he started across the pavement. *Fuck!* He weathered a powerful feeling of emptiness. *I need someone. I need to get myself fixed soon so I can.... Why does he have to be already involved? Sucks!* Sure that his evening with Alex had officially ended, he was surprised when he heard, "Hey, Theo! Can I give you a call sometime so we can hook up? Maybe do a movie or something?"

That was all he needed. His heart soared. "Yeah, you bet. I'd really like that. Call anytime."

"Will do!" Alex waved.

Keep it simple. Or maybe not. Theo floated to his truck.

CHAPTER
Five

INTERESTING! Adam's truck was nowhere in sight when Theo pulled into work. *Maybe the asshole called in sick?* Artie's Jeep was there; that was good. Grabbing his lunch cooler off the front seat, he sprinted to the door of the office. Artie was seated behind the counter going through his mail.

"Hey, Artie, welcome back!" Theo walked over to the clipboard on the wall out of habit.

"Theo, how's it going? Thanks for keeping an eye on the shop while I was away." Artie sipped from the coffee he picked up at the Pump & Grub every morning.

"You look tan. Did you go somewhere warm?" Seeing there was nothing pressing, Theo thought he'd spend a few minutes shooting the breeze with his boss.

"I was down in the Florida Keys, Key West. Great weather."

"Cool." Other than taking a few days off here and there, this was Artie's first vacation that Theo could recall since he started working for him. "Were you there by yourself?" Knowing Artie was a bachelor, Theo wondered if he went alone.

"No, I went with a group of guys I know from the Twin Cities." Artie looked up from his mountain of mail. "Say, Theo, why don't you drop off your lunch and then come back here. We need to talk about something."

"Sure, Artie." Theo's stomach tightened as he walked out to the garage. *What could this be about?* So much had happened lately it was impossible to single out one thing. *Did Adam already get to Artie? Is he going to fire me? What exactly is on Artie's mind?* He opened the large door of the shop to buy a moment to collect himself before he walked back into the office. *Take it like a man, Theo.* "What's up?" He prayed the false calm he applied to his voice would be sufficient to disguise he was scared to death.

"Anything happen between you and Adam while I was away? When I came in this morning, I found this on the desk." Artie handed him a sheet of paper.

Theo accepted it and willed himself not to show any outward sign of anxiety. *Please let this not have anything to do with me.*

Artie—Sorry to do it this way, but I'm quitting as of today. You've been a great boss, and I enjoyed working here. Something's come up, and it's time I moved on. I know it's not too busy right now, so I'm hoping this doesn't inconvenience you too much. Keep my pay.

Sorry and take care,

Adam

Theo read the note again to see if he'd missed something. *Thank you!* The note hadn't incriminated him in anyway. Shaking his head, more from relief than anything else, he handed it back. How in the hell could he tell Artie what went down yesterday? Mark's comment about not coming out to anyone until they'd had a chance to discuss it prohibited him from telling the truth. "I'm not sure what this is all about," he lied, ashamed of himself for being dishonest with his employer.

"Not a clue, huh?" Artie threw the piece of paper in the trash. "You know before you came on board, Adam and I had a few run-ins, but once you were hired, it all seemed to equal out. I just don't get it."

"If you need me to work more hours, Artie, count on it." Theo thought it best to move the topic off Adam to what was going to happen now that he was gone.

"We'll have to see how it goes. You and I can get a lot done when we stay focused. There's a guy I know from my Tuesday night meeting at the Center that does engine work. At one point he was looking for some extra cash. I can check with him to see if he could help us out if we get into a bind."

I'll be damned. Artie's a gay dude too? It hit Theo like a ton of bricks. How had he not figured this one out on his own? A bachelor in his fifties. Never any talk of a woman in his life. Not even a date here and there that Theo was aware of. And then the biggest clue— the brochure from the Men's Center. It came for a reason. There could only be one group that met on Tuesday nights at "the Center." The reason he didn't run smack into Artie last Tuesday was because he'd been on vacation. *Oh man, was that ever lucky.*

"I'm going to head out to the garage and take a look at where we're at with everything." Theo stepped toward the door. "Adam was finishing up on a rider yesterday, and I have a dirt bike started. You know of anything else I need to do before the bike?"

"Not that I'm aware of. Do your best to get us all caught up. If you need any help, give me a shout. I'm going to try and unbury myself here. Christ, can you believe how much mail this little joint gets? Amazing."

Well, it's one piece short, Artie. But you don't need to know about that now. "Sure."

"Theo?" Artie asked before he had a chance to leave the office.

"Yeah?" Theo turned, hoping this wouldn't be something that required him to lie again.

"You doing okay here? I have to be honest. I don't want to lose you. I'm too old to be doing this all by myself." Artie chuckled, but Theo couldn't mistake the sincerity in his voice.

"I'm fine. I like working here, working with you." Theo flashed an easy smile. He'd always liked Artie, but now, knowing he was gay, it made it even better working there. *The next time I meet with Mark I'm going to talk about coming out to Artie. I'd like him to know.*

"If you ever need anything, an advance on your pay, anything, you come and talk to me. We'll work something out, okay?" Artie winked.

"Thanks, Artie. I will."

"Good boy! Don't be afraid to come and get me this morning if you need help."

When Theo got back out to the garage, the first thing he checked out was the rider. It was cleaned up and put back together. Chances were pretty good it was done. Looking over to the counter, he spotted Adam's clipboard. Artie had asked them last year to sign off on each engine they worked on. He wanted something formal for his records. Picking the clipboard up, he was happy to see that the invoice for the rider was on top and Adam had signed his name to the bottom of it. On top of that was a small piece of paper folded in half. Theo's hands trembled as he unclasped it from the board. Looking over his shoulder to make sure he was still on his own, he opened it.

> Have a nice life, fag. Hope the butt flu doesn't get ya!

Theo quickly folded the paper into as small a square as he could before shoving it deep into his pocket. *What a prick!*

HARPER stretched out on the bed in his favorite cotton pajama bottoms and watched as Ian carried a massive tray piled with food into the bedroom.

"Do you think this is silly?" Ian asked, setting the tray down on the end of the bed. "Because I don't."

"No." Harper looked over the selection of tasty delights. "Especially when it involves food."

"I remember like it was yesterday." Ian fed Harper a chocolate-covered strawberry. "Andy and I were there together. This was before he remodeled the back of the garden center. We were in the tiny office flipping through the channels, trying to find a local broadcast to see if we could spot you coming out of the courthouse. You had tipped me off that you might be stopped for an interview."

Ian grabbed the bottle of champagne resting on its side and, after a momentary struggle, popped the cork. Harper took delight in watching his handsome lover dab the top of the bottle with the palm of his hand, effectively stopping the contents from exploding out like a geyser. A move he had taught Ian years ago.

Harper's memory of being shot by the lunatic wife of a guy who was convicted of a Ponzi scheme was blurred at best. What he remembered clearly were those agonizing weeks and months of recovery that followed. And the bad dreams. *The dreams were the worst of it.* Thankfully, they were history. "Ian, I love that you take the time each year to let me know you're grateful we made it through all of that."

"I know you do, and that's what makes it so fun." Ian climbed onto the bed and planted a kiss on Harper's forehead.

The first year, Ian popped for a Sunset dinner cruise on one of the big tour boats out of Duluth. They sipped hearty red wine, feasted on succulent prime rib, and toured the harbor. Last year, they managed to get away for a few nights in downtown Minneapolis. Despite the urging from friends to stay with them, Ian insisted they go the hotel route. The man had a plan. Except to dress for dinner, they barely left their king-size bed with arguably the world's most comfortable mattress. Harper remembered his naughty parts had been rubbed raw by the time they got into the car to journey back home. Several days of abstinence immediately followed to allow for healing. It was a little early to tell, but today appeared to be a move toward a simpler approach to the yearly celebration. A feast of food favorites served in bed. *Life is good!*

"I haven't had lox and cream cheese for ages." Harper grabbed a bagel half and began building his first course. "Oh, and look, you did the egg crumbles and the chopped red onion too. Just like downtown."

"Wait. Put that down." Ian handed a glass to Harper and filled it. After pouring his own, he placed the bottle on the night table. "Harp, I've probably said this a million times or more, but my life is so much better because of you. I love you so much." Ian clinked glasses and then leaned over and pecked him on the lips.

Harper reached up and cupped the back of Ian's neck in his hand and, after a few quick teases between lips and noses, enjoyed a deep, passionate kiss.

"Never get tired of that." Ian laughed when they parted.

"Nope. Me either," Harper agreed, holding his finger up to indicate he had more to say. *How can I convey to this man just how much he means to me?*

Harper too had said I love you to Ian in every way he could think of over the years. Had he missed an approach, a nuance, or a stronger, more meaningful way? There were several things about Ian that made life with him a continued blessing. On the surface, his goofy "each day's a birthday party" approach to life certainly couldn't be overlooked. It was as if his sole mission on this earth was to make sure everyone around him was happy. Sure, there were times when an existence void of practical jokes would be refreshing, but the more Harper thought about it, the more he had to admit that, no, it probably wouldn't be nearly as enjoyable as the unabridged version of Ian. Burps, farts, and all. *Okay, I think I have it.*

"I thought about this last year, and for some reason I don't remember sharing it with you. Here, let's sip. This might take a minute or two." Harper clinked Ian's glass, and they both drank from the elegant flutes they'd received from their good friends Andy and Emmett as a housewarming gift.

"Part of me would probably be lost forever if I had been on my own after the shooting. The recovery, getting through the bad parts, the dreams, it would have taken such a toll on me I don't think I would have ever been the same. Thankfully, you were there. You were there every step of the way. And you know what?" Harper reached over and caressed Ian's face. *Damn, you're a looker.*

"What?" Ian stood and, with a seductive smile, removed his boxers. "I felt confined."

"I can see that." Harper paused until Ian, clearly aroused, climbed back onto the bed. "Perfect. Your dick getting hard has much to do with what I was about to say."

Ian laughed. "Good, because the damned thing has a mind of its own when it's near you."

"Right." Harper tweaked Ian's ear and continued. "So what I've grown to appreciate over the years, and why I'm so indebted to you, is how hard you worked to make sure I got through all of that ugly in one piece. It was more than caretaking. Your coaxing me to have sex as soon as my body could handle it was a perfect way to help me to move on. And your special brand of Ian silly. You never stopped being you, and that ensured I spent more time laughing at how crazy you can be instead of falling into a deep depression. And I think you know now that, given my personality, that's exactly what would have happened. Ian, this is so long-winded, but you have to know that being with you, then and now, makes me... such a better person."

"That's cool. I don't know if I can take credit. It just kind of happened on its own. Anyway, here's to us!" Ian raised his glass in toast.

"To us!" Harper sipped and placed his flute on the bedside table. "I'm starving," he added, reaching for a fork.

"Me too." Ian removed the utensil from his hand and lifted the breakfast tray off the bed, placing it on the floor. When he sat back up, he attacked Harper's pajama bottoms, quickly pulling them down and off.

"I guess I can wait a little bit longer for the lox." Harper sighed with a wink.

Ian reached over and pulled Harper onto his side. "Look." He traced the scar from the bullet with his finger and then leaned over and kissed the spot. "I hardly notice it anymore. But when I do, it instantly brings me back to the emergency room. I can't help it. It's like the image of you lying there never fades for me. So powerful."

Harper closed his eyes and savored the sensation of Ian's tongue licking the old wound. From there, as he did so often, Ian would scoop his body up into his powerful arms and take the lead. Soon Ian would enter him and they would become one. *To us!*

ALEX had Harper to thank for suggesting tonight's dinner. *This is going to be so much fun.* Harper provided the perfect opportunity to get to know Theo without it being strained or uncomfortable when he suggested Alex invite him over as a way to say thank you for helping with the light installation at the Center. Theo readily accepted the invitation.

They rushed around the house, making sure everything was just right for their guest with a precision that only comes from spending a great deal of time together. Ian was in charge of setting the table, which, Alex was relieved to see, didn't involve his signature "penis" napkin fold. This surprisingly lifelike work of art was used for special holidays like birthdays, the Fourth of July, and the obvious, Halloween, or Halloweenie, as it was affectionately known. However, and this always brought a smile to Alex's face, it did make a rare appearance last Easter. Ian, feeling the need to cheer everyone up because of unseasonably cold weather, had insisted on it. Paired up with a nice glazed ham, the "linen dick" brought numerous comments, including Harper's hilarious "pig and a poke" remark.

Harper, the designated chef for the evening, danced around the kitchen finalizing dinner preparations. Alex had requested shrimp linguine, which Harper nailed every time.

Finished with his own designated duties, making the salad and prepping the bread, he ran a couple of bowls of munchies down to the entertainment room. The plan was for everyone to kick back and enjoy a movie after dinner.

Alex had been upfront with his roomies about his attraction to Theo, and, at least for now, they refrained from making a big deal out of it. The fact Ian hadn't jumped all over him for details showed a degree of restraint Alex didn't know existed in the man.

"Sure smells great." Alex complimented Harper, who gently stirred the sauce.

"Hey, I just remembered something." Harper placed the spoon down and reached for his beer. "What was up with the paper bag of clothes I found this afternoon by the garage door? I recognized they were yours, so I put it in your room."

"That was Todd's way of saying have a nice life." Alex was glad his sexually-aggressive boyfriend had taken a step to end their relationship.

"Really?" Harper raised an eyebrow, indicating he was intrigued.

"Before you jump to conclusions, I did try and talk with him. Several times." Alex crossed his arms and waited for a response.

"I believe you. Stop looking like you're about to be slapped."

"Huh?"

"Because if you look like you're about to be slapped, then it happens." Harper cuffed Alex playfully.

"Ouch! Stop it, that hurt." Rubbing his head, he retreated to the other side of the counter.

"I need more detail." Harper surveyed the kitchen to ensure all was under control.

"I spent an *entire* night explaining to Todd how I needed space so I could try and figure out what I wanted in a relationship. I told him his constant need for sex was getting in the way. Then I suggested we cool it for a while so we both could think about the relationship going forward."

"Sounds fair." Harper nodded. "Then what."

"He begged me to stay so we could have sex. It's like he didn't hear a word I was saying."

"It does sound like he's a bit narrow-minded. But I still stand behind what we talked about."

"I know. I agree." Alex walked to the fridge and pulled out a cold Dew. "I should have talked with him from the start. I didn't, which was wrong, and now he's angry."

"Okay, well, thanks for giving it a try."

Their conversation was interrupted by the doorbell.

"Go answer that." Harper turned back to the stove. "And don't worry. I promise not to embarrass you."

"Yeah, right." Alex knew there was little hope of that.

He was surprised at how anxious he felt walking to the door and quickly reminded himself nothing was at stake. Theo was here because he and Harper wanted to thank him for helping out. Just a simple "thank you" dinner. But even with his recent fallout with Todd so fresh in his memory, Theo was someone who intrigued him. Theo was different. He fantasized about having the opportunity to become intimate with him. He'd thought about it a lot since the night they'd spent together putting lights up at the Center.

"Theo, come on in." Alex held the door open for their guest.

"How's it going?"

"Great. We're glad you could make it." *God dang, you have a hot look, dude.* "Here, I'll hang up your stuff." *Let's start with your jeans.*

"It smells really good in here." Theo handed off his jacket and then wiggled out of a hooded sweatshirt. "Thanks."

"Follow me." Alex led them down the hallway into the kitchen.

"Hey, there he is." Harper stepped back from the stove and shook hands with Theo. "Welcome to the House of Immaturity. Fart, burp, pick your nose, it's all acceptable behavior here, but keep in mind, Ian's fiercely competitive."

Theo laughed, but it was clear he wasn't sure how to respond.

"How was that for an icebreaker?" Harper winked at Alex.

"Real special," Alex answered dryly, rolling his eyes.

"Theo, you want something to drink? Beer, wine, soda?" Harper wiped his hand on a towel.

"I'll take a diet cola if you have it."

"I got it." Alex waltzed over to the refrigerator. "Here you go." He cracked it open and handed it off. "You want a glass?"

"Naw, this is great. Thanks." Theo took a sip and smiled.

"Why don't you give Theo a tour of the house while I finish up here?"

"I can do that. Follow me." Alex led Theo away from the kitchen to the set of stairs leading up to the second level. "Harper's really proud of the house because it's a prefab. I'm not supposed to tell you that until you've seen the whole thing, so if he asks you, lie and look surprised."

Theo laughed. "Okay, will do. I'm already surprised. This place is really nice."

When they had reached the top of the stairs, Alex took the lead down the hall toward the guest bedroom at the far end. The tour was interrupted when Ian, stark naked with his towel wrapped around his neck, sauntered out of the steamy bathroom. "Hey, guys. I thought we were eating downstairs."

"Funny guy." Alex made a move to walk past his roomie but was stopped in his tracks when Ian jumped into the center of the hall.

"Check it out! I got the moves that make the menfolk cream." Ian swirled his hips around in a circle while sliding his towel back and forth behind his neck, unfazed by his lack of clothing.

"Wow, sure glad we got to see *that*." Alex folded his arms and waited for Ian to finish his show. Theo stood with his hands at his sides, mouth wide open and his eyes wild with amazement.

"Perv! Did you just check out my junk and lick your lips?" Ian cocked an eye at his roommate and folded his arms across his chest, copying Alex's stance.

"My lips were dry," Alex countered blandly. "Besides, why would I want to look at your tired old Viagra-infested fuck stick anyway?"

"Touché!" After high-fiving Alex, Ian threw his head back and roared at the snarky comeback.

"Hey, Theo, I'm sorry." Ian took his towel down and wrapped it around his waist. "Alex brings out the worst in me."

Alex turned to Theo. "Like there's a best in him. I'm the youngest around here, so it's *always* my fault. Mind if we move on, Uncle Jiggly? I'm giving Theo the tour."

"So sorry to interrupt, Ms. Thing. I'll throw on a T-shirt and be right down." Ian wiggled his ass as he walked down the hallway to his bedroom.

"You do that." Alex was delighted he and Ian were able to show off their playful comfortableness so early in Theo's visit. He forced back a laugh when he looked over at his new friend, who still hadn't recovered. *It's okay, Theo. Ian has one hell of a body, and he would be flattered you think that.*

"As you can see, both of those guys are major-league goof-offs. Hope you're not offended."

"I can't believe how crazy you guys are with each other," Theo whispered and then looked over his shoulder to make sure Ian wasn't sneaking back for a second attack.

It was zany fun. Theo was right. Alex still struggled with his decision to move out. Every day, something happened that forced him to revisit it. *Remember, you can live away and still come back for the fun.*

When they had concluded their tour, Alex brought Theo back to the kitchen, where Ian, dressed in loose jeans and a Taconknights T-shirt, stood next to his partner, Harper.

"Just a couple minutes longer and we can sit down." Harper handed over the spoon so Ian could sample.

"Yummy." Ian gave his partner a peck on the cheek.

"I like your T-shirt," Theo said, pointing at Ian.

"Are you into baseball?" Ian asked, handing the spoon back to Harper.

"I played in high school. Enjoyed it." Theo sipped his soda and smiled.

"I love baseball. Don't I, guys?" Ian walked to the fridge and reached for a beer. "Wait, are we having wine with dinner?"

"We could." Harper was preoccupied with a fistful of linguine he was about to dump into a boiling pot of water.

"Ian plays for the Taconknights. He's their star hitter." Alex made no attempt to hide how proud he was of this fact. "When do the regular games start?"

"Next week. Theo, you should come and watch. We'll go out for pizza or something afterward." Ian picked up a bowl of salad and headed into the dining room.

"Sure. I'd love that. I've gone a few times to watch you guys play. It's always a good time."

"Alex, why don't you take Theo into the dining room and fill up ice waters. I'm going to toss the pasta, and we should be good to go. Wait." Harper opened the oven and emptied a pan full of garlic bread into a basket. "Theo, you can take these in."

Theo took the basket from Harper and followed Alex. They had just sat down when Harper came in with a huge bowl of pasta. "Hope you like shrimp, Theo."

"I *love* shrimp." Theo looked around the table and chuckled. "This is great. Thanks for having me over."

"It's our pleasure," Harper said, passing the bowl over to their guest first. "There's a boatload of food here, so eat hearty."

The dinner conversation was lively, with an abundance of laughter. At Theo's request, Alex did his best to fill in the blanks—how Harper and Ian had taken this run-down resort and made it into a thriving business. The only time he faltered was when it came time to explain how he fit into the mix. Ian picked up the ball and did a great job of avoiding the bad parts, like his father's suicide, while concentrating on how the three of them had worked their asses off those first few years trying to get everything just right.

Several times, Alex had to look away, fearing he might become emotional. When his life with these guys was laid out in a timeline, it was even harder for him to believe his good fortune. These crazy, zany goof-ball roommates meant more to him than words could ever express. Tonight, with Theo as their guest, Alex truly felt like he belonged in a way that was so powerful, it humbled him to silence.

"Hey, cracker jack," Harper called out from the opposite end of the table. "Penny for your thoughts."

Alex felt his face warm. Harper had caught him drifting. He always felt bashful when this happened. It was so strange. "I was just thinking about the early days. That's all."

Everyone chipped in clearing the table. Ian and Harper insisted Alex take Theo down to pick out a movie while they finished cleaning up.

"What kind of stuff do you like? We watch everything." Alex led Theo over to a shelf stuffed from top to bottom with movies.

"I don't want to be the one to pick," Theo begged off. "I like lots of different stuff too."

Alex understood the strain it put on their guest to make the decision for the group.

"Hell, I wouldn't want to do that either." *Give the guy a break!* "What was I thinking?" They both laughed. "Okay, well, let's see—wait, here's one. I've wanted to watch this again for a long time." Alex handed over a case containing *Stand by Me*. "Have you seen it?"

"Nope." Theo examined the back for more detail.

"It's been forever since we've watched it. It's Harper's favorite movie. He'll love that you haven't seen it before."

"Will Ian like it?" Theo asked, handing the case back.

"Ian will love it for the first thirty minutes, and then he'll be asleep on the floor. Unless he's really partying, and then nobody will enjoy the movie because he'll be making these stupid wisecracks through the entire thing. It's pretty funny, usually."

"Hey," Ian said when he came into the room with a plate full of cookies. "Did you find something to watch?"

"*Stand by Me*." Alex reached for the container of remotes and powered everything up.

"Oh God, not that frickin' movie again. We just watched it last night." With an air of frustration, Ian dove onto the couch.

"That's cool. Theo's second choice was *The Sound of Music*." Alex knew he was taking a chance with Theo but sensed the time had come to stop being so careful.

"I hate that movie." Theo playfully socked Alex in the arm.

I was right. We're good.

"I'm a sap. I love it," Alex confessed. "These guys think I'm nuts."

"We do," Ian agreed. "We think he's insane, and we lock our door at night because he can't be trusted."

"Fuck off." Alex whipped an M&M from the bowl on the coffee table, nailing Ian in the neck.

"So, we have a film picked out?" Harper asked as he entered the room with two beers, handing one over to Ian.

"*Sound of Music*," everyone, including Theo, replied in unison. ·

"Are you shittin' me? God, I hate that fucking movie."

"Sit," Harper ordered Theo with a gentle shove toward the couch.

Alex inserted the disc and took the remote with him to a single chair off to the side. Ian crawled off the couch to lie on the floor in front of the big flat screen, leaving space for Harper to sit next to Theo.

"You pack of lying assholes." Harper rejoiced after discovering they were going to watch his favorite.

As predicted, Ian was snoring away soundly thirty minutes into the movie. Alex was relieved to see that Theo appeared to be enjoying it. About an hour into the film, Alex paused for a pee break. Harper kneeled on the floor and woke his partner up by licking his ear.

"Come on, my sweet prince, it's time for bed." Harper grabbed Ian's empty beer. "You guys enjoy the rest of the flick. We're calling it a night."

"I can't believe I fell asleep." Ian wiped his eyes. "That *never* happens." Picking himself up off the floor, he walked over to Theo and patted him on the shoulder. "It was great you could make it tonight. Stop by again."

"Thanks, Ian." Theo stood. "Thanks, Harper. The food, everything was great."

"Good. That's what we like to hear. We'll catch up with you soon, I hope. Don't be a stranger." Harper slapped his sleepy partner on the butt, sending him on his way.

Alex used the bathroom, and when he returned, Theo had moved over on the couch as if to suggest Alex should sit there too.

I really like you, Theo. I hope you had fun tonight. "You wanna watch it to the end?" Alex asked, sitting on the couch.

"Sure, it's a great movie. Unless," Theo quickly added with a worried look, "you're not into it."

"I was hoping you wanted to stick around. Let's do it."

Neither of them said another word until the credits appeared.

"I guess I should be heading home." Theo patted his knees and, with an initial wobble from sitting too long, stood.

Alex wanted so badly to delay Theo's exit but resisted the impulse, knowing his new friend was in the process of making such a huge change in his life. If he initiated anything more tonight, given the horny mood he was in, it wouldn't be respectful to Theo. *I think you're worth waiting for, Theo. You're sweet, you're super hot, and if I don't stop looking over at you right now, my dick is going to explode right through my jeans.*

"Thanks again for your help at the Center." Alex sprang from his seat with more energy than he knew what to do with.

"I enjoyed helping you guys. Give me a call if you have another project you need a hand with. I love doing stuff like that."

"That's good to know." Finally resigned to letting the evening come to an end, Alex ushered Theo to the door.

I want to kiss you. I want to hold you in my arms and mess around until the sun comes up. "Hey, drive safe, okay?"

"Will do. When you see those guys tomorrow, tell them again how much I enjoyed coming over. It was great." Theo shoved his hands into his jeans and then pulled them back out.

"Sure. They really liked you too, I could tell." *Let him go. He needs to get strong first.*

An awkward moment passed until Theo gave Alex a playful jab to the shoulder. "Later, dude."

"I'll call you soon to plan something," Alex called out.

"Let's do it. Bye!"

Alex waited for Theo to start up his truck and pull out of the driveway before closing the door and shutting off the light. On his way to his room, he stopped off in the kitchen for a cookie. He broke into a huge smile when he looked at the refrigerator. Ian had awarded Theo a perfect 10.

"SEE, this is where it asks you whether or not you want the entry to be linked to our contacts. If you say yes, then it will be included on the master list for mailings." Alex stood back to let Petra discover for herself what he had just pointed out.

"Wow, okay. That's so much easier than to go back and manually enter the client's name into the database. You're the smartest one, Alex Stevens."

"You're no slouch either, Petra Pavlovitch. Hey, you never told me, how did your date with the lady in Cabin six go the other night?" Alex moved from behind the desk over to the window. There was a lot at stake and he needed to make sure it all went as planned. *Oh man, this is going to be the best one ever!*

"This is between you and I. Got it?" Petra waited for Alex to acknowledge he understood.

"Sure."

"It will be a highlight of mine for many summers to come, I'm sure." Petra couldn't hold back the sigh that went hand and hand with the memory.

"Seriously? Is she, like, some really great cook or something?"

"Men. Why is it you weenie-waggers constantly think and talk about sex with each other, but when it comes to us girls, you think it's like nineteenth on the list." Petra blew her hair out of her eyes in frustration. "We skipped dinner, and I got back here at six in the morning. Does that spell it out clear enough for you?"

Alex laughed as he continued to monitor the activity outside.

"Betsy is a female version of Jekyll and Hyde. I was a virtual sex slave from the minute I stepped inside her cabin until I hauled my sorry ass back home."

"TMI, sweets. TMI." Alex was forced to step back from the window to avoid being seen. *That's right, Ian, old man, smile and yuck it up. You're going to shit your pants when you find out who you're talking to.*

"Oh, please. Don't give *me* that TMI crap when I have to stand here day in and day out listening to the cub scouts speculate on whether or not their pubes will bush out in the fall. You dudes are nonstop." To make her point, Petra slapped the counter. "What a crock of crap."

"Good point. I forget sometimes you're a woman." The minute that came out of his mouth, Alex knew he was in serious trouble.

"Dude, I know you love me, so I've decided to let you live. However, and I hope you're listening to me closely, if you ever insult me like that again I'll sever your dick from your body and use it salmon fishing. Capiche?"

When Alex looked back, Petra was staring into the air with her arms folded defensively across her chest. "I'm really sorry, Petra. Really sorry."

"You should be. That was so insensitive."

Alex watched as Petra did her best to dispel her pout. He had hurt her feelings. "Can I just say one more thing?" he asked with an overabundance of caution.

"I'm going fishing early next week, so ask at your own risk."

As bad as he felt, he couldn't help chuckling. "You fit in so well. You became a part of the team so fast. We love you and think of you as one of us. I just got a little mixed up on the fact that you have different parts than we do. *Lady* parts." Alex hoped he'd gained some ground back.

"I have to admit, that wasn't half bad."

Before either of them had a chance to say anything else, Harper came bounding through the door. "Good morning! How's everyone doing?"

"Great!" They both answered at the same time.

"Really, that's cool, because I'm great too! Isn't that a beautiful thing? Isn't it?" Harper walked behind the desk and gave Petra's cheek a tweak.

"You're truly inspirational. Don't let anyone tell you otherwise." Petra playfully shoved him away.

"If someone seriously said that to me," Harper admitted, laughing, "I'd whack them upside the head."

This cracked everyone up.

"Pretty thoughts on a pretty morning," Petra countered.

"Hey." Harper stepped over to the window. "Who are the two women Ian's touring the grounds with? They don't look like guests."

"I don't have a clue." Petra came from behind the desk to have a look. "Alex?"

"Ass Crack and her friend." Alex was so delighted with how well the joke on Ian was playing out he could hardly stand it.

"Ass Crack? As in *Ask Krak*? The misinformed garden writer for the *North Shore Tribune* Ian hates with an unbridled passion? What the hell is he doing talking to her, I wonder?"

The sincere tone in Harper's voice removed all self-control from Alex. He launched into an epic laughing fit. Unable to stay on his feet, he wandered back over to the desk for support. "I'm dying," he managed between guffaws.

"I'm just a wee bit curious, Alex." Harper walked over to him. "Does Ian know who he's talking to?"

All Alex could manage was a slight shake of the head as tears streamed down his cheeks.

Harper wandered back to the window. "Oh man, this is good. This is really good. I still can't fathom someone in their right mind would ever consider naming a column 'Ask Krak'. It defies reason."

Alex took a stab at wiping the tears from his face, but, unfortunately, they were replaced too fast for him to keep up. Laughing uncontrollably, he stumbled over to join Harper for a better view of the proceedings.

Together, with Petra looking over their shoulders, they watched Ian. By the look on his face, he was obviously enjoying himself. His exaggerated hand gestures and wide-eyed expressions made the joke on him so potent. After seconds of observation, Harper exploded in laughter and, following Alex's lead, limped over to the counter for support. "Holy crap, that's the funniest thing I've seen in years."

"I know." Alex worked diligently to regain some control. "He's going to be featured in her...." Unable to speak another word, he poked his finger in the air to indicate there was more, but it'd be a while before he could get to it.

Harper, hearing enough to finish Alex's sentence, looked over, his eyes wild with surprise. "Do you mean to tell me Ian is going to be featured in ass crack's column? Is that even possible?"

Alex fired back a tearful nod. "I told them we wanted it to be a surprise for his...." Once again, he had to stop. There wasn't enough air to laugh and talk at the same time.

"Birthday?" Harper tossed his head back and roared. "Alex, that's absolute genius."

"Holy shit." Petra narrated from the window. "The pudgy one with the safari hat has her fat arm around Ian's waist."

"That's Asssssssss—" Alex slapped his thighs in hysterics as he danced around the office.

"Oh no, this isn't good." Petra stepped back a few feet. "It looks like... yep... they're headed toward the office."

Alex reached over and grabbed Harper by the arm. They flew behind the desk and into Petra's apartment.

"I'll signal the all clear," Petra offered in a forced whisper before returning to her post.

Moving as fast as they could, they were able to reach the shower before they heard voices from up front. Leading the way, Alex climbed in and stood over in the corner. His hand smashed against his mouth so sound wouldn't leak out. Harper scurried in behind him and ripped the curtain closed.

"He's going to kill you. You know that, right?" Harper whispered when he'd finally calmed enough. "God, that's so funny."

"I know. But it's so worth it." Alex replaced his hand over his mouth and listened.

It seemed like an eternity before Petra whipped the shower curtain open. "They're gone. You guys need any conditioner?" She backed up to allow room for them to climb out. "I don't think I've ever seen anyone laugh as hard as you two. Wow, that was impressive."

"I feel sick." Alex stumbled out of the shower with Harper right behind him.

"It's not that often either of us gets one up on Ian. And such a brilliant one it is, I might add." Harper patted Alex on the back. "You might want to practice walking with something up your butt, my friend, because your ass and Ian's foot are destined to come together when he finds out."

"I'm going to be lucky to live through this." Alex led the three of them out of Petra's apartment to the office. "Oh, you know what I haven't done yet?"

"Tied Ian's shoelaces together while he's sleeping?" Petra guessed.

"No, but that's a good one." Alex ripped off a couple pieces of paper towel from under the desk and wiped his face. "I haven't gone down to introduce myself to Harold and Quentin yet."

"Go do that now." It was clear by the tone of her voice that Petra had had enough of their hijinks for one day.

"I'd better get back to the house. I have to grab some papers before heading over to the Center. Will I see you later?" Harper turned to Alex before leaving.

"Yeah. I should be over this morning." *Crap! I forgot about the faucet.* "I have to check out a faucet leak in Cabin four. Theresa from housekeeping told Petra about it when she flipped it this morning."

"Don't spend a ton of time on it." Harper was half out the door. "Call the guy we used last year when we built the new laundry facility if it looks to be a big deal. You're too busy right now. Later."

"Sounds good. Bye." Alex grabbed a large tool belt from under the desk. "I'm going to stop by to meet the guys in Cabin five, if they're around, before I play Mister Fixit."

"Let me know if you find out anything about Quentin." Petra flashed her worried look.

"Okay, later Pet. Thanks for housing the fugitives." Alex saluted as he stepped out of the office.

It was a beautiful spring morning. The warmest yet, Alex noted. *Damn, this thing is heavy.* Over the last few years, almost any tool you could imagine had been added to the belt. They joked there wasn't a single task possible the belt wasn't ready for.

Walking behind Cabin four to protect the privacy of their guests, Alex turned the corner and approached Harold and Quentin's cabin. Someone was seated in a large Adirondack near the water. *Which one is this?* The figure, bundled up in a winter coat, was hunched over a table—*that's not ours*—typing on a laptop.

"Good morning," Alex greeted with a wave, "are you Harold?"

"No, but you're very close. I'm Quentin, Harold's better half."

Petra was right. Something was wrong with this guy. *Do you really need the blanket and the heavy coat, dude?* Then he remembered his last bout with the flu. The chills. Maybe Quentin was suffering from a bad case.

"It's a pleasure to meet you. I'm Alex, operational manager. Are you having an enjoyable stay so far?" The whole reason Alex had stopped by was to meet Harold, who he knew had taken an interest in his painting hanging in the office.

"Young man, those are the most devastatingly handsome green eyes I have ever seen. And I've been around the block a time or two."

Alex chuckled. He'd been complimented on his eyes for as long as he could remember, but the way Quentin had done it struck him as humorous.

"Thanks." *Let's see, how do I find out where Harold is?* "I don't want to disturb you. Is Harold around?" *That wasn't so hard.*

"Oh, goodness, you're not disturbing me at all. It's not that often I get visited by such a handsome gentleman caller."

Ah, okay. Weird.

"If I'm not off my mark, you'll find Harold in the cabin preparing morning tea."

"It was nice meeting you, Quentin. Enjoy your day." Alex smiled and backed away.

"The pleasure was all mine, Alex. Stop by again when you can chat longer. I'd like that."

Alex couldn't help notice the way Quentin's face lit up when he talked. *It might be kinda fun to spend some time with this old dude.*

"Sure."

Harold stepped out of the cabin with a mug in his hand as Alex approached. "I wondered who that handsome young man was talking to my partner, and then it came to me—at last. You must be Alex. Do you have time to join me for a cup of tea?" Harold gestured behind him to the cabin.

"I haven't really had much tea, but yeah, I can hang for a while." Alex suddenly felt like a hick. He always associated tea with people outside of his North-woods circle. This was a good opportunity to expand his world.

"Let me run this down to Quentin. Be right back."

Alex dropped his work belt off on the side of the steps and watched as Harold delivered "morning tea" to his ailing partner. *How long have these guys been together?* Harold placed the tea on Quentin's table. Quentin reached for Harold's arm. He must have said something funny, because Harold laughed. Harold bent down for a kiss, and Alex forced himself to look away as Harold walked back to the cabin.

"Beautiful morning, don't you think? Come on in."

"It's finally starting to warm up." Alex followed the older gentleman into the cabin, where he was directed to sit in one of the chairs at the small round table.

"This is an English breakfast variety, and my guess is, unless you tell me otherwise, a spot of cream and a dollop of sugar will make it much more enjoyable for you. Should we give it a try?" Harold winked.

"Okay." Miles outside his element, Alex took a chair and watched as Harold prepared his tea.

"I'm so glad you came by, because I personally wanted to tell you how impressed I am with your painting hanging in the office. It's beautifully balanced, and your color technique is very unique. There."

"Thank you."

A steaming cup was placed in front of him along with a plate full of cookies.

"These cookies will change your life. They're chocolate chip and thimbleberry. Please help yourself."

Alex recognized them immediately. They were Audrey's. Occasionally, she would feature them at the Lip Smacker on a shelf under the cash register. They didn't last long. He eagerly took one off the plate.

"You have a very provocative smile on your face, young man." Harold circled a spoon lazily in his cup.

Alex snickered. He was caught. "These cookies are from the Lip Smacker. I worked there all through high school. Audrey Pakenpooch is a friend of mine." It sounded so strange to call Audrey a friend when she was so much more. More mother than friend, that was for sure.

"Now, there's a name that certainly needs some energy to reproduce."

"Ha!" Alex laughed. Harold had a point.

"We have met Audrey. She seems like a wonderful person. She's very kind to us. Quentin and I have fallen in love with the Lip Smacker too." Harold looked out the window and added, "Quentin went to school with Audrey's older sister."

"That's cool. Yum, this isn't anything like I thought it would be," Alex shared after he had chanced a sip of his tea. "It's really good."

"I'm so glad to hear it. Makes a nice pairing with Audrey's scrumptious cookie. So, what I'd be delighted to know is how you came to paint so wonderfully?" Harold sipped from his own cup and relaxed into the chair.

"I had an art teacher in school who was into watercolor. He taught me the basics, and I just kind of experimented on my own. I tried to stay busy in school. Home, well, it wasn't a place I wanted to be much." Alex was surprised that he could talk so frankly about something that had caused him so much pain. He remembered Harper's comment to him shortly after his father jumped off the palisade. "You probably will find this hard to believe, but time has a way of smoothing everything out."

"Are you still painting? Please, help yourself to another cookie." Harold slid the plate closer to Alex.

"I haven't painted for a few years. Seems like there's always something else to do." *Should I go for another cookie? Better not. I need to get to work soon.*

"I'm very sorry to hear that, Alex. I think you have a rare gift."

Unable to think of anything to say back, Alex sipped his tea and smiled.

"I paint. Not in your medium, watercolor, but various others, like acrylic and oil. I've never been able to master the art of watercolor, as you seem to have so brilliantly. So I guess I'm a little bit jealous too. But it would be nice for you to consider starting to paint again. I think it could end up being quite profitable." Harold reached for a cookie and bit into it while concentrating his gaze across the table.

"I never thought about painting for money." *Maybe down the road, but not now. Not with everything else I have going on.*

"Oh, don't misunderstand me. I think the rule of thumb is to paint to satisfy your artistic appetite, and along the way make a few bucks if you can. Anyway, my intention for asking you to stop by was simply to tell you how wonderful I think your painting is. The last thing I wanted to do was serve up morning tea and cookies with a lecture." Harold reached over and patted Alex's hand. "By the way, you have extraordinary green eyes."

"Quentin said the same thing. I must have gotten enough sleep last night or something." Alex chuckled, hoping Harold appreciated his humor.

"We both have an appreciation for eyes. More tea?"

"The tea is delicious, but I have a plumbing project I need to get to. Thank you very much." Alex sipped to make sure his cup was completely empty.

"Very well. Alex, will you do me one small favor?"

I wonder what this is going to be? Say yes. It can't be that big of a deal. "Sure." Alex stood and stepped over to the door.

"Wonderful. Please come and visit us anytime. I adore discussing art and technique, if you ever feel the urge."

"Thanks, Harold. I'll be sure to do that." *He's right. I miss painting.*

CHAPTER
Six

THEO felt honored to be dining with a local baseball star. A father and son had stopped by their table when they had first sat down and asked Ian to autograph the boy's glove. It was so cool. *I wonder if the world knows he's gay? Probably doesn't matter when you're that good.*

"Theo, eat that last piece of pizza." Harper shoved the pan his way.

"Naw, I'm good. Alex, here." Theo moved it over.

"I'll feel like shit if I eat it. I'm just right." Alex slid the remaining piece over to Ian.

"Well, I guess I *could* eat it. If nobody *else* wants it?" Ian grabbed the slice and chomped away. "I *love* pizza."

"We know that, slugger." Harper downed the last of his beer. "I'm still marveling at your home run tonight. You must have connected with the ball at just the right moment. It flew out of the park like a rocket."

"It was so awesome. You're lethal, man." Theo couldn't remember when he'd enjoyed a game more.

"We've been itching to get a crack at their new pitcher. I guess he's a real prima donna." The Taconknights walked away with a decisive win against the Beckersville Cormorants. "It was great to put the peckerhead in his place." Ian leaned back in his chair and patted his stomach. "That was so tasty."

"As long as we're in Superior, how about we stop off at the Main Club and shoot some darts? I feel like being out on the town for a while longer." Harper reached over and caressed Ian's shoulder.

Theo loved hanging with these guys. He could tell they liked him, and that made him feel great. Whatever happened to the rest of his world didn't seem to matter so much anymore. He no longer felt like he was alone. More importantly, he felt less dependent on his parents and his living situation. If it were all to blow up tomorrow, he'd be... well, he'd be more prepared for it. This provided him with an interesting byproduct: lately, the time he spent at home was much more tolerable. Anger and frustration at his parents' narrow view of the world took a back seat. Theo looked over at them and felt sorry. Sorry they were trapped in their ugly and hurtful beliefs. Yep, when the time came to move out, he would have the courage and strength to get through it. No matter how messy it got.

"I'll beat your ass again. You realize that, right?" Ian looked across at Theo and Alex and winked.

"The hell you will." Harper wadded his napkin into a tight ball and tossed it into the empty pan. "You're going to be crying little loser tears all the way home."

"Loser tears. In your dreams, Binky." Ian looked at his man and laughed. "I haven't called you that for a while. Not sure why."

"Damn, I thought that one had been permanently retired, Spanky." Harper beamed, obviously proud for shooting back a nickname for Ian from their extensive archive. "What are you young'uns going to do?"

The plan had been to grab pizza after the game. Going to the bar to shoot darts was an unexpected development. *Let's skip darts, Theo hoped.* Alex had driven the three of them to the game. Harper would ride home with Ian. Theo's truck was parked back at their house. Lustful intentions for Alex kept Theo from voicing an opinion on how he'd like to see the night unfold until Alex opened the door for him.

"I don't know." Alex looked over to Theo to see if he had any ideas.

He did. *I want to touch you, Alex.* "Wanna head back to your house and watch a movie?" Theo hoped his idea wouldn't come off as too lame. "I'm open," he added to cover the bases.

"Yeah, let's do that." Alex took a credit card out of his wallet and grabbed the bill. "Dinner's on me."

"We really need to go out with him more often," Harper announced to the table.

"It's about time moneybags picked up the tab." Ian leaned over the table and whispered to Theo, "Alex puts the *T* in tight. He hounded me for three weeks because I borrowed a few bucks to buy a lottery ticket."

Theo laughed. He suspected Alex was careful with his money. Nothing wrong with that. The dude's 4X4 was proof. Even though he had bought it used, it still had to have cost him a fortune. His ride was loaded—four off-road lights mounted on the roll bar, custom chrome grille guard mounted with two more off-road lights and, last but not least, the Warn winch... *hell, he could pull down a tree with that monster.*

"I found a new alternative station last week." Alex pulled out of the lot onto the street. "Do you mind if we listen to it?" He fumbled with the dials on the dash.

"Sounds good." Theo didn't want Alex to think he was an idiot, so he refrained from asking why it was called an alternative station.

"What kind of tunes do you like?" Alex found what he was looking for and adjusted the volume. The music didn't seem all that different to Theo from what he played.

"I like all kinds. Country is probably my least favorite, but I'll listen to it in small doses. Mostly, I listen to heavy metal. Some rap." Theo could take music or leave it. It wasn't something he was current on or had an interest in pursuing. He was glad Alex was the opposite.

From the minute he climbed into the truck, Theo felt something unlike anything he could remember feeling for anyone else. *It's like a connection. I can't stop thinking about this dude.* Whatever it was, this attraction was strong, and it was making him hard. *Is the same thing happening to him?* He had felt like this before—when they had said good night after he'd been over for dinner. Alex's hesitation. It was real. It had happened. Theo had driven home that night feeling sure something special was developing. Tonight, seated so close, the vibe was there again and much stronger. It was unmistakable. By the time Alex pulled off the highway and onto the dirt road leading down to the resort, Theo felt as if he might explode. The uncertainty of where this evening was headed caused his palms to sweat.

"I'm going to grab a soda. You want a diet?" Alex tossed his coat onto the kitchen counter.

"Sure." Theo whipped off his hooded sweatshirt and tossed it there too. He had on his favorite T-shirt, which had a cowboy on the front being bucked off of a bull. It fit perfectly, stretching across his chest so his pecs were displayed the way he liked. Lucy had commented on them several times, so he knew they weren't too shabby.

Alex handed him a soda. "Cool shirt. I think cowboys are really hot."

Really? I wish I'd known that. I would have worn my boots and my hat.

Theo followed Alex to the entertainment room, the whole time watching his new friend's butt shift from side to side. Theo decided then and there it was time to make his move.

"What should we watch? Got any ideas?" Alex was standing in front of the bookcase that housed their movies.

Theo stood close behind and peered over his shoulder. Sensing the moment was as good as any, he leaned his head forward and rested his chin on Alex's shoulder. Alex said nothing. Instead, he nonchalantly ran his hand across a row of movie titles as if Theo's advance was the most natural thing in the world. When he reached the end of the row, he twisted around slowly until his back was up against the shelf.

"I'm thinking a movie might not be the best use of our time." Alex reached up and began to caress the back of Theo's head. "Is that what you're thinking?"

Theo tried to answer, but his mouth had dried up. "Yes," he managed on the second attempt.

"Do you like to kiss?"

Theo was captivated when Alex's eyes searched his own for an answer. It felt like those beautiful green beacons were looking right into his heart.

Honestly, Theo didn't know if he liked to kiss. Anything sexual in the past had been forced and uncomfortable because it felt required. He and Lucy worked as a couple as long as they did because she was patient and not all that needy. Their intimate time together was mostly spent cuddling. A few times when he had been very horny and desperate for relief, his typically passive approach to sex had turned aggressive. But those times were short lived, and the moment quickly dissipated. The attempt at passion never seemed to satisfy. He was always conscious of the effort it took to be sexual. Nothing like now. He wanted Alex. He wanted to mess around with Alex, and he wanted that sooner rather than later.

Theo leaned forward until their lips met. Alex brushed noses and then kissed him lightly, the whole time massaging the back of his neck. *That was pretty cool. It's not as strange as I thought it'd be.* There was a potent energy bouncing between them. *Is this what they mean when they say that thing about sparks flying?*

Theo laughed. "I'm sorry. I'm...." he looked down at the floor.

"I'm nervous, Theo," Alex said before leaning into him for another kiss.

This kiss lasted longer. Theo felt Alex's tongue probe and gently pry open his lips. Unable to resist, he rested his hands on his friend's hips. *Touching you makes me crazy.*

Another series of light pecks, and Theo felt Alex's arm wrap around his waist. Leaning back into the shelf, he pulled Theo forward until he lost his balance and in the process pinned Alex with his body.

The shelf made a slight jolt backward and then stopped when it reached the wall. Theo's heart raced. Alex smelled wonderful. Intoxicating. He loved being this close. Alex must like it too, for his hardness pressed up against Theo's leg was all the proof he needed.

There were more tentative smooches and nibbles before the kissing finally got serious. Alex sucked Theo's tongue deep into his throat. It felt amazing. Theo returned the gesture after Alex released him.

"Would you mind if we moved into my bedroom? I'm not sure when the roomies will be home." Alex flashed a devilish smile.

Theo pressed his body away from the shelf and stood waiting timidly. "I like the bedroom idea." *You're worried. Let him know that.* "Alex?"

"Yeah?" Alex took him by the hand.

"I need to go slow." Theo released a nervous laugh. "I have no idea what I'm doing."

"Don't worry. Slow is the best way. I have a plan." Alex led Theo down the hall past the kitchen to his room. Inside, Alex closed the door and locked it.

"Why don't we kick off our shoes and make ourselves comfortable." Alex went to the desk and grabbed a remote. Soft music filled the room. He placed it on the nightstand, took off his shoes, and climbed up onto the bed, patting the spot next to him.

Before he lost his nerve, Theo climbed on the bed and scooted over to Alex. Still dressed in jeans and T-shirts, they rolled onto their sides and faced each other.

"You have the best hair in the whole world. The cut is perfect." Alex ran his fingers through it and brushed the strands away from Theo's eyes.

"I used to wear it really long, but my girl—" Theo stopped midsentence when he realized he'd gone to a place he didn't want to go.

Alex laughed. "Oh man, if you could have seen the look on your face just now. It was pure terror." Alex rolled on his back and laughed. "Okay, so not too long ago you had a girlfriend. Big deal. Not too long ago I had Todd. Sounds like we're both moving on." Alex turned back on his side. "I really like you, Theo. It feels special being with you."

Theo bit his lip. Alex had said exactly what he'd been wanting to hear. Theo wanted to say the same thing back but hesitated. He didn't want what he was feeling to come off as fake, even though, in his heart, he wanted to say the same thing. "Your eyes are amazing." *What else do you want to tell him? It's okay.* Theo didn't want to risk losing Alex because they didn't work out in the romance department. "Alex?"

"Yeah?" Alex used his finger to trace around the cowboy and then the bull.

"I don't want to ruin our friendship. I don't want to lose it if for some reason it turns out we weren't meant to be together in this other way."

"Wow!" Alex rolled onto his back.

"Wow what?" Theo inched closer.

"I'm super shitty at communicating my feelings. That was so amazing, what you just said."

Theo placed his hand on Alex's chest, unsure of whose turn it was to talk.

"Okay." Alex turned back. "A couple of weeks ago, Harper lectured me because I hadn't been fair with Todd. I didn't communicate my feelings to him as they were happening. He was totally right. I hadn't asked or said the right things to Todd. Anyway, I need you to help me with that. Please keep telling me how you feel. I promise to tell the truth back. Can we go along like that for a while and see how far we get?"

"Sure. I like that idea." Theo's hand had reached Alex's belt.

"Go ahead," Alex whispered.

Theo unclasped the belt and opened it. *Dude, your hands are shaking. Easy, man.* He moved his palm down until he found what he was looking for. It wasn't easy to miss. Alex was rock hard. Theo closed his eyes and savored the sensation of resting his hand there. *Oh yeah.* He could feel Alex pulsate beneath the fabric.

Stretched out on the bed, Alex placed his hands behind his head, which Theo took as a sign to continue.

Undoing the button of Alex's jeans, Theo slowly brought the zipper down as far as it would go. *Breathe. Oh my God....* In need of a more comfortable position, he slid down the bed and propped himself up on his elbow. He leaned in closer until he was hovering over Alex's crotch. With a nervous hand, he peeled the faded denim back, exposing a pair of bright orange boxer shorts. *So close.*

Theo smiled as he looked up to Alex, who smiled back and nodded. *I think I just got the green light.*

The outline of Alex's constrained dick was impressive. Theo's own cock throbbed, but he didn't care. He wanted to see and touch Alex. He had waited so long for this. Careful not to rush, he grasped Alex in his hand and squeezed. It was obvious Alex was very eager for attention.

As if to confirm all was well, Alex unleashed a sigh of contentment, the bed barely able to accommodate his long, relaxed body.

It was the moment of truth. *Alex wants me to touch him here.* Sliding up closer, Theo brought himself up onto his knees and parted the slit in Alex's boxers. *Wow! There it is. Looks bigger than mine.* He could see most of it. After several false starts, Theo reached down and worked the warm, hard shaft from its orange prison. *That's it. There we go.* The dick bounced a few times in the air, as if testing its newfound independence, and then rested flat on Alex's stomach.

Alex laughed, and so did Theo when he realized he'd spent the last few moments mesmerized by Alex's boner.

See? You're doing just fine. Alex will let you know what he likes and what he doesn't.

Alex placed his hand on the back of Theo's neck and gently pushed him down. A sure sign he wanted Theo to continue.

Theo traced his finger up and down the underside of Alex's cock. *Dude, this is so awesome. It's so warm and hard.* Like before, it reacted by springing up in the air. After several trips up and down its length, Theo moved in closer and took the entire dick in his hand.

Alex moaned and curled toward Theo. While Theo held him, Alex began rubbing his hands over the parts of Theo's body he could reach. Theo didn't have to be told what to do next. He began to slowly jack Alex.

"That feels so good. Please don't stop." Alex reached over and hugged as much of Theo as he could get his arms around.

Oh man, hug me harder. Theo couldn't wait for Alex to hold him in his arms. There was so much to this. *I can't get enough of you. I'm so starved to be loved and to love someone back.*

A glistening bead of precum appeared. Theo, an expert at satisfying himself, launched into a tried and true technique guaranteed to please. Starting at the base of the shaft, he slowly squeezed as he moved his hand toward the tip and was rewarded with a much larger release. *It's so wild to be doing this to someone else.* Starting with the plump head, Theo generously coated Alex. Clasping his fingers together in a circle around the shaft, he began to brush up and down over its sensitive scar.

"Oh man, you're really good at this. Yes!" Alex once again reached for Theo and pulled him tight to his body.

Discovering the confidence he thought he might have lacked, Theo increased his efforts. Soon Alex was gliding smoothly, the entire shaft wet and glistening.

Rapid thrusts in and out of Theo's hand caused Alex's balls to emerge from his boxers. Shifting his weight, Theo now had two hands to work with. As he loved to do with himself, he kneaded Alex's sac while at the same time stroking him.

Alex responded by reaching down and pulling his T-shirt up to his neck. Seconds later, he tensed. Alex's upper body came up off the bed as a huge spurt of cum shot high into the air.

Theo could hardly contain his joy. "Wow!" He kept his hand moving up and down until Alex, struggling to catch his breath, grabbed it and stopped him from continuing.

"Stop. I can't take any more."

For a second, Theo thought he might have taken things too far, but the warm smile from Alex, followed by laughter, dispelled his fear.

"I don't think I've ever cum that hard before. That was amazing," Alex complimented.

Theo laughed, keeping his sticky hand in the air so he wouldn't mess up the bedding.

"Fuck, I don't know where it all went. I don't care." Alex climbed off the bed and removed his jeans and his boxers. Theo got his first look at one of the hottest asses he'd ever seen. Alex removed his T-shirt and walked several feet to his closet, coming back with a towel.

"Here." He tossed it onto the bed with a smirk. "Sex is messy."

Theo wiped his hands, placing the towel on the nightstand. At once he felt—*I feel dirty. What are you doing, Theo? Are you sure this is what you want? Your whole life will be so different if you let this continue.*

"My turn." Alex hopped back onto the bed.

Theo wanted to relax and enjoy the attention Alex was about to give his body, but a guilty inner voice threatened to ruin the experience. Seconds after being on top of the world pleasuring Alex, he suddenly wanted to leave. His face warmed, unable to understand or process the guilt he felt for allowing himself to enjoy being with another man. Theo turned and sat on the edge of the bed, facing away. *Why won't these feelings go away? Nothing is wrong with me. Please stop. Please!*

"Theo. Don't go there. I think I know what's happening." Alex scooted behind and brought Theo up into his arms.

"I used to feel so ashamed right after I had sex with another dude. I knew it was okay to enjoy it, but no matter what I did, I couldn't stop the bad feelings. I felt really crappy. It took time, but that doesn't happen anymore. I know I deserve to feel good about being naked with you. You deserve it too. There's nothing wrong with us, Theo."

Theo willed his body to relax. Being held by Alex felt so wonderful. *You have to face this head-on. Mom, Dad, the church. The nasty is coming from them.* Theo's unexpected bout of vulnerability caused him to frown. It was a disappointment his parents still held such a firm grip on him. The disappointment came from knowing that as far along as he had come, there was still so much farther he needed to travel to enjoy the freedoms Alex and his roomies enjoyed. Alex would help him escape. He was sure of it. He needed to trust.

"Does that make sense? Is that where you're at?"

Theo felt Alex's lips on the back of his neck. Soft, gentle kisses. He turned and hugged him with all of his might. The faint scent of sex coming from the naked, still-panting body seemed to blast away the evil. "It's exactly what I feel, but I didn't know how to say it."

"So—" Alex nibbled on his ear. "—can I have a turn?" Alex dragged his tongue down the back of Theo's neck, sending shivers through his body. "Don't think for a minute I'm going to pass this up. You're not getting away from me. No siree. I've been dreaming about this, dude."

Theo giggled. Twisting around, he looked up to Alex and wondered, *How does this start? Do I lie on my back? What does Alex want to do?* He had a million questions but soon found out he needn't worry.

"Let's start like this." Alex reached for Theo's T-shirt and lifted it up over his arms. "Lie down on your back. Let me do the rest. Your chest and stomach… you're so ripped. Damn!"

Theo reached for the pillow above him and placed it under his head. He stretched his body out and, for the moment, closed his eyes. His thought was, if he had his eyes shut, he was less likely to be nervous or apprehensive. He was less likely to be visited by those icky thoughts again.

Seconds later, he felt his belt being unbuckled. Like Theo had done, Alex brought down his zipper. This is where the similarity in their initial approach ended.

Alex slid off and walked to the bottom of the bed. Theo felt the cuffs of his jeans being tugged, and before he knew what was happening, Alex had removed them, leaving only his navy boxer briefs.

"Aha! Boxer briefs. I guessed right."

Theo laughed, hoping Alex liked what he saw.

"Gooey, *wet* boxer briefs."

In another fast move, Alex had Theo's underwear down to his ankles and off. His cock was throbbing, begging to be touched. "Dang! You have an awesome dick."

Unable to locate the shame that had attacked him earlier, Theo raised his head and smiled. He shot a quick glance down his body to make sure everything below was as he remembered it. Satisfied all was well, he rested his head back on the pillow.

Climbing up from the bottom of the bed, Alex positioned himself between Theo's legs. Seconds later, Theo felt Alex's warm tongue trace the vein on his dick from his balls to its tip. A charge raced through his body. *I'm so ready for this.*

Theo gasped and involuntarily hunched his body up when Alex, in a surprise move, plunged his mouth down on him until his entire cock was engulfed. In another unexpected move, Alex thrust his hands underneath his butt.

"Oh yeah," Theo voiced with complete approval.

Alex cupped and squeezed his ass as he held his cock captive in his throat. In response, Theo reached behind for the pillow and hugged it tight to his chest.

Slow and deliberate, Alex's assault intensified, his lips clasped tightly around Theo's shaft while at the same time his warm hands were working him from below. With the exception of his momentary bout with guilt, Theo had been aroused for a very long time and knew from experience he wasn't going to last long.

As Alex's efforts increased, Theo buried his face into the pillow. He inhaled the intoxicating scent of Alex that lingered in the soft fabric. *I love how this dude smells.* The combination of smell and touch proved to be too much for him. It was all happening so fast. He felt out of control. His body was being bombarded with wave after wave of pleasure, and all he could do was hang on for the wild ride. This was uncharted territory. Someone he was beginning to care for was pleasuring him, and it felt amazing.

Before Theo realized it, he was there. "I'm going to cum," he hollered out, feeling the need to voice a warning. This only seemed to kick Alex into a higher gear. A hand was removed from his ass. It grasped Theo's cock at the base, and, together with his expert sucking, Alex brought him to the promised land.

Theo slapped the bed with his hands as he emptied himself into Alex's mouth. He thrashed and twisted but was unable to halt the attack. Alex continued to suck and pump until Theo could do nothing more than whimper his total satisfaction.

For several seconds, the only sound filling the room was soft music and his panting. He was totaled. Annihilated by the power of his orgasm, Theo removed the pillow from his face and gasped for air. Alex kept his mouth tightly clasped around his dick.

Feeling the need to be close, Theo reached down and found Alex's soaking wet head and neck. Locating an ear, he gently tugged. Alex responded by easing himself up and off.

"How'd I do?" the man with the handsome, smiling face and the insanely cool green eyes asked, as if the answer couldn't be predicted.

"You've done that before, dude." Theo laughed at his own joke. "Wow! That was worth the wait."

"Let's cuddle."

Cuddle? How weird is it for a guy to ask me to cuddle? Guys cuddle?

Alex pulled the blankets back. Theo, still too befuddled by shooting his load into Alex's throat, crawled into bed, bringing the sheet up to his chin. As strange as this seemed, it was also exciting. Theo's heart raced once again.

Alex climbed in, reaching over for Theo's head, bringing it up onto his chest while at the same time wrapping his arms around him.

"Theo?" Alex whispered into his ear, "This will probably sound weird, but... what do you think about us being boyfriends?"

Boyfriends? He was thankful he was faced away from Alex. He needed time on this one. *What would Mark tell me to do?* One thing he knew for sure, he already had stronger sexual feelings for Alex than he'd ever had with Lucy. If tonight was any indication of how good it felt to get off with another dude, he was ready for more.

Theo, what can it hurt? Say yes and you can figure out the rest of this later. "It's cool."

"Good. I don't know what I would have done if you said no."

Thinking out loud, he offered, "I felt something... not sure what it was, from the moment I met you at the Center. I guess something told me to try and get to know you better." Theo was brought back to those tentative moments when he wasn't sure he would even have the courage to attend his first meeting. Seemed like years had gone by since then when, in fact, it was a very short time.

"I know it's the middle of the week, but any chance you can spend the night? I have to get up early to help Ian with the gardens. We make a mean breakfast around here."

Theo felt Alex nibble his ear. *Adam would shit his pants if he saw me now. This is frickin' insane.*

"I don't think I've slept in a bed with another guy since scouts," Theo admitted. "This is so strange." Aware that what he just said could be interpreted wrong, he quickly added, "Good strange. You know what I mean?" He hoped that Alex understood on some level how different this was to anything he had known in the past.

It was Alex's turn to chuckle. "Stop being so careful with me. I promise to tell it like it is. And to answer your question, yeah, I know what it means. But for me, it feels more... right than anything."

Theo reached back and tugged Alex's arm tighter around his chest. *I think you're good for me, Alex.*

"DUDE, where are you?" Alex had walked away from Harper and Tiffany to place his call to Ian. This was too big a decision to make without *both* Harper and Ian's input.

"I'm less than a mile away. See you in seconds."

"He's almost here. Sorry to keep you guys hanging." It felt really odd to have everyone focused on him.

"Don't worry about it, Alex. This isn't a decision you want to rush." Tiffany Marks, his realtor, was wonderful. She had sold Harper and Ian the resort and over time had become a good friend.

Today was their third house-hunting trip with her. The previous two afternoons hadn't yielded anything close to his expectations. Harper, understanding he was discouraged, took him aside midway through the second outing and reminded him that not only were homes scarce in the area, but his wish list was packed. Combined, this made Tiffany's job challenging. Harper was careful to add that he shouldn't give up hope. Finding a home that fit the bill might take them awhile. He pledged to Alex that both he and Tiffany were in it for the long haul. He needed to relax with the process.

When Tiffany pulled up to the second house on today's list, Alex's heart did a somersault. Before he put a foot inside the place, he sensed something special about it. The setting, the structure, it was exactly what he'd imagined. *Yes! I think this one could be it.* Alex held his breath as he stepped out of the car.

Nestled back in the woods, eleven miles north of the Beach Cabins, sat a rambler built in the 1950s with, according to Tiffany's spec sheet, a walk out in the back.

"This is a good period for homes around here. The materials tend to be of high quality, and the homebuilders had an integrity you don't often find nowadays." Tiffany took a piece of paper out of her purse and entered the code to retrieve the key so they could get inside for a look.

All of that was good, but what mattered most to Alex was how the house was laid out. It had most everything on his list, with the exception of a garage and screen porch. Both could be added on later. The kitchen had been updated recently, and a large fireplace was located on the lower level. There were three bedrooms, two up and one down. Alex hadn't thought of it originally, but it might be nice to set up an art room, a place to paint and be creative.

True to his word, Ian pulled up and hopped out to join them. "Sorry, Team Alex, for being late. They had a long-underwear sale at Pamida, and the fitting rooms were jammed. What's shakin'?"

Alex, with help from Tiffany and Harper, filled Ian in as they walked through the house one more time.

"The rooms are nice and large. I wouldn't have thought they'd be this big. I like the open counter from the kitchen into the dining room. The kitchen is really nice, don't you think?" Ian patted Alex on the shoulder.

"Yeah, I think so. I like how it opens up to the other room. And the two windows in the corner are a plus. Lots of light."

Today was so exciting. Alex didn't care if he sounded like a little kid. Harper and Ian knew what a big deal this was for him. Both would speak up if for any reason he wasn't being practical. They'd also never embarrass him in front of Tiffany when he was so vulnerable. Once he was alone with them, it would be a shit storm of abuse he'd gladly weather.

"If it were me," Ian offered, "I'd think about reducing the size of the master bedroom and install a walk-in closet. Also, I'd think about knocking out a wall so you can enter the bathroom from the master, and if you reduced the size of the second bedroom, you could create a poop palace. But that's just me."

"Bingo!" Harper weighed in. "I really like that idea too."

"Let's show Ian the lower level." Tiffany led the way down the narrow stairs. "You have eight-foot ceilings, high for this period, which helps to wipe away the cave-dweller effect. Also, and maybe you haven't noticed, but it doesn't smell damp down here. With all the rain we've had recently, if there was a problem with moisture you'd be able to tell. It would smell funky. And you have the walk out, which is really cool. You could do a patio or a deck. I'm surprised there isn't one already." She peered out the glass door again to make certain. "Yeah, I don't see any remnants of a pad."

"Alex, what do you think about the fireplace being down here and not upstairs?" Ian walked over and knelt down to inspect it.

"I'm just glad there is one." Alex laughed. "I guess I like it better down here, because I'd do what you guys did and have it in the same room as the television and entertainment stuff."

"I agree." Harper joined Ian to inspect the brick. "Sure, it would be nice for your guests to enjoy a fire while visiting in the living room, but come on, for most of the time you're going to be down here kicking back, if my guess is right."

"Sounds like he has your ticket, Alex." Tiffany laughed.

"I know." *Stop sounding like an idiot.* Alex was overwhelmed. So much to consider.

After the house tour was complete, Alex grabbed Ian to tour the surrounding property, leaving Harper and Tiffany behind.

"You have a creek running back here? Alex, that's so cool." Ian walked further into the lot so he could get a better view.

"Yeah, so the property runs right up to the creek, and then, see that huge pine over there? The one past that clump of birch?" Alex pointed over to the far right. "That's the property line on this side, and you can't even see the property line on the other side. Lots of privacy."

"I would buy this house. I think it has a lot of potential. You're handy, plus you and I can tackle a bunch of projects this winter after the resort is closed." Ian turned around and looked back to the house. "What are they asking?"

"Tiffany said it's listed at $195,000, but because it's been on the market for several months, she thought I might be able to offer $180,000." Alex studied Ian's face for his reaction.

"Well, it's a serious amount of coin. But I think it's worth it." Ian surveyed the lot and smiled. "What did Harper say?"

"The same thing. He thought it was priced maybe a little high, but because the house was in such good shape it was still a good value."

"Well, I'm in if you decide to go for it. Like I said, we can do a lot of the improvements ourselves. You know from the remodeling we've done at the resort, there're local dudes who will work for a reduced rate during the winter months."

"That's true." *Ian's the big brother I've always wanted.*

Alex traded punches with Ian as they walked back to the house. Harper and Tiffany were waiting by her car.

"Should we keep on looking?" Tiffany asked when they were all back together.

"Naw, this is great." Alex couldn't help himself. He knew he was smiling like a deranged person. "Let's put in an offer."

"I think that's a good decision." Tiffany surveyed the group to see if there were any objectors. Confident everyone was in agreement, she asked, "What should we go in with?"

Alex looked over to Harper. Of the three of them, he was relied on the most for these kinds of decisions.

"Let's go with the $180,000 and see where it gets us."

"Sounds like a plan. I'll put the offer in tonight, if I can get it all drawn up. If not, for sure in the morning. I'll be in touch, gentlemen."

"I think I'm going to be sick." Alex looked over to Harper, who was driving them back to the Center. He was only half kidding. "That's so much money."

"This might help put the whole thing in perspective for you." Harper glanced over and then back to the highway. "You're so damn young. You have longer to pay this off than anyone I've ever known. Plus, this isn't just a place for you to run around carefree in your skimpy designer undies with a tambourine in one hand and a Dew in the other. Your home is an investment. Hopefully, down the road you'll see a return."

"The tambourine's a good idea. Thanks." Alex sighed.

HARPER yawned large. Recently, he'd noticed a slight change in the way his pants were fitting. Nothing serious, but alarming nevertheless. *You're getting to be that age, my friend, when things start to change. Some you can control, others, not so much. This would definitely be one you can control, so move your lazy ass.*

Stepping into the large walk-in closet, he nabbed his running shorts off the hook next to Ian's freshly laundered Taconknights' uniform and lumbered back into the bedroom. He looked over to the bed one last time to make sure he'd made the right decision before he committed to putting them on.

He crept closer to the scene of last night's spirited love romp. *I'm the luckiest man alive. Don't even try and argue it. I am. End of story.*

Ian was still sound asleep. He'd arrived home from a big win against the Virginia Oarblasters with only one thing on his mind. Harper had begged him to shower first, and of course, this wasn't anything Ian was up for doing by himself. The last moment he remembered having any control over the proceedings was reaching out of the shower and handing his partner a towel. From there, he'd been flipped in the air, twirled like a baton, and bounced around the bed like a rag doll. *What do the simple folk do?*

Hot nights only made Harper hungry for hot mornings too. It never failed. *Go run! Your man's got a long day ahead of him, and he needs his sleep.* Over the course of a few days, Ian, with a small crew including Alex, would plant thousands of brightly colored annuals around various beds on the property. Much of the planting was made up of perennials and ornamental shrubbery that came back every year. Ian used the popular bedding plants as if they were the icing on a cake. He was particularly skilled at clumping various varieties and colors together which, year after year, gave his gardens a distinct look. Ian's talent had a great deal to do with the resort's popularity.

Throwing on his shorts, Harper stepped back into the closet to grab a T-shirt and a hooded sweatshirt. The mornings were still cool enough to warrant the additional layer. After stopping off in the kitchen to toss back a glass of juice, he walked through the house, exited out of the screen porch, and began stretching. His warm-up time before a run had increased significantly. Two months ago, he had pulled a muscle in his thigh—a painful experience he hoped he'd never have to go through again.

Limber and ready to go, he switched up his routine and started down a path he and Ian had put in that followed the lake on the opposite side from the resort cabins until it ran into the end of their property line. From here, it curved back into the woods and continued until it reached the highway. They used it in the winter for cross-country skiing and for hiking the rest of the year.

The lavish attention Ian displayed last night energized him. But he couldn't ignore a twinge of guilt for not reinvesting this energy back to his partner. *Maybe after my run.*

The sun had just crept over the trees when he reached the highway. If he ran early, like today, it wasn't that unpleasant to jog along the shoulder. A single hour could make a huge difference. He hated it when semi trucks and RVs blasted past him.

Sprinting up to the resort entrance, he left the shoulder. About midway down the private road leading to the beach cabins, he turned onto a path that would eventually bring him to the lake and the palisade. He loved this trail. There were times, after a rainy spell, when it was impossible to use. Today it was perfect. Spring exploded everywhere he looked. The songbirds filled the air with music. *And you still miss the city?*

He did miss living in the city from time to time. Over the winter, they spent a considerable amount of time staying with their friends, whom they never seemed to find enough time to be with since making the move to the North Shore. Long, conversation-filled dinners, the theater—they gulped it all down when the opportunity presented itself. But Harper knew in his heart that, despite all the trappings of city life, nothing could compare to these wooded surroundings on such a beautiful spring morning.

The sound of waves crashing signaled his arrival at the huge formation of rock. From here, the trail followed the lake in front of the ten cabins that made up their resort. The other bonus to getting an early start—he could avoid intruding on the privacy of their guests. Or at least that was what he had hoped. Nearing Cabin six, he spotted Quentin seated down by the lake. Normally he wouldn't stop to chat, but the older gay couple fascinated him. Quentin, in particular.

"Quentin, you're up early. Beautiful morning." Panting, Harper stopped a few feet from where he was sitting.

"Good morning, Harper. I see I'm not the only one taking advantage of the beauty this early hour offers. It's my favorite time of the day. The energy—it's all so invigorating." Quentin smiled and adjusted the blanket tucked around his lower body. He'd been hovering over a laptop placed on the center of his lap.

"Are you a writer?" Alex and Ian had both reported sightings of Quentin typing away. *Never hurts to ask.*

"I dabble here and there." Quentin smiled but seemed anxious to get back to his work.

Conscious of intruding on his privacy, the awkward moment resolved itself when Harold called out from the steps of their cabin. "Harper, if you have a minute, stop on by."

"I'm so glad he spotted you. I was supposed to tell you to stop by if we crossed paths, and I completely forgot." Quentin sighed. "We have something to ask you. I'll let Harold take it from here."

"Be right there," Harper hollered back. "I'll let you get back to your work. Have a great day, Quentin. Remember, if you need anything, please let us know." *You're looking healthier this morning. I hope the resort has something to do with it.*

"We're having a lovely stay. Thank you."

Harper sprinted up to the cabin, where Harold stood waiting on the stoop. "Yes, sir, what can I do for you?"

"I wish my legs would still allow me to run. I've had some issues with my knees. Had to say good-bye to running several years ago. I really miss it," Harold admitted. "But that's not the reason I wanted to talk to you. Do you have a few minutes to chat?"

"Oh sure." *Hm, I wonder what this is all about?*

"Are you a tea drinker?" Harold held open the door.

"I am, but honestly, haven't had tea in a long time." Harper stepped inside. The table at the front of the cabin was set for two, with a small vase of roses. He stifled a snigger. The setting could have easily been a tea party for a child's dolls.

"Please have a seat."

Harold brought over a tray with an ornate tea set and carefully unloaded it onto the table. "This is a wonderful green tea. Very cleansing to the body." He joined Harper at the table. "I had a marvelous visit with young Alex. He has a remarkable talent."

"It's interesting." Harper waited for Harold to finish pouring his tea. He bent over and inhaled the earthy aroma. *I should really drink more of this.* "Alex came into our lives very unexpectedly. I'm sure he wouldn't mind my telling you a little of his history."

"Oh, please do." Harold sipped and then sat back in his chair.

"Alex was waiting tables at the Lip Smacker when we moved up here. He was living with his father who... well, let's say it wasn't a good situation for Alex. This strikes me so funny now." Harper laughed and sipped. "Ian and I had the crazy notion we would spend that first winter living in the small office apartment that Petra now has. When we finally came to our senses and figured it wasn't something we could make work, an opportunity opened for Alex to live there over the winter and caretake the property for us."

"Isn't it interesting how things work out for the better?" Harold mimed zipping up his lower lip and chuckled. "I'm sorry. Please go on."

"Well, the situation with Alex sort of organically progressed from there. Harold, I can say this in all honesty, had Ian and I raised that young man from birth, we could not be more in love with him. Alex means the world to us."

"How sweet." Harold sipped.

"We try very hard to treat him as an equal. After all, next week he'll be turning twenty-one, but it's hard. We're extremely protective and, in our hearts, consider him our own." Harper chuckled. It always made him feel good to think about Alex and the role he played in their lives. It was special. He was family.

"Alex appears very lucky to have you both." Harold nodded knowingly. "When I visited with him, we talked mainly about his art. You don't know this, but I've made my living as a painter. I know talent when I see it, and Alex has it in spades."

"You're a painter by profession?" *So that's it. Yeah... I can see it.* "I've never met a painter before. Well, except for painters who work on walls and trim." Harper laughed. "That's wonderful."

"I've been very fortunate," Harold said. "But please, continue on about Alex and how you came to know of his talent."

"Well, that was like a bonus. The first season we opened, he presented the painting that hangs in the office as a thank you, I guess, for taking him under our wing. To say we were blown away by how good it was would be an understatement."

Harold sipped his tea and looked out the window to his partner. "Quentin and I had a dear friend who painted in watercolor. Sadly, we lost him to AIDS. Gosh, it must be almost twenty years now. Very sad. Roland Templeton was his name. He's quite famous in local painting circles. Many of his works hang throughout the Twin Cities, and across the country, for that matter. When he died, we were the beneficiaries of his equipment. A beautiful easel, brushes, even paints, virtually his whole studio. For years now, all of this has been collecting dust in our basement. It's a crime."

Harper nodded, understanding where this was headed. "He'd be honored. I can say that without any hesitation. And the other thing, Alex takes great pride in his belongings. He's very respectful."

"I sensed that. It's Quentin and I who would be honored. And of course, Roland. We'd love for Alex to be the beneficiary of Roland's studio. It sounds to me as if you would approve."

"Not only approve...." Harper gestured to the pot of tea. "Do you mind?"

"Oh, absolutely. There should be plenty, and, if not, it only takes a moment to brew more." Harold poured for Harper and then himself.

"Ian and I would be thrilled if your wonderful gift somehow motivated Alex to begin painting. He's got a lot on his plate, I have to be honest, but I think there's room for painting too. We would encourage him to make room."

"Oh, I'm so glad to hear you say that. We artistic types, sometimes we lose track of what's really important in life. Alex should take advantage of his gift."

Harper inhaled from his cup again. *Mmmm.* "When were you thinking of doing this?"

"We have a friend driving up tomorrow who has agreed to transport Roland's supplies. Do you think I should talk to Alex first, or surprise him?" Harold leaned forward in his chair.

In typical Callahan fashion, an idea blossomed in Harper's mind like a time-lapse flower photograph. *Invite Quentin and Harold to Alex's birthday party.* "We're throwing a birthday party for Alex next weekend. We'd be honored if you and Quentin would attend. Alex would love it, and if you wanted, you could use the opportunity to gift your friend's artist tools to him then."

"A party. We would love…." Harold stopped midsentence and visibly slumped in his chair.

Something's being covered up here. This might be a good chance to find out what's going on with Quentin. Call it instinct, but Harper knew from the time they had first arrived there was much more to this couple than they were letting on. "Harold, is everything all right? Is there anything I can help you with?"

Harper watched the older gentleman's face. *He's crumbling.*

"I'm sorry. I'm very sorry." Harold was struggling to keep it together.

Harper reached across the table and patted Harold's hand. "Harold, what is it? Please tell me what's wrong."

As the first tear streamed down Harold's face, he looked across the table at Harper and said quietly, "I'm losing my precious Radish."

Radish? What on earth does he mean by that? "I'm sorry, Harold. What did you say?"

"Quentin… his nickname is Radish. We received some very bad news Friday."

"Bad news about Quentin?" Harper leaned into the table in hopes it would make it easier for Harold to go on.

"He has level-four throat cancer. We thought this last…." Harold was consumed with emotion.

"I'm here for you." Harper held both Harold's hands in his own while the man across from him cried.

"We had so much hope this last round of chemotherapy would knock it out. On Friday, we got the news it had spread. There's... no hope... now. Oh God. I'm going to miss him so much. He's my world."

It was all Harper could do to keep his own emotions in check. *This is terrible.* He didn't know what to say. *My heart is breaking. I'm so sad for you both.*

"Look at him sitting out there... he'd never let on he was so sick." Harold wiped his eyes dry. "Not his style."

Harper glanced out the window. Quentin was still hunched over his laptop, typing away.

"He's a very famous writer, you know. Well, you probably don't know."

"Really? What does he write?" Harper sat back and listened.

"He writes love stories involving gay men. He's been doing it for years. Nobody knows because he's always written under a pseudonym. You were forced to do that back when he started, or you ran the risk of someone making trouble for you. You know, it wasn't like it is now. You can be open about so many more things today. Jack Simms."

"Jack Simms is the name he writes under?" Harper sipped from his cup. The tea was cold but still enjoyable.

"Search the Internet sometime under that name. You'll be surprised. His books are known around the world. Translated into many different languages. Even Braille. Excuse me." Harold stood and walked over to the little side table that hosted the warmer he used to make their tea. He wiped his face with a hand towel. "I can't let him see me like this. Not when he's being so strong."

Harper was at a loss for words. He wanted to help but wasn't sure what he could do. He needed more information. "Have you thought about what you might do? Will you be able to stay with us for a while longer? We'll do anything here to help. Whatever you want. I'll see to it."

"I think he might want to stay here until the end. It won't be very long. Not from what we were told by the specialist. We understand if that is a problem."

"Certainly. That's not a problem. I'd like to do whatever I can for you both."

"It feels good to share this with you. I feel so alone sometimes." Harold forced a weak chuckle. "I'd better get used to that feeling."

How long have the two of you been together? Harper knew he had to do something. Anything. He felt so helpless. "Do you have a piece of paper I can write on?"

Harold reached into his shirt pocket and pulled out an index card and a pen. "I have so little memory to work with these days. I have to write virtually everything down or it's gone. Poof!"

"These are our cell phone numbers," Harper said while he jotted them down. "I want you to promise to call if there's anything we can do to help you. Day or night. Will you do that, Harold?"

"We'll try not to be a bother. I just...." Once again, Harold was overcome with emotion, but this time he was able to get ahold of himself before it got the best of him. "I don't know what to expect. The doctor really couldn't provide much detail. It will all depend on Radish, I mean Quentin." Harold accepted the card and held it out in front of him so he could read it. "Thank you, Harper. I'm overwhelmed by your generosity."

"We want to be there for you both. I want to be there." Harper stood and smiled "Please let us help you." *This could be us. Remember that, Harper.*

Back out in the fresh morning air, Harper walked behind the cabin out of sight and broke down. *God. I can't believe how fucked up this is.* Two lives so completely intertwined. The thought of them being separated by death was more than he could take. It was several minutes before he could stop the flow of tears and walk over to the office.

"Good morning, Harper. How they hangin'?" Petra looked up from the paperwork she had laid out on the front desk next to her coffee and sweet roll. "Are you sure you guys won't mind covering for me next Monday and Tuesday? I feel guilty."

Next Monday and Tuesday, what is she talking about? Harper walked behind the desk. "Hey. Oh, oh right, next week. You're going to head over to Bayfield to spend some time with... Betsy. Betsy, right? Not a problem."

"Harper, look at me." Petra moved in closer. "Have you been crying?"

"I have been crying. Yes. I'm okay." Harper tried to catch a glimpse of his reflection beaming off the window. "God, life sucks sometimes."

"You're going to have to level with me about what happened to you, or, the alternative, I'm going to be totally worthless for the remainder of the day."

"Quentin is dying. I just came back from talking to Harold."

"Like right now dying?" Petra shot him a panicked look.

"No, but I got the impression it's not far off. Apparently they received some bad news last week. He's battling level-four throat cancer." Harper walked back out into the office and sat down in one of the chairs at the small table.

"What are they going to do?" Petra came out and joined him.

"They want to stay here until the end. I already told Harold we were fine with that. We'd do whatever it takes to make things easy for them. Christ, I don't even have a clue what we can do other than be there. I feel terrible." Harper sighed and folded his arms across his chest.

"Whenever I hear something like this, I always think about what it must be like to have received bad news, really bad news. I can't imagine."

They sat in silence for several minutes, staring out the window. The shadows had slowly diminished as the morning sun rose higher into the sky. Brilliant rays of light streamed down through the massive pines and birch. It was impossible to imagine a more beautiful place, Harper thought as he worked to process Harold and Quentin's situation.

"If we're going to be there for them, then let's not shit around with this." Petra sat up in her chair. "Let's make sure we are on top of it. Almost like, well, like we are dealing with our own family, if that makes any sense. See where I'm going with this?"

"Exactly." Harper sat up from his slouch. "That's what I want to be for them."

"Behind the scenes, we can start organizing. Meals, all of it. We can try and anticipate what they will need. Harper, I want to do this too. I feel, in a good way, that it's kind of our duty."

"I have another idea." Harper rose from the table and walked behind the desk. "Can you pull up the reservations so we can take a look at Cabin ten? Just Cabin ten?"

"Oh, I know where you're going with this. Sure." Petra joined him.

"Let's dedicate Cabin ten to Quentin and Harold for however long they need it. I want Quentin to have the very best."

"The only problem—there's no road leading that far down. Do you think it might be an issue?" Petra moved the computer mouse around as she navigated through the reservation program.

"I'll talk to Ian, but I don't think it matters. If someone needs to pull right up to the cabin, they can go behind it. And the grass is kept short, so it would be fine to drive on. What are you seeing for reservations?"

"Well, I was concerned if anyone had specifically requested Cabin ten. I'll have to go through each reservation and look. If they did, I made a point of noting it just in case we needed to switch things around."

"You're the best, Petra. That's awesome." Harper rubbed her shoulder.

"Well, for as many things as I get right, I get at least as many wrong. I'm just very good at hiding them from you." Petra gave Harper a pat back. "We'll make this happen. If I run into a party or two that has specifically asked for Cabin ten, do I have your permission to give them a call to see if they will accept one of the other cabins?"

"Sure. Just don't talk about why. Actually, that brings up a point." Harper tapped his finger on his chin while he took a minute to think. "Let's plan on meeting tonight up at the house. The whole team. What is it, Thursday? I think everyone's around. Let's put some planning into this so, from the beginning, we're all on the same page."

"Yeah, that's a great idea. What time?"

"Here's what we'll do. I'll throw some burgers on the grill. Why don't you pop up around six thirty. We can have a dinner meeting and scam on how we can make life a little easier for Harold and Quentin. Transfer the guest call button to one of our phones. Hopefully, it will be a quiet night." Harper walked to the door.

"Got it. Six thirty. I'll tell the other dudes if either of them wanders by. See you then."

"Thanks for being so agreeable to this, Petra. I spoke for the group before consulting anyone. I'm not happy about that. I... I didn't know what else to do."

"I think we'd all have made the same decision. Poor Quentin. Let's give him our best shot." Petra smiled.

Harper caught a rare glimpse of the softer Petra. *Could be her maternal side shining through all that armor.*

CHAPTER
Seven

ALEX scooped a heaping glop of artichoke dip onto his cracker and wolfed it down. The portable table set up in the screen porch was overflowing with tasty delights. *Man, what a spread!* Never in his wildest dreams would he have anticipated Harper, Ian, and the rest of his friends coming together to celebrate his twenty-first birthday in such a huge way. Everyone was here. Audrey and her husband, Bud, from the Lip Smacker, Andy and his partner, Emmett. It must have taken some real planning for both of them to be away from their south Minneapolis garden center, Jungle Gems, during such a busy time of the year.

Colin, his best friend, drove up from the Twin Cities with a new girlfriend, Marla. Alex met her during the holidays when Colin had her classified as date material. She hadn't reached the lofty status of girlfriend yet. Alex thought right from the start Marla was a keeper. He looked forward to getting to know her better.

Allison and Spencer, more friends from the Twin Cities, had pawned off their one-year-old daughter, June, on Allison's parents and were spending the night. They had become the equivalent of a cherished aunt and uncle. Family.

"So, Alex," Spencer asked, filling up a plate full of goodies, "how's it feel to officially be an adult?"

Alex had to think about this. Other than the fact he could finally go into a bar and order a drink, which wasn't his deal, he'd been acting and operating as an adult for years. "That's a good question, Spencer. Can I get back to you on that one?"

"It's silly, I know. What the hell does reaching the magic number of twenty-one have to do with anything? I know fifty-year-olds who act like they're seventeen. Well, and then you have Ian. Need I say more?"

They laughed at Spencer's well-aimed jab at Ian. The comment was funny because yes, Ian, at thirty-one, could act more juvenile than just about anyone they knew. But he was also such a cherished friend to them both, they understood Ian's antics would be sorely missed if they should ever go away.

"Where is Ian?" Alex hadn't seen him since they returned earlier from the Main Club. His roomies had insisted on taking him to the bar as part of the birthday proceedings. They had also talked him into downing a shot, a Mountain Dew Me, to make the visit official, even though he had done everything in his power to refuse. Surprisingly, it hadn't tasted all that different from the diet Dews he consumed in mass quantity. He did feel a little unbalanced on the drive home.

"Not sure. Say, Allison and I were both thinking of you when we found out you lost the bid on your house. That really sucks." Spencer leaned over and gave him a friendly hug.

"Thanks. Yeah, that was some devastating shit, Spencer."

Alex wasn't sure when or *if* he'd ever get over the fact the seller had, after Alex put in his bid, unexpectedly yanked the house from the market. What had been communicated to Tiffany, who was furious, was the seller's daughter was divorcing and relocating to the North Shore. *Bitch!* Harper and Ian had put everything they had into damage control, but Alex still spent a few late nights crying into his pillow. *It wasn't fair.* Tiffany assured him there would be others, and more often than not when these things happened, it was for the best. Something even better would pop up. He just had to be patient.

"We lost our first house because of, get this, five hundred bucks and a refrigerator. We bid low and insisted the fridge remain in the house. Don't ever mention this to Allison, because she'll erupt like it happened yesterday. Christ, I thought I was going to lose my mind. Good luck with the hunt. Something will turn up soon, I'm sure."

"Hey, birthday boy," Allison greeted as she joined her husband. "I don't think I've gotten a hug from you yet. March those gorgeous green eyes over here and rock this married woman's world, you hunk a hunk of man love."

"Good God, where the hell did that come from?" Spencer laughed. "Honey, have you gotten into the Buttershots?"

"Nope. Those days are long gone. Happy birthday, Alex."

"Yeah, right." Spencer rolled his eyes.

"Thank you, Allison. Hey, have you seen Ian?" Alex gave the party the once-over.

"Not for a while. I'll let him know you're looking for him. Have you guys tried this shrimp toast? Audrey brought it from the Smacker. Incredible. Come, Spencer, let's walk down to the lake before it gets dark."

"Sure, let me grab a beer." Spencer patted Alex on the back and followed his wife as she weaved through the guests.

Missing from his party was Theo. Harper made sure Alex knew he'd been invited, but earlier in the day, Theo's family had driven into Wisconsin to celebrate his grandmother's seventy-fifth birthday. Theo had tried to get out of it, but feeling the pressure that comes from still living at home, he was forced to participate. Theo had promised he'd stop by as soon as he got back into town.

I think I'm in love. Really in love.

Not missing from his party was Brent Burns. He was over in the corner of the porch, yukking it up with Harper. Brent had been Harper's assistant at the Minneapolis firm when Harper had been shot. Brent was now in his second year of law school, and Harper had become his mentor.

What am I going to do about Brent? I have to tell him about Theo.

Since meeting Brent the summer the resort opened, he and Alex had shared a comfortable "fuck buddy" relationship that had been remarkably free of drama. The sex was great, and Alex always looked forward to their time together. *Can't be doin' that anymore.*

It was a coincidence that they'd been unable to hook up during the time Alex had been seeing Todd. *It's probably not good to go there, but you would have fucked Brent anyway. Admit it.* Brent was spending the night on the couch in the entertainment room. *Which is where you're going to have to stay, dude.*

Alex headed back toward his own room to pee and collect his thoughts. When he rejoined the party, Harper, with Ian in tow, nabbed him by the arm, hauling him into the center of the room. Alex waved over to Harold and Quentin, who had arrived while he had stepped away. Petra was busy fussing around them, making sure Quentin was comfortable. Ever since Quentin's health issue had been discussed at their staff meeting last week, everyone had eagerly pledged to be there for the couple in any way they could. They both looked dapper, dressed a step above the rest of the party guests in sport coats and slacks. Alex felt honored they were there.

"May I have your attention please," Harper shouted out.

I want to die! This is so embarrassing. Alex, aware of Ian's death grip on his arm, knew he wasn't going anywhere.

"We are gathered together tonight to celebrate a milestone. Our dear friend, Alex"— Harper stepped aside and with both hands made a flowing gesture— "has turned twenty-one."

While the room exploded in cheers, Alex could feel the blood rush like a tidal wave into his face. To make matters worse, Ian poked and jabbed him mercilessly.

"Allison, my dear, what was the line you said to me earlier?" Harper looked over to their friend.

"I said I had shoes older than Alex." Allison laughed along with everyone else in the room.

"Ah yes, that's it. Well, anyone who knows the real Alex, and I think we all do, some better than others—nice of you to make it, Brent."

If Alex felt the urge to crawl into a hole when Harper started his speech, he was, by this point, numb. Brent, in the hot seat as everyone turned to acknowledge him, laughed at Harper's inclusion.

"Everyone here," Harper continued, "is well aware that Alex is wise beyond his twenty-one years. He's traveled a considerable distance in that short time, and, well, let me be the first to say it's not Alex who is the lucky one tonight, but all of us who have the honor to call him our friend. If there were any more love in this room, I daresay we'd probably all be naked and in the morning more embarrassed than words could express."

The room exploded with naughty sounding chuckles.

All right already. Quit, Harper! The only thing Alex could think of to do at the moment was stare at his feet until Harper finished, which from experience, he knew could be ages from now.

Harper ended his Alex tribute by leading the room in a spirited rendition of "Happy Birthday." As the crowd dispersed, the doorbell rang.

"Hey, Alex," Ian said, leaning over his shoulder, "can you get the door? I have to fill the punch bowl."

"Sure." Alex stopped off in the kitchen for a second to hug Audrey, who was plating another round of her much-sought-after shrimp delights. "Thanks for coming tonight, Audrey."

"Oh, sweetie, I wouldn't have missed this for anything. Bud either. You know how we feel about you." She reached up and gave Alex's arm a tug.

Hope this is Theo! Alex opened the door to find the stoop empty. He expanded his view out onto the driveway and nearly fainted. *Oh... my... God! Oh my God! Is this seriously for me?*

On a trailer hitched to his truck sat a powerboat with a pink bow on it. Stepping down the stairs on legs he could barely keep under control, he moved in for a closer look. A huge tag hung down from a strand of ribbon.

"Happy Birthday, Alex! Love from your pals, Ian and Harper."

Turning back to the house, he discovered Harper and Ian spying on him from the doorway.

"Now, it's gonna need some work," Ian cautioned as he jogged down from the door. "It's a 1980 Chris-Craft."

"Yeah, actually a ton of work," Harper added, joining his partner. "The windshield needs to be replaced. And what else?"

"Besides all the wood, the engine," Ian added. "But, man, after some tender loving care this 160 horse-powered screamin' bitch is goin' to skim across the water like a rocket. We had the engine checked out, and it's fine. Just needs a little attention. And don't worry, we'll help."

"I can't believe you guys did this." Alex rediscovered his voice. "I love it."

"Screamin' bitch?" Harper rolled his eyes. "Isn't it stylin'? The minute we saw it we knew it had to be yours." Harper grabbed Alex and gave his head a good, hard knuckle rub.

"A Chris-Craft, right?" Alex leaned over the edge of the sleek little speedboat to scope out the inside. "Wow, the upholstery looks pretty cool yet. It's red. I love red."

"There's a few tears in the vinyl, but it's definitely salvageable. Say"—Ian playfully slugged Alex in the arm— "I know you'd like to stay out here all night, but we need to go back to the party in a few minutes."

"Why?" Alex didn't want to leave. *This is so amazing.*

"Because you need to start on the dishes and clean up, or you'll be at it all night," Harper teased.

Alex laughed. "Shut up."

"Harp, you want to run in and make sure they're ready?" Ian looked over his shoulder.

"Sure. Hold back for a minute." Harper sprinted up the stairs and into the house.

"You really like the boat, eh?" Ian patted Alex on the back.

"Are you serious? I know there's work and stuff, but can you imagine what this thing is going to look like when it's all fixed up?" Alex stood on his toes to look deeper inside.

"The chicks are gonna frickin' cream." Ian leaned over next to Alex.

Alex strolled around the trailer a couple of times until Harper poked his head out the door and hollered, "Okay, we're ready."

Ian grabbed Alex's arm, pretending he was pulling a sack of rocks toward the house. "Great, come on birthday boy, you have another surprise waiting. You might like this even more than the boat. I'm serious."

Ian led him into the house and down the hall to the entertainment room. Harold and Quentin were seated on the couch with little plates of food and their glasses of punch.

"Happy birthday, Alex," they said together, raising their glasses in a toast.

"Thank...." Alex was silenced when he realized the room was filled with art supplies. Everywhere he looked. It was as if someone had purchased an entire studio. "What...."

"Here, take my seat next to Quentin." Harold stood and gestured to the space now open next to his partner.

"We're going to leave you guys alone." Ian, already on the move, gestured for Harper to join him.

"Alex, we have a favor to ask of you." Quentin spoke first after Alex had plopped down next to him on the couch.

What could this be all about? It was as if an art store exploded. There were wooden frames of various sizes stacked up against the wall. Reams of what could only be watercolor paper were stacked by the fireplace. Several containers held just brushes and other painting instruments. And books. Dozens of art books. *Awesome!*

"This is very important to us, so if for any reason what we propose makes you uncomfortable, you need to let us know." Harold glanced around the room as if conducting an inventory.

Alex barely knew these two men. He was as uncomfortable as he was excited to find out what this was all about.

"Alex"—Quentin patted him on the knee—"many years ago, we had a friend who made his living painting divine watercolors. Perhaps you've heard of him."

"Oh, I doubt he has, Quentin," Harold interjected.

"Well, you never know. This world can be as small as it is large." Quentin patted his knee again and winked. "Tell him the story, Harold."

"Our dear friend, Roland Templeton, who we lost years ago to that dreadful AIDS—"

Harold was interrupted when Quentin added, "I cried for a month. I couldn't eat, I couldn't write. He meant so much to us, you understand."

Alex nodded he understood. He'd seen documentaries both in health class and on television that described the early days of the disease. He'd never forget the images. And he'd never take a chance with his own body, no matter how hot the dude was. It wasn't worth the risk.

"When he died, he left his studio to us, knowing we would treat it with the respect it deserved and, eventually, hand it on to someone we felt worthy. In short…." Harold paused and smiled.

"We think that someone is you!" Quentin exclaimed, clapping his hands together and stealing the thunder from his partner.

"Me? Seriously?" Alex couldn't believe his good fortune.

"May I continue?" Harold looked over to Quentin with a pained expression on his face.

"Yes, of course." Quentin giggled and sat back into the couch. "Go on, Harold, tell him the rest."

"Thank you, Quentin." Harold walked over and picked up what appeared to be an old wooden toolbox. "If you accept this gift, Alex, you need to know it comes with a caveat."

"That means there is a string attached." Quentin took a healthy sip of his punch and then covered his mouth while he weathered a series of coughs.

Alex suppressed a giggle. He knew what caveat meant, but only because Harper used the word all the time.

"Perhaps you should rest your voice for a few minutes," Harold cautioned when Quentin had regained control of himself.

Unable to speak, Quentin was forced to nod in agreement, but it wasn't lost on Alex that the gentleman next to him wasn't happy about it.

"We want you to continue to paint. As I explained to you when we met up for tea, you have a gift, and it would be an absolute shame if you were to ignore or waste that talent."

Poor Quentin, Alex could tell he wanted so badly to add his two cents worth but was reduced to another pat on Alex's knee to emphasize the importance of what Harold had just said.

"It will be a gentleman's agreement between us, Alex," Harold continued. "We won't be hounding you at every corner to see if you have made good on your word. Someday, when the time is right, we hope—this is the selfish part of our agreement, isn't it, Quentin? We'll hopefully get to see more of your terrific work."

"Yes," Quentin agreed in a weak voice.

"This box is filled with paint. It's exactly as Roland left it." Harold brought it over to Alex and opened it on the table in front of him.

"See... er...." Quentin was debilitated by another coughing jag.

Alex looked over to Harold to see if there was anything he could do. *Poor guy. I wish I could make him well.*

Quentin rubbed his throat and looked up to Harold in despair, his eyes moist from the fit.

Sensing it might be good to get Quentin home where he would be more comfortable, Alex took the box and placed it on his lap. "You can bet that I'll paint. I promise you guys. Ask Ian and Harper. I keep my word." Alex looked over to see if he was being believed. Quentin smiled and reached for his glass, taking a tiny sip before setting it back down.

"That's all we had to hear, my young friend. Roland would be so happy to know someone with your talent is taking possession of his brushes. Quentin, may I help you up?"

Harold moved over to the side of the couch and offered his hand, which was accepted. Alex placed the box back on the table and stood, in case the ailing old guy needed help from both sides. Wobbly at first, once he was up for a moment and found his balance,

Quentin stepped slowly out from the couch to stand at his partner's side.

Alex walked over and extended his hand. "Thanks, Quentin, for thinking of me. I'm honored." He felt a surprisingly firm squeeze back. Moving over to Harold, he said, "I can't wait to go through all of Roland's stuff." Alex surveyed the room. "Wow! It was so cool you guys came tonight. Your friend's art supplies have a good home now. Thank you so much." Alex discovered a lump in his throat. *How cool is it these guys think enough of me to leave their friend's stuff in my hands? Paint something for them. It's the least you can do.*

"Better make our rounds before heading home. Last night there was a beautiful full moon shining above the palisade. We have a marvelous view from our new vantage point at Cabin ten."

"Wasn't that a cool thing they did?" Harper asked when Alex joined a small circle of guests that included Brent, Andy, and Emmett.

"Oh man, this is one totally awesome night." Alex shoved a brownie into his mouth.

"Once you get your studio up and running, we'd love to feature some of your work at the garden center. You know, act as a gallery for you. There wouldn't be any problem selling them, would there, Em?" Andy reached over and ruffled his partner's nest of hair. Emmett frequently changed the color and added streaks of bright accents. You never knew what to expect.

"I can't wait to see your paintings. They would be easy to sell." Emmett had, much to everyone's delight, overcome his shyness and was contributing regularly to the conversations these days. However, only when Andy was at his side to bolster his confidence.

"Thanks, Em." Alex patted him on the shoulder. "I need a Dew. Be right back."

Alex needed a Dew, but what he really needed was to slip outside and take another look at his new boat. *This is whacky. How did they know I wanted one so much?*

When he opened the fridge, Allison and Marla were engaged in an intense conversation in the corner of the kitchen. Exiting with a wave, Alex made a beeline for the back door. "Hello, boat," he announced when he'd reached the trailer. "I'm Alex. I'm going to make you look brand new again. You're going to be so hot all the other boats will be jealous." Alex walked to the back of the trailer. "Wow! I'll have to come up with a name for you."

He ran his hand along the chrome rub rail. It felt so smooth and cool. *I'll have this shined up in no time.* It was hard to see much of the boat's detail. The light from the back of the house faded before it reached the area where it was parked. Maybe once the party wound down he'd come out with a flashlight to get a better look.

Ian said the engine needed work. *I wonder how long that will take. Hey! Maybe Theo will get into helping me. That could be really cool—working on it together.*

"Hey, green eyes."

Alex twisted around to face the direction of the voice.

Brent had snuck up on him. "So, this is the boat I've heard so much about."

Brent. He hadn't spent much time with his friend. Now was as good a time as any to bring him up to date. *Get it over with.*

"I can't believe those guys went out and bought me a boat." Alex leaned over for a better look at the interior.

"Oh, baby. That's what I've been waiting for."

Alex felt Brent's crotch rub up and down against his ass. *Oh God, how do I start this? I don't want to hurt his feelings.*

After he stood up, Brent snuggled his head into Alex's back. "I've been thinking a lot about us lately. Damn, I hate we have to live so far apart."

Alex couldn't let this go any further. Pushing himself away from the boat, he turned and faced his overly eager friend. "Brent…."

"You have someone."

Alex couldn't believe he had figured it out so quickly. "Yeah. How did you deduce that, Sherlock?"

"Deduce. I haven't heard that word in forever." Brent chuckled. "When you didn't back your ass into me, I knew it could only be one thing." Brent smiled and tapped Alex on the chest. "I'm *much* too handsome a catch for you to ignore. Your ass has a name on it, and it isn't Brent."

"Theo." Alex returned the chest tap.

"As in Theodore?"

"Theodore Engdahl." Alex found it impossible not to look away. *This is tough.* "He's from around here."

"Well...." It was Brent's turn to look away. He coughed into his hand. "I'm happy for you. I want to crawl into bed with a box of chocolates and a bottle of wine and cry my heart out, but I'm happy."

"We've been seeing each other for a few weeks. I'm surprised he hasn't shown up yet. He had family stuff going on he couldn't get out of."

"Theo. He'd better be fucking hot as hell or I'm *really* going to be pissed off."

Alex could tell Brent was hurt, but he was doing his best to shake it off. "Brent, I really like you, and I feel I should say more."

"You can say more. As long as the more has nothing to do with *Theo.*"

Alex loved how Brent could be honest and funny at the same time. "I don't think there's any way to say this that won't sound lame, but I'll miss our sex. I've never had better. And I'll be more than bummed out if we can't continue to be friends. I love ya, dude. I really mean that." It was a struggle, but Alex was proud he had managed to keep eye contact with Brent through his entire little speech.

"I didn't find that to be lame at all. In fact, you said many of the exact same things I was trying to get to once I had my emotions in check. Come here, you little fucker." Brent opened his arms, and

Alex walked right into them. "Your friendship means more to me than our sex. It was close, but yeah, to lose you as a friend would hurt more. Much more. Dude, I love you too."

Alex gave Brent a hearty hug.

"Alex?"

"Huh?"

"Would one last kiss be too strange a request?" Brent pushed away, waiting for Alex's answer.

Alex cupped the back of Brent's neck and brought him forward. At first the kiss was hesitant, as if it might have been a bad idea, but with both men realizing it would most likely be their last, lips parted, and just as they began to relax into each other, headlights from an approaching vehicle stole the moment away. Turning, they both stared into the bright beams and stepped apart.

THEO stared at the two illuminated figures in disbelief. *No! No, I can't believe this. Seriously? No!*

He'd been punched in the stomach once or twice and had no problem remembering how that felt, but being stomach punched had nothing on what he was feeling inside right now. *It's betrayal. Plain and simple.*

As shock gave way to reality, he knew he had to bolt. His body began to tremble as he threw the truck into reverse and backed onto the side of the narrow access road. Turning around, his tires spun in the loose gravel as he pushed the pedal to the floor and headed toward the highway.

I knew this was too good to be true. God hates gays. God hates you, Theo, because you're a weakling. God is punishing you. You deserve this, you piece of shit.

Gasping to catch his breath, he stared at the road ahead while he struggled to keep himself together. Turning onto the highway, he realized he was incapable of driving. The next exit was the palisade overlook. He'd park there until he could get a grip on himself.

I'm in love with you, Alex. In love! How could you fuck with me like this? Oh God....

Surprised and caught off guard by how hurt he felt, he broke down. Deep, painful explosions of emotion he couldn't control rocked his core. What he'd seen back there devastated him. And what made this so terrible, he never in a million years would have thought Alex capable of messing around behind his back. He knew a lot of guys, girls too, who, just by the way they acted around other people, flirting and teasing, you knew they were a risk. Not Alex. He had completely snowed him.

You're stupid! You're a loser. A fag loser!

Minutes that felt more like hours passed before Theo was able to pull himself together. Grabbing an old sweatshirt from behind his seat, he wiped his face dry. *What a prick. What a little fucking prick.* He bounced between feelings of hurt and anger like a rubber ball.

Theo started the truck. At the same time, a light flashed in his rearview mirror, the reflection of someone pulling into the small parking area. A car roared up alongside of his. It took only a second to realize it was Alex. Before he had a chance to back out, Alex was out of the car and knocking on Theo's window.

"Theo, you have to listen to me. Theo," Alex pleaded as he knocked. "I can explain. It's not what you think."

A soft rain started to blanket his windshield. Theo stared ahead, unable to bring himself to even acknowledge Alex.

"Theo, I'd be pissed too. Come on, Theo. Roll down the window so I can explain."

God, he wanted to roll down the window. But he was hurt. He was hurt bad, and his trust for Alex at this point was zero. And he couldn't talk. Because he knew if he tried, he'd be a weeny and start to cry again. *No way am I going to let him see me cry.*

Seconds passed. The tiny droplets had doubled in size. *Maybe I should at least hear him out. Then I can call him a fucker to his face and be done with it.*

Just as Theo pressed the button to lower his window a crack, he heard a loud thump from behind. *Huh? What's he doing?* Alex had hopped into his truck bed.

Oh, this is just great. Now what am I going to do? "Get out of my truck," Theo hollered out the tiny crack of window. The angle of the rain caused it to come right into the cab and coat his face and neck.

"Not until you let me explain what you saw," Alex hollered back.

Theo knew himself to be stubborn. Was it possible he'd met his match in Alex? "It's fucking raining out. Get out of my truck."

"No. I'll die out here before I get out."

Theo rolled his window back up. He needed Alex out of his truck. Alex wasn't planning on getting out until Theo listened to what he had to say. There it was. *I give, or he gives. It doesn't sound like he's going to give. Goddamn it anyhow.*

Frustrated and out of options, Theo rolled down his window. "All right. You can come in and talk, but you have to leave the minute I ask you to. Or...." *Or what, Theo? Are you going to punch him?*

He didn't have time to finish. In a split second, Alex had come around to the passenger side and hopped in. "Thanks."

"What is it you want to say?" Theo refused to honor Alex by looking over to him.

"Okay. When you pulled up, I was kissing my friend, Brent."

"Tell me something I don't already know."

"Brent and I have had a casual sexual relationship for several years now. We're fuck buddies. Nothing more."

Theo thought for a moment about what Alex had just said, and his anger raged on with a newfound vengeance. "I'm not, and never will be, some dude's fuck buddy! God, how could you think I would agree—"

"No. Let me finish," Alex cut him off. "I would never think that or ask that of you. We were saying good-bye, Theo. You have to believe that. We were saying good-bye as lovers. I told him about you, even your name. Brent asked if he could have one more kiss.

His friendship means a lot to me, but we're never going to have what I want with you. So the kiss—it was harmless until you pulled up." Alex reached over and rested his hand on Theo's shoulder. "Theo, I would have assumed the same thing—that I was cheating on you or messing around behind your back. All of that shit."

Theo wanted to believe what Alex was saying. He wanted to believe it so badly he didn't trust himself. *It sounds like he's telling the truth. If he wasn't, would he go to this trouble?*

"Theo, when I asked you to be my boyfriend the other night, I wasn't just asking it to make our night special. I was asking because I want you, just you. I know this is hard to believe, but when I realized it was you who had pulled up, I was so angry for risking something so important to me I wanted to puke. Please don't give me the silent treatment. I don't know what else I can say."

Theo gave in and looked over to Alex. The man sitting next to him was soaked and shaking. "Let me turn some heat on." *Theo, take a chance. You're in love with him, and you know it.* "Are there any more of these fuck buddies I need to know about?"

"Nope. Honest. I'd tell you if there were. I don't ever want anything like this to happen between us again. This is fucking awful."

Alex's voice, already laden with emotion, broke. And so did Theo's heart. "Come here. You're fucking freezing." Theo took the sweatshirt he'd brought up to the front of the cab and wrapped it around Alex's shoulders. He wrapped his arms around his chilled friend and held him tight. "I felt so lucky to have met you. When I saw you kissing that dude, I thought it was God punishing me. My mind, it immediately went there."

"We're going to have to work on that God stuff with you. It's jack."

Theo felt Alex's body begin to relax in his arms.

"Theo?"

"What?"

"Remember the first night we talked? It was raining, and we were sitting in your truck, just like now. Being there next to you, I wondered what it would be like to have you hold me in your arms."

"I thought about that too. But mostly, back then, I wanted to touch your dick."

"Nice." Alex laughed and shook his head.

"I hadn't touched any dick other than my own. Give me a break." Theo, relieved that this whole mess had diffused itself, kissed Alex's neck.

"That's fair."

"Are you starting to warm up?" Theo renewed his hold on Alex.

Alex, you're starting to mean so much to me. I don't know what boyfriends are supposed to be, exactly, but I'm willing to keep going with this.

"I could stay here all night. This is awesome."

"Is the party still going on?" Theo hoped this horrible misunderstanding hadn't ruined the night for either of them. And he felt guilty for misjudging Alex. But only a little. *Who wouldn't have jumped to the same conclusion?* "I'm thinking I'd better meet this Brent dude." Theo nibbled on Alex's ear. *Lucy loved when I did this.*

"Really? You're okay doing that? He's a nice guy, Theo. He felt really bad when I told him it was you. Seriously. He gave me his car to go after you."

"One more thing," Theo whispered.

"What?"

"I wasn't planning on going home tonight."

"I wasn't planning on letting you go home tonight," Alex fired back. "It's my birthday, dude. You're going to have a very busy night. Man, I hope you're ready for it."

"All of me is ready." *I think.* "Bring it on."

"I'M FAMISHED," Harper admitted. *Oh no. I'm in one of those moods again when everything looks good.*

"Thanks, Francine." Petra sipped from her tall ice tea that had just been delivered. "God, I love this stuff. Alex, hand me over a fake sugar packet. Nope. Not the yellow, the pink one, please. There we go. Thanks."

"I wish it was pot pie day," Alex lamented. "I used to chow those down all the time when I worked here."

"They are tasty. When is pot pie day anyway?" Harper peered over his menu.

"Whenever Audrey gets a little ahead with her pies and muffins," Alex explained.

"I've never ordered one. I'm not sure I've been in here on pot pie day, come to think of it." Petra glanced over her menu. "Salad—I'm trying so hard to eat healthier, but to save my soul I never seem to be able to fire up for salad."

"I can never order a salad either. Too many other things always look better," Alex piped in.

"I don't get out much. This is so nice of you guys to invite me to lunch." Petra sucked half a glass of tea down through her straw.

"We thought it was the least we could do with all the shenanigans you have to put up with." Harper looked over to Alex, who nodded in agreement. "We're buying your affection."

Francine returned, and they placed their order.

"So, details about the overnight in Bayfield with Betsy have been few and far between. Did you have a good time?" Harper asked after a steaming cup of split pea soup had been placed in front of him.

"Betsy's been bitten by the special. She's a breath of fresh air, and you know the best thing?" Petra asked.

"Harper?" Alex whispered across the table. "Brace yourself. I think this next part involves girlie parts."

"Listen, sweet pea," Petra challenged, "I could fire off a list of girlie parts a mile long, and you'd probably confuse them for burger toppings."

Francine delivered their lunches, and after she had unloaded them from an enormous oval serving tray, Harper asked, "Do you think you'll be seeing more of her?"

"I'm fighting it every step of the way, but the truth is I'm falling in love with her."

"That's awesome, Petra." Alex reached over to her, initiating a high-five. "I think she's really pretty. She's pretty in a natural way. Not in a made-up or fake way."

"Thank you, Alex. That's what I think too."

Petra, if you could see your face right now. You're radiant. "I know with your schedules you haven't had a chance to spend much time together. Are you talking a lot on the phone?" Harper bit into his green olive burger. "Oh, I'll be ordering this again. Damn, talk about tasty."

"I wish I liked green olives. Just can't go there." Petra dunked her French dip in a cup of au jus and bit off a large hunk, savoring the taste for a moment by closing her eyes. "Here's the deal with Betsy." Petra placed the remainder of her sandwich on her plate and brushed her napkin across her mouth. "The thing that's so refreshing about Betsy is I don't have to sell myself to her constantly."

"Not sure I'm tracking, Pet," Harper admitted.

"Oh God. What the hell am I doing having this discussion with you two, of all people?" Chuckling, Petra shook her head and picked her sandwich up.

"What?" Alex looked over to Harper, completely lost.

"Petra, we're not really sure what just happened." Harper leaned into the table, as if trying to will himself to understand.

"Okay. That's fair. And honestly, this isn't your fault. Sit back, because I'm going to explain it to you. You're my friends, after all."

Alex and Harper did as they were told. Alex brought his leg up onto the seat and squished into the corner of the booth. Harper relaxed his forward thrust and sat back.

"You guys are two of the most handsome men I have ever come in contact with. Ian is right there with you. I'm including him because I know when you dorks get back and you replay this lunch, that's the first thing he's going to ask, and if I hadn't included him, my life would be a living hell. So, we were talking about looks."

It didn't take a roadmap for Harper to see where this was going. And it wasn't the first time something like this had been said to him. *Just let her say it.*

Petra sipped her tea down to the bottom of the glass. "My guess would be, neither of you had to think much about whether or not someone you had an interest in thought you were attractive. It's not that you're arrogant. You have this comfortableness about yourselves. See, I never had that. I grew up knowing I had to compensate for not being cheerleader material. Hell, I wasn't even media room material."

"Petra, you're very good looking…."

"Alex, you're a gem, but you and I both know that isn't true."

"I think Alex was commenting on your inner beauty." Harper explained on behalf of his young friend.

"I was. Inner beauty is so underrated." Alex shared a nod with Harper.

"Alex? Remember when I told you a while back to watch yourself or I'd have your dick for bait the next time I went fishing?" Petra looked at Alex and raised an eyebrow.

"Yes, ma'am." The sassy smile on Alex vanished.

"Whoa. That's a conversation I'm sorry I missed out on." Harper looked back and forth between Petra and Alex, anxious for more detail.

"So," Petra continued while at the same time flagging down Francine for more tea, "every woman I've *ever* dated or seemed to get close to, I've had to fight for. It's like I've had to talk them into seeing that I'm a really cool chick despite the fact that my nose is too big and I have a sturdy build. But with Betsy, it's different. She wants me just the way I am. I know this because she's told me. You pretty boys have no idea how comforting that is to hear. How refreshing. At my age, I'm tired of campaigning. Now, did that make any sense to either of you?"

"Please don't threaten to cut off my dick, Petra, but I think you're being too hard on yourself based on the self-evaluation I just heard." Harper sipped from his straw. "But I get what you're saying. And I'm happy for you. But more importantly, I'm really happy to hear that Betsy is smart. Smart enough to pursue a good thing when she sees it. We see it. Don't we, Alex?"

Poor Alex. The helpless look on his face was priceless. "That's okay, sport," Harper whispered out of the side of his mouth. "I know where we can get these solid metal nut cups. We'll be safe. No worries."

Everyone at the table laughed mightily as Francine deposited their check.

"You know, it felt really good to say all that. It's like cathartic. So, what in-depth topic can we sink our teeth into next time? Maybe we should make this lunch a monthly thing. Whattaya say?"

"I'd be up for—" Harper was interrupted by his phone. "Hang on." He fished it out of his pocket. "It's Tiffany. Hey, Tiff."

Harper looked over to Petra and winked.

"Well, I'm not sure, but I'll let you talk to Alex." Harper handed his phone over.

Alex listened, staring intently at the condiment container. Harper pointed over to him and mouthed the word, "Watch."

I wish Ian were here right now. This is going to be so good. Green eyes is about to crap his pants.

Seconds later, Alex started to squirm. Small movements quickly grew into body twists, and then finally all hell broke loose. "They accepted our offer! The daughter isn't moving back after all. Oh boy! Oh boy, they accepted our offer. Can you believe it!"

Harper grabbed his phone out of Alex's hand and slid out of the booth. Alex scooted out right behind him.

"We'll call back, Tiff, when we've got ourselves under control," Harper announced before pocketing his cell.

"Are you shittin' me? For real?" Petra squealed.

"For real. For real, Petra!" Alex gave her a big hug.

"Dude, you're making my eyeballs bulge. Easy," Petra begged until Alex released her.

Harper took Alex into his arms, bent backward, and lifted him in the air until his feet left the ground.

"Everything okay over here?"

The commotion had brought Audrey out from behind the cash register. The other patrons of the restaurant were staring too.

"The house I wanted but lost? Tiffany… I mean, our realtor just called, and they changed their mind. They've accepted our offer."

"Your offer," Harper corrected.

"Oh, honey, that's the best news ever. Listen up, everyone, Alex just bought his first house. Isn't that exciting?" Audrey clapped her way back to the till.

Even the grumpy old curmudgeons sipping coffee at the counter turned in their direction to smile and clap.

Shit! That means he's moving out. Harper was still struggling with the empty-nester concept.

REALITY was banging on the door. Frightened, Harold stared out of the cabin window. The full moon shining through the tall pines teased him into thinking it was dawn, but the clock on the small nightstand told him otherwise. He flipped his pillow and willed his body to relax, a process that had been repeated several times over the course of the night.

Since receiving the dreaded news that Quentin's cancer was on the move, spreading at an accelerated clip through his weakened body, the enormity of what he was about to face, the inevitable grand finale that he'd barely allowed himself to contemplate, was imminent. *How long do we have, Radish? A month or two? A couple of weeks?* Small but noticeable changes had begun to appear in both his partner's body and his mind.

Harold slid over toward Quentin until his nose came in contact with his partner's pajama sleeve. He inhaled. The sweet, fragrant smell of laundry detergent melded with the essence of Quentin, a smell Harold would never tire of. He snuggled tighter, his face now buried in the soft cotton fabric. *I need you.* Harold teetered on the brink of sleep.

The loud, incessant chirping of birds brought him back from slumber. *What time is it?* Quentin's side of the bed was empty. *Quentin?* Glancing over to the clock, which now read seven thirty, he bolted up and swung his feet around to the floor. Blinking his eyes to clear his vision, he stood slowly and walked to the corner of the small room where his robe lay draped across the back of a chair. The sound of splashing water came from the tiny bathroom. Harold knocked on the door before opening it.

Seated on the plastic shower stool they'd picked up in Duluth at the medical supply shop last week, sat his naked partner.

"Good morning, Harry," Quentin said in a rough, raspy voice.

One of the most alarming changes in Quentin over the last several days was the change in his speech. His clear, bell like voice had lowered and taken on a coarse quality. Harold could tell at times it hurt him to speak. At the doctor's recommendation, Quentin had begun to drink lemon-lime soda through a straw to help stimulate taste and saliva.

"You're up bright and early. Feeling better today?" Harold continued to hope for a miracle. As risky as it was to allow himself to hold out for some divine intervention, he needed a powerful thought to keep him going when all the odds were stacked against them.

"I'm taking advantage of my energy. I thought if we got an early start, we might stop off and have breakfast before my appointment with Dr. Routhier. How does that sound?" Quentin winked and turned off the water. "Be a dear, Harry, and hand me a towel." He slapped his naked knees with his hands and shook the water out of his wispy white hair.

"Here, let me help you." Harold reached over to give his partner a hand standing up.

"Not on your life. I can do this." Quentin closed his eyes for a second and then, after a forced effort to fill his lungs with air, slowly rose to his feet.

"I sure like the looks of that," Harold cheered. "Now come here, whether you like it or not, I'm going to help dry you off."

"Quit now. I can manage." Quentin took one tentative step out of the shower.

"I don't care if you can manage or not, I want to hold you, and this gives me a perfect excuse to do so." Harold opened the towel, and Quentin stepped into it. "Are you just exerting your independence? Or have you finally come to your senses and decided that, after all these years, you could have done better in the partner department?" Harold teased as he hugged the frail body to his own. When the sassy response he'd counted on failed to materialize, he looked down and removed the warm terry cloth that was covering up Quentin's head.

"Mmm... I almost feel young again." Quentin wrapped his arms around Harold's waist with a surprising grip. "Harry, you're such a naughty boy. How could you say that about yourself? I got the best man in the whole world, and I'm never giving you up. Never."

Harold chuckled to combat emotion as he resumed brushing the towel up and down Quentin's back.

After splitting an order of eggs Benedict at the Lip Smacker, Harold drove them into Duluth for their appointment with the cancer specialist. Harold suspected Quentin's burst of energy this morning was an attempt on his part to fight the disease and mask his fear. Unless that miracle Harold had been hoping for chose this very moment to make itself known, the news from today's meeting wasn't likely to be good.

"Dr. Routhier is finishing up with another patient and shouldn't be more than a few minutes. Can I bring you anything while you wait?" Debra, the doctor's assistant, was only slightly personable, opting instead for a level of professionalism that had no rival. At first it had annoyed Harold and amused Quentin. Over the last few weeks, it was a trait that had managed to become endearing. Her eyes were kind, even if she lacked the proverbial bedside manner one comes to expect from care providers.

"I'd like a glass of water, if it isn't too much trouble," Quentin said, looking over to his partner. "Harry?"

"I'm just fine." For all the calmness Quentin displayed, Harold found himself in a more desperate state. The impending doom of what most likely would be communicated was taking its toll.

"I'm good, Harry."

Harold looked over to Quentin, who winked and managed a small smile. "You're good?"

"Yes. I'm where I need to be."

"And where exactly is that, honey?" Harold still wasn't sure he understood.

"Gentlemen," Dr. Routhier greeted them in a soft, compassionate voice as he entered the warm wood-paneled office. For all of the coolness displayed by his assistant, the doctor made up for it and then some. They had felt comfortable with the young specialist from their first meeting.

Younger than them both by a good twenty years, the doctor wasn't blessed with the striking good looks one would expect from all of the medical dramas on television. Dr. Routhier was on the plump side and had a head of hair that refused to be tamed. But never once did either Harold or Quentin question his expertise. And he was an effective communicator who made it a point to make sure what was discussed was fully understood.

"Good morning, Dr. Routhier." Quentin's voice was reduced to a low, raspy whisper.

Debra was right behind the doctor with Quentin's glass of water. She closed the door as she exited the office.

"Beautiful morning, isn't it?" The doctor looked up from his notes and smiled.

"Yes. Absolutely gorg—" Quentin was forced to stop midsentence when he was silenced by a coughing fit. Harold removed the glass of water from his hand until he had calmed enough to sip.

"Are you feeling any pain when you cough? We can give you something to soothe your throat if you are."

Quentin, considerably deflated by the disruption, could only nod back. Unsure of himself, he handed his glass back to Harold for safekeeping after taking a small sip.

"Are you eating?"

Understanding Quentin's inability to answer the doctor, Harold took over for his partner. "It's spotty. We have the best success in the early afternoon. Mornings and evenings he doesn't seem to have much of an appetite."

"Most likely, Quentin, you'll find that your appetite will diminish even more until you'll hardly feel the need to eat at all. Of course, this is a trend that I'm hoping you'll fight. It will help you to have foods that are diverse and easily consumed. Did you see the list of suggestions I sent along with you last week?"

"That was very helpful," Harold acknowledged.

"Good. And the lemon-lime soda? You're keeping that handy as well?"

"Yes." Harold answered while Quentin nodded.

"The progression at this stage of the disease is always difficult to predict. I think we should discuss a few things to anticipate." The doctor looked down to his notes.

Harold closed his eyes briefly when Quentin reached over and took his hand. The grip was weak, and the hand trembled slightly. *You have to stay strong, old boy. Quentin needs to know you have the strength to see him through this. You're all he has.*

"It's going to get more and more difficult for you to talk. You might want to practice using a pad and writing notes to Harold before you get to the point when speaking isn't an option. Or, I know you're a writer, perhaps your laptop would work better for this. You'll have to decide, but I would recommend you begin the transition now."

Harold shared a look with Quentin and patted his hand.

"Your need to rest and sleep will increase over the next few weeks. I wouldn't fight it unless you have an obligation you absolutely need to keep. And of course, keeping your body nourished will help combat this to some degree. At least at first. What has your sleep pattern been like this week?"

Quentin rubbed his throat and then looked over to Harold, who once again spoke for him. "Nothing too out of the ordinary. You've been sleeping longer in the morning. I've noticed that. We both have gotten in the habit of napping during the day. That seems to be about the same. The evenings...." Harold hadn't paid much attention to it, but Quentin had lost his interest in most things after attempting to eat in the evening, preferring instead to lie in bed and read while

Harold watched television. "I think he's tiring earlier now at night," Harold finished.

"Have you discussed a plan for when it's no longer comfortable for you to remain at the resort?" Dr. Routhier asked as if it was nothing out of the ordinary.

The question devastated Harold, who up until now hadn't had the courage to think that far into the future. If what the doctor had asked affected Quentin at all, he didn't appear to be fazed by it. Harold wasn't sure how to answer. In his mind, and he was fairly confident it was Quentin's hope as well, they would stick it out until the end. *Christ, is this even possible? Were we fooling ourselves?*

"I certainly don't expect either of you to have all the answers today. However, it wouldn't be prudent or practical for me not to open this up for discussion. Maybe I can help you decide."

Dr. Routhier turned and opened a drawer in the large credenza located directly behind his desk.

"It's not uncommon at all for patients to choose their homes, where they feel the most relaxed—the resort you're staying at, in your case," the doctor added, personalizing their situation, "as the location to spend their remaining time. The disease will undoubtedly play a role in helping you decide what is best. If you feel you'd like to stay out of a facility for as long as possible, you can certainly do this. Remote care is available to you."

Harold was handed a folder.

"In there"—Dr. Routhier pointed—"you'll find a list of services by the clinic as well as a few by the county if you find yourself in need of financial assistance. As with the other materials, look it over and call my office if you have questions. Personally, if it were up to me, I don't think I'd want to spend the time I had remaining in a clinical setting. However, I encourage you both to give this some consideration so you have the necessary elements in place when they are needed."

Again, Harold and Quentin shared a look between themselves and nodded they understood.

"I know from experience there are questions, well, one question in particular you're hoping I can answer for you." The tone of the doctor's voice changed slightly. Harold noticed it had softened even more from what was typical, and the delivery had slowed. "Everyone's body reacts differently, and therefore it makes it extremely difficult to predict the future. Based on everything I've looked at, and I should tell you I went over the tests from last week before today's meeting, my guess would be that we are talking anywhere from a few weeks to a few months. I wish I had better news, but unfortunately I don't. Your cancer is extremely aggressive. Now it's my job to make sure you're comfortable, Quentin. You'll need to let me know if you are in pain. I can remove most of that for you."

There it was. The answer to the million-dollar question. It was the news Harold had anticipated hearing ever since they'd gotten the other news, that the cancer had begun to spread throughout Quentin's body. *Weeks. He said weeks.*

Harold fought off the urge to scream. This time, it was Quentin who patted his hand.

"I fully understand"—Quentin reached for his throat and rubbed it before continuing— "What you said."

"Quentin, promise me that you will let Harold know if you are in pain. It's my number-one priority to make sure that the time you have left is spent as comfortably as we can make it for you." The doctor stood. "Harold, this isn't going to be easy for you, as I'm sure you're well aware. We have services here, professionals who can help. If the going gets too tough, or even if you just feel the need to talk, call me and I'll put you in touch with the right individual. Do either of you have any further questions?"

Dr. Routhier walked from behind his desk over to Quentin and gently rubbed his back. "Call me if you need anything, promise?"

Harold watched as Quentin nodded.

Before leaving the room, the doctor paused at the door. "Take your time. There's no rush to leave here."

CHAPTER
Eight

AND a dozen shorties should do it for plugs. Theo wrote down the amount and looked over the new inventory sheet he'd created with Alex's help. *Sweet!* He'd found time over the last few weeks to change up some things in the shop. Theo was motivated in part due to guilt, guilt over Adam quitting so suddenly. Mark from the Men's Center had advised it was Adam's decision to quit and that even though Adam was using Theo's disclosure he was gay as an excuse, they were two separate events and should not be linked. Emotionally linked, Mark had added.

The inventory sheet wasn't the only change he'd made. He and Alex had dropped by the shop after closing Monday night, and, together, they completely did away with Adam's old space, merging it with his own to create one large area where more projects could be worked on at the same time. The shop seemed much bigger now. Artie was pleased and thanked him.

Theo swept the last small pile of dust and dirt out of the garage door and returned the broom to its new designated spot next to the other neatly reorganized cleaning supplies.

The sound of tires on gravel caused him to glance back out to the parking lot. Alex pulled his truck up to the side of the building and parked. "Hey, boyfriend," he said when he'd rolled down the window.

"Dude, what's happening?" Theo laughed as he approached the truck. "What are you doing on this side of town?"

"Ian sent me to Daryl's Plumbing and Heating to pick up tubing for a new pond at the resort. He was going to go himself, but I volunteered. I thought, hell, I'm going right past your work, I'll stop and bug you for a minute. How's your day going?"

"Good. We're kinda slow." Theo gestured back to the garage to indicate the lack of engines needing repair.

"Cool. Did the boss like your new inventory sheet?" Alex leaned out of the window and beckoned for Theo to step closer to the truck.

"He hasn't seen it yet. I'm turning one in this afternoon so I'll…. Hey!"

When Theo had gotten close enough, Alex reached out and grabbed him by the shirt and pulled him in for a quick kiss. "It's been a long, lonely drive, stud, and you were on my mind the whole time."

Theo fought off panic, thinking someone could have seen them, but it dispersed without a fight a second later. "I'm glad you stopped by." He felt on top of the world. "I missed you the last few days. Talkin' on the phone isn't enough. I need the real thing." Alex had just returned from a trip down to the Twin Cities to hang with his bud, Colin.

"I need the real thing too, if you know what I mean." Alex laughed. "So, what are you doing tonight?"

"You thinkin' about headin' into Duluth to watch Ian play?" Theo stuck his hands in his pockets.

"Yeah, we could do that. I don't know. I was just thinking it would be fun to hang, and…."

"And…." Theo laughed.

"Well, maybe we just hang out in my bedroom for a while and get to know each other better." It was Alex's turn to laugh.

He didn't have to think twice about accepting Alex's offer. "I like your idea." Theo raised his eyebrows a few times in quick succession to indicate he totally got the hidden meaning. "How about this? I'll pick you up after work and we can grab a burger and then go back to your place and… *talk*." Theo blushed. Images of

Alex naked were racing through his head, making his jeans tighten. He pulled his hands out of his pockets to create more room.

"Works for me. Think about what you want to *talk* about." Alex licked his lips and demonstrated his own skill at eyebrow fluttering. "Hey, boyfriend, can I have one more kiss before I go?"

Theo gave a quick look around to make sure the coast was clear and hated himself for being such a wimp. "Sure." He leaned into the window, Alex met him halfway, and they kissed.

"Theo, you out here?"

"Fuck!" Theo jumped back a few feet from the truck. "It's Artie."

"So?" Alex laughed. "Don't ask me how I know this, but I don't think you have anything to fear there."

Artie walked out of the garage. "Alex? Is that you?"

"Hello, Artie!" Alex smiled and waved.

"I didn't know you guys knew each other. I didn't mean to interrupt, but we have a rush coming in. A guy's dropping off a wood splitter in a few minutes. I told him I thought we could look at it while he waited."

"Sure, Artie." Theo had a hard time looking his boss in the face when he knew his own was bright red.

"Great. Take care, Alex. It's nice to see you."

"You too, Artie." Alex had a grin from ear to ear as they watched Artie walk back through the garage and into the office.

"Dude, you think you have me fooled." Theo smirked.

"I don't think I have you fooled." Alex laughed innocently.

"Yes, you do. You think it was a surprise for me to find out you knew Artie." Theo took a step toward the truck.

"Well, maybe a little." Alex laughed harder when he realized Theo had discovered Artie was gay on his own.

"Artie's in the group that meets on Tuesday night with Mark at the Center."

"Oh, wow, did he tell you? That's cool." Alex seemed a little surprised.

"Not exactly, but I figured it out. I know he's gay." Theo moved another step closer.

"No comment. I can't talk about that shit." Alex shook his head in all seriousness.

"Then talk about this." Theo reached in the window and grabbed Alex by the back of the neck, pulling him out until their lips met. "Fuck, you're hot," he whispered when the kiss had ended.

"You're hotter, boyfriend." Alex traced his finger down Theo's chest. "Speaking of hot. It's been kind of hot in my bedroom lately. I might have to remove some of your clothes tonight."

"Oh yeah? Don't start anything you can't finish," Theo challenged.

"Shit, I think I have a wet spot on my jeans. I have to go or this is going to get worse. See you later." Alex put the truck in gear and backed out.

"I'll be over by six," Theo shouted as Alex pulled onto the highway.

After the truck had sped out of sight, Theo fetched his phone from his front pocket and went to his contacts. He scrolled down the list until his thumb rested on "Home." Home: he could tell by the way his parents were acting that they had questions. Questions he wouldn't be able to answer. At least not yet. But soon. Fear of their reaction to his coming out was being displaced by the challenge it presented. As frightening as it was to contemplate that inevitable confrontation, the benefit of having the burden off his shoulders was starting to make itself known. Theo wanted to come out to them soon, but the timing had to be perfect. There was a real possibility the encounter would become explosive. His mother would freak; that was a given. And his father, well, that was the wild card. He would have to start looking for somewhere else to live before he risked losing his basement cave.

Screw it! Theo slid the phone back into his pocket. He didn't have to call home. Having spent so many years following his parents' extensive rulebook to the letter, it was tough to break the mold. *You're a man now, Theo. Act like one.*

He and Mark had determined the time was right to expand the people in his life he thought capable of handling the news.

Artie. Now's probably as good a time as any.

But Artie would have to wait. A battered old pickup pulled into the lot and Grizzly Adams stepped out. Well, Grizzly's brother. *I wonder what hole this guy crawled out of.*

"Called you folks up. I got me a splitter that's hell-bent on holdin' me up. Waz it you that said you'd look at the damned thing while I waited?"

"Sure." Theo helped Grizzly unload the machine, and together they carried it into the shop. The whole time, the old man ranted on and on about how it had just stopped. "You can wait out there." Theo pointed to the parking lot in hopes Grizzly would take the hint and not hover over him the entire time he worked on the codger's splitter.

"I'm gonna stand right here and see what you do to that thing. Maybe the next time it goes on the fritz, I can fix it myself."

Lucky me!

After checking out a few things, Theo determined it was a clogged fuel line. Once this had been cleaned, he gave the engine a pull, and it started right up.

"Lord's sake, I drove all the way over here for that? Now I suppose I have to give you some of my money."

No, dipshit. We work for free. I bet you don't give away those fireplace cords you're stockpiling for next winter. Huh? Gotcha there, didn't I? "Why don't you head in there." Theo pointed to the office. "Artie will let you know what you owe. Tell him it was the fuel line." *You can share in the fun, Artie. I've had it with this dude.*

When the machine was loaded back in Grizzly's pickup and he was on his way down the highway, Theo wiped his hands and walked into the office.

"Did Grizzly Adams hassle you about having to pay?"

"Grizzly Adams, yeah right." Artie laughed. "His real name is Sedgwick Tipple. Isn't that a corker? Must be some weird immigrant thing. Thanks for getting him out of our hair so fast. You're right; a little Sedgwick goes a long way."

Just tell him.

"Artie, there's been something I've been meaning to talk to you about. You gotta minute?" Theo didn't want to start anything if Artie was in the middle of something.

"For you, Theo, I've always got time, you know that. What's on your mind?"

"Alex." Theo chuckled and then panicked. He hadn't planned on his "coming out" discussion to start out with Alex as its introduction. It just happened.

"We both know Alex. Small world, isn't it?" Artie pushed his chair back from the little desk in the corner. "Those are some eyes that young man has, eh?"

Artie's comment about Alex's eyes made Theo feel awkward. *Can't go there with you, Artie.* "Yeah. I met Alex at the Men's Center about a month ago." His face warmed. "Is that where you know him from too?"

"Yep. I attend a support group on Tuesday nights. Theo, let me save you some trouble here. I'm gay. It took going to the group for me to get up the nerve to begin living my life in an honest way. I'm not all there yet, but I'm making good progress. Back when I was young, well, you know this. Things were different."

"I'm gay too." Theo was surprised at the surge of emotion that suddenly erupted. He felt his lower lip quiver.

"It's a tough one for some of us. You're wise to have mustered up the courage to admit this so early on. Damn, Theo. I'm a little jealous here."

"You are?" Theo didn't have a clue what his boss meant.

"Sure I am. You're so young. Why, you've hardly wasted any of your life living a lie. For me, there were years wasted. Well, not really wasted, but they sure as hell could have been a lot better if I'd been able to be myself."

Oh, Artie. You're so cool. "Not many people know yet. I'm working on getting the word out too."

Artie's face wore a look of concern. "Have you told your parents?"

"No." As had been the case so many times since accepting he was gay, a movie-like glimpse of telling his parents flickered in his mind, and the scene chilled him to the bone. "That's going to be huge." Theo tried not to show worry, but the thought of confronting them made him edgy. *It's going to be like jumping off a cliff. Once you make the move, there's no turning back.*

"I don't expect telling them is going to be an easy one, given what I know about your folks. They're good people. It's a tough call how they'll react. Take your time. No real rush."

"I want to get it over with, but I have to organize some before I tell them."

"Maybe I can help with that. You've been over to the house. I have that spare bedroom down in the basement. It's yours, Theo, when you need it, and for however long it takes you to get something of your own."

"Oh, Artie, I wasn't asking—"

"I was offering." Artie cut him off before he had a chance to explain. "It would make me feel good to have helped you. If you can give me day or two heads up, that's great. But no worries if it doesn't work out that way. These sensitive matters sometimes have a life of their own."

"Wow." Theo felt his lip tremble again. "That's nice of you. Thanks, Artie." Theo resisted an impulse to walk over and give his boss a hug. "I hope this doesn't piss you off, but I found out about the Men's Center when I was going through your mail. Wait. Be right back."

Theo ran out to his truck. The red brochure was in his glove box. He ran back to the office. "Here you go. Sorry, it's not so new looking anymore."

"I was thinking when you were outside how glad I am I had something to do with you making the move to be honest with yourself. Oh, gosh, look at that." Artie took the brochure into his hand and admired it. "It's the Center's first one, I think. I remember

174   Joel Skelton

a few years back"—Artie placed it on a pile of papers behind his chair—"a guy I was seeing from Duluth talked me into going to Gay Pride. At that point, I was starting to get angry about having to hustle around in secret, so I agreed to go. We came across a booth for the Men's Center." Artie laughed. "I didn't know it at the time, but Alex was there along with Harper Callahan. He's the director of the Center. I thought to myself, Lordy, those are two of the most handsome men I've ever seen."

Theo was very proud Alex was his boyfriend. But at the same time, this discussion made him uncomfortable. It was weird getting to know his boss in this new way. Theo wondered whether or not he should mention something about him and Alex.

"I have to ask this, Theo. Are you and Alex…?"

"Yeah," Theo piped in enthusiastically, the shit-eating grin on his face destined to remain at least as long as Alex was the subject.

Artie sat back in his chair and roared. "Well, good for you. Listen, I'm sorry to act like such a horny old dude, but mostly, I was hoping the best for you. Alex is a sweetheart. He'll treat you right. I'm sure of it."

"Thanks."

A car pulling into the parking lot brought this odd encounter to an end. "I'll check this out, Artie. Hey, and thanks for offering your place. That's really great." Theo smiled and turned to leave.

"It's yours if you need it. No strings attached, if you know what I mean."

"Thanks." *Oh God. I never thought of that.*

FOR the last several minutes, Alex had been preoccupied with the scenery. Half of Theo was submerged, while his lower body was stretched out over the seats displaying his hot bubble ass in all of its glory. *I've got plans for you, butt.*

"It's not as bad as we thought." Theo's muffled voice came from deep within the engine compartment. "I think we could put this baby in the water right now and it would start up."

Alex was aroused. Antsy to get his hands on those round, firm globes... naked. *There's a good time to be had in Buttville,* he thought but answered, "That's great." *Hurry, I need to play. Now!*

"Hand me another clean rag." Theo's hand dangled out of the opening.

Bored and in a silly, playful mood as he daydreamed about Theo's rump, Alex complied and, in the process, bent down and mimed with bold, broad moves licking Theo's ass. *Lick. Lick. Lick. Oh yeah.... Licky, licky, I'm going to lick you all—*

"Hey, what's goin' down?"

Alex sat up, mortified. "Oh! Hey... Ian." *I'm so fucked.*

"Wanna practice on my butt, dude? That was soooooooo funny." Ian, dressed in his Taconknights' uniform, roared. Doubled up, he staggered around the driveway, barely able to stay on his feet.

Aware he would live out his entire life having to listen to and watch Ian recount this stupid incident, Alex sat on the edge of the boat with his head in his hands, debilitated from embarrassment.

"That's okay, slurpy. It's a nice specimen. I'd have to agree. Mercy me, that was funny." Ian was off again, charging around the blacktop howling with laughter.

"What's going on?" Theo slid out from the compartment and looked around, clueless.

"I was pretending to lick your butt, and Ian caught me." Alex knew from experience it was best to just come clean.

"Alex, you bring me so much joy, dude. So much joy." Ian had finally regained control of himself. "Hi, Theo. So, how does the engine look? Are we going to have to junk the boat?"

"Hey, Ian. It's in pretty good shape. I was telling Alex we could probably plop it in the water and it would start just fine. It needs a little attention, but not too much."

"Sweet. Well, boys... Alex... behave yourself. I've got to haul ass to the field, or I'm going to be late."

"Knock one out of the park for me, dude." Theo whacked the ball with his imaginary bat.

"You're on, my friend." Ian hopped in his truck and tore off down the road.

"Ready to call it a day?" Alex, despite being humiliated seconds ago, was still hot for some action.

"Yeah. Now that I know what needs to be done, I can stop by with the right oil and a few tools and we should be good to go. But seriously, there's nothing wrong with the engine. Whattaya want to do?" Theo attempted to wipe the grease off his hands.

"Hmmm… maybe take a shower for starters?" *This is insane.* Alex was so damned horny he could barely stand it.

"A shower? Together?" Theo collected the few tools he had laid out on the floor of the boat.

"Yep." *Hurry now, boyfriend.*

Theo handed the duffle bag he had loaded up to Alex and jumped out of the boat. Taking it back, he waited for Alex to hop down, and together they walked into the house.

"Is Harper around?" Theo kicked off his shoes when they had reached Alex's bedroom.

"Nope. He's at the Center, working, and then he's headed over to Duluth to watch Ian play." Alex removed his T-shirt and stepped out of his flip-flops. "Here, allow me." He tugged Theo's T-shirt over his head, leaving him naked except for his jeans.

"Ah, I see. Okay, I guess it's my turn." Theo undid the button of Alex's cargo shorts and brought down the zipper. With a quick yank, they fell to the ground, and Alex stepped out of them.

What's mine is yours, Theo. Just let me know if you're feeling uncomfortable. Sex can be so much fun. I'll be your tour guide and take you to new and exciting places.

"Here, feel." Alex reached for Theo's hand and placed it on the front of his boxers. "This happened when I was watching you work on the boat."

Theo stroked and petted Alex until he looked up and, with a smirk, pulled Alex's underwear down, exposing his plump and eager dick. "This can never get old," he confessed. "I love touching it." Theo, maybe feeling guilty for going right to the prize, removed his hand and placed it on the back of Alex's head, bringing him close for a kiss. "Kissing is good too. I never really liked it before."

"Here's what *I'm* into." Dropping to his knees, Alex unbuttoned Theo's jeans and pulled them down, helping Theo step out of them. Reaching around, he cupped Theo's butt in both hands and buried his face in his crotch. "Your ass is like a rock, dude," Alex complimented when he came up for air. "I can't wait to play with it. First things first—it's shower time." Alex hooked his thumbs inside the waistband of Theo's boxer briefs and hauled them down. Before getting up off his knees, he kissed the tip of Theo's dick. "I've got plans for you too."

They took turns circling under the spigot until they were warm and relaxed by the spray. Alex squirted a glob of shampoo into his hand and worked it into Theo's hair and then his own. Suds raced down their bodies. "I love shower sex, but I want to play with you on the bed."

Theo grinned. "Shower sex? I can't wait for the day when I know what to do. There's so much to all this."

Shutting off the water, Alex stepped out and handed Theo a towel. When they had dried themselves, Alex led the way back to the bedroom. "Whattaya say we try a few new things tonight?"

"Sure, I guess."

The hesitation was back in Theo's voice. Alex had to keep reminding himself that his boyfriend had only been out for a month. Except for the basics—hand and blowjobs—sex with another man was still a new frontier.

"Ah, don't worry. You trust me, right?" A gentle push here and there couldn't hurt, Alex thought as he moved over to the dresser. "Hop on the bed."

"Okay."

His request set off a few nervous glances from Theo.

"Don't worry. You're going to really like this. I know it seems kind of strange"—Alex climbed on the bed and onto his knees—"but do this." Spreading his legs slightly, he brought his head down onto his pillow, leaving his ass high in the air.

"Seriously? Okay. You're the boss." Theo, sporting a look of apprehension, shuffled back and forth on his feet.

"Dude, relax! I'm gonna worship your butt. I've been waiting for this all day. You'll love it." Alex stepped off the bed and gestured for Theo to take his place.

"My butt? Really?" Theo sheepishly positioned himself as Alex had demonstrated.

"Wow! I can't say enough about your ass. It's soooo hot." Opening a drawer, Alex pulled out a large flesh-colored dildo and a small purple vibrator, setting them on the night table. "This little baby is so much fun." He held the plastic toy in his hand for Theo to see.

Climbing onto the bed, Alex began by massaging Theo's legs and thighs. They were covered with a soft blond fur. His calves were muscled and well defined. Sitting back to take in the view, Alex admired Theo's impressive cock and balls, dangling low between his legs. He allowed his hands to occasionally brush up against the plump sac. A playful tease he hoped would make Theo want more. *I'll get to you guys soon enough.*

Unable to resist any longer, he leaned forward and presented each cheek with a kiss. The skin was smooth and warm and the scent, a little bit of heaven. Using his hand, he signaled for Theo to spread his legs out more. "Ah, there it is." He parted Theo with his hands and flicked his tongue over the dark ring.

"Whoa!" Theo's entire body rose off the bed in surprise.

"Relax. Relax, I'm not going to hurt you. This is just play, nothing serious. I promise." Alex waited while Theo reluctantly repositioned himself. Reaching to his side, he picked up the purple vibrator and turned it on. He brought it up to the circle where his tongue had just been and gently pushed forward.

"No! Stop! Stop it right now."

Alex leaned back on his haunches in reaction to Theo, who twisted his body around until they sat facing each other.

"I... I don't want to do this." Theo's panicked eyes darted around the room.

"Theo, I'm sorry. I didn't mean—"

"I'm not ready for that," Theo admonished angrily. "Don't rush me." He jumped off the bed and turned away.

"I'm sorry. I wasn't going to…." Alex slumped. "Theo, come back here. We don't have to do anything you don't want to."

Several painful moments of silence passed. Alex was too ashamed of his behavior to look at Theo. *What the fuck were you thinking? Idiot. Idiot.* Stunned by how suddenly a playful romp could sour, he weighed his options. *I bet he wants out of here.*

"Please come back." Alex didn't want Theo to leave angry.

"I don't like being touched there. I don't think this is going to work."

"What isn't going to work? Theo, don't leave." Alex, crestfallen, watched as Theo went over to his pile of clothes and began to dress.

"I'm turning into Todd." *I'm a total idiot.* "I'm pawing you and treating you like shit. Like Todd used to treat me. I can't believe I just tried to force you into doing something you obviously didn't want to do. Theo, I'm so fucking sorry. It won't happen again." Alex was so angry at himself he could hardly breathe.

"I've got so much to learn. You'll just get bored with me. I'm going to be a beginner for a long time." Theo stepped into his underwear.

"No." Alex jumped off the bed and grabbed the toys. "I shouldn't have coaxed you into trying something without first talking it out with you." This was even worse than rushing Theo. *He feels bad now because he's so new at this. I'm such an asshead.* Alex opened the drawer and threw the toys in. "I'm so mad at myself." He searched for a way to salvage the rest of evening.

"Remember that first time together I told you your friendship meant more to me than sex? I wasn't kidding." Theo stepped into his jeans. "I've got so much going on in my mind right now." He pulled his T-shirt over his head. "I need some time to sort this all out."

"Theo, I'm the one that fucked up here. Not you. You'll always be my friend. I just thought we'd try something—"

"Give me time, Alex." Theo cut him off as he walked to the door. "Maybe our differences are too much for us to go the boyfriend route. I… I just don't know. I don't know what I want."

"Theo?" Alex, feeling awkward at still being naked, took a step forward. "Please don't go into hiding. I'll miss you… I'll miss you as a friend."

"I'll call you. I'm just really messed up." Theo unlocked the door, turned, and forced himself to smile before walking out.

Alex plopped down on the corner of his bed in despair. *I'm the one that has the most to learn, Theo. Please don't get so far away that you lose your way back.*

"PET, I brought you one of those tasty jelly rolls from Maxwell's Bakery you like." Harper placed the plastic-wrapped plate next to a stack of envelopes on the front desk. "Have you already been up to get the mail?"

"Not me. I think I heard Ian in here earlier while I was in back making coffee. It's funny. I'm starting to tell you guys apart by the noises you make when you're in here. Ian's louder, if you're wondering." Petra undid the plastic and took a bite of the rich pastry. "Yummy! It's blackberry. This is the best yet."

"I had their Mandarin orange muffin this morning before I came down. Loved it!" *No paper today?* Harper shuffled through the mail but looked up when somebody or something flashed past the window. "Did you see that?"

"I saw something," At the same time Petra came strolling around from behind the counter, Ian flew past the window with a pruning shears in his hand.

"What the hell is he doing running with that thing? Talk about dangerous." Harper looked over to Petra in hopes she would have an explanation, but it was clear by the look on her face she wasn't going to be too much help.

"Holler at him, Harper. You're right. That's just stupid."

Harper made a move to step out of the screen door but stepped right back in again when Alex came whizzing by at full clip, followed only seconds later by Ian.

"Ian, are you crazy? Drop the pruning shears. Now!"

"Are you thinking what I'm thinking?" Harper asked, stepping back in with a wink.

"Ass crack?" Petra chuckled.

"If Ian went up to grab the mail, he probably got his hands on the Gazette before the rest of us could see it."

"The coast is clear. Let's watch the show." Harper held the door open for Petra.

"Oh, good. Ian dropped the shears." Petra strolled a couple feet further from the office for a better view.

Alex, with Ian hot on his trail, tried to lose his pursuer by squeezing through a small bank of lilac. Ian bulldozed past the shrubs, dramatically decreasing Alex's lead. Desperate to get away, Alex committed the huge mistake of running through a newly planted bed of blue Salvia.

"Alex, tell me I didn't just see you run through one of Ian's flower gardens." Harper shook his head, fully understanding the severity of the crime.

"Wait until I get my hands on you… you little bastard!" Ian shouted, taking the time to go around the large kidney-bean-shaped bed.

"Nice. Our guests and everyone in a five-mile radius probably heard that." Harper shook his head.

"Do you think he'll catch up to him?" Petra asked and then acknowledged how stupid her question was. "Wait, what do you think Ian will do to Alex *when* he catches up to him?"

"Hard to say. It's not going to be pretty." Harper stuffed his hands into his pockets and cheered Alex on. "Run, Alex. Run your ass off."

"I don't think he heard you. He's starting to slow… oh God. I don't know if I can watch."

"Ian loves you, Alex. Remember that," Harper yelled, bringing his hands out of his pockets to form a megaphone.

"Did you see that? Harper, did you see that?" Petra was beside herself.

"Yeah."

In what appeared to be a last burst of energy to try to outrun Ian, Alex must have hit a piece of lawn still wet from the morning dew, and although he managed to make a remarkable adjustment to stay on his feet, the slip cost him the lead. Before he knew it, Ian was on top of him. In a move as impressive as any professional wrestler's, Ian grabbed ahold of Alex by the waist and tossed him in the air and over his shoulder.

"Poor Alex." Petra looked over to Harper, full of worry.

"Poor Alex is right. Ian's headed toward the lake."

They couldn't make out the actual words, but it was clear from the tone, Ian was giving Alex a good piece of his mind as he stomped toward the beach with the young man dangling over his shoulder like a rag doll.

"Should we try and stop this?" Petra advanced a few more steps in their direction.

"Naw. Alex knows Ian well enough to have understood the risk involved. Besides, Ian needs some resolve, and if we don't let him run with this, life will be hell until he gets his revenge. Better to just sit back and let this one play out. But, damn, that water is cold."

As if on cue, a high-pitched scream confirmed that, in all likelihood, Alex had just taken an unexpected plunge. When Ian exploded out of the shore scrub solo, both Harper and Petra bolted back into the office and scurried behind the desk, pretending to be hard at work.

"This is stupid, Harper." Petra laughed. "Ian heard you call out to him. He knows we were watching."

"Not necessarily. See, when Ian gets really wrapped up in something, he's not always sure how he got from point *A* to point *B*. Think of it as if you were out on a walk and heard birds in the trees.

We probably made the same impression. He's too mad to confront us now. Tonight in bed, I'll be interrogated."

"Do you think Alex is okay?" Petra moved over to the side window.

Harper was impressed with Petra's maternal concern. "Ian is mad; there's no doubt about that. But Alex means too much to him, which is a good thing for Alex. Trust me. The man can bring on some serious hurt if he wants to."

"Harp! Look! There he is…."

They both watched as Alex, dripping from head to toe and with one shoe missing, trudged up from the shore with his head bowed.

"I bet he's asking himself right now if it was worth it." Petra raised her eyebrow knowingly.

"He is. And he's answering himself that it was. He and I are a lot alike. Stubborn as hell." Harper grinned as they watched a hunched-over Alex turn onto the trail leading to the house.

"There was so much excitement going on I forgot to ask." Petra left the window and walked back behind the desk. "Have you noticed something different about Green Eyes lately? He doesn't seem happy. Is there something else going on with him?"

"Yeah, Ian and I were talking about it last night in bed. We think something's going on between him and Theo. We aren't sure what, but maybe one of them is getting cold feet. Ian," Harper laughed, "before he found out about the ass crack stunt, thought we should confront him. I didn't think that was such a good idea, so for now, we've agreed to just let him be. Alex has a knack of coming to you when he's good and ready. It's hard seeing him unhappy, isn't it?"

"Yeah, the little shit can really brighten a day. I guess I've grown to count on it."

"I don't know if you've had a chance to get to know him, but we both really like Theo. Between you and I and the fence post, he's in the process of coming out. Alex might be a little too advanced for him right now. Hope not. I think they could both benefit from each other. But you can't control how the heart works, now can you, my dear?"

"You got that right. I have years of unpredictable heart research to back up your statement." Petra sighed and blew the hair out of her eyes.

Harper grabbed his keys off the counter and headed for the door. "If anyone's looking for me, I'm off to the Center. Call if you need anything."

"Will do. Have a good day. Whoa...."

"Whoa, what?" Harper walked over to Petra, who was looking out the window.

"Here comes an ambulance." Petra stepped aside so he could get a better view. "I think they might be lost."

Harper flew out of the office and approached the emergency vehicle. "I'm the owner. Can I help you?"

"Is Cabin ten directly ahead?"

Oh shit, Quentin. "Yes. The road ends at Cabin six, but keep going on the grass until you get to the last cottage."

"Thank you."

"Quentin?" Petra joined him.

"Yeah. I'm going to head down there and see if I can help them out. Damn, I hope he's still with us. Poor Harold."

"Call if you need anything." Petra turned to head back to the office.

"Pet?" *The other guests.*

"Yeah?"

"I'm not sure who's even going to know there's an ambulance down there, but if one of the guests asks, assure them there's nothing to worry about."

"Sure."

Harper jogged toward Cabin ten, following the same path as the ambulance. By the time he got there, the medics had already entered. He peered into the window and heard voices coming from the back, the bedroom. He opened the screen door and entered.

He didn't get far before one of the medics rushed past him, returning a moment later with an oxygen machine. Looking through the narrow doorway into the bedroom, he could only see the backs of the emergency guys and just a little glimpse of the foot of Quentin's bed. *Where's Harold?*

The mystery was solved when both paramedics exited the room. Harold, who must have been huddled in the corner, came around and sat on the side of the bed. Harper inched his way so he could peek inside the room. Quentin was hooked up to oxygen, which was a good thing, Harper thought, because his face was blue. Harold stroked his partner's cheek tenderly.

Figuring out the appropriate thing to say at this point was a challenge. Part of him wanted to simply back out of the room to give Harold some privacy. *Thank God! He's still alive.* When the ambulance had pulled up, in his mind, he assumed the worst-case scenario.

Before he could make a decision on what to do, the paramedics came back in with a gurney. Harper stepped out of their way as they worked to load Quentin onto it. A few minutes later, with the oxygen now hooked to the side of the portable bed, they wheeled him out, and Harold followed.

"Oh, Harper, I'm so very sorry." Harold grabbed his arm and squeezed. "I waited too long. We have all these resources to call for help and I just couldn't bring myself to do it."

"Harold, please." Harper rested his hand on the weary gentleman's shoulder. "Please don't worry about a thing. How can I help? What's going on?"

"They're going to take Quentin into the hospital so they can make him more comfortable. I guess I'll have to decide what to do from there. At this point…."

Harper watched Harold's lip quiver. It was clear the man wasn't going to be able to continue with what he had planned to say.

"Are you riding with Quentin?" *Be there for him, Harp. That's probably the best thing you can do at this point until you know more of the details.*

"I hope I can." Harold brushed away a tear that had tumbled down his cheek.

"Excuse me. We're ready to leave if you'd like to ride with your partner," one of the medics said through the screen door.

"You should be there with Quentin. I'll meet you at the hospital. We'll know more then, and we can talk about what's best. Can I bring anything along?" Harper gestured into the bedroom.

Harold thought for a moment. "Please pack up Quentin's laptop and bring it with. I'm not sure if he'll be able to use it, but it might be good to have around. I doubt he's going to be able to talk. He hasn't for the last day or so."

Aware they were waiting for Harold, Harper took him by the arm and led him to the door. He watched as the medic helped him up into the ambulance and closed the door. Reaching into his pocket, he pulled out his cell phone. "Hey, it's me."

"Here comes the ambulance. What's going on?" Petra's voice was rich with concern.

"I don't know very much. They're taking Quentin to the hospital in Duluth. Harold is in the ambulance with them. I think there might have been a problem with Quentin's breathing. He was blue in the face when I got here."

"Oh no, that makes me so sad. What can I do?"

"I'm going to gather up a few of their things to bring to the hospital. Hold down the fort until Ian or Alex come around. I'll call back when I know more."

"I'll be here. Hey, Harper?"

"Yeah?"

Petra's voice cracked. "Please tell Harold and Quentin I'm thinking of them. I feel just terrible."

"I promise I'll do that. I'm going to run up and grab my car so I can load a few things into it. I'll call Ian on the way. Bye!"

Jogging past the office, Harper sprinted up the path to the house where he climbed into his car and drove back down to Cabin ten. He found the laptop on the table near the bed and the case over against the wall. Looking around, he spotted Harold's jacket, noting a wallet was in the side pocket. He placed a cell phone, probably Harold's, in the jacket and then climbed back into the car.

Harper pressed the phone to his ear. "Petra, I don't see a cabin key. Can you come down here and lock up?" He started the car.

"Sure. I'll be right down."

Backing the car around, Harper rolled down his window and waved as he passed his office manager. "I'll update you as soon as I know more. Thanks."

"Drive safe." In his rearview mirror he watched as Petra jogged down the road.

"I'M PROUD of you, Theo." Mark smiled across the table. "You're listening to yourself. When you felt out of control, you put on the brakes. What I'm trying to tell you is, you did the right thing."

Theo was having a hard time buying into Mark's reassurances. This whole mess came about because, as much as he wanted it, the truth was he wasn't ready for a relationship. *I hardly know the dude, and he asked me to be his boyfriend.* Especially with someone so comfortable with who he was—like Alex.

"Look, we're going to talk about a few things tonight that I think you'll benefit from. But before we do that, you have to give yourself some credit."

Credit for what? Keeping a fake dick from being shoved up my ass? That was pretty damn brave. He felt almost as screwed up now as when he first started the process of coming out.

"A month ago, Theo, you walked in here a very confused man who needed help. Don't get me wrong, you've come a long way in a very short time, but to some extent, you're still confused and you still need help." Mark laughed.

"I know." Theo couldn't have agreed more.

"Yeah, okay. Tell me what you think I want to hear." Mark winked.

I don't want to lose Alex. I don't know if he'll wait for me to catch up.

"I know that look, Theo. The way this works is you share with me your thoughts, and then together, we work on them. I can't read minds."

There was a direct tone to Mark's comment that couldn't be ignored.

"I was thinking…." Theo looked around the room to find the right words and then settled on his original thought. "I don't want to lose Alex. I don't know if he'll wait around for me to catch up."

"That's a legitimate concern. However, I would value your mental health and happiness over a relationship with Alex or anyone else right now. Think of it this way. You need the proper foundation first. Building a relationship on shaky ground isn't advised."

Nodding he understood, Theo couldn't hide his disappointment. Wrong place at the wrong time, he thought, stealing a line from his dad.

"Theo, you haven't lost Alex. You just need to talk to him and be honest. Let him know you and I have talked, that's fine, and tell him you were advised to slow things down. Use me as the bad cop. Slowing down doesn't mean not seeing Alex. It means proceeding forward with you in control. Confidence. Trust me. It will all work out. I promise you that."

That's a little better. Theo couldn't stop the smile from spreading across his face. "I understand."

"Good. Now let's roll up our sleeves and talk sex." Mark sipped his coffee and sat back.

Theo's face flushed. *Seriously? This is so embarrassing.*

"Let's start with the myth about anal sex."

Mark… Theo was dying.

"Don't give me that look. We're both adults here, and how many times do I have to remind you? I've heard it all and experienced most of it firsthand. So come on. I'm not Dad, I'm a therapist. People, not you, but some people pay good money to talk about sex with a guy like me."

"Sorry, it's just kind of embarrassing." Theo sat up in his chair.

"At least as many gay men oppose anal sex as those who are into it. Non-gay folk seem to believe that it's the only kind of sex gay men have, and this perpetuates the myth. With all the talk and hype about what gay guys supposedly do to each other, it was natural for you to find fault with yourself."

"I've never thought about... you know... being touched there."

"Yep. I get that. And when you were being forced to go there, you did the right thing. You let Alex know, at least for now and maybe forever, it might not be your thing."

"I think he's really into it, though." Theo couldn't hide his concern. How would it be possible to get around this?

"I think you're probably right. Especially given the fact he's gone to the trouble to obtain a few toys specifically for anal play. I want to make sure I'm clear on this and you understand what I'm advising." Mark leaned forward and placed his hands on the table. "Having something shoved up your backside doesn't ever have to be a goal for you. You may wake up one morning and think, hey, let's give it a try, or you may not. This is entirely your call. Now, had Alex approached you, or let's say at some point he approaches you and draws a line in the sand, stating that it's his way or the highway if you guys are going to stay together as boyfriends—then, you'll have a decision to make. And as much as I like and enjoy Alex, I'll be disappointed if you give in just to keep the relationship going. Happy people make happy relationships."

"I don't think he'll do that. I mean, I'm not certain, but he was pretty upset with himself." Theo experienced a pang of guilt at the thought of walking out on his friend.

"Okay, here's something that might help you deal better with this. There's nothing in the rule book that says you can't give Alex what he wants. Unless you're totally opposed to playing on that end. This might be something you can do for him that he'll enjoy in exchange for something special you like. And again, I know you might not have gotten far enough down the road to even know what that is, but at least you know what Alex likes. That's a good starting point." Mark sat back again after taking another sip from his paper cup.

"Yeah, that's cool. He's got a really nice butt." Theo's unexpected confession caused him to blush.

"There you go." Mark laughed. "Sounds like you're not opposed to providing Alex some pleasure if he indicates it's something he enjoys. You know the other thing, Theo—you have years of negative exposure to all things gay, including what people think gay men do to and with each other. Remember, you're a man who has needs too. As long as they're safe and consensual, there's nothing wrong with any of these sexual activities. The sky's the limit. Be safe, be proud of who you are, and don't brag to others how wonderful your sex life is, because it's really annoying to us who are still single."

"You're a really good looking—"

"I'm kidding, Theo. I'm single because right now I choose to be. But thanks for the compliment. Now is there anything else regarding gay sex you'd like to discuss?"

"No. This helped. I'm kind of charged to talk to Alex about what he likes. I never thought to do that." Theo found himself smiling for the first time in a long time.

"Good, now let's move on to something else I think we need to touch base with. Have you given any more thought to coming out to your parents?"

Theo had thought about it plenty. He wasn't ready for that one. Not yet. Having a place to stay at Artie's was good, but it didn't do a thing to lessen his fears about confronting his mother and father. "I can't do that yet. I'm starting to think about it, but I'm not ready to face them."

"I understand. I'm not going to let you off the hook here, though. It's something I think you should do, but as I advised you earlier in our sessions, the time has to be right for you. So, you'll have to work toward that one. I guess I'm asking you to start thinking of it as a goal. Okay?"

"Yeah, I want to do it. I just need some time. I'd like to find out where I'm at with Alex first, and then if that still works, I should be ready to take on the 'rents. That's going to suck, I'm sure."

"Take your time, that's fine. I just don't want you to shove it under the rug and move on with your life without being honest with your family."

"Artie, my boss, has offered me a room at his house until I can get something of my own. That helps. I'm pretty certain once I come to out to my parents they won't want me in the house. It's a tough one to call."

"I was wondering about that. Good. Nice to know a roof over your head won't get in the way. What else? Anything you want to talk about?"

"No, not that I can think of." Theo felt good about this session. The whole mess-up with Alex didn't seem like such a huge thing. He planned on following Mark's advice.

"Let's call it a night, then. You're doing good work, Theo. It might not seem like it now, but I see it. Be proud, okay?" Mark sat back and smiled.

"Okay." Theo felt the return of a grin. *Time to face the world again.*

"I'm going to stick around and finish some notes. See you next week."

"Thanks, Mark." Theo got up from the chair and walked to the door. "See you next week."

On his way out, he heard clanking coming from the big hall. *Maybe it's Alex. It would be good to talk.* As he had guessed, Alex was in the far corner by the large window wrestling with an old set of blinds. He turned at the sound of Theo's footsteps on the old wooden floor.

"Hey." Alex stepped down from the window sill he was standing on.

"How's it going?" Theo sheepishly approached, not sure if he should initiate anything or just let Alex be.

"It's going good. I got a wild hair up my ass to start tearing down these old blinds. There are new ones to replace them in the storage room."

"Cool. Well, I don't want to disturb you. Just wanted to come by and say hi." *Probably not the best time to talk.*

"I need to take a break or go home or something. I'm done for tonight. Feel like hanging out in Harper's office for a few minutes? I'm dyin' for a soda." Alex collected his tools and put them into a box.

"Yeah, that sounds good." They walked in silence across the large room and down the short hallway to the office. Theo fought off an urge to touch Alex. *You can't have it both ways.*

"Here." Alex handed Theo an ice-cold soda from the little fridge Harper kept in the corner. "I'm still so mad at myself." Alex sat on the small chair and gestured for Theo to take the seat behind the massive oak desk.

"Don't be." It felt strange to sit in Harper's chair. "Mark helped me understand a few things tonight." *You can't just leave him hanging. Go for it. Be honest.* "I really like you. Nothing's changed about that. But I need to be comfortable with myself. I mean, I need to know who I am before I start a serious relationship."

Alex sipped from his can and then placed it on the corner of the desk. "Can I ask you something? You don't have to tell me if you don't want to."

"Sure." Theo took his hands off the desk and placed one on each knee, bracing himself for whatever Alex had on his mind. He couldn't get a read on his friend, and that caused anxiety.

"Do you have to stay away from me for a while?" For the first time since they'd sat down, Alex looked him in the eye.

"Fuck, no. I don't want that." Theo wasn't sure why Alex would think that. "Why do you think that?"

Something about his response caused Alex to laugh. "I thought maybe Mark might have told you to stay away or something. Or maybe you thought you had to stay away from me while you were working things out. I know. I'm a paranoid freak."

It was Theo's turn to laugh. "I think I'm the freak. I thought you might want to stay away from me because I'm so screwed up." Theo brought his hands back onto the desk when he realized Alex was still interested in something more than a friendship. "It takes me a while to catch on sometimes, but I want to work at this, Alex. I want us to work out."

"I'll take what I can get with you, Theo. I don't care how long it takes. I'm there."

Theo watched as Alex bolted from his chair and began pacing around the office. "I've been with other guys before. I know what I like, what I want," Alex continued. "I want you. That is, if you're still interested. And...." Alex stopped behind his chair, placing his hand on the back of it and leaning forward. "I don't mean sex. I mean your friendship first, and then, well—okay, I'm just going to say this—I'm hoping it will grow into more."

"That's what I want too. I just don't have my shit together yet to be a good boyfriend to you. Let's start over, kind of. Hang out. Get to know each other better as friends and then let what happens, happen." Theo was proud of how that all had come out.

"Deal."

Alex appeared relieved as he sat back down in the chair.

"And maybe I can touch your dick every now and then just for shits and giggles." Theo burst into laughter as Alex struggled to keep from spitting out his pop.

ALEX sat up and grabbed the remote, turning down the volume. *Damn, Harper. You look so drained.*

"I'm glad you guys are still up. We need to talk." Harper plopped down in the chair across from the couch where Alex and Ian were sitting watching the Twins game.

Ian sat up too and removed his bare feet from the table. "How's Quentin? How's Harold?"

"They're going to keep Quentin overnight. Maybe longer. According to Harold, he had a bad coughing jag this afternoon and couldn't breathe. Scared the hell out of them both." Harper got up. "I need a beer. Anyone need anything?"

Alex looked over to Ian, and they both shook their heads.

"Be right back." Harper left the room.

"The old boy is lookin' a little ragged, wouldn't ya say?" Ian stood, stretched and yawned, and then dropped back down.

"Petra said the ambulance left here about one. What is it now, eight thirty? He's got to be dragging." Alex still couldn't come to terms with Quentin being on the edge of death.

"Okay, where was I?" Harper reentered the room with two beers in his hand.

"You were telling us about why Quentin was taken to the hospital. He couldn't breathe." Alex brought his leg up onto the couch.

"It must have been bad. He was blue when I got down there. One of the first things they did was put him on oxygen."

"How's Harold holding up?" Ian reached for his own beer.

"He's scared. Guys, can you imagine? He's losing his partner."

Harper's observation silenced the room.

"Is Harold back here?" Alex asked. "Is there anything I can do?"

"Nope. He's spending the night with Quentin. If everything goes as planned, they both should be back tomorrow."

Alex shot Ian a look. Ian returned his trademark "I don't fucking know" shrug.

"There's a plan, and I'll need you both to help me out."

Harper detailed for them what he had in mind. Early tomorrow, before their guests were milling around the grounds, they would use Alex's truck to remove the bed from Cabin ten. The whole space needed to be rearranged. Sometime later in the day, before Quentin and Harold returned, a hospital-quality bed would be delivered, along with various other things, like an oxygen machine, that would enable Quentin to spend the last of his time there rather than the hospital.

"They were all set to throw in the towel, but I wouldn't hear of it. We need to make this happen." Harper wasn't soliciting a discussion on this one. That was for sure. "I know I'm kind of revved up right now, but guys, if you could have seen them…."

"Do we want to do it tonight?" Alex was getting revved up too.

"I thought about that, but I think it's best if we wait." Harper took a long pull off of his first beer. "It's almost dark, and, honestly, I need to unwind. Let's shoot for really early, like dawn, and then we can come back and crash for a while if we want. You guys okay with that?"

"Hell, yeah. I'll make sure we're up." Ian was the early riser of the group. It was rare for Alex to get up and not find Ian either already at work on the grounds or futzing around the kitchen. "Harp, how much time does Quentin have left?" Ian cut right to the chase.

"I don't know. It's not going to be in the next day or two. He could go a couple of weeks, from what I heard discussed, or maybe even longer. With the stuff that's delivered tomorrow, he'll be much more comfortable. There's also going to be a nurse stopping by for a few hours each day to help Harold out."

"Oh, that's good, the nurse." Alex was still having trouble wrapping his mind around Quentin coming back to the cabin if he was coming down the homestretch.

"I'm going to talk to Petra in the morning, but one of the things we can do as a team is come up with activities for Harold to keep his mind off of Quentin, if that's possible. Although they're going to be together, in a way, they're not. Harold mentioned that the doctor had told him that Quentin would start sleeping more and more as the end comes. Think about things we can do for Harold so that he doesn't lose his mind."

"I could put him to work." Ian chuckled but shut it down the minute he saw the look on Harper's face. "Sorry."

"Hon, you never know. That might just be the ticket. Alex, I had an idea."

"I know what you're going to say." Alex looked over to Ian and smiled.

"No you don't," Harper challenged, finishing his beer and exchanging it for a replacement.

"I'm going to paint with Harold."

Ian got up from the couch and stepped into the room. "Mister smarty-pants lawyer just got his ass nailed by the brilliant and terribly annoying Ms. Alex Stevens. Bravo, butthead!" Ian leaned in so that Alex could swat him a high-five.

"I wasn't being a smartass. Harper always challenges me like that, and this time I knew I had it." Alex felt proud. What he said was true. Harper, in his infinite wisdom, occasionally got a little full of himself. The fact it was Alex and not Ian who brought him back down was a testament to their solid relationship.

"I know I totally deserved that, but I still have this tremendous urge to punch you… both." Harper yawned.

They sat in silence until Ian interrupted, "Home run. Look!"

They all focused on the screen as the hitter began his trip around the bases after rocketing a ball out of center field and into the stands.

"Hon, let's go to bed. I need some time alone with you." Harper stood, waiting.

"Sure, babe." Ian got up from the couch and ruffled Alex's hair. "'Night dick-lick."

"Night, guys." Alex stretched out. "I'll see you in the morning." *Hang in there, Quentin.*

CHAPTER

Nine

THAT should work! Alex had spent much of the morning setting up a makeshift space in the screen porch he and Harold could use as their studio. *This is going to be a really good opportunity for me.* It didn't matter to him that they worked in two different mediums— Harold in oil and he in watercolor—there would be plenty to talk about. *Hope Harold enjoys our time together.*

At first he had been worried about the light in the large, open room. Except for a brief period in the morning, it was shaded for the remainder of the day. But then it dawned on him that the porch could be used to discuss and experiment. If it worked out that he and Harold could actually start painting something, maybe they'd paint on location. In front of the palisade or somewhere else cool. *He'd be close to Quentin there.*

Lifting a small tray out of the *very cool* paint box he had inherited, he brought the photograph out from under for one last look. It was a picture taken at his birthday party. Seated in portrait fashion were Harold and Quentin, all stylin' in their sport coats. Alex smiled. *Make this one really special, dude.*

Placing the photo back in its hiding place, Alex pulled out his phone.

"Theo." The voice answered. Theo always answered the phone the same way—with zero emotion. Alex had kidded him that he could be in the middle of a twister bearing down and he'd still only offer up a soft "Theo."

"Hey, it's me. Are we still on? What time are you coming over?" Alex left the porch and strolled into the house, totally stoked.

He and Theo had worked until dark the night before on "My Woody," the name for the little wooden speedboat they both favored over any other. The double meaning had just the right silly. Ian had campaigned hard for "Spunk Missile," which Alex had to admit was kind of catchy.

Theo went through the engine, making sure it was oiled and ready to roll. Alex installed the new windshield that had been special ordered from a supply house in Florida. He had to dig a little deeper into his savings for it than he would have liked, but it was worth it. *Damn, you're a good lookin' boat.* The only thing left to do other than spend time on the wood—*My Woody*—was to repair a few rips in the red upholstery. He was thinking about approaching Audrey. She could sew just about anything. Everyone said so, and she'd know the best way to patch it up.

"I was just going to call."

Shit. Alex closed his eyes and banged into the wall with his back. He could tell by the tone in Theo's voice that something had come up.

"We just got a call from a nursing home in Silver Bay. They did a test on their emergency generator, and it wouldn't start. Sorry, man. I can't get out of this, or, believe me, I would."

Try harder. No, it sucked, but he understood. "No worries. I'm bummed, but I completely understand. We'll get it in the water soon, right?"

"Hell yeah! I can't wait to jet around the lake in that thing. Anyway, I've gotta run. Wanna grab a burger or something tonight?"

Alex smiled. This was Theo code. The subtext to Theo's invitation was "let's spend time together, but not in the bedroom." Alex had to admit he longed for another romp around the sack, but this waiting thing was working. With the pressure off to make that part of their lives exciting and hot, it was nice just kicking back. The last few times they had gotten together were fun and relaxed. Alex was really getting to know Theo. The report was good. Quiet and sweet. Masculine, but not in a forced way, which made him *so, so hot*. And the best part, Alex could tell Theo enjoyed spending time with him. It was too early to call, but a few times now when they'd been talking, he'd had kind of a déjà vu moment because he was reminded of the easy way Harper and Ian were with one another. *I'll take more of that. You bet.*

"Sure. I'll be here. Don't worry about the boat, Theo. Really, I'm cool. Later, dude."

Alex shoved the phone in his pocket and walked the rest of the way through the house and out the door to the driveway. They had hooked the boat and trailer onto his truck last night after wrapping up. This morning, before working on his art studio, he had given the truck a wash. *Dang it.* The shiny pickup, the sporty little speedboat, it was so sad that today had to be postponed. *But maybe.... Hey, it doesn't. Not exactly.*

He'd never considered it before. What if he took the boat out on his own for a quick spin? Theo might be disappointed he wasn't on the maiden voyage, but probably not. He didn't seem like the sensitive type. *I should go for it. It's been weeks since my birthday. Haven't I waited long enough?*

There'll be someone at the marina if I need help getting it off the trailer. That shouldn't be a problem. He and Theo had discussed the process several times, and, having grown up on the lake, this wasn't his first encounter with walking a boat off a trailer. Although he did have to admit it was kind of strange how few times he'd been on Superior in a boat. A small boat. Theo, while going through the engine, had also explained the whole starting process and how the throttle worked. It wasn't brain surgery.

Back in the kitchen, he grabbed a small cooler and put a couple of Dews into it, along with a bag of chips and a candy bar. *Should I make a sandwich to bring along?* Naw, he decided when he looked at his watch. It was already close to noon, and Theo would be over sometime around five to head out for a bite to eat. *Ready, set, go.*

The tiny marina was just a few hundred feet away from an iron-ore processing plant. The plant where his father had once worked. *Let's put that memory back in the attic and lock the door for good.* Alex had been angry at his dad for so many things, including how selfishly he'd taken his own life, that Harper had insisted he talk to someone. Alex spent four months meeting with a therapist to learn how to process his anger and live with it in a way that wasn't harmful. Jarring images, like the ore plant, were unwelcome challenges.

He backed his truck to the edge of the water. Alex ran up to the little makeshift office to see if anyone was around. *Locked. Everyone must be at lunch. Should I leave a note? It's cool. They'll let me know if I owe them anything when I get back.*

Alternating between his side and rearview mirror, he carefully inched the truck back until the trailer had entered the water. He had to get out of the truck several times to gauge how much further he needed to go. With the boat positioned in what he thought to be the right depth to glide it off and over to the dock, he shut off the truck engine.

Dressed in shorts and a T-shirt, Alex kicked off his flip-flops and went about releasing the boat from the frame. Once *My Woody* was free, he had no problem walking it over to the dock and tying it up. Alex parked the truck and trailer on the side of the marina where there were a few other vehicles. *This is good. I'm not in anyone's way.* He grabbed his sunglasses and the cooler, locked the truck, and walked down to the boat.

This is so frickin' awesome. He couldn't believe how cool the boat looked tied to the dock. It sat low in the water poised to leap up and fly through the air at a moment's notice, chasing the larger boats and leaving them in its wake as it roared by.

Alex reviewed the startup steps Theo had covered. *It's now or never.*

Giving the key a first turn, the engine rumbled to life with a puff of smoke, alternating between gurgle and growl as the exhaust bobbed in and out of the water. *Nice work, Theo.* Alex let out a joyous whoop. *Music to my ears.* He untied the rope from the cleat on the dock, and, confident the boat was operating properly, he eased the throttle into reverse, forcing the stern against the chop. Clearing the dock, Alex snapped the throttle forward and was greeted by a smooth purr. *Okay,* Woody, *it's time to show me what you can do.* Anxious to get out on the lake, he pushed the throttle further. The sleek hull rose out of the water until it got on plane, reducing drag and increasing speed. *Oh, baby. This is livin'!* The bow sliced through the water as Alex set a direct course for Devil's Island.

"KNOCK, knock."

Perfect timing. Giving the sweet mixture a last stir, Harold put down the spoon and walked to the door. "A fine good afternoon to you, Ian."

"Hey, Harold. I come bearing gifts." Ian opened the screen door and handed him a paper bag. "Is Quentin sleeping?" he whispered. "Sorry."

"No, he's awake." Harold held the door open. "Please, come in and say hi."

"Great!" Ian stepped into the front room of the cabin. "Hello, Quentin. I know it's hard for you to talk. I just wanted to say hi. This looks like a much better setup for you."

"Yes, having the bed in the front works very well," Harold confirmed.

A few days earlier, before Quentin came home from the hospital, Harper, Ian, and Alex switched around the cabin. They began by taking out the double bed in the back room and replacing it with a cot. Harold thought to request this in case it became difficult for him to sleep next to Quentin. So far, it hadn't been needed. Next, leaving a small seating area across from the sink and counter, they moved back what they could from the front area to make room for the hospital bed Quentin now rested in.

"Why don't you show Ian your new toy," Harold suggested, walking over to the bed and handing Quentin his laptop.

Harold watched with glee as Quentin began typing. Soon after, a mechanical voice filled the room. "Hey, handsome! New in town?"

Ian, his mouth wide open from surprise, threw his head back and laughed. "That's fantastic. I love it."

"I bet all of the boys are after a tiger like you!" the voice continued.

Enjoying the moment almost as much as Ian, Harold cautioned Quentin, "That'll be quite enough of that sass, young man."

"Sorry, boss," the voice apologized. "It's not every day we have such a fine specimen of manhood pay us a visit."

"Well, I'd have to agree with you there." Harold looked over to Ian and winked. "As you can see, I've had my hands full ever since Dr. Routhier presented him with this software. Before you came by, he was amusing himself by typing every naughty word in the book just to hear how it sounded."

"Weiner licker." Quentin took cover behind a pillow.

This struck Ian as being so funny he backed into the wall for support.

"Quentin! That's quite enough." Harold walked over and snatched the laptop away. "I warned you."

Harold and Ian watched as the pillow was slowly lowered, revealing a face Harold had fallen in love with decades ago. Quentin displayed a textbook example of mischief that faded quickly into an award-winning pout.

I'm so thankful you're enjoying yourself, Radish. Harold couldn't remember the last time he saw his partner this animated. "Do you promise to be a good boy?" Harold asked, aware they were putting on a show for Ian.

Quentin nodded slowly with playful remorse.

Walking over to the bed, Harold offered back the laptop. Quentin, in a surprising burst of energy, snatched it out of his hand and began typing. "Thank you, Ian, for helping to make my stay here so comfortable. I'm so grateful to you all."

Harold couldn't help noticing the kindness that radiated from the youthful face across the room. *You have a kind soul, Ian.*

"We're so glad to have you back, Quentin." Ian wiped the tears from his eyes. "It was a little lonely knowing you weren't with us anymore."

How sweet, Harold thought, until he saw the look of horror overtake Ian's handsome face. He must have initiated an instant replay of his last comment and realized the opportunity his words had for misinterpretation. *You don't have to be so careful, my young friend. We understood your thoughtfulness. I'd better rescue the poor lad.*

"You're right about that, Ian. It was lonely not having Quentin here. I'm so happy to see him back and doing so well." Harold joined Ian and patted him on the shoulder.

Ian shuffled in his spot. "You said that so much better than I did." An anxious moment lingered about the room before Ian added, "Well, I should be heading home so I can change. I've got a game."

Quentin typed, "Good luck, tonight. I'll be there in spirit."

"The next homer I hit has your name on it, Quentin. Have a good afternoon, gentlemen."

"Thank you." Harold watched as Ian stepped out of the cabin and jogged down the path. "I have a surprise for you," Harold said, turning back.

"You do?" Quentin typed, looking over to the paper bag sitting on the counter.

"Yes. Courtesy of Ian." Standing with his back to the bed, effectively cutting off Quentin's view of the counter, Harold removed a clump of fresh radishes and began cutting them into paper-thin slices.

"What a nice man he is," Quentin opined. "He and Harper make such a beautiful couple."

"I couldn't agree more." *Remember, Harry. He's probably not going to be able to eat much. It's the thought that counts.* Harold stopped after cutting up only a few of the bright red, super-crunchy vegetables. "In many ways, they remind me of another couple." Reaching into the bag, he pulled out the special brand of rye bread Quentin favored and removed several of the slices.

"Oh, Harry," Quentin replied in his mechanical voice.

Harold was momentarily stunned by the realization that this strange sound coming from his partner would be his only voice, from now until the end.

"Remember when we were younger?" Quentin asked.

"Of course I do. We had the world by the tail." Harold carefully cut away the crusts. "I was thinking back, a few days ago, to when you found out you'd sold your first book. I don't think we had ten dollars between us, but that didn't matter. We bought the biggest steaks we could afford and a bottle of some cheap red table wine and dined like kings."

"Oh my, that was so long ago."

A cool breeze blew through the room, rustling the plastic blinds on the window he faced. Harold ladled a generous amount of the honey-butter spread he'd been secretly preparing under his partner's nose. He chuckled. Quentin was so disinterested in food these days, his covert attempt at hiding his surprise was hardly necessary. *It's the last thing he would be curious about.*

"When you sold your first painting, we were in better shape." Quentin remembered. "We used the proceeds to fund our first trip to Europe. I was so excited."

"Oh my. Paris. I remember thinking we were special. None of our friends had been." Harold carefully layered on the radish. Joining the two slices together, he cut the sandwich into four smaller squares. "Okay, close your eyes."

"Yes, sir."

"Are they closed?" He looked over his shoulder to make sure Quentin had complied. "Voila!" Harold exclaimed after he had placed the plate next to his partner on the bed. "Radish sandwiches for my *special* radish. They're fresh from Ian's vegetable garden."

"Well, would you look at that?" Quentin clapped his hands together and, after typing, added, "This will make you very happy, Harry. I'm hungry."

"That's wonderful. How is your beverage? Do you need more? Ice?" Harold waited for a response.

"I need you right here." Quentin patted a spot on the bed next to him.

"I thought you'd never ask. It's been a while since I had an invitation from a handsome man such as you."

Quentin reached for a sandwich as Harold came around the other side of the bed. Taking a bite, he placed it back on the plate and typed, "Harry, will you hold me?"

"Sure. Here, let's put this away for a while. I don't think we need it." Harold took the laptop off of Quentin's lap and placed it near the end of the bed. "Scoot up a little, and I'll get behind you."

After Quentin had slid his body a few inches closer, Harold, his back against the metal railing of the bed, reached under his partner and brought him tight against his chest. Reaching over, Quentin fumbled around for a minute until he had located the oxygen mask that had fallen to the side after he'd removed it for Ian's visit.

"Make yourself comfortable, sweetie. I could hold you forever." Harold felt his eyes grow moist. *There won't be many more moments like this. Savor them.*

With the exception of children's voices in the distance, they lay together in silence. Quentin finished off his first sandwich and started on a second, which he never finished. Harold felt the body resting on his begin to rise and fall, his breathing deeper, a sure sign that his ailing partner had fallen asleep. *The combination of the late afternoon warmth and the gentle breeze got the best of you, didn't it, Radish.*

Harold rested his chin on the top of Quentin's head. *What am I going to do?* He couldn't put it off any longer. The time had come to make plans for the future, when once again he would be navigating through life on his own.

Sell the house?

Most likely. It would be too agonizing to stay. Sure, as time marched on, the pain would dull, and after a certain period, maybe as little as a year, Harold speculated, he'd have moved on enough to begin feeling comfortable there again. *But why do that?*

Removing the emotion from his situation, it was probably healthier for him to view this as another phase of his life. Phase one, life prior to Quentin. Phase two, life with him, and finally, phase three, life on my own.

Palm Springs. How many dinners had he and Quentin sat across from their friends, Carl and Edward, and listened to them go on and on about how wonderful a place the desert community would be to retire. Each time they'd gotten into the car for the short drive home after one of these get-togethers, either he or Quentin declared to the other that Palm Springs would never be their first choice. It had been easy to dismiss Carl and Edward's plan when you had someone else to share life with. Faced with being alone, it didn't seem like such a bad idea. *It would be a fresh start.*

Once again, his eyes pooled. *I'm so scared.* He didn't want a fresh start. He wanted to go somewhere, find someone, and negotiate more time. The first tear journeyed down his cheek, dampening his shirt collar. More followed. The miracle he had hoped for needed to happen now—today. This was it. Tomorrow, Quentin had to wake up with newfound energy. The day after that, the soreness in his throat should vanish. By next week, he and Quentin would be taking walks together, possibly exploring the trails in and around the palisade. And when December hit, Harold would rent out the swankiest room in town for Quentin's birthday.

Harold cried out in desperation. Not wanting to wake his partner, he gently moved Quentin's head off his chest and onto the pillow. Gasping, with tears streaming down his face, he slid off the bed and rushed to the back of the cabin and into the bathroom. Shutting the door, he collapsed on the stool and cried.

SHOOT! It looks like a few other people had the same idea. Alex pulled back on the throttle and cruised past the rock ledge he had hoped to tie up to. Other boats occupying the space made it impossible even for *My Woody*, a small boat, to slip in. He had fond memories of Devil's Island. Once, while in scouts, his troop camped overnight here. The next day they kayaked through the sea caves the island is famous for.

Navigating a large circle in front of the landing, Alex tried to get a read on the activity. Did anybody look like they were packing up and ready to move on? *Nope. Okay, what's plan B, buddy?* "Nice boat!" someone hollered out to him. Alex waved and, unable to resist showing off, thrust the throttle forward. The boat rose out of the water like a skipped rock, and, in seconds, he was on to a new adventure.

Man, I don't want to take you home yet. Leaving the Devil in his wake, he flew across the water until he came to the next island. *If I remember right, this is Rocky.* Again, he eased back on the throttle so he could enjoy the shoreline as it passed. Reaching the northern tip, Alex continued to hug the scenery until he came to a beautiful little bay on the other side of the big lake. With virtually no wind to rough up the water, he made the snap decision to chill out there for a while and grab some sun.

The boat idled while Alex opened the bow compartment and hauled out an anchor. Theo had commented it really wasn't much of an anchor when they'd first discovered it buried under a tattered boat cover, but for today, with the lake so calm, it was just the ticket.

With the engine still running, he crawled out onto the bow and tied the anchor line to one of the cleats positioned at the very front. After testing the knot to make sure it was secure, he heaved the hunk of lead over the side and climbed back to the cockpit. *Let's take a little rest here, Woody.* Alex shut off the engine and enjoyed the sound of the gentle waves lapping against the rocky coastline.

I wish Theo was here. At least now I know of a cool place to bring him when we come out together. Alex laughed out loud. His next thought was a vision of him and Theo having sex here. *Oh yeah.*

Reaching for the cooler, he pulled out a Dew and popped the top. *This is livin', buddy boy.*

Climbing into the backseat, he tugged off his T-shirt and rolled it up in a ball, using it as a cushion for his back. Every now and then, a gentle breeze charged across the water, turning the little speed boat around its anchorage. *So great. It's like being flipped on a grill.*

It wasn't long before his thoughts drifted back to Theo. *My yummy Prince Theo.* Alex released a huge sigh, content that his life was good. The future was bright. And even though it might have started out a little on the rough side, his relationship with Theo was starting to gel. It was starting to feel comfortable. The last few times they'd been together, Alex was almost certain he could sense Theo wanting more. *He wants my dick.*

Alex sipped his soda as the boat lazily turned so the sun was at his back and he was facing the island. He wasn't done with Theo yet. *I think what's happened,* Alex told himself, *is Theo's ready for more, but he doesn't know how to ask for it. That's it!* Alex sat up and acknowledged the light bulb that had just exploded. *Talk to him. Tell him that sex is still important to you, and ask him if he's ready. And if he is, then make damn sure you take it slow.* "Stay away from his ass, Alex." Alex could finally laugh at his earlier blunder.

The sun felt awesome. He'd been so busy the last few weeks with everything going on, there'd been no time to work on his tan. *Semper Fi!* He leaned back against his shirt and closed his eyes to savor the moment until a rustling on shore caught his attention.

Using his hand as a shield against the bright reflection of the sun off the water, he scanned the shore until he spotted the source of the noise. His jaw dropped open as he watched a bear work itself down the rocks to the lake. *I can't believe I'm watching this.* The bear was on the small side, he thought as it dipped its head into the water. *Are you a baby?* Seconds later, it came up with a fish in its mouth.

That was amazing.

The fish had to have been dead or dying, because there didn't seem to be any fight left. The bear repositioned it in its mouth and backed itself up the rock before disappearing into the dense woods. *Totally unbelievable!*

Downing the rest of his soda, Alex stood and peed over the side of the boat. Spotting the bear had made his heart race, but the warmth of the sun coaxed a large yawn to the surface. Checking his watch, he still had an hour to kill before he needed to head back to meet up with Theo. *Make the most out of days like this,* he told himself. *You're here. Enjoy it.*

Alex moved his shirt to the other side of the seat and stretched his legs out until they reached the side of the boat. His body was longer than the width of *My Woody,* which caused his knees to jet up to the sky. He was plenty comfortable. Alex closed his eyes in hopes of catching a snooze before leaving paradise.

"HOLY crap, is it ever dark over to the west. We'd better batten down the hatches. Petra, pull up the weather on your 'puter." Harper threw his keys onto the desk and walked behind her to join his office manager for a look. "We might have to gather up our guests and herd them over to our house for safety."

"Let's see," Petra switched gears and went to her favorite local weather site. "Oh yeah, this isn't lookin' too good. There's a band of red and orange heading right for us. Hang on, I'm reading the National Weather Service bulletin."

Harper couldn't wait for the relay of information. Not only did he love severe weather, he could stare at weather models until the cows came home. "That's impressive," Harper mumbled over her shoulder. "I tell you what. I'm going to jog down to Cabin ten to alert Harold and Quentin. Stay by your cell. If anyone stops here to inquire about storm protection, tell them to gather here or stay if they can, and we'll walk up to the house as a group. Once I'm done with Cabin ten, I'll work myself back to the office and, in the process, hopefully touch base with all of our guests on the way."

"Sounds good… Wait, they just issued a new warning." Petra stood back to protect herself from Harper, who came flying back to her side for a peek.

"Golf-ball-size hail… winds in excess of sixty miles an hour. All of this directly in our path." Satisfied he had the latest and greatest, Harper headed for the door. "Okay, I'm off to Cabin ten. I have my cell if you or anyone have questions."

"Ian's on the grounds somewhere, but I'm not sure where." Petra looked across the room with concern.

"I'll keep my eye out for him. If we don't cross paths, I'll give him a call on his cell. I have no idea where Alex is. He might be up at the Center." Harper opened the screen door.

"I haven't seen Alex since early this morning. I'll try calling him."

"Thanks, Petra. See you back here in a few."

The air was at a standstill when Harper stepped out of the office. *This isn't good.* The rumbling of thunder in the distance confirmed the storm was nearing the resort.

Harper Callahan! Were you born without a brain? It makes absolutely no sense to go all the way down to Harold and Quentin's cabin and then, once it was determined what they were going to do, head back up and touch base with the other guests. Harold and Quentin are going to be your biggest challenge. End with them.

Cabins one and two were vacant. There were no cars around, so Harper had to assume the occupants were on a day trip somewhere. *Hope they're safe. Wait.* He dialed the office.

"Palisade Beach Cabins, this is Petra."

"Pet, it's me." Harper didn't let her respond. "Print off a few sheets of paper that give cell phone numbers for you, Ian, and me. Also say something to the effect that, in the event of threatening weather, you can seek safety at the owner's permanent residence, located on the south side of the property. If you are unable to locate the house or need assistance, please feel free to contact one of the staff, and we will be happy to assist."

"Yep. Got it. Anything else?"

"Yes. When you have these printed, grab some tape or something and tack the notice onto the doors of one and two. They might come back from hiking or somewhere and not know what to do. Also, I'll call you and tell you which other units are empty, and maybe either you or Ian can repeat the process where needed." *That should work.*

"I don't know why we didn't think to do this before. I'm on it. Call me if there's more."

"Thanks." Harper pocketed his phone and continued to Cabin three. As he approached, he could hear the television from inside.

"Hello!" he called out. "Anyone home?" Harper stood away from the screen to respect the occupants' privacy.

"Hi, can we help you?" A woman stepped out of the screen door while another looked out from behind.

"Sorry to bother you," Harper said with a smile, "I'm Harper, one of the owners. There's a pretty strong storm coming our way, and I wanted you to know that, if you'd feel safer, you're more than welcome to take shelter in the lower level of our home. It's located a couple hundred feet past the office."

"We've been watching the radar on the television. Doesn't look too good, you're right." The two women exchanged looks of concern.

"Well, why don't you gather up anything you want to take along and head to the office. Petra is there, and once we get everyone rounded up, we'll be heading over to the house." Harper waited for a reply.

"Thanks. I think we'll do that."

He had similar exchanges with the folks in Cabins four and five. Cabin six was empty.

"It's me again. Add Cabin six to your list. They're gone." Harper held onto his phone in case he needed it at the next stop.

Cabin seven was rented to a young family of four—Mom, Dad, and two boys. Ian had spent some time playing Frisbee with them and brought back a good report. "I heard thunder, Momma. Did you hear it?" he heard a young voice ask when he got up to the door.

"Hello. Anyone home?"

Dad appeared at the door. "Hey."

"Hi. I'm Harper, one of the owners. We have a bad storm approaching, and if you want, you can take safety in the lower level of our house. It's located on the south end of the property."

"Thank God! You just saved the day. My wife is near hysterics. You never plan for stuff like this. Where do we go? Angela, come here," Dad turned and hollered.

"I think the best thing is to gather up your family… oh, hi!" A woman with a textbook look of worry appeared next to her husband. "I was telling your husband I think the best thing to do at this point is to gather up what you want to bring along and head over the office. It will be much safer to ride this out in our lower level." She nodded while holding two excited boys at bay. "One of us will take you over to the house as soon as we have everyone notified."

"Oh, thank you. Boys, go grab your packs. Now!" Mom shooed the kids back into the cabin.

"Thanks for letting us know," Dad said with a salute.

The front door to Cabin eight was closed. Harper opened the screen and knocked. Moments later, he heard footsteps.

"Hello," he greeted when the door opened. Standing inside the screen was a woman who looked to be in her seventies.

"Hello. Is there something I can help you with?" She smiled through the screen.

"I'm Harper Callahan, one of the owners. I'm not sure if you're aware, but we have a storm approaching that has the potential to be threatening. You're more than welcome to take cover in the lower level of our house, located on the south side of the property."

"Well, I guess we really had no idea. Please, I'll only be a minute." The woman left the screen. *Come on lady. We haven't got all day.*

"Bernard thinks we're fine," she said with a smile that screamed for someone to rescue her. "He's been watching it on the television. I've been reading."

"Okay." *Suit yourself.* "If you change your mind, head over to the office in the next few minutes. We'll be leading a group of guests over to the house from there."

"Well, we do appreciate your offer. Bernard adores storms. If we blow away to the heavens, it's his fault."

Harper was struck by the false confidence in the woman's voice. *Bernard rules the roost. And he's a selfish asshole.*

Cabin nine, rented to a thirtyish single guy, had been the topic of conversation up at the office since the guest had arrived. Ian was convinced he was some kind of minor celebrity who was trying to get away from his hectic life. Or, Ian was quick to add, trying to hide from an intervention. Petra thought he might be a poet or a writer. "He has that look," she said knowingly. Alex thought he was just a regular dude and offered that maybe someone would join him later in the week. "A girlfriend," he tacked on to support his assumption.

Harper leaned toward Petra's hypothesis. He had that loner look Harper had always associated with literary types. Well, poets to be specific. *You're so full of shit, Harper.*

Just as he stepped up to the door, it opened, a cloud of fragrant, organic smoke tumbling out.

"Oh, hey, dude, what's goin' down?"

Ian's the winner. The guy had a beer in his hand and was well on his way to happy land.

"Hi. I'm Harper Callahan, one of the owners." Harper thought it responsible to establish he was in charge.

"Cool." The stoner looked around, his eyes darting here and there as if he were expecting others to show up.

"There's a storm approaching that could be dangerous. If you want, you're more than welcome to take cover in the lower level of our house. It's located on the south end of the property." *If you even give a rip!*

"Dude, I fucking hate storms. They scare the shit out of me. I'm not lying."

Harper backed up. Barefoot, the guy stepped out of the cabin and marched out onto the lawn. He was dressed in cut-off sweat pants and a Pennzoil T-shirt. He looked up to the sky just as mother nature, never one to miss an opportunity to show who's boss, chose that particular moment to send down a bolt of lightning in the very near vicinity. The crack of thunder made even Harper jump.

"Holy fucking mother of Jesus," the stoner cried out, waving his arms up and down. "Where the fuck do I go? I gotta get my sorry ass out of here, like now!"

"You know where the office is?" Harper asked, not sure what state of inebriation this guy was in.

"Yeah. Over there." The dude pointed frantically.

"Go there and wait. We'll be walking over to the house shortly."

"Gotcha. I'm fuckin' not lyin'. This is serious shit, this weather shit."

"The office," Harper ordered, confirming its location by pointing down the path.

Now it was on to Harold and Quentin. "Harold?" Harper called out as he approached.

"Harper. I bet you've come to warn us of the approaching storm. Please come in." Harold held open the screen door.

"Sorry, Harold, but I have to see to all of our guests. Things could get pretty wild around here in a minute. It's a serious storm, from the way it looks. Why don't we bring a car down here, and you and Quentin can ride it out in the comfort of our lower level. We have some other guests who will be doing the same thing."

"Oh. Well… just give me one second."

Harold moved away from the door. Rumblings of thunder close by made it hard for Harper to hear what he was discussing with Quentin. "If that's what you'd like to do," he heard as Harold returned to the door. "You know I love storms."

"I know this is reckless," Harold stepped outside the door and whispered, "but I think we're going to stay put. We both enjoy storms, and…."

"No worries. I understand." With Quentin so ill, maybe they felt the stakes were different. *I sure hope you guys will be safe.* "Listen, if you change your mind, call my cell. We'll have someone down here in a flash."

"Thanks, Harper. We appreciate your concern. I think we'll be okay, won't we, Radish?" Harold turned toward his partner. "He's having a good day," Harold said after turning back.

"That's wonderful. One of us will be here in a heartbeat if you decide staying is too risky. Hang on tight." Harper forced himself to chuckle as he turned away. *Hang on tight. There's nothing you can do, Harp.*

When he arrived, the office was empty, with the exception of Ian, who sat glued to the computer. "Bink. I was waiting for you."

"Where is everyone?" Harper stepped inside.

"I sent Petra up to the house with our guests. The dude from Cabin nine was poopin' his pants. I'm not shittin' ya." Ian flashed his "did ya get it?" look and smiled.

"That was very clever—your back-to-back usage of both poop and shit. But you had an advantage. Come on, admit it."

"Okay, they're two of my favorite words. I know, I know." Ian nodded he understood.

"Let's get up to the house. I know we both love storms, but I have a bad feeling about this one for some reason." Harper motioned for Ian to get a move on.

"No arguments here. This thing has the potential to be a real bitch." Ian jumped off of the stool. "Okay, let me power the system down and we can go."

Harper stepped out of the office to wait for Ian. The wind was really starting to kick up. Trees were beginning to bend over, searching for relief. By the time Ian joined him, the first drops of rain had begun spattering around them.

A COOL, steady breeze off the lake woke Alex. *Holy shit!* Flying out of the backseat, he plopped down on his knees on the front cushion and turned the key to start the engine. *Please start.* The little anchor that had been perfect as long as there was no wind had traveled a considerable distance. *My Woody* had moved to within a few feet of the rocky shore.

The engine started right up. *Thank you. Thank you.* Alex climbed out on the bow and hauled the anchor up. Not wanting to waste time by trying to untie the line up front, he brought it into the boat. Pushing the throttle forward, he steered clear of the rocks, and after putting his T-shirt back on, headed toward home. Alex followed the shore until he came to the island's point.

Holy shit! Holy fucking shit!

Clearing the tip of the island, tall pines no longer blocked his view of the western sky, now a dark, menacing mass. Bolts of lightning stabbed the horizon. *What the fuck? What am I going to do?* The storm and the marina were in the same direction. Alex tried to visualize the layout of the islands. *Think, Alex. Try and remember.*

He had passed a small dock on the leeward side of Rocky minutes ago. *Should I go back or try for something closer to home? What's the island directly ahead? Is it Bear? Yeah, Bear sounds right. If I remember, there's a dock on the calm side of that island too.*

Alex gunned the engine and headed toward Bear Island. A considerable stretch of open water separated him from his destination, but if he made a quick beeline to where he thought the dock was, there was a good chance he would be able to make it before the storm hit.

The calm, smooth lake he had skimmed across on the way out was starting to morph into a caldron of angry water, with waves now over a foot high and steadily growing. Making matters worse, the waves were hitting the boat broadside, and as their height increased, so did the chance of capsizing. Alex felt his skin crawl. *This is serious shit, dude.*

To lower the risk of being tipped by a large swell, Alex was forced to adjust his course. Cutting directly across the open water wasn't possible now that the wind had increased. He needed to keep control, and this required a gradual approach to Bear so the waves were hitting as much of the bow as possible. *This sucks. The waves are forcing me to head right into the storm.*

When he had the chance, Alex gunned the boat directly at the island, but as the waves grew in size, he couldn't risk this maneuver any longer. The other development, the tiny boat was being picked up in the large swells, causing the engine to come out of the water. *Go back to Rocky. That's what you need to do.* Alex scolded himself. *Why didn't you do this in the first place? What were you thinking?* His fear mounted as he unsuccessfully tried to turn the boat around.

The waves had increased until he found himself surrounded by a wall of water, only to be lifted high into the air on the crest. Lightning bolts were dropping down everywhere. Large droplets pelted his head and face. He struggled to maintain control. Heading back to the little dock he had passed up earlier was no longer an option. Alex was forced to head into the storm in hopes he would still be able to reach the western end of Bear. *Give me a break here!*

Fear turned to terror as the storm barreled down on him. *Focus.* Every second was a challenge. Alex had to keep the bow pointed into the waves. To break concentration now would be his demise. One wrong move could easily be his last. *Help me. Please!*

At some point, Alex lost the ability to distinguish the surface of the water from the air. The wind howled, whipping rain at his face with such a force he could hardly keep his eyes open. The only thing he could do was continue to keep the bow pointed into the waves. *You might not make it through this,* Alex told himself when pellets of hail were added to the mix. The roar of the storm was so loud now it drowned out the sound of the engine, which alarmingly spent more time out of the water than in.

Because the wind was blowing the rain and hail directly into his face, Alex was forced to shut his eyes. *This is it.* Terrified, he began to sob. His vision was reduced to nothing. The only hope was to go by instinct. Guide the boat into the wind. The constant battering had taught him to anticipate the adjustment in steering needed to keep the bow facing into the storm. Blindly, he kept at it, hoping to save himself from being thrown into the dark, cold water.

His hands ached from the fearful grip he had on the wheel. "Do not give up! Alex, do not give up!" he screamed into the wind. "You'll die. Die!"

Sidetracked momentarily as he fought with himself to keep it together, Alex allowed the bow to veer slightly off its direct course into the wind. The penalty for this error was unimaginable. The boat was pummeled from the side with such force he was unable to direct it back into the wind. Water cascaded into the cockpit. Nothing he tried was successful in regaining control. *Please... please help me. Somebody help me.*

Alex took his hands off of the wheel and sat back on the cushion. There was nothing he could do. He had lost control of the boat, and all it would take now would be one large wave to send him to the bottom. At the brink of total despair, he heard a new sound. It caused him to sit up and grab the wheel. Shielding his eyes from the blinding rain, he cocked his head and listened. *What is that sound?*

Visibility was poor. At best, he could see maybe three, four feet in front of the boat. The mystery sound grew louder and louder. Turning around, he tried his best to identify the source. A huge wave slammed into the side of *My Woody*, and he went flying forward, smashing into the dashboard and, in the process, killing the motor. Scrunched between the wood-paneled instruments and the seat, he moaned. He was sitting in half a foot of water. A sharp pain in his back kept him down for a minute, until he could bring himself to rise up on the seat.

I know that sound. It's waves splashing onto the rocks. Fueled by alarm, he forced himself to get off the floor of the cockpit. When his head had cleared the interior of the boat, he looked out and screamed just as the boat slammed sideways into the jagged rock.

CHAPTER
Ten

THEO was relieved to finally turn onto the road leading down to the resort. The brunt of the storm had hit while he was driving from work to hook up with Alex. The wind whipped the rain sideways so fast and furious he couldn't see the road and was forced to pull his truck over to wait it out. It was creepy being stopped on the side of a busy highway. Any minute he might be rear-ended by a semi truck and knocked into another county. With his emergency lights activated, he sat, hoping it let up soon so he wouldn't be such a sitting duck.

Several intense minutes passed until the worst of the storm blew over and he could once again see well enough to continue on. The road was littered with branches and debris. He drove by several recreational vehicles that were pulled over. *Probably just being overly cautious.*

When Theo arrived at the resort, he turned onto the short driveway to the main house. Alex's truck was nowhere in sight. *Huh? That's strange. Maybe he parked it somewhere safer so the boat wouldn't get messed up in the nasty weather.*

Turning around, he headed back down and parked behind the office. When he entered, Harper and Petra were huddled over the computer.

"Hey," Theo greeted. "Everyone make it through the storm in one piece?"

"Oh, hey, Theo. No news is good news," Harper said, looking up with a smile. "Man, that was one hell of strong front."

"Harold and Quentin are fine," Ian reported as he charged into the office. "The grandpa and grandma in Cabin eight are safe too. There're a ton of branches down, but, as far as I can tell, no trees bit it. I'll have Alex help me clear up the mess when he shows up. By the way, anyone heard from pencil dick?"

"I seem to remember Alex saying something about... well I guess I really don't remember *what* he told me," Harper mumbled from behind the counter.

"I haven't seen his truck all morning. I tried calling him," Petra added.

"We we're supposed to head out for a burger," Theo offered. "Did he park the boat somewhere to keep it out of the storm? We hooked it up to the truck last night."

Ian came around to join Harper and Petra on the other side of the desk. "If the truck is gone, so is the boat, I guess."

"What?" Harper jerked his head up from the screen.

Theo watched as the expression on Harper's face changed. The easygoing smile vanished.

"Oh God. You don't' think…." Harper stopped midsentence.

"I kind of screwed things up," Theo admitted. "We had planned to take the boat out for its maiden voyage, but I had an emergency call at work and had to stay back. When I talked to Alex, he was bummed, but it sounded like he understood. We agreed to take it out as soon as we could. That's really all I know."

They all stood in silence.

"He hasn't been here all afternoon." Harper dug out his cell and checked it for messages. "Nothing. Shit!"

"He took it out on his own. I know he did." Ian started pacing around the office. "He's such an independent little shit. That's exactly what he did. Oh God. I can't believe this."

"We don't know that for sure. But I have to agree. Knowing Alex, that's probably what he would have been inclined to do." Harper joined Ian and Theo in front of the desk.

"Okay, I don't mean to be snarky here, but has anyone tried calling him again?" Petra appeared to be the only one who still had a level head on her shoulders.

"Here." Harper fished his phone out again. After dialing, he waited. "It went directly to voice mail. He must be talking to someone."

"What are we going to do if he's out on the lake?" Ian asked. "The boat is so small. I don't even think there were life jackets on board. He had it on his list to pick a few up at Pamida."

"Where else could he be?" Petra looked out the window. "Try his cell again."

Harper put the phone to his ear and waited. "Nope. Same thing. Goes right to voice mail. What time is it, Petra?"

Petra walked back behind the desk and looked at her computer screen. "Five on the nose. Why?"

"Are you thinking about how much daylight is left if there needs to be a search?" Ian plopped down in one of the chairs by the window.

"Yeah, something like that. I don't know what I'm thinking. I feel sick." Harper leaned into the desk and rested his head in his hands.

"Oh God." Ian bolted out of his chair to resume pacing. "What a fucking nightmare. What are we going to do?"

"We should call the police." Harper glanced around the room. "They're probably familiar with this kind of thing. There's only a few hours of light left, so we need to get something happening now."

"I'll call." Petra began typing on the keyboard.

"No!" Harper barked as he came around the counter. "I want to talk to them. I'm sorry, Petra. Let me introduce you to Harper the control freak. I've no ability right now to try and filter myself."

Theo had never heard Harper speak in such a harsh way. The tone of his voice had an immediate effect on Ian, who threw a punch at the wall.

"Ian, don't go there." Harper wasn't any less direct with his partner. "Keep it together. Alex is strong and resourceful."

"Harper, here's the number." Petra gestured to the computer screen.

"Dial 911." Ian yelled. "Christ, dial 911."

"Why don't I take a spin over to the marina? If his truck is there with the boat trailer, well...." Theo wasn't sure how he could help, but it was clear the atmosphere in the office was disintegrating into a barely controlled panic. *I have to get out of here.*

"Good idea," Harper agreed. "Call us when you get there."

"Sure." Theo crossed the room to the door.

"Theo?" Harper followed him. "If Alex's truck *is* there, check to see if anyone around saw him? It's possible he talked to someone and they might know something that could help."

Alone in the truck, Theo couldn't dodge the fear that was starting to manifest itself. *Please don't be there, Alex. Call me or someone back at the office to let us know you're in town somewhere where you could back the boat into a shed to protect it from the storm.*

The minute he turned into the marina, his worst fears were realized. Alex's truck was parked next to an old van. The boat trailer was empty. *Fuck!*

His first reaction was to hop out and head toward the water. *Maybe now that the storm has passed he's on his way back in.* Running to the end of the dock, his hopes were dashed when he saw the dark bank of storm clouds still over the water. One lone sailboat with the sails down crept toward the Duluth Harbor.

There was nothing wrong with the engine. Theo tried to comfort himself, but it didn't work. The combined disappointment of finding the empty trailer and not being able to spot a small boat with a handsome green-eyed boyfriend speeding toward the marina overwhelmed him as he walked back toward Alex's truck. For the first time since leaving the others back at the resort, Theo slipped up and permitted his fear of losing Alex to surface. *Stop that right now! You know the rule. When you think bad things, they happen.*

Reaching Alex's truck, he peered into the cab. *That explains it.* Alex's cell was sitting on the seat. Leaning his head against the window, he stared at the phone. *What were you thinking, Alex? I've never seen you without your phone.* Theo closed his eyes in an effort to corral the tidal wave of emotion on the verge of crashing over him.

He was brought back to the moment when a beat-up old station wagon came roaring into the lot. It parked next to the little marina office. A dude in dirty overalls got out and stepped into the shabby building. Following Harper's instructions, Theo jogged over and knocked on the banged-up screen door. "Hey." He waved to the dude, who had just lit a cigarette.

"What can I do for ya?" the man asked, blowing a thick cloud of smoke into the air.

"I think a friend of mine might have launched a boat from here earlier." Theo pointed over to Alex's truck and trailer. "Any chance you saw him or he told you what his plans might be?"

The man walked over to the door and peered out. "Can't say that I seen anything. Never seen that truck before either. A friend of yours, you say?"

Even through the screen, Theo could smell the pungent fumes of whiskey. "Yeah. I was hoping he might of checked in here and maybe told you what his plans were."

"Bad weather kept everyone away. Like I said, ain't seen nobody around here today. What he look like?"

Theo stepped back. The smoke was hitting him right in the face. "Never mind."

"I'm just askin' so that if I see someone, I'll know to say somethin'. That's all."

Pour yourself another drink and go fuck yourself. Theo turned and, without answering, walked back to his truck.

"If your friend was out on the water durin' that storm, there's a good chance he's not comin' back."

Theo stopped. *Don't. If you go after him, you'll end up killing the dude. He's an idiot.* Desperately hoping for a positive sign that Alex was safe, Theo walked down to the edge of the water. *One last look.* There wasn't a boat in sight. The imposing bank of clouds appeared to be out in the big part of the lake. *Alex. Please come home to me.* Theo got into his truck and picked up his phone. "The truck and trailer are here," is all he managed to get out to Harper before he was forced to end the call. Choking back sobs, he headed back to the others.

WAVES continued to batter the boat into the jagged shore. Alex was too stunned to move at first. When *My Woody* had come into contact with the rocks, he had been thrust headfirst into the dashboard. He reached up to explore a throbbing sensation above his right eye and was horrified at the amount of blood on his hand. Understanding the need to stop the flow, he removed his soaked T-shirt and wrapped it around his head bandana fashion.

A loud crack coming from the hull made him jump. *The boat is breaking apart.* The waves showed no signs of letting up. Looking down to his feet in response to the sound below, he spotted the tiny anchor. Hoisting it up onto the bow, Alex hung onto the windshield and tossed it as far as he could. The boat had been turned so that its stern was pounding against the island.

I need to get the hell off of this thing before I get hurt even worse.

The shore was flatter over to his left. A wave crashed into the boat, and after it retreated, Alex climbed onto the rock before the next one could hit. Careful not to slip or get his leg trapped in one of the deep crevices, he climbed over to the anchor. He carried it up to one of the trees lining the bank, wrapping the line around the trunk so the boat would stay put at least for as long as it held together.

He reached into his pocket, and his heart sank when he discovered his phone was missing. *You dink! You left it in the truck. Now what are you going to do?* The sky was beginning to lighten up. The storm was moving away. If he had any luck at all, the sun would come out and at least warm the air.

What happens now?

Alex tried to visualize what might be happening back at home. *Theo should stop by looking for me soon. They'll find out I took the boat out and send help.* Judging by the angle of the sun, he had at least a few hours of light left. *They'll find me. Harper and Ian will be mad as hell, but they'll send someone out to find me. Alex, you are one lucky dude. You could have gone to the bottom of the lake.* "Fuck."

The waves appeared to be lessening in strength. Alex walked back down the rock to see if he could determine the damage. "Shit." Right away, he spotted a crack in the hull where a sharp, protruding rock had stabbed through the wood. *There's no way I'm going to be able to get this thing running again. I'm shipwrecked. How long will I be stuck here*, Alex asked himself. *Maybe overnight.*

Now that the adrenaline from fear of drowning had dissipated, Alex felt chilled. *I need to come up with a survival plan.* It would get cold tonight, and if he didn't figure out a way to stay warm, he wouldn't be around in the morning. *Hypothermia.* Growing up near the lake, a very cold lake, stories of fishermen dying of hypothermia were abundant. Parents taught their kids early on to watch for the signs or, better yet, never to put themselves into a situation where they were at risk.

Fucked that up. What am I going to do?

"The boat tarp." Alex remembered an old canvas boat cover was stored down where he had found the anchor. It covered the entire boat and would at least offer protection from the cool air. A plan was starting to gel. The cooler was still on board. At least he thought it was. There were two more Dews left, a bag of chips, and a candy bar. He'd have to ration his supplies, but his chances were getting better. He'd be able to make it through the night if he had to.

You won't be here all night. The guys will figure it out.

Alex spent the next few minutes making trips in and out of the boat. He located the tarp, and although there were a few rips in it, there was plenty of material to wrap up in for warmth. The cooler was on the floor in the back with its contents spilled out. He repacked it and ran it up to the shore. Next, he went after the cushions. If he could keep his body off the cold, damp ground, he stood a better chance of staying warm.

I wish I had something to build a fire with. If he was still here tomorrow and the sun was out, maybe he could use something on the boat as a reflector and start a fire on shore so anyone passing would be more likely to spot him.

Having just tossed the cushions onto the rock, he heard the sound of a motor. *Where the hell is it?* Alex searched the lake to find the source. *Please let someone see me here.* A sailboat under motor with its sails bunched around the mast rounded the point and headed out over open water toward Duluth.

"Help!" Alex hollered as loudly as he could. "Help me! Help me!" Jumping up and down, he waited to see if anyone onboard had heard him. *Where is everyone?* "Help! Help me!" he screamed out. The boat was as close now as it was going to get. "Anyone there? Help! Help me!" And then it dawned on him why nobody was out on the deck of the boat. *Autopilot.* They were probably all snug and warm below, having hot chocolate and laughing about how fun it was to weather the storm in a big boat.

Placing the cushions on the closest flat surface, Alex wrapped himself up in the tarp and watched the boat round the corner of the island and vanish. *Hang in there, buddy. This could be a long night.*

"PLEASE call my cell with any updates." Harper rattled off his cell number and then repeated it to the dispatcher in an overabundance of caution. "We appreciate everything you can do. Yes, I'll call if we find out anything more on this end. But right now, were not sure what Alex's plan was. Right. Thank you."

"What did they say?" Ian had spent the entire time Harper was on the phone inches from his partner's ear.

"They're going to start searching right away. The dispatcher said they would send out their own boats from Two Harbors and also involve the Coast Guard. Most likely they'll send out a plane too." Harper placed his phone on the counter and tried to collect himself.

"What do they do when the sun goes down?" Hopelessness seemed to ooze out of Ian's every pore.

"They search until they find him. They go all night if they have to." Harper turned and rubbed his partner's neck.

"Hello, is Betsy Bender there? This is a personal call."

Harper and Ian both looked over to Petra to see what she was up to.

"Hey, sweets, it's me." Petra listened for a moment and then appeared to interrupt. "We have an emergency here. I need your help."

Petra started in on the details of Alex, but this time she was cut off.

"Betsy says they've received the call and are already preparing a boat to head out. They just came back from rescuing some folks who were in a small sailboat when the storm hit."

"Ask her to call you if she hears anything." Harper was thankful they had an inside connection with the Coast Guard. The more attention this search got, the better for Alex.

"Betsy wants us to call the station if we find out anything about Alex's plans." As Petra listened, she shifted her focus back and forth from Ian to Harper.

"Thanks, honey. We really appreciate all you can do. Bye." Petra attempted a smile. "They're the experts. Guys, they'll find Alex. They treat someone missing as a really big deal."

"Where do you think he'd go?" Ian walked back behind the counter, trading places with Petra, who had been standing in front of the computer searching for a website that would offer more information on the area islands.

"From my understanding, the boat can really fly. I suppose he could have traveled quite a ways in a short time." Harper walked back and sat in the chair.

The screen door opened, and the dad from Cabin seven walked in. Roger. They all had learned his name from their brief time together in the basement waiting out the storm. Roger's wife was Angela, and the two boys were Anthony and Kurt. "Hello."

"Hi, Roger," Petra greeted him. "Can I help you?"

"I was wondering if I could buy a few more of those S'more kits."

"How many would you like? They're complimentary." Petra stood by the door to the apartment.

"Could I trouble you for three? They're a huge hit with the boys." The dad looked sheepishly over to Ian and Harper, hoping they understood where he was coming from. "We're really enjoying our stay here," he added. "I'd be happy to gather up branches if you need some help."

"We can manage on our own, but if you're looking for a little exercise, sure, we'd love it if you gave us a hand." Ian glanced up from the computer for a millisecond.

Harper could see that both Ian and Petra were trying very hard to appear as if nothing was going on when, in fact, at least for Ian, he was shitting his pants with worry. Although rare, the look was unmistakable. The last time Harper witnessed it was about a year ago. Ian's sister Monica called to tell them Ian's nephew, Kyle, had been seriously injured during a high school football game. Thankfully it had turned out to be a bad bruising and not something more serious.

"Why don't I start by cleaning up what I can from around our area and stacking it behind the cabin? I'm looking for anything I can involve the boys in that helps to burn off a sugar high."

"Perfect." Ian smiled.

"Here's the S'more kits. Enjoy!" Petra slid them across the counter.

"Thanks again. Have a nice night."

"You too." Harper felt compelled to say something for, up until then, he'd sat silent, allowing Ian and Petra to deal with their guest.

"Here's a map of the Apostle Islands. He could have easily crossed over to Sand Island. That's relatively close. It has a dock, from what I can tell from this image. York Island is close too, but no dock." Ian pulled the stool out from under the counter and sank onto it, shaking his head.

"What's wrong?" The look of fear on Ian's face challenged Harper to remain composed.

"There are so many places he could be. I don't know where you would start. Harper...."

Ian had reached the wall. He thrashed his arms back and forth, sending papers flying off in all directions. His eyes filled with tears. "This can't be happening," he hollered out in despair.

Petra was closest and came to the rescue first. "Honey, they'll find him. They have systems and techniques for this that we can't even imagine. It's their job."

As Petra tried to supply comfort from her side, Harper leaned over the counter and held Ian's face in his hands. "Ian. We can't ever give up hope. Not for a second. Alex is very smart. Very practical. We have to believe in him, sport. We have to."

THANKFUL he was finally starting to get warm, Alex kept up hope a boat would come close enough to where he was stranded for him to hail it and catch a ride home. His hopes were sinking at about the same rate as the sun, which had just dipped below the trees on the horizon. *It's gonna be a long night, buddy. Don't freak. You'd better make good use of what light remains.*

Unwrapping himself from the tarp, he climbed up the rock to where the island's vegetation began. The first few steps were difficult. His body hurt all over, and the pain from the injury above his eye caused his head to ache. *Push yourself.* The brush was very dense but for a few openings that gave him a glimpse into the dark edges of the forest. The perfect setup would be to find a spot to put down for the night that still offered him a view of the boat and the water directly in front of it. The last thing he wanted to do was miss out on being rescued because he couldn't see.

On the walk back he found what he'd been looking for. Moving in deeper, he stood in the spot he hoped would shelter him from the wind that had picked up over the last hour, yet provide a clear visual path out to the water. *This will work. Not as windy back in here.*

It was starting to grow dark when Alex finished his preparations. Everything he thought he would need for the night was hauled up into his little camping spot. Earlier, he had made the decision to refer to this whole ordeal as one big camping adventure. Somehow the mess he found himself in didn't seem all that bad that way. *The camping trip from fucking hell!* It was almost comical. But not. *Damn, do you know how close you came to biting it out on the lake? You're one lucky dickhead.*

Although it wasn't his favorite way to sleep, Alex thought it best if he were propped up against the trunk of a tree so he could keep his eyes on the water. He placed one cushion against the tree and positioned the other on the ground. The tarp was spread out and then refolded into a smaller, thicker mass of material he hoped would keep him warm as the temperature dipped through the night.

Time to call it a day, buddy. We have a full schedule of hiking tomorrow. Hey, but what about dinner?

Anxiety had kept his appetite at bay, but his practical gene told him it might be wise to eat something. *Treat yourself. You deserve it.* Alex crawled over, took out a soda, and opened the bag of chips. *Naw. Save these for later.* He grabbed the candy bar, leaving the rest in the cooler until later that night or early in the morning. *Can't hike on an empty stomach, buddy.*

Wrapped back up, he extended his elbows to create a space for his hands to move around. *I need a bigger tent.* He tossed the candy bar wrapper outside and took the tiniest bite he could manage. He closed his eyes and savored the rich chocolate taste before swallowing. Over and over, he repeated this process of small nibbles until the bar was completely consumed. By eating slowly, he had eliminated the feeling of hunger. *At least for now.*

Shit! With the light almost gone, Alex had to sacrifice comfort one more time to pee. *I hope it doesn't get much colder than this. Damn.* Several feet away, he gave the plants a good soaking. "Yes!" He voiced to the open air as he stuffed himself back into his shorts. He was cheered up by a large, bright moon that had crept over the trees, its reflection sending waves of light off the water onto the island. *This isn't going to be so bad, buddy.* He cracked open his soda and rewrapped his body in the musty fabric, leaving only a small opening to see out of. As with the candy bar, he savored every sip of his Dew.

You forgot to pack the television. Idiot! What would you watch if you had a television? Alex mulled this over for few minutes and then realized that the stupid trick he was playing on himself to keep his fear and anxiety at bay wasn't worth the effort. *Well, what should we do next? Theo. Let's go visit Theo.*

This would be the perfect time to think about how to move forward with his inexperienced new boyfriend. One of the first things he would do when they were back together would be to have a talk about sex. Why? *Because Theo needs to be reassured I can wait. I have to make sure he understands I'm in no hurry.* Alex admired Theo for putting the brakes on that aspect of their relationship. The last thing he wanted was to disrespect Theo's need for them to move at his pace in that department. *Thank God he likes your dick, buddy. Stop it!*

So the sex talk had to be top of the list. After that, they would discuss what else they needed from each other. Alex was surprised he didn't already have this list prepared. But the more he thought about it, his needs boiled down to two things. Two people, actually. Ian and Harper. *If I could have what they have, I'd be the happiest person in the whole world. So, what do they have? They trust and respect each other. They're both good people with big hearts.* And they were both honest. Alex couldn't come up with a single instance when he thought one of them might not be telling the truth. It wasn't in their game plan. So, if he and Theo could be honest, respect each other, and always trust, they would be off to a good start.

What's next? Alex was interrupted by the sound of a plane. For a brief second, he thought about crawling out of his safe, warm haven but then remembered there was enough boat tied up to the rocks for anyone who was looking to spot him. The new windshield would reflect any light that shone on it. That was a plus. Curiosity finally got the best of him. He pulled his head out to listen. *Is that plane searching for me? Is it getting closer or moving on?* His ears got cold, so he ducked back into his shelter. The plane roared overhead a second time. Alex tore his tent away from his face and listened. This time, the noise diminished much faster, until the only sound he heard was from the light chop coming in from the lake. Every now and then it would move the boat tighter against the rock, causing a sound that made him wince. The boat was in agony, voicing its anger for having been wrecked.

The next most important thing, other than Theo, Alex thought as he repositioned himself for maximum comfort, was his new house. *You've hardly thought about it, and it's coming up soon.* On some level, he understood why the house didn't occupy a more prominent place in his thoughts. First: for weeks he was led to believe he had lost it, his bid being rejected so the owner's daughter could move in. Second: the argument for moving into the house was as strong as the one that nagged him to stay put. Why give up something as good as having Ian and Harper for roomies? Then it hit him like a ton of bricks. *Hell, I never thought of that. Damn!*

How wrong was it *not* to think that maybe Ian and Harper were ready to have the house back for themselves? *Buddy, how could you have not figured that one out?* The thought made him angry and mad at himself for being so insensitive. *Those guys love you so much they're willing to open their lives to you. Give you anything you need. What's theirs is yours. No questions asked.*

Maybe I've overstayed my welcome. This was too painful for Alex to dwell on. Closing his eyes in the hope it could be deleted, he found himself drifting. *Just close your eyes for a few minutes. It'll be okay.*

THEY had hung out in the office for as long as possible, but when word of Alex's rescue wasn't immediately forthcoming, like zombies, Harper led everyone back to the house. Petra had placed the sign on the desk informing guests to call if they needed anything. Harper was glad to have her around. Theo too, but he was hard to read. Stoic. The look on his face seemed frozen, and other than to nod or voice agreement, he kept pretty quiet. *Theo must be terrified, and he's trying so hard not to let on. The quiet types are always so strong.* Ian was becoming more and more of a challenge, as Alex's fate was still unknown. For himself, Harper knew he couldn't go there. *Hope. You owe Alex your strongest hope for his survival. That's all you can do for him from so far away.* He had to be strong. Experience had taught him that, once he allowed emotion to enter the room, there would be no turning back. That's how he was put together. Ian was born without a shield. You almost always knew how he was feeling. The only exception to this rule was when he was pissed off. He got quiet. But even then, you knew what was going on because, even quiet, you could always spot the anger. Ian was simple in a very good way.

"Betsy didn't know anything more since the last time I called. The search is beginning to go deeper into the Apostles. They're hoping to spot the boat tied up at one of the docks. Many of the islands have them, but not all. Stockton Island has a ranger station, and they've asked personnel there to talk with the other boaters to find out if they may have seen him. There's a lot of territory to cover. The last thing she said to me was that we should be thankful nothing has been found yet. That's almost a better place to be right now. Anyway"—Petra filled her glass from the pitcher of ice tea she had made earlier—"she promised to call if she hears anything."

"Thanks, Petra." Harper stared at the plate of food on the counter. Ian, needing something to take his mind off of Alex, had thrown together an assortment of sandwiches. They sat untouched. No one had an appetite. "Theo, are you sure you don't want anything to eat? How about a soda?"

"I know where they are. You don't have to wait on me."

"Okay, then I'll trust you have what you need." Harper walked over and patted the young man's shoulder. "He's a toughie, Theo. You'll get him back. I'm sure of it." Harper couldn't help how corny this last bit sounded. Honestly, he didn't care. He said it more for himself, he realized, than anyone.

"I'll be back in a minute." Ian wandered out of the kitchen.

"I wish I could help him," Petra whispered after Ian had left the room.

"I know. He's so torn up right now. I don't know what's going to happen if…." Harper caught himself. He and Petra jumped when Harper's phone went off. "Harper Callahan."

"Oh, Andy, hi. Listen, we have an emergency going on here. I can't talk long."

Harper did his best to bring Andy up to speed without going into unnecessary speculation.

"I'll make sure one of us calls you to let you know they've found him. Sure. I don't mind if you tell them, but don't have people calling here. We need to keep the phones open. That's sweet, Andy, but why don't you and Em stay put. We're just barely managing here, and the whole atmosphere is just, well, it's fragile." Fearful they had already spent too much time tying up the line, Harper began to pace in hopes of speeding Andy up. "He just left the room, but I'll tell him. I'm sure he'll appreciate you're all thinking of him, of us. Bye."

"It must be hard to hear news like ours and not be able to do anything to help." Petra, with her glass of tea in hand, sat on the stool at the end of the breakfast bar. "I'd be going crazy if I was Andy."

Harper agreed but didn't have the energy to waste on furthering this line of thought. He took a sandwich off the plate, reached for a napkin, and spread it out. Taking a bite, he placed the sandwich back on the napkin. It didn't taste good. Ham and cheese. His favorite in happier times, but now, it did nothing for him. He glanced at his watch. Ten forty-five. *Where are you, Alex? Are you warm? Are you safe? Are you alive? That's it. I have to keep moving.* "I'm going to find Ian. I'll be back in a minute."

"Take your time." Petra reached for a cooking magazine and began paging through it.

"Ian?" Harper called down the hall. When there wasn't any answer, he walked all the way to the entertainment room. *Maybe he's watching television. Trying to keep his mind off of Alex.* Harper was encouraged when he heard the sound of a baseball game, but the room was empty. *Bathroom? Nope.* The door was open, which wouldn't be all that unusual for Ian even with guests in the house, but not this time. He wasn't there. *Oh, come on. I don't need this shit right now. If you went for a walk or something and didn't tell us, I'm really going to be pissed off. The last thing I need is to worry about you too.*

Surprised at how easily he angered, he charged down the hall, passing through the kitchen. "Any sign of Ian?"

"No. You mean he isn't down there? I could have sworn I saw him leave in that direction. I'm so fucked up right now," Petra admitted wearily, "I don't know if I'm coming or going. I *thought* I saw him go that way, but maybe not."

Theo shook his head to indicate he hadn't seen Ian either.

"Yeah, me too. But I'm in the same state. I'm halfway here and halfway somewhere else." At the same time Harper finished his sentence, he had solved the "where is Ian" problem. "Hang on. I think I know where he is."

Harper braced himself. This was Alex's hall. He peered into the bathroom, but it was empty. When he got to Alex's room, he stopped. The door was open, but the room was dark. Harper leaned forward and listened. *I knew it. Oh, sweetie. I don't know what I can do for you other than to let you know I love you.*

He stepped into the room. Enough light filtered in from the hallway to make out most of the details. The bed was empty. The chair was pushed up snug against the desk. The sobbing came from the corner near the closet. Moving around the bed, he almost stepped on Ian, who was huddled on the floor.

"Sorry. I'm…." Ian struggled. Deep, heart-wrenching sobs robbed his partner of the ability to speak.

"Don't apologize. I have no idea why I'm not emotional. In my heart, I am. I'm very scared, Ian."

"I'm… so scared… right now," Ian cried out. "We can't lose him. I can't. I love him so much."

Harper was on the verge of breaking down. *Hang tough.* He eased himself down onto the floor. His eyes had adapted to the dark. He could see that Ian was crying into Alex's hoodie. "Don't give up hope. That's all we have. Alex needs us to shine a light his way." Unable to buy into his own argument, he added, "There's no easy way to get through this."

"Part of the reason…." Ian had something he had to say. "I was thinking back to when you were shot and I thought I was going to lose you. Oh...." Ian wailed, and Harper scooted up to hold him, fully understanding the link.

"Let it go, honey. Just let it go. Alex knows that he's your special friend. He's going to come back to us. I know he is. He loves you too much to let you get away."

"I hope he isn't cold and scared...." Ian cried out again.

"Me too. I hope that so much." Not knowing how long he'd be able to last, Harper got back up on his knees. "Stay here as long as you want. I promise to run and get you if I hear anything. Just do what you need to do. I have to keep going or I'm going to self-destruct. I love you, Ian."

"I love you so much." Ian reached out and squeezed Harper's hand.

"Did you find him?" Petra asked when Harper had returned to the kitchen.

"Yeah. Ian's in Alex's room. He's not doing very well. I told him to stay put. That we'd come and get him if we heard any news."

"I was thinking about what Betsy said earlier. I know you latch on to whatever you can at times like this, but, given the circumstances, I guess I like the no-news-is-good-news theory more and more." Petra looked over and shrugged.

Petra's comment carried Harper back to when he practiced law. Specifically, what it was like to read a jury. You thought you knew, but many times you were taken by surprise. The jury was out on Alex.

THEO moved about the house as if he were in a trance, too stricken with fear to stay in the same spot for long. He was going nuts and had to do something. Anything to take his mind off of possibly losing Alex. Racing past a handful of stations dedicated to local broadcasting, he landed on a reality show where an accident was being reenacted. He watched with interest for several minutes until an interview with a surviving family kicked in a new wave of anxiety. *This could be me, us.* It hit too close to home, and he sprang from the sofa and bolted from the room. Midway down the long hallway, he stopped.

It's worth a try. At least I'll know I did everything I could to help Alex.

Theo remembered spotting a pen and paper on one of the end tables next to where he had been sitting. Walking back to the entertainment room, he sat and, after only a moment to decide what he wanted to write, carefully printed his message. When he was finished, he pocketed the piece of paper and headed toward the kitchen, which had become ground zero.

Petra was seated at the counter, staring at a magazine. Harper and Ian were nowhere in sight. Sensing the time was right to make his move, he placed his note on the kitchen counter and made a direct path to the back door.

Coming to the end of the road leading into the resort, Theo turned onto the highway. He drove in silence without seeing another car in either direction. It wasn't long before he slowed, signaled, and pulled into the parking lot, empty, except for a bus used for field trips. He parked behind the large vehicle to prevent anyone from the road spotting his truck.

The sky, littered with stars and anchored by a bright moon, seemed surreal to Theo. *Does Alex see what I'm seeing?* In a group of low-lying shrubs, several feet from the front door, he kneeled on the concrete and, after a few swipes of his hand beneath the undergrowth, found what he was looking for inside of a small plastic container. *Yes! At least my mother is good for something.*

Sliding the key into the lock, he pushed open the large oak door and stepped inside. The smell was at once familiar and triggered a barrage of images from his past. Moving through an entrance hall, he palmed the wall until he located a bank of light switches.

What if someone sees a light on and stops to investigate?

Peering into the cavernous space, his eyes soon adjusted to the dark. With the added help of moonlight seeping in from the narrow side windows, he was able to see well enough to continue inside. He crept down the wide aisle, sliding onto a wooden bench near the front.

Theo had a lot on his mind. There were many things he wanted to say. Where to start was the problem. Minutes passed as he tried out in his mind various ways to begin. Resting his hand on the pew in front, he looked up and witnessed something that made the hair on the back of his neck stand on end.

The moon, so full and bright, had shifted just enough in the sky to begin illuminating the large stained-glass window behind the altar. *Wow!* The rich, jewel-toned image of Christ hanging from the cross was no stranger to him. The ornate work of art had been there longer than he had lived on this earth. Where it had once offered comfort and, on occasion, distraction from boredom, now it fueled anger and rage. Theo's heart raced.

"You heard right." He sat on the edge of the pew. "I said, you heard right!" Theo shouted. "I'm gay!" His voice reverberated through the church. "I'm proud of who I am," he continued. "No apologies or repentance, if that's what you're looking for. Not a chance!"

The adrenaline was pumping. Unable to manage the surge of energy seated, he stood. His anger roared back. "It's just you and me now. So strike me down if you want," Theo hollered out. "I'm all alone. I don't have you. I don't have my family. It's just me. Gay me." Pacing between the rows with a vengeance, he added, "You were no help to me at all, God. Thanks for fucking nothing! Thanks for making me feel like shit."

Half expecting a response, he paused. When only silence answered, he slumped back down in his seat. Tears filled his eyes. "I deserve to be loved. And you know something else? I don't feel like this is my home anymore. Haven't for a long time. I don't trust what they say here." Not really thinking, he added, "That's my problem, I guess, not yours." His train of thought softened his voice. Theo focused on the majestic back-lit window and wept. "I'm working on it. I'm working on a lot of things right now, but that's not why I'm here."

Wiping the tears from his eyes, he stood and stepped out into the aisle. Walking up the small bank of stairs, he moved to the center of the altar.

"I need your help," Theo whispered. "You see, someone loves me. Alex. His name is Alex. You might take him away. Please," he pleaded, "if you have any mercy, spare his life." Tears streamed down his cheeks. In another burst of defiance, he raised his voice and begged, "Do whatever it is you have to do, but please don't punish me by hurting Alex."

Silenced by emotion, Theo brought his hands up to this face and bawled. How wrong this was to come here. How could he ask for help after he'd turned his back on his church, on his God? When he removed his hands and looked out, he was awash in color. The moon had moved enough distance in the sky to shine directly onto the center of the glass. He'd never seen anything quite like it.

Staring up into the radiance, he voiced his thoughts. "Part of me misses you so much. You meant so much to me. I trusted you." Aware of his rambling, he relaxed his shoulders and decided to continue. "I miss so many things. I miss my dad. I miss how it felt to be held by him, knowing he loved me. I don't think he does anymore. I don't miss Mom. Can't talk to her anymore about anything. She seems so angry all the time." Theo laughed through his tears, the absurdity of the moment catching up. "She's not your best effort, and you know it. You have to. Don't bring harm to her, but come on, be honest—there're a lot nicer people walking around.

"So anyway"—he struggled to focus—"when I met Alex, I fell in love... I am so happy. He's kind, Father, and he helps people. And he loves *me*. I *need* him."

Feeling as if he'd said all he could, he turned and stepped down from the altar. It felt good to let go. Pulling the key out of his pocket, he strolled toward the entrance. As if to say a final good-bye, he turned back. The moon had moved now, and the image of Christ had faded. Not sure what to make of it, he exited the church, locking the door and replacing the key, returning it to its home under the shrub.

On his way to his truck, a shooting star with a brilliant trail streaked across the sky. He took it as a sign. A good sign.

AT FIRST, Alex thought he might be dreaming. A loud sniffing sound came from somewhere very close. Todd used to snore in his sleep. *What the*.... He opened his eyes and quickly realized his ex-boyfriend wasn't lying next to him after all. It took a few seconds to wake up to the point where he remembered where he was. But the sniffing, followed occasionally by a low grunt, continued.

Fear blossomed into panic. *It has to be a bear. Don't move! He might attack. A deer*.... A deer wouldn't make these types of noises. *Please no.* Alex wasn't sure what a bear sounded like, but he had a feeling he wasn't wrong on this one. Panic crashed over him when he remembered the can of Dew nestled between his legs. *Oh, please don't go after it.* Alex stifled a cry when whatever it was brushed the fabric next to his face and grunted. He felt the warmth of his own piss.

Holding his breath, he used every resource he could pull from not to cry out. The only option was to stay completely still and hope the bear lost interest. *Leave me alone, bear.*

To his great relief, the bear sniffed a few more times and then, if he could trust his ability to hear, appeared to be moving away.... *The cooler!* Alex listened as the bear attacked the cooler. Eventually, the cover dislodged. He heard a crinkling sound. *He's going for the chips. Thank God. They're yours. Just please go away.*

Alex had to sit silently for several more minutes as he listened to the chip bag being ripped open and then the bear eating. At one point, he entertained the idea of running for it. Running into the water or taking refuge in what remained of the boat. It's the middle of the night. You won't be able to see. He shifted slightly to release the ache in his back and discovered his peek hole in the fabric had closed while he was asleep. *That might be what saved me.*

Wait. What is that? Alex forced himself to listen. *Is it a boat?* The rumbling grew louder, and Alex was able to determine it was an engine. *Yes! And it's close by.* The bear was still so close he couldn't risk aggravating it, especially if it was eating. *You're fucked. You can't do anything. Hopefully, they see my boat. How could they? It's still dark. Get the fuck out of here, bear.*

Alex was beside himself. The chance of getting rescued was ruined by a bear. *At least your arms and legs haven't been ripped from your body.* There was nothing he could do. He listened as the boat got closer, and then, to his dismay, the sound of the engine faded away. It was passing by. And then he was unable to hear it at all.

The bear gave out a few satisfied grunts. *Finished with the chips? What are you going to do next? Come after me?* Livid at having missed his rescue, Alex geared up for a fight. After another series of snorts, he listened as the bear padded off into the woods. *Finally! That's it. Go somewhere else, bear. Somewhere very far away.*

When he felt enough time had passed, Alex reached up and located the opening in the fabric and was surprised to discover it was starting to get light out. He forced himself to wait a little longer before he popped his head out for a look around.

He was right about the cooler. It was lying on its side, with the chip bag and the unopened can of soda not far away. Alex almost messed himself again when he spotted his candy bar wrapper lying next to the tarp. *You idiot. That's what probably brought him so close to you.*

Steam rose off the lake into the cool morning air, creating an eerie effect like you'd see in a slasher movie. *The boat probably didn't even see* My Woody *through the fog.* To avoid another unwanted visit from Boo Boo, Alex hauled his makeshift tent, cushions and all, down to the rocks. The boat hadn't changed much from when he last saw it. The lake had calmed. *I hope* Woody *doesn't get ripped up any more than it is already. There still might be a chance to salvage it.*

The worst was over, but he needed to stay warm. He had made it through the night in one piece. His shorts were soaked with pee, but he wasn't going to do anything about it until the sun came out. Then he'd wash up and dry them on the rock while he waited. *Okay, you can rescue me now. Anytime. This was a blast, but I've had enough of this camping trip to last a lifetime.* He sat down, wrapped the tarp around his shoulders, and stared out into the mist.

"WHAT are you thinking?" Harper joined Ian, who was standing on the porch staring into the woods.

"I'm happy it's getting light out, I guess." Ian's voice was weak.

"I bet the air search has already started up again. I wonder how many of the islands they still have to cover."

Harper didn't have much energy left either. He had been operating on this strange plateau of squelched emotion for so long now, he was getting used to it. Petra had at some point managed to fall asleep at the kitchen counter. Theo, the last time he had checked, was staring blankly at the television. The night had been horrific on so many levels it was hard to identify a low point. On and on it went, with very little outside communication. Petra had several calls with Betsy. They were nothing more than reassurances that everything possible was being done to find Alex.

"Harper. Get in here. It's your phone."

Startled initially by the breach in silence, Harper raced into the kitchen with Ian hot on his trail. "Harper here."

With his head bowed for strength, he listened. His eyes reacted first by welling up, and tears spilled over onto his cheeks. His legs were next, forcing him down onto the floor. "They found him. He's safe. He's *alive.*" All of the emotion he had so valiantly fought back through the course of the night exploded out of every pore. Tossing his phone across the floor, he sat hunched over himself and cried. Ian joined him. He felt his partner's strong arms wrap around his shoulders. They were joined by Petra, who wept like a baby.

"Theo," Harper screamed when he could. "Theo!"

"What is it?" Theo, wide-eyed, brought his hand up to his mouth when he walked into the kitchen.

"They found Alex. He's fine."

"I thought he was dead." Theo stumbled over to the counter. For a second, all eyes were on him. "Thank you, God! Thank you for listening to me. I owe you big time!" he hollered, thrusting his arms into the air. Sitting at the counter, he buried his head in his hands and wept.

Harper wiped his face on the sleeve of his sweatshirt and, after a few staggered steps, got back on his feet. "Oh, my lord, I'm so relieved."

They moved about the room in silence. It was the news they had all prayed for. The amount of energy it had taken to get through the night left little for celebration. Raising his head and arms to the ceiling, Harper cried out, "Thank you! Thank you for watching over our Alex. I'm so very thankful!"

"Who was on the phone?" Petra was laughing now through her tears. "I'm just going to say this... I sincerely hope you ground green-eyes for a year."

Everyone cracked up and nodded in agreement.

"The Lake City rescue squad. A fishing trawler on its way back from emptying its nets early this morning spotted the boat on the rocks of Bear Island. I think that's what the dispatcher said."

"I've been on Bear Island before," Theo said. "It's a huge island."

"The fishermen radioed his location to the Coast Guard. I guess they had a boat pretty close. They rushed over, picked up Alex, and took him to someplace called Roy's Point, where he was met by medical—"

Harper was interrupted by Petra's phone. They watched and listened along with Petra.

"Thank you, Betsy. You have no idea how relieved we all are. I'll call you later. Thank you. I love you too." Petra smiled. "She wanted to make sure Alex was fine before she called. They checked him out, and he's already been released. Someone is driving him home."

Harper considered saying something to the group about how to react when Alex stepped through the door, but then, as quickly as the thought entered his mind, he dismissed it. *Everyone will be fine. Worry about yourself.* His thought was Alex would be exhausted, scared, and maybe disorientated. The last thing he needed was to be bombarded from all sides when he arrived. *Let Alex see for himself how much he means to us.*

"Did anyone say anything about the boat?" Petra emptied the last few drops from her second pitcher of tea.

"Alex no longer owns a boat." Ian was all over this one. "I don't fucking care if the fucking thing is in pristine shape. The boat was a fucking dream. End of story."

The look on Ian's face was so intense that the room fell silent as they all contemplated what he had just said.

"I'd have to agree with you on that one," Harper offered with a weak smile.

THEO wandered into Alex's bedroom and sat on the edge of the bed. The intense fear and worry for Alex's safety had battered him to the ground. The thought of losing his boyfriend was unbearable. In desperation, he had prayed to the same God he had scorned and discarded, in the hope this God would show mercy and bring Alex back to them alive.

When the squad car pulled up a few hours earlier and deposited Alex in one piece, there wasn't a dry eye in the house. The first order of business had been to inspect Alex for injuries. Two stitches above his darkening right eye plus a few bruises was the extent of the physical damage. Extreme hunger was the most immediate issue that needed his attention. Ian whipped up breakfast. They all sat around the kitchen, feasting on blueberry pancakes and bacon as Alex shared the many highlights of his brush with death. Theo wasn't the only one who went silent as Alex described the storm, the lake, and losing control of the boat. When he finally got around to telling about his close encounter with the bear, you could see the smiles reemerge, even though the threat to him then was as real as the storm.

The whole scene reminded Theo of the powerful bond parents have with their children. He watched Ian and Harper react to Alex's story, and he was brought back to an earlier time when he shared the same bond with his own parents. *How did it all get so screwed up? They must know I'm different.*

After breakfast, everyone dispersed to catch up on much-needed sleep. Theo didn't want to leave. *I never want to leave.* When the news had gotten to them that Alex had been rescued, he placed a call to Artie. After a brief explanation of what had gone down, Artie insisted he take the day off. Alex, who was running on some kind of borrowed energy, seemed genuinely happy he was sticking around.

I want to hold you, Alex. I want to tell you what you mean to me and to say… I'm sorry.

Stretching his arms out, he yawned. At some point he would need to shut down. *Not yet.* He was still too wound up. Throughout the night, Theo had experienced spells where he felt physically ill, sick with worry he would never see Alex again. Faced with this frightening prospect, several things crystallized for him. If there was any doubt before now what his real feelings were for his new friend, *boyfriend,* he felt certain he knew the answer. *I love Alex.*

"Hey," Alex called out when he came into the room with a towel wrapped around his waist. "Thanks again for taking the day off. I'd suggest we take the boat out, but oh, wait. I no longer have a boat." Alex chuckled and shrugged.

Ian had made it crystal clear during breakfast that whatever was left of the boat after it was towed back to shore would be of no concern to Alex. The parental tone in Ian's voice was a stark contrast to the jovial inflection Theo had come to expect from him.

Theo watched Alex saunter over to his closet. He bit down on his lip when Alex dropped his towel, exposing his firm, muscled butt. That was all the show he was going to get. *I'm so ready for you.* Alex stepped into a pair of boxers, then picked the towel up from the floor and ran it through his hair a few times. Throwing on a T-shirt, he walked around to where Theo was sitting and plopped down next to him.

"So, did you miss me?" Alex punched Theo in the shoulder.

Maybe it was the lack of sleep, but Alex was full of the devil this morning.

"I missed you, Alex." *This is the perfect time to let him know what's on your mind.*

"Are you mad at me?" Alex pulled his leg up onto the bed and looked over.

"Huh?" *What does he mean? Am I mad at him? Hell no.*

"For putting the boat in the water without you?"

Theo dragged his foot up on the bed so they could face each other. "I never thought that. Maybe it was because there wasn't time. When I got here yesterday, everybody was so freaked out. I guess it never crossed my mind." Theo couldn't resist. He reached over and petted Alex's knee, still warm from the shower. It was a miracle he wasn't killed. "I wasn't surprised you went out on your own. I'm starting to get to know you pretty good."

"I hate it when I'm no longer a mystery." Alex rested his hand on Theo's leg. "We're in the bedroom."

Theo laughed but had to look away. Alex zeroed in on his own thought. "It feels good to be here." *Tell him the rest.* "Listen, I need to say a few things, Alex."

"Okay." Alex brought his other foot up onto the bed and sat cross-legged. "I'm sorry I caused so much worry. I never intended to hurt you or anyone else. I wasn't thinking."

"That's not it at all. I was thinking more about us." Theo looked around the room, searching for what to say next.

"Theo, please give me a chance to make it up to you. I want us to work out. I'm willing to fight for it."

"Alex, stop it. It's not that either. I'm not breaking up with you. I'm giving myself to you, if you'd just let me fuckin' finish." This was an odd comment, and the minute it left his mouth, Theo acknowledged it and laughed. "I mean, you're bouncing all over the place here."

Alex laughed too. "I had a lot of time on the island to think about the future. I've got us pretty well planned out."

Theo smiled. *You're an amazing man, Alex Stevens. Sign me up.* "Sign me up. That's what I want to tell you. I'm over being careful and protective of this whole coming-out shit. When I look around this place and see you, Ian, and Harper, I can't imagine not having the same life. It's so cool to see how you guys act together. I want that too, Alex."

"I can't even think about those guys right now. I owe them such a huge apology for being so reckless. The way Ian looked at me when I walked in the door just about broke my heart."

"I don't think I've ever seen that kind of love before. It was amazing. But what I'm trying to tell you is, take the lead. Show me the way. I think it was a mistake to back away from you sexually, or in any way. You're a great teacher. A great dude to hang with. I need to trust."

Alex looked away. Theo wasn't sure how to read him. *Maybe he thinks the responsibility is too much.*

"Theo, you make it sound like I can't learn from you." Alex turned back. "That's so not true. I think, together, we can find a balance. One of the things I thought about when I was stranded out there was how much I've gotten to know you over the last few weeks because we took sex out of the picture. And don't get me wrong, I'm starved for a piece of you, but I'm willing to wait. So don't rush yourself."

"I'm starved for a piece of you too." Theo leaned in and kissed Alex. *Oh man, I've missed this so much.* "Does it hurt? The cut on your eye?" Theo brushed away Alex's hair and leaned in for a closer look.

"It kind of aches, but not too bad." Alex looked up so Theo could see it from a better angle.

"Well, it looks like you're going to get one hell of a shiner out of the deal. Makes you look kind of butch." Theo winked.

"It does?" Alex leaned over so his head was centered in the mirror on the wall across the room. "Can I guess what piece of me you're starved for the most?"

Theo threw back his head and laughed. "Your dick. It's the truth. I'm starved for your dick."

"Come here." Alex stood and offered his hand to Theo. With a multitude of tender kisses and a few nibbles, they stripped each other. "Theo, your body is so mighty fine I can't believe you share it with me."

Theo stood and watched as Alex traced his finger around each nipple and then journeyed down his chest to his belly button, where it was inserted and pushed a few times. "Sorry, I thought for a minute you were a soda dispenser. Where was I… oh yeah."

Theo needed to hold Alex, but before he had a chance, his boyfriend had dropped to his knees and was reciting some kind of love poem to his penis.

"Hello, Theo's penis. I'm your biggest fan, Alex. If you don't have any other plans, I'm going to give you a tongue bath and then take you out for a nice long walk. It's a beautiful day, and recently I learned that it's a big deal to make the most out of each day because, in a flash, it can all be over." Theo bent his head and watched Alex kiss the tip of his cock.

"Alex," Theo said with a chuckle, "come here." He reached down and pulled Alex back up onto his feet. "I need more of this first." Wrapping his arms around his naked waist, Theo brought Alex up into a tight embrace. "God, it feels so good to just hold you."

"It feels good to be held."

A large yawn, originating from the tip of his toes, reminded Theo of how tired he was. "Sorry. I'm not used to being up all night."

"I don't know where this energy is coming from. I should be crashed by now. I'm so thankful. Thankful to have gotten through that mess. Theo, you have no idea how scary it was. I thought I had bit it."

"I can't imagine. I've never been on the lake during a storm. I have nothing to compare it to." Theo bent forward and placed his lips on Alex's. They took turns kissing one another, their tongues sliding lazily past teeth, the passion between them on the rise. This time Alex stopped the action.

"I know my last attempt at introducing you to something new was a bust, but I think I might have just the ticket for right now. I mean, I don't know about you, but I'm equal parts horny and tired. Let's sixty-nine." Alex stepped back to catch Theo's response.

"Lead the way, Mister Wizard."

Alex guided Theo up onto the bed. "Make sure you're comfy. We're in no rush." Grabbing the pillow next to Theo's head, Alex placed it at Theo's feet and climbed into place. After a few minor adjustments, Alex reached between Theo's legs, cupped his ass in hand, leaned forward, and throated his cock. "Perfect," he announced after Theo glided out of his mouth.

"Let the feast begin," Theo joked. Alex's dick was begging for attention. Theo thought about using his hands but, feeling adventurous, leaned forward and, after a few tentative licks and kisses, eased his boyfriend down his throat until his lips brushed up against a mass of sandy brown pubes.

"Oh yeah...." Alex encouraged between his own licks and plunges. "Take your time. I've been waiting so long for this."

Theo couldn't have agreed more. *This is heaven.*

They sucked and teased each other. Theo felt the familiar build-up in his body. In hopes he and Alex could reach the ultimate goal at the same time, Theo increased his effort, but Alex stalled him, placing his hand on Theo's head to slow him down.

"I'm there too," Alex purred.

Without warning, Alex bucked his body up off the bed and dispensed himself deep into Theo's throat. Seconds later, Theo wrapped his arms tightly around Alex's legs and came in a series of violent body spasms.

They lay side by side panting, lacking the energy to do anything else. Eventually, Alex scooped up his pillow and rested his head next to Theo's. "You know what I enjoy so much about sixty-nine?" he whispered.

"What's that?" said Theo, who was still struggling to catch his breath.

"No fuss, no muss. I'm blessed with an overactive neat gene."

Theo tried to come up with an appropriate response, but halfway through the process, his lights went out.

CHAPTER
Eleven

ALEX sat back in his chair and stared at the canvas.

"See, this is what I'm talking about." Harold pointed to a spot on Alex's paper where he had, in a few simple brushstrokes, created a marvelous tree trunk. "By adding that touch of green to the bark, you've made it come to life. Your color choices and... wait." Harold sat back in his chair. "It's not only your use of color, but it's how thrifty you are with it that really sets your painting apart from so many others. Alex, you treat color like it's money." Harold laughed, and so did Alex.

At the beginning of the session, Harold had shared a book containing some of his most ambitious works. His paintings were in collections all around the world, and, from the photos, Alex could see why. They were wonderful. Bold and expressive. Harold had a thing for color too.

"Well, my young friend"—Harold glanced at his watch—"Quentin's nurse should be packing up about now. When can we meet again?"

Alex had to think. Between the Center, the resort, the closing on his new house, moving, and finding time to be with Theo, his calendar was jam-packed. *You need to set aside time for Harold.* It was only a few hours here and there and not really that big of a deal when he actually thought it through. "Let's see, today is Sunday. Does the nurse visit Quentin on Tuesday morning? If not, I guess Wednesday would work. Thursday would be tough. I close on my house Friday, and I'm planning on moving in over the weekend. I have to pack and organize."

"Next week already? Purchasing your own home is one of those milestones in life that you'll never forget. I hope to see it. You'll make sure to have us out when you're all moved in." Harold winked.

I'd love for you guys to see it. I hope Quentin hangs around long enough.

"Absolutely. Thanks for spending time with me today, Harold. I'm going to write down some of the pointers you went over. It was super helpful." Alex stood and stretched.

"My pleasure. Let's plan on next Tuesday morning. Say hi to the other fellows when you see them, and have a good day." Harold smiled and left through the porch, opting for the wooded trail near the lake as his route back to Quentin.

"Harp, it's me." The minute Harold was out of earshot, Alex fished out his phone from his pocket and dialed Harper, who was already at the Center, working.

"Me! How the hell are you?"

"Me's fine. Say, I'm thinking of hanging around here today. I've got a few things I'd like to take care of." It would surprise Alex if Harper had a problem with this.

"Is Theo's thing on your to-do list?"

"We must have a bad connection." Alex suppressed a chuckle. "Thanks. Call if you need anything."

"I will. Enjoy the day. I'll be here. Here working. Working hard to keep the entire operation up and running. Have lunch by the lake. Maybe head into Two Harbors. Enjoy a slushy at Pamida."

Alex rolled his eyes. "Is there more?"

"Nope. I think I'm done. Seriously, we're fine. We do have to put our heads together and talk about the flier for the fall dance. I want to make sure we get to people well in advance so the turnout is huge. Oh... fuck."

"Fuck what?" *It's not like Harper to have an "oh fuck" moment.*

"We have Pride weekend sneaking up. Do you think Colin might come home and help *man up* our booth?"

"Not sure, I'll ask him. Now that he's got Marla on his mind, the rest of us are second-class citizens."

"Ah yes. She's very attractive. I enjoyed getting to know her at your party."

Alex heard the rustling of paper in the background.

"I need to get back to work. Will you be around for dinner?" Harper had a thing about everyone eating together. Alex made a mental note to call him on it. *What's the deal with that?*

"Yeah, I think so. Theo and I haven't made any plans. How about this? I'll pick up something to throw on the grill." *Maybe some steaks. Yum!*

"Works for me. I'm looking at the Taconknights' schedule. They don't play tonight, so Ian will be around too. Okay, enjoy the day. Bye!"

"Bye."

Alex moved about the porch, rearranging his supplies. When everything was organized to his satisfaction, he removed the photo of Harold and Quentin from his paint box and clipped it to a fresh sheet of thick watercolor paper. *You guys look so handsome.*

One of the things Alex noticed as he sat and stared at the picture was skin tone. Harold's was pink, almost red in places. Quentin—*he's sick*—had hardly any red tone but more blue and gray. Because this was a portrait, and the last thing he wanted to do was paint Quentin not looking his best, Alex would find a balance and paint both faces using the same shades, with maybe a degree or so of variance.

The composition of the photograph was off. What Alex had intended to do all along was place the faces of the two men on a palisade background. He felt it important to link their images with the surrounding scenery. *Kinda to commemorate their stay here. Something like that.*

To begin, Alex watered down his paper. Next, he brushed in the outline of where the faces would go. Once the faces were painted, he would work on the background. It was important to begin the images of Harold and Quentin on white paper so he could capture the detail in each of the subject's eyes.

Starting with a dab of raw sienna, Alex added a light red to the mix until he had a suitable skin color. Working with quick, precise strokes, he outlined the faces. *Yep. Just like riding a bike. It all comes back to ya.*

From there, he moved to the eyes. Quentin's were easier to capture than Harold's, who had a pronounced squint. *Take your time with the eyes.* After prepping his trusty squirrel mop, a brush that holds a lot of water and pigment but still comes to a very fine point, he went to work. *This is going well.* It was the subjects—Harold and Quentin had come to mean so much to the gang that it made painting their portrait easier. His session earlier with Harold had him jazzed to start the project. Alex made a promise to himself that, if, after finishing the painting, it wasn't his best effort, he'd try again and again until he had it just right.

Keep going, he told himself. This could be a keeper.

IAN was about to fuck with Alex. Theo was getting better at reading this goofball.

"Dude, you have clothes here I've never even seen you wear. What the frick is up with that?" Ian unburdened himself of a bundle of hangers, storing them in the entrance-hall closet. The plan was to begin on the walk-in off the master bedroom right out the gate, so it made sense to keep stuff away from that area of the house until the remodel was complete. "This top is simply *adorable*." Ian held up a pink and green rugby shirt and turned from side to side so everyone in the room could get a good look. "Pair this up with your jean skirt for a smashing ensemble. Huh? Guys, am I right?"

"Shut the hell up, Ian." Alex grabbed the shirt out of his hand, hanging it back up and closing the closet door.

"There's a few more things in the back of my truck. Be right back." Theo was impressed with Alex's new house and surprised by all the room. *My parents' house isn't this big.* Alex had invited him to the closing, but the shop was so busy he had to pass. Artie would have let him go if he had pushed, but it was probably more important to Alex that he was available to help move him in. *Maybe this will be your home someday too.* The thought had crossed Theo's mind. This being an option for him hadn't come up in a conversation yet. Theo wasn't in any kind of hurry. He was comfortable where he was. Home was much closer to work, and by living at home, he was saving a ton of money. If he moved in with Alex, he would insist on paying rent. *You're not a freeloader, Theo Engdahl.*

Loading himself up with a pair of cross-country skis, poles, and ice skates, Alex's last remaining items, Theo walked back into the house and, for reasons unknown, brought whatever conversation was happening to an abrupt stop.

"Well." Harper got up from the lawn chair he had placed in the middle of the room and walked over to a cooler. "Anyone up for a beer? Alex, here's a frosty Dew."

"I'll take a beer." Theo walked over and accepted a cold one. *I wonder what those guys were talking about? Probably finances.* Alex had mentioned Harper cosigned on his mortgage. This was stuff Theo didn't need to know about. "Ian?"

"Sure." Ian stepped forward and took Theo's beer, which Harper immediately replaced.

"Really, compared to some of the moves I've helped with, including my own, this was a piece of cake." Harper closed the cooler. "You're lucky, Alex. Having so little to schlep around means you get to go out and buy new stuff."

"I went over my budget last night after the closing. I'm cleaned out. I hope you guys like that lawn-chair look. Casual but colorful."

"Just like you." Ian winked.

"Everyone starts out that way. No one is going to expect you to throw a formal dinner party for at least a week." Harper clinked bottles with his partner. "So you and Ian are going to start right in with the bedroom and the walk-in?"

"We should at least be able to knock out the walls, and then maybe we can talk one of the dudes from town into coming out and helping us shell it in." Ian looked over to Alex for a comment.

"I'm in no rush. Like Ian said before, if we do a little here and there, it will get done eventually."

"Count me in to help. I enjoy stuff like this." Theo had helped his dad remodel their kitchen. It was one of the better experiences he had had with his father. And the before-and-after pictures made it all worth it, knowing you had a hand in the final product.

"Here's what I think." Ian walked over to the window and released a fart that went on for much longer than anyone in the room could believe. "Hey! That was a record setter I'll bet."

"Thanks for breaking in the house, dick lick." Alex was laughing so hard he could hardly talk.

Harper's face was what sent Theo into hysterics. It was the look of a man who had experienced firsthand so many of Ian's farts over the years he just couldn't humor him by acknowledging it. *God dang, that's funny.*

"Well, make sure to write, Alex. Let us know how everything is going." Harper tossed back the remainder of his beer and got up from his chair. "Ready to roll?" He looked over to Ian, who was still trying to devise a way he could get further mileage out of his record breaker.

"Yeah, I guess. I should do a walk-through of the gardens and make a list of what needs to be done. I have a full crew tomorrow." Ian finished his beer and placed it next to the cooler. "You guys need anything else before we take off?"

Theo smiled when he saw the satisfied look on Alex's face. *You're pretty damn lucky. This is all yours. And you're twenty-one years old. Not bad.*

"I think we're good. Thanks so much, you guys, for helping today." Alex stood and followed Harper and Ian to the door.

"This was the easiest move I've ever helped with," Ian said. "Seriously. Try lugging a hide-a-bed up three flights of stairs. Or a two-ton solid oak entertainment center. Andy moved three times in one year. I almost disowned him as a friend."

"Ew… hide-a-beds are really nasty. I had to move one of those too. Okay, we'll catch you guys later." Harper stepped out of the front door. "Wait." He poked his head back in, causing Ian to back up a few feet. "Why don't you guys plan on coming over Sunday afternoon, and we'll have dinner together. I'm in the mood to cook something special."

Alex looked over to Theo for a response.

"That sounds great. What can I bring?" Theo loved hanging with these guys.

"Buns?" Ian deadpanned directly at Alex.

"Fruit salad?" Alex countered without missing a beat.

"Brats?" Theo added, delighted he was starting to fall into the groove.

"How about root beer floats?" Harper grabbed Ian and yanked him out of the house.

"Call Petra and invite her too," Alex called out before they hopped into Ian's truck.

Those guys are, like, the coolest. They watched the truck round the corner of the long driveway and vanish into the woods.

Theo had an idea. "Come here." Stepping outside the door, he waited for Alex to join him.

"What?" Alex laughed.

Before Alex could protest, Theo swooped him up in his arms and carried him back into the house. "There. I know this isn't exactly the right moment for this, but what the hell. Welcome to your new home, Alex Stevens."

"Our home?" Alex searched Theo's face for a response.

Our home. Theo placed Alex back on his feet. "Hmm, are you inviting me to move in with you?"

"It would be so great. It's also me being selfish. This is too much house for me to be roaming around in on my own." Alex gestured to the large living room. "And, I don't really like living alone."

"That could work." *Don't sound too excited. Come on, dude. You know this is what you want. You know what's standing in the way?* Theo opened his arms for Alex, who stepped right into them. "It would be really cool to live together."

"That's what I was thinking." Alex planted a kiss on Theo's neck.

And what else? "I have to come out to my folks first." Theo returned the kiss. "I'm almost there."

"I know. I just wanted you to know you're wanted here." Alex licked Theo behind his ear.

Theo laughed. "Hey, I have an idea. Come here." Theo led Alex through the house and down to the lower level. Because the plan was to start working on the master bedroom upstairs, Alex decided he would use the guest bedroom until the work was completed. "I don't know about you, but the project I could really fire up for would be to set up the bed and...."

"Bloody hell. That crossed my mind too." Alex adjusted himself in his jeans.

Theo grabbed a box of tools from his truck. It wasn't long before the room started to take shape. The biggest dilemma was where to put the television. Alex only had one. He was used to watching it in bed but also wanted one in the entertainment room so they could build a fire and throw in a movie.

"The problem is solved," Theo announced proudly after he had returned carrying two lamps for the bedside tables.

"The television problem is solved?" Alex looked up, not understanding.

"I wanted to get you something for a housewarming gift. How about we put your old television in here, and I'll pick up a fancy big flat screen for the other room?"

"Theo, you don't have to do that." Alex frowned.

"How about I want to? You decide. It's either a television or a set of pot holders. You can take a few minutes to mull this one over." Theo watched as Alex put a finger to his lips, as if giving this ridiculous choice some serious thought.

"Damn, this is tough. Okay, I guess I'll go with the television."

"Let's do that tomorrow. We'll drive into Duluth if we have to. Tonight we'll decide where it should go and how big it should be."

"Great. Now what should we do?" Alex sat on the side of the bed.

"Do you have any puzzles?" Theo looked over to his boyfriend to see if he could be coaxed into messing around. "Seriously, I have a plan if you don't."

"Maybe... we have the same plan." Alex got up and walked over to Theo.

"Maybe we do...." Theo savored the sensation of Alex's hand resting on his crotch. "I'm thinkin' we're on the same page, dude."

Careful not to rush one of his favorite new things, stripping each other, Theo took turns with Alex removing each article of clothing. When they were both naked, Theo wrapped his strong arms around Alex and held him tight to his body. They swayed together until Theo took the lead. "Someone's anxious." He looked down at his eager dick and speared it into Alex's thigh.

"Do you and your cock have the same plan?" Alex reached down and petted Theo's hard-on.

"Yeah, I'm pretty sure we do. Can I ask you something?" Theo removed his arms from around Alex's waist.

"Sure."

"The night you tried to...." Theo blushed. *This is Alex. Just say it.*

"Play with your butt?" Alex chuckled.

"Yeah. Thanks. Is that something you enjoy?"

"I love having my butt played with." It was Alex's turn to avert his eyes. "I also like being fucked sometimes. Honestly, Theo. I enjoy sex." Alex laughed. "I'm pretty adventurous. Does that freak you out?"

"Nope. Get on the bed," Theo ordered.

Alex climbed onto the bed and sat Indian style.

"Now get into that position you showed me before." Theo reached for Alex's arm, guiding him onto his knees.

Alex did as he was told, pausing to look over to Theo to make sure this is what Theo had meant. Theo answered by gently pushing his head down. "I think it's you who has the hot ass." Theo got up behind Alex and began palming his butt cheeks. "Do you like this?" Theo's hands moved up and down, squeezing and pinching, petting and patting.

"Oh yeah. You could do that all night and I wouldn't mind." Alex buried his face in the pillow.

Theo worked over his ass, legs, and thighs until he heard Alex purr. "Man, I've been waiting for this for a long time."

"Hang on."

Theo climbed off the bed. "Let's see, where did I see those things?" *Dang it. Where are those rubber dicks?* He searched several boxes that had yet to be unpacked. "Oh yeah, here they are." Theo held them behind his back and crawled back onto the bed.

"What're you doing?" Alex turned his head in an attempt to look behind him.

"Alex, don't look. Head down. I've got this. Just because *I'm* not ready doesn't mean you have to wait."

"I'm lovin' it, what you're doing. Love it all. Surprise me." Alex unleashed a huge sigh of contentment and lowered his head.

"Let's try this." Theo reached for the long flesh-colored dildo. *Man, this thing is big.* Squirting a glob of lotion from the bottle on the table, he coated it. Theo studied his target. He'd never really seen this part of the body close up. The more he looked, the more interesting it appeared. *A lot happens back here; that's for sure. Okay, let's rock my boyfriend's world.* Positioning the tip of the fake dick right at the center of Alex's butthole, Theo plunged it deep into his boyfriend's ass.

"Yeeeeeeooooowwwww! Eek! Eek!" Alex punched the bed with his fists. "Oh, oh... God. Mother fuck. Motherfucker."

Damn, he really gets into this.

"You like that, eh?" Theo enthusiastically twisted and pushed the hard rubber toy until it couldn't go any further.

"Stop! Stop, Theo. You've gotta stop!" Alex reached behind, yanked the dildo out of his ass, and tossed it across the room, where it hit the wall with a loud thump and rolled behind one of the unpacked boxes. Hugging his stomach, he curled into a fetal position on the bed. "I think I'm gonna die."

"What'd I do? Alex… what'd I do?" Theo bounced around the room from one side of the bed to the other. "I'm sorry. I thought you liked that. What'd I do?"

"Theo…." Alex moaned. "Sit down."

Theo sat next to Alex on the bed. Alex uncoiled his body and stretched out on his stomach. "You can't just…." Alex looked to the ceiling, "You can't just shove it in like that."

"What do you do, then?"

"Oh… I have to stand up." Alex got off the bed and limped around the room. "Christ, did that hurt."

"I had no idea. I'm so sorry." Theo stood. *What the fuck did I do?*

Alex started to laugh. "It's so funny. You're so new at this. Oh, I can't believe that just happened."

Theo tried to laugh, but he was still too freaked out.

Alex continued to tour the room with his hand on his ass. "Give me a minute, and then I'll explain it to you." After pacing back and forth and laughing so hard tears rolled down his cheeks, he slid back onto the bed.

"Can I do anything?" Theo sat down again along Alex's side.

"That, boyfriend, was some funny shit. Painful, funny shit. Damn, my ass hurts. Okay"—Alex sat up against the headboard—"here's the deal with butt play."

Alex detailed for Theo how to use his toys. He covered the foreplay and preparation steps several times for added emphasis.

"Okay, I got it. Jeez, I feel so bad." Theo reached over and patted Alex on the thigh.

"No worries, it was just my butt. I have an idea." Alex reached for the smaller purple vibrator sitting on the nightstand. "Before you break out in a sweat, don't worry. This is completely different. Slide up, and we'll have ourselves a little demonstration."

Alex waited for Theo to move up, and when he did, Alex moved his head over so they could share the same pillow. "I bet I can make you shoot using only this. And before you get all freaked, I'll do it, and I won't get anywhere near your ass. You game?"

"Really?" Theo shot him a skeptical look. "Hell yeah, let's give it try. Wait."

"What?"

"So, you're talking no hands, just that little purple Barney dick?"

Alex laughed. "Yeah, just this little Barney dick. Wanna give it a go, Sponge Bob?"

"Sure." Theo snuggled up close, his head nestled in the crook of Alex's neck.

Just as Alex turned the vibrator on, his phone went off. It took him a minute to figure out where it was. "Oh, wait, it's still in the pocket of my jeans." Alex got up and fished it out. "Weird, it's Harper. Hey there, what's up?" Alex looked across the bed at Theo while he listened.

The change on Alex's face was immediate. "We'll be right over." Closing his phone, he sat on the end of the bed. "Quentin passed."

HARPER felt the hair on the back of his neck bristle. As long as he could remember, the sight of a hearse never failed to produce a shiver. Gathered together in the office, they all watched in silence as it crept past them, turned, and headed up to the highway with Quentin inside. Alex and Theo had followed the hearse from McGregor Funeral Home into the resort.

Bye, Quentin. It's not just Harold who is going to miss you. Harper leaned against Ian, who responded by wrapping his arm around his shoulder.

Harold had been surprisingly calm when he called to inform Harper that Quentin had passed. The days leading up to his death had been very hard for Harold. Quentin was given morphine the last week of his life to help him rest comfortably. He slept almost continuously. The few times Quentin was awake, his mind was so muddled all Harold could do was offer water and caress his face. A prolonged good-bye for a cherished loved one, Harper had thought. Unwilling to sleep for fear he would miss being there for Quentin, Harold was numb from exhaustion. He rarely left Quentin's bedside, holding his hand right up until the very end.

Harper and Ian rushed down to Cabin ten after receiving the call. Quentin, who was still lying in bed, appeared so peaceful. Harper contacted the local mortuary, and together they waited. After the funeral home had tenderly moved Quentin into the hearse, Harold broke down and wept. Through tears of their own, Harper and Ian did their best to console him. Once calmed, Harold placed a call to friends from the Twin Cities, who had been alerted to Quentin's rapidly declining condition. They were already on the way to take Harold back home until arrangements could be finalized. Ian went up to the house with Alex and Theo after he had made the rounds to the other cabins to explain the situation if anyone had questions.

Feeling as if his own life had been sucked right out, Harper collapsed on the chair near the window and stared out to the lake. Meeting and getting to know Harold and Quentin over the course of the summer had been a blessing. Everyone had benefited. That the Palisade Beach Resort staff was able to step up to the plate and make a difference in the older couple's stay was a huge source of pride. This loss was hard for everyone to accept.

"Harper, there's something I need to tell you." Petra came around the desk.

"What's up?" *Shit! Is she quitting? Oh, please don't let it be that.*

"I haven't said a thing to anyone about this. Not even Betsy. Remember the first week we started spending time with those guys so Harold would have a break to go off to do his own thing?"

"Of course I remember. What's your point?" Harper reached over and gave her hand a shake. "I'm sorry. I'm just not myself right now. What is it you want to tell me?"

"Quentin entrusted me with this." Petra reached into her pocket and pulled out a small purple velvet bag. After undoing the tie on top, she expanded the opening until she could reach in and remove its contents—a flash drive.

"A flash drive?" Harper raised his eyebrow, requesting more information.

"It's Quentin's final wishes. He typed them and put them on this drive so, when he was no longer around, I could hand it over to Harold and he would know what to do."

"Really? They struck me as the type of people who talked everything out." Harper said.

"I thought that too. What Quentin told me is that Harold will be in denial right up to the end, and he'll be so grief stricken when it happens, he won't know where to turn. Quentin thought he was doing Harold a favor by placing it all on this."

"That's amusing, actually." Harper shook his head and managed a weak laugh. "So, to follow through with the plan, you have to hand this over the Harold and explain to him what it is."

"Well yeah, that...." Petra looked away.

Harper picked up on her hesitation and pulled the rug right out from under her. "You've already opened it up, and you know all the details. You're feeling guilty for being a snoop."

"It gets worse." Petra got up from her chair. "Be right back."

Worse? This should be interesting.

"Here." The office manager returned with a large envelope.

"Stop being so elusive, Pet. What's going on?" Harper's patience was being tested.

Petra reached into the envelope and pulled out a bound stack of paper about an inch thick. She slid it over so he could read the title.

"Kang-Dae: A Story of Love by Quentin Devereux." Harper sat back for a moment. "Oh, I get it. This was also on the thumb drive. You printed it out and read it."

"Every page. I'm very sorry, Harper. I really don't know what came over me. When I saw it, my curiosity got the best of me. I feel terrible."

"What is a Kang-Dae?" Taking the manuscript in his hands, he began paging through it.

"It's a young Korean man. The name means strong and big. Oh, Harper, you can't believe how amazing this story is."

"First, let me alleviate any additional anxiety you might have for checking out the content on this drive. Truthfully, I would have done the same thing… probably."

"I'm not usually like this, Harp." Petra wore the face of complete remorse.

"I know that. I'm a little surprised you pursued his book to the extent you did, but there again, given the chance, I can't sit across from you and say I wouldn't have done the same thing. We're born with only so much restraint. Hell, think of it this way. It was a 'Petra' tax for taking on this responsibility."

"There was no way I could have said no to Quentin. I mean… as much as I wanted to make an excuse and turn my back, more of me realized it was a duty. No, wait, the more I've had time to think about it, it's an honor."

"The book is good?" Harper flipped a few pages before settling on one.

"Kang-Dae is the son of a prostitute. He learns early on that he can make money too, making his body available to those who show interest. Anyway, the whole Korea thing, the setting, the dynamics between him and his mother, it's all so well done. Eventually, he connects with an American soldier who, at first, you think wants to try and help Kang-Dae, you know, by coaxing him away from his crappy life. For a while, this goes on, but ever so slowly, the soldier, Mac… they fall in love. When the war ends, Mac disappears, leaving Kang-Dae back where the story had started—a male prostitute. It's a life-sucks kind of read with lots of great stuff in between."

"Sounds like something I'd enjoy. Here." He held it out for Petra to take.

"Turn to the third page." She gently pushed his hand back.

Harper turned to the third page and read, "I lovingly dedicate this book to Harper, Ian, Alex, and Petra. Their generous and unending support brought more happiness to me than they'll ever know. To each of them, I offer my heartfelt thanks." Harper stared down at the page and mumbled, "Unbelievable." He handed it back after reading the dedication for a second time. "This will be our little secret."

"Thanks, Harper. Seriously, thanks for understanding." Petra replaced the manuscript in the folder and sealed it. "What do you think? Should I walk down to Cabin ten and hand this over to Harold now?"

"Keep the book for yourself. No one will benefit from knowing you've already read it. Maybe they have some kind of tradition where Harold is always the first person to read Quentin's work. I would hate to spoil that for them. Him." Harper corrected himself and stared blankly at the wall.

"I understand."

Harper stood and walked to the door. "Unless you want to do this on your own, let's walk down there together. I feel a need to be around Harold right now."

"Thank you. I would really appreciate that." Petra was obviously relieved.

Harper opened the screen door. "Ready?"

"Yeah. I was thinking earlier, back to the scare with Alex. This will easily go down as the summer of unexpected drama."

"One thing I know for certain." Harper let the door close after Petra had stepped out. "I've had just about all the drama I can handle for a lifetime."

"THE turn is on the right, at the bottom of this hill, Carl."

Harold, seated in the back, was being driven to the resort by his good friends Carl and Edward. Per Quentin's wishes, there would be a brief memorial service this morning at the resort, where his ashes were to be interred. Quentin had also requested a party in his honor in the Twin Cities. He specifically requested this event to be held after the holidays, when a well-planned party would help take the chill of winter off. Very detailed instructions had been left for Harold, detailing everything from music, to the style, contents, and color of the table arrangements. *Radish, you are so particular. That's only one of the million things I adore about you.*

"This is the resort office. Keep going down this road behind the cabins," Harold instructed.

"It's so beautiful here. I can't wait to see the grounds." Edward looked back and smiled.

"Harold, it looks like the road ends up here." Carl slowed the car.

"It does, but continue on the grass until we get to number ten, which is where Quentin and I stayed. It has the most incredible view of the palisade," Harold added as the car left the gravel.

"Here?" Carl asked as they pulled up behind the last cabin.

"Yes." *There's Alex.* Harold waved to his friend, who looked devilishly handsome in a black suit, white shirt, and lavender tie. "The young gentleman walking up to us is Alex, the watercolor artist. He's an absolute delight."

"It's so nice to see you," Alex said after he walked around and opened Harold's door.

Harold stepped out of the car and into Alex's arms. "It's nice to see you too, Alex."

Introductions were made, and Alex led them around to the front of the cabin.

"Good morning, Audrey." Harold walked over and embraced the owner of the Lip Smacker. "These are our friends, Carl and Edward."

"It was so sad to hear about Quentin." Audrey squeezed his arm.

"Thank you. What a lovely fall day we have for him." The fall color was spectacular. The trees had yet to drop their leaves. Harold looked up to the sky and watched a bank of puffy white clouds float gracefully over the top of the palisade.

Audrey gestured to a woman who stood quietly by the entrance to the cabin. "Harold, this is my sister, Marie. She went to grade school with Quentin."

"Ah yes." Harold accepted her hand. "I can see the family resemblance. So nice to meet you, Marie."

"I had every intention of getting over to see Quentin. I'm so sorry it didn't happen. I can remember him so vividly. Independent. That's what I remember most." Marie shyly smiled and stepped back.

"Oh, I can see you had his ticket even back then," Harold quipped. "Quentin would have enjoyed seeing you again. Thank you so much for coming."

Oh look. Here come the others.

Harper, Ian, and Theo came strolling across the grounds, all wearing black suits and all looking fabulous, Harold observed. *Radish, did you ever expect to have such a handsome group of men sending you off?*

After heartfelt hugs, Harold introduced the men to his friends.

"It appears everything is ready, Harold." Harper gestured down toward the water. "Do you need anything before we start?"

Harold felt his lip quiver as he looked to the area Harper had indicated. *Stop this right now. You've been crying for a week solid.* Chairs, lined up neatly in three rows, faced a lectern and a marvelous view of both the lake and the palisade. On the left was the urn containing Quentin's ashes, along with a wonderful photo of him taken only a year ago when several of his earlier books were released in his own name. On the right, a harpist and flutist stood waiting patiently.

"I'm fine." Harold linked arms with Harper, and together they walked down, with the others following behind. "Is this the garden?" Harold asked before taking his seat.

"Yes," Ian replied. "I was hoping to have a plaque ready, but unfortunately it didn't arrive in time. We have decided to call it

'Quentin's Garden'." Ian patted Harold on the shoulder, then, along with Harper, took a seat directly behind him.

"Quentin's Garden. Oh, that's lovely." Harold reached for Carl's hand. Edward, because of his lovely baritone, had been asked to speak this morning.

That's it. Petra. Harold knew someone was missing, but it took until now to realize who it was. "Was Petra unable to make it?" Harold asked over his shoulder.

"She wouldn't miss this, Harold. She's back at the house organizing the food." Just as the words left Harper's mouth, she appeared. "Speak of the devil." Harper tapped Harold on the shoulder so he could see Petra approach.

"Hello, Harold. It's so wonderful to see you again. I've missed you." Petra leaned over and gave him a hug.

"Hello, sweetie. You look so lovely." Harold stood to give her a proper hug. "Petra, these are our friends, Carl and Edward, from home."

"Pleased to meet you." Petra shook hands.

"You might think the gentlemen behind me are responsible for this lovely resort, but let me tell you," Harold whispered loud enough for everyone to hear, "Petra makes it all happen."

Blushing, Petra walked around and sat next to Ian.

When everyone was seated, Harper walked over to the lectern. "I'd like to welcome Quentin's friends and loving partner, Harold. On behalf of all of us here at the resort, please know we are honored to be hosting this memorial. When Harold first approached us about him and Quentin spending an entire summer here, I have to be honest, we weren't really sure that was something we wanted to do. I'm so thankful we had the good sense to say yes. Had we not, we would have never had the opportunity to get to know Quentin and Harold, and that would have been a tragedy."

Harold's lip began the tremble once more. He knew today was going to be hard but hoped he could make it through the memorial in a dignified way. Thankfully, Carl must have sensed his struggle. His dear friend looked over and put his arm around his shoulder.

"We are blessed with a remarkable fall day on the North Shore. I can't imagine anything less to help us celebrate a remarkable man, Quentin Cornelius Devereux. Let us take a minute to remember our dear friend."

Harper nodded over to the musicians and took his seat.

It was surreal for Harold to be here, he thought as the musicians began a lovely harp and flute duet. Periodically, a cool breeze from the lake dislodged a leaf from one of the many surrounding trees. Brightly colored leaves floated lazily to the ground.

When the music came to an end, Edward rose and took his place in front of the group.

In a voice deep and passionate, Edward told Quentin's story. Harold often lost track of the fact it was Edward who had introduced him to Quentin. They were roommates at the time. Harold had been invited, through an acquaintance, to a New Year's party hosted by Quentin and Edward. Back then, the only comfortable place for gay men to meet was in homes or apartments of friends. There were a few bars in the Twin Cities who catered to gays and artists, but the atmosphere prohibited men from cutting loose and really enjoying themselves. The fear of being arrested did a more than adequate job of keeping most people subdued back then. *I remember it as if it happened yesterday.* Harold stepped through the door that evening into an explosion of noise and energy. Quentin was the unmistakable ringleader. *I thought I'd stepped into a vast fortune when I laid eyes on you, Radish.*

Edward closed with a passage from Quentin's first novel. Harold closed his eyes and listened. He could almost visualize the words on the page, he had read it so many times. Seated next to his window, the main character, Dash, looks to the street below and watches as a pair of lovers stroll along in the soft rain. Goose bumps formed on Harold's arms. As Quentin could do so well, his prose magically transported you to the moment.

A pat on the hand by Carl brought him out of his trance. Harold reached across Carl and squeezed Edward's hand after he had sat back down. "Thank you, Eddie."

As the musicians started their second piece, Ian rose from his chair and walked over to the urn. Lifting it off of its pedestal, he carried it over to the garden and carefully lowered it into the ground. Harold had anticipated this happening, had even rehearsed it in his mind, but the power of reality was more than he could manage. As if on cue, a handful of red and orange leaves hovered in the air over Quentin before gently floating down to the garden bed. Carl held him in his arms as he wept.

Edward reached over and offered his handkerchief. When Harold had dried his eyes, Harper was back at the lectern. "It would be our pleasure if you would join us back at the house for refreshments."

That was rough. I hate to admit it, but I can really use a drink.

"Harold, this is for you." Alex, who had just stepped out of the cabin, handed him a gift.

"What do we have here?" Harold asked.

"It's a rendering of Quentin's Garden. Ian and I worked together to show you what it will look like next summer. We thought you would enjoy having it."

"Oh, Alex, this is wonderful. Thank you so much." Harold hugged his talented friend.

Quentin had made the right call by keeping the interment brief, Harold thought as they drove from the Cabins over to the main house. *I don't think I could have taken much more.* When he had first read Quentin's notes about today's memorial, Harold worried there should be more. He had to remind himself that the grieving part of Quentin's good-bye was something his partner understood and knew necessary. But the real tribute to Quentin would come later—the big party this winter when everyone they knew and cherished would be invited to enjoy themselves in his honor. *That's more your style, isn't it, Radish?*

Harold weathered another wave of emotion when he walked into Harper and Ian's home and saw what a marvelous and tasteful presentation they had assembled. The large dining room table was laden with sandwiches, salads, and platters of beautifully presented sweets. Vases of flowers were everywhere you looked. A bar in the kitchen featured wines, beer, and Bloody Mary fixings. *Quentin, look how much you meant to these people. Isn't this delightful?*

Making the rounds, Harold made it a point to spend time with each guest. He got great pleasure from his brief visit with Marie and Audrey. Because Quentin had been so vague about his past, she was the key and, surprisingly, could recall quite a bit of it. Before moving on, they agreed the next time Harold visited the North Shore, he and Marie would meet at the Lip Smacker for lunch so he could hear more about his partner.

By midafternoon, Harold signaled to Carl he was ready to call it a day. Quentin had only been gone for a week, and each day was a grueling task to get through. *I'm exhausted.*

"Please don't be a stranger," Harper requested as he and Ian walked Harold and his friends to the door.

"I'll never be able to stay away from this place and you kind people for long," Harold confessed. "Ian, I'd like you to consider putting me on your landscape crew next season. I'm a very thorough weed puller, if I say so myself."

"You're already on the crew," Ian joked.

"Good. Now I have a reason to stay in shape." Harold was suddenly reminded he had one final piece of business to take care of before heading back home.

"Harper, do you think you'll be at the center on Monday?" Harold asked.

"Sure," Harper answered. "I should be there all day. Why?"

"My accountant and I have something we would like to discuss with you. It's too involved to get into here. Can we give you a call on Monday?" Harold asked.

"Certainly. If for some reason I'm not around, call my cell. You have the number, right?" Harper patted Harold on the shoulder.

"Yes. This was lovely. I can't thank you enough." Harold wrapped his arm around Harper and hugged him tight. "Ian, thank you so much for all you've done for us," he said, moving over to hug Harper's handsome partner. "Quentin would have been so proud."

"We know that," Ian said. "We... *all* of us felt honored."

CHAPTER
Twelve

"HOW much is left in the truck?" Alex extended the legs on the folding table and placed it right side up. With fall on the doorstep, the morning had started out on the cool side, but the remainder of the day was supposed to be spectacular. *I love Pride.*

"This is it," Ian said. "Theo, let's tackle the tent." Ian carried a large pack over to their designated spot.

Alex remembered back to the first year. They were late to register, and their booth was stuck between the bathrooms and a Pronto Pup vendor. The combined smells could be challenging, depending on the direction of the wind. Every year they borrowed the tent from Audrey and Bud. The only other time it got used was in early August for Crazy Days in Silver Bay. Audrey peddled baked favorites from the Lip Smacker, and Bud sold humungous barbecue sandwiches for two dollars each.

"Sure, but I have to pee first. Where are the cans?" Theo glanced around and then back to Alex.

"Right over there." Alex pointed to the edge of the park.

"So," Ian asked when Theo had gotten far enough away from them to not hear, "did you ask him?" Ian held the pack in the air, letting its contents fall to the ground.

"Huh?" Alex looked over as he went about taping a plastic rainbow cloth over the table's surface.

"Have you said anything? Did you ask Theo to move in with you?"

"Yeah." Alex started on the second table. The plan was to do exactly what they did last year and the year before. Place the tables side by side to make one table so at least three people could sit behind it to assist anyone who stopped by with questions. It also had to be large enough to hold brochures and other marketing materials. For the second year, they would be distributing coupons to the Lip Smacker. It was the least they could do. Audrey insisted on spending one afternoon at Pride manning their booth.

"Lookin' for a slap?"

"What?" Running late, Alex tried to ignore Ian. He wanted to get the booth set up before it got busy. The crystal-clear fall day would ensure a healthy attendance.

"What did he say?" Ian went about laying out the poles.

"It's going to happen, but he needs to come out to his folks first."

"Oh shit, I forgot about that. Yeah, it's probably better he take care of that before moving in." Ian walked around the canvas, distributing the stakes.

"I can't believe how many people are already here." Theo shared his observation as he walked over to inspect Ian's tent prep. "What can I help with?"

"Grab that corner of the canvas, and I'll take the opposite end. We should be able to get the poles under it and then secure the lines."

Twenty minutes later, they were ready for business. Alex poured out a few bags of miniature candy bars into a large bowl, placing it at the end of the table. *I wonder what Theo thinks of all this?* "Hey, you doin' okay?" Alex asked in a whisper so Ian couldn't hear. He didn't want to put his boyfriend on the spot. The look on his face was hard to read. "If this gets to be too much, let me know."

Theo looked over and smiled. "I'm cool," he whispered back.

"I have to head home for a few hours for a meeting with a bride, and probably her mother. That's how these things typically go." Ian shook his head to convey his total lack of interest. "But hey, they're paying good money, so I'm there. I'll be back this afternoon with Harper." Ian walked into the tent and sat in one of the folding chairs. "Why don't you guys scope things out? I can handle this until you get back."

"Okay. We'll see you in a few. Come on, Theo. Let's introduce you to Pride."

"Later, dude." Theo waved good-bye.

It would still be a few hours before the live music started, but all the food vendors, the booths, and the entire celebration appeared to be open for business.

"Let's check out some of the vendors." Alex led them down a row of tents filled with artisans and their work intermixed with various groups, like the Center, who were using the event to drum up support. "Hey, this is pretty cool." Alex waved for Theo to join him. "Check it out."

They ducked into a tent lined with feathers with images painted on them. A strong American Indian theme permeated the collection.

"This is so awesome." Theo had his eye on a large feather with an Indian chief in full headdress painted brilliantly in the center.

I'll have to remember to sneak back and buy this for him. Theo's birthday was coming up in October, and Alex wanted to make it special. He made a note to talk to Ian and Harper. He wanted the whole gang on board to help celebrate.

"Yeah, I thought you'd like that. Hungry?" Alex stopped before heading down a row dedicated to food.

"Yeah, I could eat something." Theo waited for Alex to lead the way.

"I think I know what I want. Do you like gyros?" Alex stopped in front of a truck named Athena's Tasty Delights.

"I had one for the first time at the fair last year. It was really good. Sure, let's do it. I got this." Theo retrieved a wad of cash from his pocket. "You're broke, remember?"

"I am broke. Thanks." Alex chuckled.

"Let's sit over there while we eat." Theo cut across the grass to the vacant bench.

"How's the gyro?" Alex asked, with milky cucumber sauce squirting out the sides of his mouth.

Theo laughed. "Man, if you could see yourself right now. So damn funny."

"Why's that?" Alex took another jumbo bite.

"Ah, nothin'."

Alex could tell by the way Theo was looking at him that he was laughing at something to do with his face. It took a second before he figured it out. "You are a dirty boy, Theodore Engdahl."

"I know. It's the first thing I thought of."

They sat in silence, eating and watching the people go by.

"Can I ask you something?" Theo walked over and threw his wrapper in the trash can and sat back down.

"Sure."

"One thing I can't figure out. If gay people want to fit in and be treated like everyone else, why do they dress so fuckin' crazy at this thing? I'm not talking about the guys who take dressing up like women seriously. That I think I get. It's everyone else. I mean, look at that dude over there." Theo pointed to a heavyset middle-aged man who was walking around in dingy briefs that were more gray than white. "I think that's disgusting."

"Me too. But…." Alex finished his last bite and got up to throw away his wrapper. "Let's walk and talk."

They headed down one of the avenues they'd yet to visit.

"Harper and I seem to have a discussion about this every year. Here's what I think. Gay people are very diverse. Part of the culture has to do with uniforms, and I'm not talking military. I mean, there're certain distinct looks associated with our specialized groups. That's part of it, I think. There are really flamboyant gay folk, there's the leather crowd, and Pride is one of the only times when all these different people come together to celebrate diversity." *I bet he's happy he asked. Wind it up, dude.* "The drabby underwear dude is part of the drabby underwear group." Alex looked over to see if Theo was buying any of this. "I don't fucking know."

They both laughed.

"Okay." Theo shifted in his seat. "But how about in everyday life? I see people who, by their looks, the way they dress, you just go, wow, it's a gay dude. Or a lesbian chick. It's not pride. It's everyday, and they stick out like a sore thumb."

Alex had to think about this. He wasn't so sure he had an answer. "That's a good question. I guess, and honestly I haven't really thought this out, but I think the people you are talking about are showing the community a couple of things. They're proud of who they are. They're not afraid to be individuals. What else.... I don't know. Let's bring that one up at the next group dinner. I'd love to hear Petra's take on it."

By the time Alex noticed who was headed in their direction, he'd missed any chance of avoiding them. *Todd. This should be interesting.*

"Theo?"

"What?"

"See the two guys coming toward us? The shorter dude in the yellow shirt is Todd." *Relax. You have a new boyfriend to show off. I bet he doesn't.*

"Got it. Who's the dude with the camera?"

"Not sure. But we're about to find out." Alex feigned surprise. "Todd! Hey, how's it going?"

"Alex! Wow, what a surprise." Todd was all smiles.

Fuck off. The only reason I didn't turn and head the other direction is I know you saw me.

"Todd, this is my friend Theo." Alex moved over to the grass so they wouldn't all be blocking the path. *I wonder if Theo is pissed I didn't introduce him as my boyfriend. Why didn't I?*

"As in boyfriend? My how time flies by. Hey, Theo." Todd was all about the warmth. "And this is my *friend* Phillip. You guys working the booth for the Center this year? We haven't seen it yet."

"Yeah, Ian's there now. It's down toward the other end."

"Oh, I'll have to stop by and say hi to Ian. Phillip, wait until you meet Ian, Alex's roommate. He's *gorgeous*. And... he's a *baseball* player. You know how much you *love* baseball players."

"I have a thing for baseball players," Phillip was forced to admit.

Okay, that was a little rude.

"So, Theo, what do you do?" Todd wasn't in any hurry to move on.

"Huh?" The question was lost on Theo.

"Theo repairs engines." *Anything else, Todd? His dick is bigger than yours by at least two inches, which is probably the only thing you're really interested in, and his ass is like a rock.*

"Well, we should probably be moving on." Alex rested his hand on Theo's shoulder. "It was nice to meet you, Phillip."

"It was nice meeting you too. Hey, before you go, do you mind if I get a shot?"

Anything to get away from Todd.

"Yeah, that's cool." Alex looked over to Theo, who answered with a "what the hell" shrug.

"Great." Phillip twirled around and then spotted what he was looking for. "How about in front of that Pride banner?"

"Works for me." Alex and Theo moved over to where Phillip had pointed.

"Perfect. This is going to be a really nice shot, I think. I'll have Todd send you a copy."

"Yeah, I'll send you a copy." Todd stood back, eyeing the crowd as they passed by.

"Okay, one more if you don't mind. Why don't you guys kiss? That would be so hot."

Theo laughed. "Seriously?"

"Come on," Phillip goaded, "one more and I'll let you guys go."

Alex looked over to Theo and got another shrug. *Okay, but after this we're outta here.*

"Ready?" Alex placed his hand on Theo's hip.

"I guess." Theo turned to face Alex.

"You get one shot at this, Phillip." Alex placed his hand on the back of Theo's neck and planted a wet sloppy on him.

"Sweet. Another nice shot. Thanks, guys." Phillip flashed a thumbs-up.

"Bye, Alex. Nice to see you again. And nice meeting you, Theo. Happy Pride." Todd gave them a little wave good-bye and walked away.

"Happy Pride," Alex and Theo responded in unison.

"Sorry about that. I didn't see him until it was too late."

"No worries. I *liked* Phillip more than I *liked* Todd." Theo punched Alex in the shoulder.

"Me too." Alex back kicked Theo's butt as they walked toward their booth.

"Christ almighty, I thought you guys went home. I almost pissed my pants waiting here." Ian was joking, but you could tell he was anxious to get back to the resort. "Harper and I will both be back this afternoon for the second shift. What are you guys doing later?"

"I don't know. We haven't talked about it." Alex came around the table and took his seat next to the bowl of candy. "Theo, any idea what you want to do later?"

"Whatever you want to do. This is all great. I'm lovin' the crazy."

"Okay, well I've got to bounce or I'm going to be late for my client meeting. Happy Pride, gents. Catch ya later." Ian hugged each of them and then sprinted down the path to his car.

"Gay Pride." Theo sat back in his seat and looked over to Alex.

"Pretty amazing, isn't it?" Alex rested his hand on Theo's knee. "This Pride is special."

"It is? Why?" Theo asked.

"I have you." *I wonder if you believe me, Theo.*

Alex received his answer when Theo leaned over and kissed him tenderly on the lips.

ON TOP of the world is how Theo felt driving home the next day from Alex's new house. *So this is what it feels like to be in love? Damn, it was worth the wait.*

Thirsty, he pulled off the highway and walked into the Bait and Bake for a diet soda. A father and his two daughters were ahead of him in the checkout line. Theo reached into his pocket and pulled out a wad of change he'd scooped up from his truck. Glancing down at the newspapers while he waited to pay, his heart nearly stopped. His hand involuntarily sprang open, and change went flying everywhere. Blown up to epic proportion on the front page of the Silver Bay Gazette was a picture of him and Alex, lip-locked, with the brilliant Pride colors in the background.

His first instinct was to bolt out of the store and hide. *I'm so screwed. There's no way in hell this is going to get past Mom and Dad.*

"Thank you," he managed to mumble as the two little girls scurried around picking up the coins. Stepping up to the counter, on impulse he grabbed a paper.

"Did you have gas too?" the woman at the till asked.

"Just the soda and paper." Theo's knees began to shake.

Dashing out of the store, he climbed into his truck and forced himself to take several deep breaths. *Well, I guess this is it. No more secrets. I need Alex.*

Pulling up behind Alex's truck, Theo shut off the engine. Alex was back at the resort to help Ian with a landscaping project. The enormity of the situation came crashing down. *These guys aren't going to be able to help. Sure, I can run and hide, but eventually I'm going to have to go home. They can't help me with that.*

Looking up to the house, Theo spotted Harper wave from the kitchen window, and then Alex came into view. Seconds later, the door opened and Alex came bounding down the stairs.

"Hey, what's up?" Alex smiled. "I missed you too."

Theo held the paper outside the window. "Front page. Can you believe this shit?"

Alex reached for the paper and gasped. "Oh my God." He looked back to Theo and added, "This is Todd's doing. I know it."

"Not too worried about Todd right now," Theo admitted. "I'm fucked."

"Hey, Theo." Harper walked out and joined Alex. "Everything okay?"

"Look." Alex handed Harper the paper. "Todd's friend took our picture at Pride. What a prick."

"Todd had something to do with this?" Harper flashed his signature skeptical look.

Harper opened Theo's door. "Out!" Harper gestured for Theo to get out of the truck. "Let's go in the house and talk this one over."

On the way inside, Alex told the rest of the story of running into Todd with his friend Phillip and the whole picture incident.

"There's no way my parents could not have seen this picture," Theo explained when they were all seated at the table.

"Okay, so let's go with the assumption they have seen it and now they know you like guys." Harper was interrupted when Ian came in the door.

"Hey, Theo. Cool! Are you going to help too? I bet we have everything done by lunch if someone else would get his ass out of the chair and outside." Ian turned to Alex and said, "Oh, Alex, there you are."

"Sit down, Ian. We're having a family crisis." Harper pulled out a chair and slid the paper over so his partner could see the picture. "Theo's been outed."

"It's a nice picture, though." Ian ruffled Theo's hair as he sat down next to him.

Once again, Alex detailed how it came about that he and Theo were on the front page of the paper engaged in a passionate wet sloppy.

"Theo, have you ever met Todd before?" Harper asked, getting up for more coffee, bringing the pot back to the table with a cup for Ian.

"No. That was the first time I'd met him." Theo looked over to Alex and shook his head. *Stop it. Alex had nothing to do with this.* "Don't feel responsible for this, Alex. I don't think that at all."

"I'm going to kick his ass the next time I see him." Alex puffed out his chest and folded his arms. "Seriously? How could anyone be so fucking mean?"

"So, Alex, how is it that Todd intentionally outed Theo with the help of this dude Phillip's photo? That's kind of a mystery to me."

What's Harper saying? This Todd dude definitely had something to do with this.

Theo kept his mouth shut while Harper went on to point out that it was Pride weekend, a celebration, and couldn't it have been possible Phillip was actually doing something special for them by taking the shot and not anything mean spirited or premeditated. *Harper's right. The dude didn't know. But that Todd is still a dick.*

Theo explained what a morning was like at the Engdahl house. "Mom and Dad get up early, hours before they are due in church, and Dad reads the Sunday edition of the paper while Mom cooks a larger breakfast than usual. They love the paper," Theo added, as if to make sure everyone at the table fully understood there wasn't a chance in his own hell they had missed their son locking lips with another man.

"Right." Harper looked over to Ian to see if he had anything to add. When he didn't, Harper continued, "By eliminating or reducing Todd and Phillip's role in this mess, it makes it easier to see the real issue at stake here. Guys?" Harper pushed his chair back. "I'm going to ask you both this, and I apologize in advance if it puts either of you on the spot, but it's for the best. How serious are you about cohabitating?"

Theo's face warmed. Alex's turned red as they both chuckled out of nervousness.

"I wanted to come out to my folks first," Theo confessed.

"Well, glory hallelujah! Today you just took one giant step toward making that a reality." Harper seemed miffed they all didn't see the advantage in having the picture published.

"Harp, I get where you're going with this, but it doesn't do anything to make a face-to-face between Theo and his parents any easier." Ian sipped his coffee and patted Theo on the shoulder.

"That's very true." Harper leaned forward. "Before I address that concern, we need to hear from Alex. Are you interested in having Theo live with you? Is this something you wanted prior to this happening?"

"Definitely." Alex leaned over and kissed Theo on the cheek. "I've wanted that from the minute I…."

"Laid him?" Ian quipped, the drama around the table obviously testing his ability to remain attentive.

"Close, but no cigar. Laid eyes on him," Alex corrected. Turning again to Theo, he said, "Seriously, I'm so ready for you to share that house with me."

Theo smiled and returned the kiss. "I hate the part that's left." Theo slumped back in his chair.

"You hate the part that's left because you think you have to do this on your own."

The entire table looked over to Harper, confused.

"All this time, Theo, you've had it in your mind it was up to you and you alone to come up with the huge amount of courage you assumed it would take to tell your folks you're gay. To me, just coming out to yourself like you did was the hardest part. This next step, although it might be dicey, is, I think, easier."

Another round of confused looks prompted Alex to blurt out, "What the hell exactly are you trying to say? What's the plan?"

When Ian spit his coffee back into his mug, Alex laughed too. "Jeez, Harper. We're all pooping our pants here."

"Okay, sorry. I thought for a minute I was back at the law firm. If you'll have us, we're coming along for the ride on this one. I want to be there for you. Ian, this water feature thingy you and Alex were going to work on today, can you put it on hold?"

"Hell yeah, I'm in. I was going to try and get Alex to do most of the work anyway." Ian stuck out his tongue as far as it could go.

Shit balls, that's a long tongue. Theo forced himself to look away.

"Theo, you okay with this?" Alex asked.

"You guys don't have to come with me." Theo squirmed. *This is my problem.*

"Oh, yes we do," Harper countered.

Theo looked down at the table. *You don't want to do this alone, dude. Let them help.* When Theo looked back up, his eyes were moist. "I need some help with this one, I think."

TIME was on their side, but they'd have to hurry. Even though his parents would be greatly affected by the photograph, Theo felt confident they would still attend church. They'd be hurt and embarrassed, but the church would come to their rescue.

"It's a place for healing," Theo had tried to explain. "Mom, even though she's probably very angry and hurt, will thrive off the attention. She's sacrificed so much of her time helping others, she's hungry for a chance to have the tables turned."

"How about Dad?" Ian had asked.

Theo wasn't sure. His father could go either way. Mom had always been predictable. Dad, the wild card in most situations, took the time to put some thought into his reaction. Theo was reminded, as he gave the table a crash course in all things Engdahl, how in the last couple of years his father had mellowed. Theo thought it might even be a countermove to his mother's increased insanity. Her dedication to the church, in Theo's opinion, had surpassed that for her husband, and certainly Theo.

Harper had asked to ride with Theo on the way over to his house. Ian drove separately in his truck, and Alex brought up the rear of the caravan. It was estimated that three trucks should be sufficient to accommodate all of Theo's belongings. They would use the time while Theo's Mom and Dad were at church to move him out of his basement bedroom. He had stuff stored in the garage, but there really wasn't much else to worry about. It was mostly sports-related gear he wasn't ready to part with but never thought about until it was staring him in the face.

Harper used the drive over to coach Theo on various ways he might respond to his parents' reaction to his moving out and, more importantly, coming out. They would have had some time to stew about this, so the reaction could be defensive. Harper pretty much covered all the bases, including how to react to the silent treatment. "Don't lose your temper, no matter what. Remember, you may not think this important now, but you don't want to permanently close the door on them. They're your parents."

It was good to have Harper with him on the ride over. His voice of reason had a calming effect. "The other thing," Harper continued, "We're all pumped up for a fight. They might see the trucks are all loaded up and walk in the house and shut the door on you." Harper was trying to touch on all the possible scenarios. They discussed the sting this reaction could cause. "Don't take it personally. It's them and not you that has to deal with this."

With his hand gripped tightly on the steering wheel, Theo turned the corner and pulled up in front of the house. *Thank you.* His dad's truck was gone. They always took the truck to church. No particular reason. Sometimes, right after service, they would run into Two Harbors or even all the way to Duluth to shop. The truck ensured whatever bargain they might stumble on could be brought back home.

Once Theo had opened the door and led everyone downstairs, they started carrying things out to the trucks. "I feel like we're all ants at a picnic and we're hauling away lunch," Ian joked as he stuffed clothes into one of the boxes Alex had thought to bring along for loose items. With four of them attacking one small bedroom, they had it cleaned out in no time. The only items left were the bed and dresser set. Theo had thought about taking it, but Alex convinced him to leave it behind.

"We're starting fresh here, dude. We'll shop together and get exactly what we want. It might take some time, but it'll be worth it. Plus, you're not adding any fuel to the fire if your parents decide to put up a stink."

When it was all said and done, including the sports gear from the garage, Theo's worldly possessions only filled up two of the trucks. They left Ian's empty so he and Harper could head straight home. All they had to do now was wait for Mr. and Mrs. Engdahl.

"What time did you say they usually get home?" Harper asked, leaning up against Ian's truck.

"Anytime." Theo checked his watch again, although it wasn't necessary. He had glanced at it every few minutes the entire time he had been home, out of fear his folks would return and catch them in the act of moving out.

"I could run and get some sodas," Alex offered.

"I'm good." Ian leaned back on his truck next to Harper.

"I'm too nervous to eat or drink anything." Theo couldn't suppress the laugh that had been building inside of him for the last several minutes.

"What's so funny?" Alex asked.

"There's no way in hell I would have ever made it through this on my own. Even with you guys here now, I'm a mess."

"Naw, you don't look like a mess," Harper said, looking to the others to weigh in. "I think you look fabulous. You have a fresh thing going on, and your energy… I can feel it from here."

"Yeah." Ian gave Theo the once-over. "I see that fresh thing you're talking about, Harp. Daisy fresh."

"They're trying to take your mind off your folks," Alex explained, rolling his eyes.

"Shit, here they come." Theo walked toward the truck as it pulled into the driveway. At first, his parents just sat inside. He could see them talking. His mother was much more animated than his father, who appeared to be doing more listening than talking. His mother was the first to get out.

"Theodore, who are these men on my lawn?"

"They're my friends, mother." Theo held his ground as she came barreling toward him.

"I want them to leave *now*. Do you have any idea the shame you have caused your father and I?"

Oh man, she's really worked up.

"The shame you feel is your own," Theo said calmly. "There's nothing wrong with...."

Before he had a chance to finish his sentence, his mother brought her hand across his face with such force he staggered backward to stay on his feet.

"Darla! That's enough. Get in the house." His dad stomped a direct course to his wife.

Water filled his eyes as he watched his father grab his mother by the arm and drag her toward the house. The left side of his face was numb.

"I don't think you have any idea, mister, what the good lord has in store for you," Darla hollered over her shoulder. "No idea! And when judgment comes, the only person you'll have to blame is yourself."

Alex was the first to reach him, followed immediately by Ian and Harper.

"You okay?" Alex wrapped his arms around Theo's shoulder.

He couldn't talk. Not yet. The last thing he wanted to do was cry. There was no way in hell he was going to allow himself to be harmed by her hurtful words and actions. If he opened his mouth to say anything right then, he wasn't sure if he would be able to keep it together.

"Here comes your father," Ian informed the group when they had walked Theo back to the truck.

"Oh, great." Theo stopped rubbing his face and stood to face his father.

Lay a hand on me and you'll regret it.

"Your mother was wrong to strike you." His father gestured back to the house.

Theo couldn't think of any way to respond. *She's the devil.*

"Your mother is upset."

His father was making excuses for her behavior again, and Theo hated this more than anything. He looked away. His emotions bubbled at the surface, and the same rule applied to his father as his mother. *I will not give you the satisfaction of seeing me cry.*

"Hello, I'm Eugene Engdahl, Theodore's father." Theo watched his dad make the rounds, shaking hands. Everyone was respectful and introduced themselves.

"I assume all this stuff loaded on the trucks is yours? Where are you going?" His father looked to the others, inviting them to answer.

It's a fair question. "I'm moving in with Alex," Theo answered evenly.

"I see. It's probably all for the best, given the circumstances. Do you gentlemen mind if I have a moment alone with Theo?"

"We'll be right over here, Theo." Ian's reassurance brought a smile to Theo's face. *I love you guys so much.* With his face still stinging, Theo looked his father directly in the eye as the others dispersed.

"Theo, now's probably not the best time to have this discussion, but there're a few things I want you to know before you leave here."

"I'm gay. I can't change that." Theo swallowed a few times before continuing, "I won't change, so don't waste your time."

"I'd be lying if I told you I understood any or part of what you're going through. I will tell you that I've suspected something for a while now. I don't have a clue what this gay thing is all about, and, frankly, I don't plan on investing much time on it in the future."

"I don't care what you think." The anger from being embarrassed by his mother was surfacing. Theo realized he was directing it toward his father. *You married the bitch.*

"Theo, you haven't cared about what your mother or I have thought for quite some time, so this isn't a new revelation. What I want to tell you is that, no matter who or what you are, you are my son. I put you on this earth, and I will continue to be your father through this and anything else that life brings your way. I love you."

His father's words were gentler than he had anticipated. All of the comebacks he and Harper had discussed in the car were worthless now.

"Theodore. Promise me you will come to us if you are in trouble or in need of help. Despite her actions today, your mother loves you. I know you don't believe this, but she does. She's hurting. You can't imagine what that picture did to her this morning."

"We should be going." Theo waited to see if his dad had anything else to say.

"Good luck, and please keep in touch. Call me at the office if you want."

For the first time in as long he could remember, Theo felt an urge to give his father a hug. *I've forgotten what a father sounds like.* To his surprise, his dad stepped forward and took him into his arms. "I love you, son."

Theo felt his eyes fill with water a second time as he turned and walked toward his friends.

"PICTURE time. Come on, you guys, it will only take a minute." Harper motioned for everyone to get up against the wall. "Allison, where's Spencer?"

"I'm here. Sorry, had to visit the little boy's room."

"Okay, here's how we're going to do this." Harper gazed over the group assembled. It was all of their nearest and dearest friends. "Ian, Alex, Theo, Spencer, you guys are the tallest so you're in back. Ian, save room for me."

"I guess I could if I have to." Ian blew Harper a kiss.

The dress code for tonight's event, the Fall Harvest Gala, was strictly formal. Tuxedos and dark suits for the men, evening dresses for the ladies. This requirement had been advertised with the understanding that gender identity would be respected. Those who felt the need to mix it up had the nod to do so. This was the first time Harper had seen his partner in a tuxedo, and the results were stunning. *Damn, you're one handsome man.* Everyone looked great.

"Bud, you and Audrey start the next row. Brent, you're next to your new best friend, Audrey."

"Come here, sweetie." Audrey linked arms with Brent.

"Harold, I want you next to Brent. Allison, you can stand in front of Spencer. Colin, you and Marla on the end of the row."

Harper waited for everyone to shift around. "Perfect."

"Petra," he continued, "you and Betsy in front. Andy and Emmett, you right next to them.

"Look at that." Harper singled out Emmett by pointing. "Don't think I didn't notice your attention to detail, Em. I love the hair matching the cummerbund. Two enthusiastic thumbs up!"

"Thanks, Harper," the small voice replied.

"Okay. I think that's everyone." Harper turned to face the photographer more out of embarrassment than anything. *Think before you speak. It's not everyone. Quentin.* Sneaking a peek back to the group, Harold and Audrey were sharing a laugh. *You got lucky. Watch it.*

"Get the hell over here, Harp," Ian barked. "We've got a party to get back to."

"I'm comin'." Harper slid in alongside Ian, holding his hand as the photographer did a little fine-tuning on the positioning.

"Okay, let's see great big smiles." The photographer adjusted his lens.

Being the first major event sponsored by the Center, Harper wanted it well documented, so he decided at the last minute to have a professional stroll through the festivities and capture the evening. It was pricey, but there might be some gems out of the rough he could use later on for marketing and publicity.

"Great. I've got what I need." The photographer saluted the group and stepped back.

"Hang on." Ian came out from the back row. "We need a couple more before you call it a wrap."

"Call it a wrap? What the fuck?" Spencer sidled up with Andy.

"I know. He's like, all of a sudden, Mr. Hollywood in that tux," Andy quipped. "We'll mess with him later after he's had a few beers."

"We need a picture of the executive director and the program and event coordinator. Harper, Alex, you're up."

Alex walked over to the wall and motioned for Harper to join him.

"Hey, smarty pants. See what a little hard work and inspiration can achieve?" Harper gave Alex a hug.

"This is so cool."

"And one more, please." Ian grabbed Theo by the arm and led him over to join Harper and Alex. "The Four Musketeers."

"More like the Four Mouseketeers if you ask me," Spencer corrected.

They all laughed as the photographer moved in and snapped their shot.

The evening, billed as a fundraiser for the Center, had a suggested donation of fifty dollars per couple highlighted on the invitations. Harper and Alex had reached out to the surrounding community by placing calls for area businesses to provide food and drink for the event at a reduced rate. The response was better than they had expected.

Harper and Alex, along with Ian and Theo, had spent several late nights decorating the large hall. Harper had suggested they adhere to the traditional rainbow theme, but Alex talked him out of it, and, boy, was he ever glad he did.

After much discussion, they had settled on the title, "Fall Harvest Gala." To support the fall theme, Alex assembled a color palette of rich, warm tones that, when paired with the extensive wood in the old building, created a classy, elegant look for very little cost. Bouquets of leaves, accented with long gold streamers, were attached to each wall sconce. Arrangements of yellow, red, and orange roses, mixed with leaves, adorned the tables. Tall, potted branches wrapped with white lights flanked both sides of the makeshift stage.

I don't think we could have gotten any luckier than we did by scoring this building for the Center. It's perfect.

Music pulsated out of the speakers placed strategically around the hall. It was starting to get crowded, and, judging by the number of attendees already present, there were still many who hadn't arrived. Over a hundred parties had RSVP'd.

"I'm thinking we wait a few more minutes before kicking this thing off," Harper suggested after meeting up with Alex.

"That should be about right. How about Dr. Jive? Isn't he great? I'm lovin' the mix of tunes so far. Great energy, something for everyone." Alex tested out a few moves.

"I agree. I have to remember to thank Colin for sending him our way. So, once I get this going, are you all set to roll?" Harper snagged a white wine off the tray of one of the roaming servers. "Thanks."

"Yep. I'll wait for your cue."

"Great. I have to use the can, and then I think it will be just about time to get the show on the road."

Harper shook hands and greeted a few of the guests he had met over the years on the way to the bathroom.

"Hey, handsome."

For a moment, Harper thought he might have mistakenly wandered into the wrong bathroom. *Joke's on me.* "Hi there," he greeted the six-foot drag queen he passed on his way in. *Shit, I love this!*

Harper dried his hands on a towel and paused for a minute to inspect the image looking back at him. *Wrinkles? Where'd they come from? Ah, don't be so hard on yourself, old man, you're holding up pretty damn good. You ready for this?* He was excited.

When the big-band favorite "In the Mood" had finished, the music was temporarily put on hold. The DJ handed Harper a wireless microphone, and he walked over to the riser that had been set up at the far end of the big room.

"Good evening," he began. "I'm Harper Callahan, director of the Men's Center, and I would like to welcome you to our first, and I hope annual, Fall Harvest Gala."

A hearty round of applause erupted from the guests, who had congregated around the small stage.

"This is a very special evening for us. It's been a long road to get here."

More whistles and cheers.

"As I'm sure you all know, our mission in the community is to provide services for, primarily, but not exclusively, men. I don't want to waste any time tonight going into the details. Our brochure, located at the entrance to the Center, does, I think, a pretty good job of explaining what we do."

Harper paused for a minute to look out at the crowd assembled. *This is absolutely a dream come true.* "As I look out at all of you—and you are one very attractive group. In fact, I think a round of applause is in order. You're all fabulous."

Harper laughed along with everyone as they cheered and clapped wildly.

"And you're all very modest, I see." More laughter. "What I wanted to say—" Harper paused again to make sure he had the words organized in his mind before continuing. "—What isn't detailed in the brochure is the sense of community the Center hopefully provides. Events like tonight, the meetings, all of the support groups the Center offers, both now and in the future, work collectively to create a community we can trust and rely on. I look forward to the future."

Keep up the pace. So far so good.

"Of course, the services provided by the Center come at a cost. We're talking donations. And so far, the generosity of the community has far exceeded all of our estimates. So I want to thank you, first and foremost. And, I want to ask for your support in the future so we can continue to grow."

The response from the crowd delighted Harper. *This is fantastic.*

"With that said, I would like to share with you a very special development. Harold, are you... there you are. Would you please join me? Everyone, please give a warm round of applause for Mr. Harold Benedict."

Alex escorted Harold to the stage and helped him step up onto the platform.

"Harold holds a special place in the hearts of many here tonight. Thank you for joining us."

"It's my pleasure." Harold looked to be a man who, over the years, had gotten very comfortable being at an event in a tuxedo. The dapper gentleman owned the look.

"I met Harold and his partner, Quentin Devereux, because we were privileged to have them as guests at the Palisade Beach Resort this past summer. Unfortunately, Quentin came to us ill. He passed away in August and will be very much missed by everyone who had a chance to get to know him. I should add that Quentin grew up here on the North Shore."

Harper paused, giving the moment the respect it deserved. He reached over and patted Harold on the shoulder. "This is a very special moment for me," Harper whispered away from the mic. "Would you like to do this, or do you want me to continue?"

"You're doing marvelously. Please go on." Harold returned a pat on the back.

"Because of their interest in the Center and Quentin's connection to the community, the Center has been made the benefactor of a very generous gift. When Harold first told me what he had in mind, I had to sit down. I was overwhelmed."

As Harper looked out, he could tell the crowd was eating this up, their eager faces begging for more.

"I'm very pleased to announce that, beginning next spring, the Center will offer a yearly scholarship." Harper looked over to Harold and mouthed the words "Thank you." He continued, "It is with great pleasure that I announce the Quentin Devereux and Harold Benedict Scholarship for Artistic Excellence."

Again the hall erupted in thunderous applause.

"This generous gift will be awarded to a qualified local *gay* artist. The sole intention is to promote and support those individuals in the area who show artistic promise."

Another wave of cheers and applause.

"So, Harold, in appreciation for this wonderful opportunity you are providing our community, we would like to say thank you not one, but two ways. First—"

Harper signaled the DJ, and a drumroll filled the room. "From tonight on, this great space we're all standing in will forever be known as Devereux Hall, in honor of the late Quentin Devereux."

Alex, who had been standing on the sidelines, pulled a cord to expose a handsome nameplate placed above the bank of windows behind them.

"Welcome to Devereux Hall, everyone!"

The partygoers clapped. They looked to each other, as if to acknowledge the importance of the evening and their good fortune in being a part of it.

At Harper's request, Harold had turned around to witness the unveiling. "Quentin would be so proud. Thank you." Harold wiped the tears from his eyes and stepped forward to give Harper a hug.

"Alex?"

Harper and the rest of the guests watched as his young associate took the stage carrying an easel covered in gold fabric. He handed the microphone to Alex.

"Hello, everyone, I'm Alex Stevens, program and event coordinator here at the Center. My friend Harold"—Alex rested his hand on Harold's shoulder—"is an artist, a painter. A very accomplished painter."

Harper bit his lip as he watched the gears in Alex's head spin. *You're doin' just fine, sport. Just keep up the pace.*

"Anyway, I paint too," Alex continued after receiving a nod from Harper, "and this summer I had the chance to work with Harold and to benefit from his incredible talent."

More shoulder pats to Harold from Alex.

Sensing Alex was struggling, Harper motioned toward the easel.

"Harold, you'll always be an inspiration, and, in my own way, I wanted to say thank you." Alex looked over to Harper for further direction.

Never one to miss an opportunity for levity, Harper frowned and gestured once again toward the easel. Laughter warmed the big hall.

"Okay…. Man, Harold—I hope you don't think this sucks." Alex handed the microphone back to Harper and walked over to the easel and removed the cloth.

Harper, Ian, and Theo were the only ones to have an advanced viewing of the painting. Alex had captured the images of the two men beautifully, with the rich tones of the palisade as the background.

The unveiling elicited oohs and ahs from the crowd. Harper thought about handing the microphone over to Harold for a comment, but by the look on his face, and given the size of the tears that streamed down his face, he decided to let the moment play out.

Way to go, smarty pants. You nailed it. I'm so damn proud of you right now, Alex.

In lieu of words, Harold took Alex into his arms and held him tight.

"Nice job!" Ian complimented his partner after they had all dispersed from the stage to enthusiastic applause. "I'm so proud of you, honey." He pulled Harper in for a kiss.

"Thanks, sweetie. Are people having a nice time?" He had been so focused on his part of the evening, Harper needed an update.

"What do you think?" Ian pointed to the dance floor, where an impromptu conga line was forming in response to a lively calypso number.

"Sweet!" Harper took Ian by the hand and made a mad dash to join in.

ALEX looked across the table at his boyfriend and grinned. *Just wait until I get those clothes off of you, Theodore Engdahl.*

"That was *mighty* delicious." Ian patted his stomach and sat back on the folding chair.

"This was my first crock pot turkey dinner. How cool was that? Theo, nice job." Harper wiped his mouth with the paper towel that had originally been wrapped around his silverware.

"I think we have some ice cream if anyone is looking for dessert?" Theo collected their plates off the card table and brought them into the kitchen. "Shit. Sorry, guys, I lied. No ice cream." Theo returned to his chair.

"Should we test out the hot tub?" Harper looked around the table.

Alex clenched his jaw. *Nope. Come on, Ian. It's late. You have a big day tomorrow putting the beds down for the winter.*

"What time is it?" Ian looked over at his partner's watch.

"It's only nine thirty. The night is young." Harper smiled.

That's pretty late. Maybe I should yawn.

"A relaxing hot tub sure sounds inviting." Ian tilted his head the way he always did when he was mulling something over. "We didn't bring any suits."

"Oh, I bet these guys have extras. I mean, come on, do we even need them? I'm not shy."

We take turns sharing a suit. One suit. And Theo's really shy.

"I have so much to do tomorrow, Harp. We should really get going."

"Damn! Really?" Harper was obviously disappointed.

Give it up, Harper. Let it go.

"Sorry, guys. Do you mind if we take a rain check on the hot tub?" Ian took a final swig of his beer, stood up, and stretched his arms high in the air, then released a full-bodied belch.

"Ah, really? We'd love it if you stuck around." Theo collected a few more dishes.

Theo! Alex screamed inside his head. *Shut up. We're walking a fine line here.*

"Well, if not tonight," Theo added over his shoulder, "promise you'll stop by sometime soon to give it a try. Thanks for helping us with the deck and getting the tub set up."

Good, Theo. That's my boy.

The four of them had spent the entire day working like dogs on a small deck outside the screen door on the lower level, which included a little port overhead to protect from the elements. It was a temporary solution to something more permanent down the road. Theo had scored a great deal on a hot tub through Artie and had surprised Alex with it. It wasn't the prettiest setup, but at least they didn't have to go all winter without being able to enjoy the luxury of lounging outdoors in warm, bubbly heaven.

"All right, you win." Harper stood and pushed in his chair. "You coming into the Center tomorrow?"

"I wasn't planning on it. I wanted to do a few things around here, and then I was going to come over and help Ian." Alex had been so busy with the events at the Center that he felt guilty for not spending more time at the resort.

"Seriously? You're helping me tomorrow?" This perked Ian up.

"I'll be over before lunch." Alex and Theo followed their guests to the door.

"Maybe tomorrow won't be so bad after all?" Ian joined hands with his partner.

Crap. They're not changing their minds about staying, are they?

"I didn't realize how tired I was until I stood up. Drive daddy home, please." Harper handed the keys over to Ian and opened the front door.

"Okay, but the minute we get home I'm going to teach you who the *real* daddy is." Ian turned and gave Theo and Alex a hug.

"Thanks again, guys." Harper exchanged hugs with his hosts.

"Drive safe." Theo stood next to Alex. They watched their friends climb into Harper's Smart Car and drive off.

Alex slammed the door and locked it. "Last one in is a rotten egg."

Theo strong-armed Alex until he got around him and then bolted toward the stairs leading to the lower level.

"No fair," Alex hollered, hot on his trail, and then slipped on the stair midway down and finished his descent on his ass. "Son of a bitch."

"Are you all right?" Theo was doing his best not to laugh until he knew the extent of Alex's injuries, if any.

"I'm not sure." Alex rubbed the small of his back.

"Where does it hurt?" Theo sat on the step next to Alex.

"It doesn't. Ha! Ha!" Alex jumped up but found himself back on his ass before he knew it.

"That's the oldest trick in the book, boyfriend." Theo held him in a death grip and planted kisses all over his face.

"Quit it." Alex was laughing and squirming at the same time. "Ew, come on, Theo. I'm sorry. Quit it."

"Here." Theo pulled off Alex's T-shirt and then ripped off his own.

They both kicked off their shoes and removed their socks. Alex stood and dropped his jeans, pushing them to the floor. Theo's jeans followed an identical route. Panting from all the racing around, the two men stood in their underwear, facing each other.

Theo slipped his hand in the waistband of Alex's boxers and, in one quick move, brought them to his knees. Alex returned the favor.

Alex stepped out of his shorts and watched Theo push his down to his ankles and off. "I can't believe this body is all mine." Alex stood back and admired Theo's nakedness.

"If we stick around here any longer, I'm not sure we'll ever make it into the tub. Come on." Theo took Alex by the hand. "Wait here," he ordered. "I'll get the cover off."

Alex waited until Theo opened the door and poked his head in. "Turn on the outside light. It's snowing. This is going to be great!"

"Wow, really?" Alex flipped the light on and joined Theo outside. "Damn, it's cold."

"That's going to make this so fun. The water is soooo warm."

Alex stared at Theo's sculpted ass as he climbed up the small stair unit that came with the tub.

"Oh man, this is awesome." Theo eased himself into the steaming water.

Alex followed him in. "Damn, it's hot." He flashed Theo an exaggerated look of panic.

"I'm used to it already. Seriously, it's great. Come here."

Theo reached over and guided Alex up onto his lap so they were facing each other. There was no mistaking what Alex was sitting on. Alex leaned forward until their lips touched. At the same time, Theo wrapped his strong arms around his waist.

"I like this position." Theo reached up and pulled Alex in for another kiss.

"Me too. Isn't this great?" Alex kissed Theo's nose.

"Yep, but I have a better idea. Here, turn around." Theo waited while Alex stood and turned. "I could kiss you all night, but this is too sweet for you not to see. Here."

Theo guided Alex around until his back was snug against Theo's chest. Once again, Theo wrapped his strong arms around Alex's waist. "I'm going to slide down a little more so we're both covered with water. There, how's that?"

Are you kiddin' me? Dude, this is heaven. Alex relaxed in his partner's embrace. Theo's chin rested on his shoulder, and the best part of all, his rock-hard cock was wedged nicely into his ass crack. *Heaven might not even be* this *good.*

The backyard light put up by the previous owners did a good job of illuminating the huge expanse directly in front of them. Large, plump flakes were falling everywhere. It was one of those rare times when you could hear them hit the ground. Alex could remember when he was a young kid, walking with his mother. She had a thing about getting out and celebrating the first snow. It was a wonderful memory, made even more special now that he was secure in Theo's embrace.

"Isn't this beautiful?" Alex bent his head forward and kissed Theo's arm.

"Yeah, it really is. I could sit here all night." Theo placed Alex's ear in his mouth and nibbled.

"Should we turn on the jets and give them a test?"

"We could. The quiet is nice too, though," Theo whispered between nibbles.

"Theo?"

"Yeah."

"I love you."

"You do?"

"Yep." Alex felt another playful nibble on his other ear.

"Alex?"

"Yeah?"

"I think I love you more."

"Sweet."

"Alex?" Theo whispered directly into his ear. "Are you looking at what I'm looking at?"

Alex looked up from the steaming water to discover a deer, a huge buck with a majestic set of antlers, standing on the edge of the forest. Scared he might frighten the large animal off by talking, he reached down and squeezed Theo's arm.

"Isn't he gorgeous?" Alex could feel Theo's lips move against his ear.

They both gasped when an even larger buck, sporting an enormous rack, stepped into the light and cocked its head, staring toward the house.

Alex was mesmerized by the incredible tableau until Theo's body began to shake beneath him. *What's going on?*

The shaking increased. When squeaks and hisses started to come out of Theo's mouth, Alex finally figured it out. *He's giggling.*

"What's so funny?" Alex whispered, causing Theo to gasp so loudly that both of the male deer looked in their direction and then bolted off into the dense woods.

"Oh God. I'm dying. That's the funniest thing I've ever seen."

Theo's laughter was infectious, and now Alex was laughing right along with him but had no idea why.

"Two bucks. *Together!*" Theo roared. "Holy crap, even the deer around here are gay."

JOEL SKELTON lives with his partner in the thriving Minnesota arts community commonly referred to as the Twin Cities. Writing is the latest destination in the author's tour of the arts. When he's not writing, scamming on a character, creating a chapter outline, or editing a portion of his manuscript on the bus in and out of the city, he's playing law firm—a whacky, highly entertaining way to put food on the table.

Visit his web site at http://www.joelskelton.com.

Also from JOEL SKELTON

Beneath the Palisade

Reliance

Joel Skelton

Also from JOEL SKELTON

dress up

joel skelton

http://www.dreamspinnerpress.com

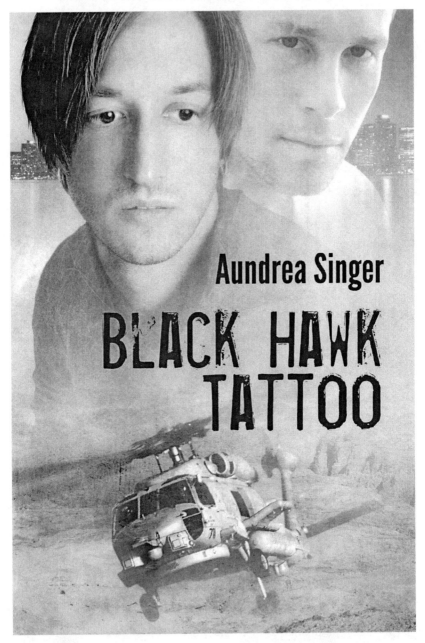

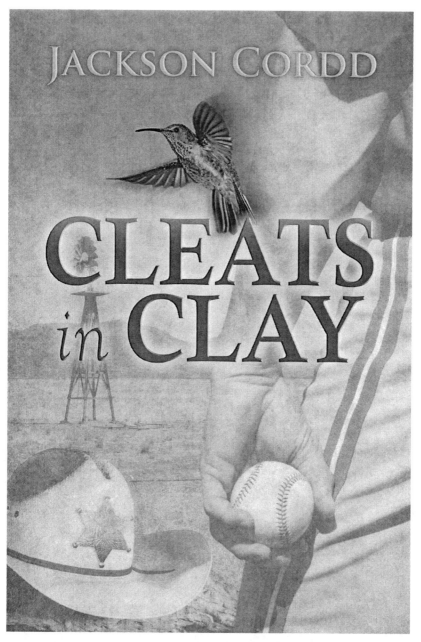

CPSIA information can be obtained
at www.ICGtesting.com
Printed in the USA
FFOW01n0931120216
21404FF